GOD'S BLOOD

Volume Three of *The Fallen*

K.N. Nguyen

To F.N. And L.N.

With your blessing, I have been able to soar.

Thank you for being my wings.

THE REALM OF
CORINTH

GOD'S BLOOD

I

ZAA'NI PACED around the dirt-packed back of her mother-in-law's home, her constant steps beginning to create imprints of her steps in the usually smooth, sweet-smelling earth. It had been barely two weeks since Len left Fa'Tinh, yet she struggled to keep calm in the cities. Wyrd left the capital, going to the outer districts to find followers and stir up the people. Zaa'ni tried to talk with her people, but had to stop after a few days due to sharp pains in her belly. At Intan's behest, she spent most of her days on her bed, resting so that she didn't stress her baby. Now, she waited.

Pram met with the leaders of the Hanzo and Thurlish tribes, the Great Heart's Feet and Mouth of Xan, respectively, to see if they could be persuaded to take action and provide aid to the Qu'ari. Pak from Thurl made no commitment, preferring to remain a neutral party. Yettan, the Hanzo lord, offered to spare some of his. Neither of these tribes were known for their combat skills amongst the rest of the clans. Their support helped, but not so much.

Hroth wandered about, keeping his ears open for news, while Pram traveled to Yshan, his homeland, to convince the mighty Tuk-kan to lend their strength. Pram seemed confident that his people would support the Great Heart and help keep the clans unified. Zaa'ni prayed that it was enough.

For now, she paced.

Bermet danced through the trees, kicking up dust as she frolicked. Her dark hair played behind her as her dress fluttered around her little legs.

Zaa'ni glanced over at her daughter, smiling at the child's innocence as she played.

She won't be able to play much longer, she lamented. *Bloody days are ahead.*

"Mommy!" Bermet called out, waving to her mother. "Join me."

"Not now, my little pearl," Zaa'ni replied, motioning for her to continue her fun. "Mommy is busy and needs time to think."

"But, the blue-haired girl said we should play."

"Blue-haired girl?" Bermet had her mother's attention now. On more than one occasion, Bermet claimed to speak to the gods. Zaa'ni had even seen her dancing with the holy Windstrider, Freyna of the Ayr, herself. The child was god-chosen, Zaa'ni was sure. "If she says we should, then we shall. Come to me; I am too tired to walk much further."

Bermet's face lit up as she hurried to her mother's side. She planted a kiss on her mother's belly before dancing around once more. Zaa'ni waved her arms around gracefully, encircling her little girl as the child bounded around her. Bermet laughed as the two played. Zaa'ni allowed herself a rare smile. Surely, she could relax just for this moment.

A sharp pain in her stomach caused her to double over with a groan. It didn't last long, but the feeling was intense and took her breath away. Bermet stopped mid-twirl and looked at her mother with wide eyes.

"Mommy, are you okay?"

Zaa'ni waited for the pain to pass before responding. Time went by slowly as she hugged her stomach, waiting for the agony to cease. Finally, it stopped and she was able to straighten up once more. Wiping her damp brow, she tried to flash her daughter a reassuring smile. It came out more like a grimace.

"Mommy is fine, my pearl. Just a little discomfort. Now, where were we?"

Bermet stared at her mother questioningly before resuming her spinning. Zaa'ni half-heartedly waved her arms over her daughter. Her trepidation was replaced with fear. She remembered the pain, hoped that Len would return before she felt it again. It didn't seem like he would.

The pair danced for almost an hour with Zaa'ni feeling only mild discomfort semi-regularly before she had to stop again because of the pain. Bermet let out a tiny squeak of pain as she yanked her hands out of her mother's. Zaa'ni didn't notice, however, because her hands were clenched tightly, her nails digging into the palms. The little girl's eyes widened once more and she ran off screaming for her grandmother. Zaa'ni placed her hands on her knees and waited for the pain to subside. Gradually, it went away and she was able to straighten up. Looking down, she noticed that she'd wet herself.

"Zaa'ni, my dear," Intan cried as she hobbled out towards the woman, young Bermet in tow. Pram's wife, Altansari, raced ahead of the two and wrapped her arm around Zaa'ni's waist. "Come, we must get you inside now. The little prince will be here soon."

"I've got you," Altansari added. "Lean on me."

"What about Len?" Zaa'ni asked. "Have you heard anything from him?"

"Now's not the time," Altansari replied. "We need to focus on bringing your son safely into the world. Berkah," she called out as they entered the home, "get me some hot water and then watch the kids."

Zaa'ni let out another groan as the pain intensified. Altansari guided her to the bed and gently laid her down. Zaa'ni struggled to breathe regularly, her breath coming out in deep gasps as the agony in her body increased in frequency and strength. Sweat beaded on her brow as she tried to curl into a ball.

"No, no," Intan soothed as she rubbed a damp cloth on Zaa'ni's forehead. "Let's make it easy for him to come."

Zaa'ni clenched her teeth as pain wracked her body, a groan escaping her throat. Altansari shooed the children away from the room before checking how far along Zaa'ni was. Intan finished lighting some incense in the window and brought the stick to the laboring woman. Delicately, she waved the stick over Zaa'ni's body, chanting as she chased away the bad spirits that may try and harm the babe as he entered the world. Zaa'ni's groans turned into cries. Tears ran down her cheeks as she pushed.

"Keep pushing, Zaa'ni," Altansari said down by her feet.

Pushing herself upright, Zaa'ni got into a deep squat and pushed. Intan put a piece of leather into her mouth for her to bite down upon.

"It's almost time," Altansari said.

Suddenly, Zaa'ni felt a pain that lanced through to her core. She let out a shriek of agony as she doubled over. Somewhere in the distance, Altansari and Intan were talking, but Zaa'ni couldn't understand them. She felt her body rip open as she screamed in anguish. Zaa'ni could only breathe in ragged gasps as she struggled to remain upright. Overcome by pain, she dropped onto her back, a sob escaping her lips. Everything around her was muted as the pain receded. Then, she heard a cry.

Looking down at her legs, she saw Altansari rubbing the baby's back. Another high-pitched cry sounded feebly from Altansari's arms. Zaa'ni saw a tuft of dark hair before Intan swooped down to cut the cord.

"A boy," Intan said proudly.

"Careful, Great Mother," Altansari said as Intan placed the cord on a bowl on the floor for later. "The cord was around his neck as he came out. He seems to be breathing though," she added as another cry cut through the room.

"He's all right?" Zaa'ni asked breathlessly.

"We will pray to the Ayr," Intan said. "But my son is protected by the Windstrider. I do not see her letting this baby die."

"Good, good," Zaa'ni replied weakly. She felt drained after the sudden labor. "Let me see him."

Altansari brought the babe, now wrapped in a cotton cloth, over to Zaa'ni. Intan waved her incense over the mother and child to make sure that bad spirits did not attack the two while they were vulnerable. Zaa'ni reached out to grab the bundle.

The babe sighed as he smelt his mother, his head turning towards her in hopes of finding her breast. Zaa'ni filled with a warmth that overshadowed her exhaustion. Tears welled in the corner of her eyes as she beheld his cobalt eyes peeking out from behind his eyelashes. The baby made a tiny coo as he closed his eyes once his skin touched hers.

"Heru," Zaa'ni said.

"Heru?" Altansari asked. "Didn't you and the Great Heart want Telan?"

"No, no, it's Heru," Zaa'ni replied. "That name feels right."

"This isn't his first life in Corinth," Intan broke in. "Heru is a good name for him. I see a great future for him."

"Mommy?" Bermet's voice could be heard behind the door.

Rising, Altansari shooed Bermet and the other children away from the room. Zaa'ni could hear the woman telling the children that everything would be okay. Her eyelids felt heavy once more. Intan guided the babe to Zaa'ni's nipple so he could have his first meal. Closing her eyes, Zaa'ni let out a sigh as she leaned back into the pillows.

II

Cienna strode down the hall in her riding pants, her mouth set in a determined line. Her wavy hair was tied back, hanging low on her back in a loose tail. The quick gait should've been heralded by her boots. Instead, they were muffled by the din surrounding her. People bustled around her, getting everything ready for Pharn's forces' departure. Servants ran about fetching supplies to bring down to the soldiers, bumping into each other occasionally in their hurry. Young recruits, some who hadn't even experienced their first assignment, looked about frantically as they tried to find their new posts.

They're so young, Cienna noted as a pair of baby-faced soldiers scurried to their spots, their eyes wide in panic.

Turning down a corridor, Cienna made her way to her mother's room. This hall lacked the chaos of the rest of the caer. A trio of grizzled guards stood outside a door at the end of the hallway.

No way they're leaving the queen unattended. Especially after what just happened.

A healer exited the room as Cienna approached. Nodding to her briefly, the woman flashed a quick smile at the princess. The guards made room for Cienna, one opening the door for her. Cienna walked into her mother's room, a lump forming in her throat as she crossed the threshold.

The room was dark — darker than usual thanks to the curtains that covered the windows and blocked the sun. A fire burned in the hearth, casting a dim glow in the room. The gentle scent of crushed lavender combined with the warmth made Cienna feel drowsy. A handful of healers surrounded her mother's bed. Master Urthro motioned for the princess to join them once he saw her. She made her way over, nodding to a couple of her classmates.

Queen Hera lay under several thick quilts and a large fur, her face pale. The waning light from the flames cast shadows on her face, making her features look gaunt. Cienna's breath caught in her throat momentarily. A soft cough from her mother eased her fears, loosening the knot.

"She is doing better, Princess," Urthro whispered to her. "However, she is still weak and could slip. We *believe* we've isolated the poisons, but it is hard to tell. It's just too early."

"Someone said she is fine though," Cienna replied. "I can't leave her. What if she dies?"

"What if she doesn't?"

"She needs my help, Master. I can't turn my back on her."

"Your Highness," Urthro said, guiding her away from her mother gently with his hand on her elbow. "If I may. What were your plans if she was healing? Would you still stay with her? Would you do what it takes to ensure the kingdom's safety?" His eyes lingered on her clothes. "Because there is nothing shameful with doing what needs to be done."

"But... I can't lose my mom," Cienna replied, her voice catching in her throat. Her eyes stung as tears threatened to flow freely down her cheeks. "Everything has gone so wrong. I can't risk losing someone else."

"Your mother is in good hands."

"But what if she needs me?" Cienna asked, a little more loudly than she intended to. Several of the healers looked her direction, their faces concerned. Lowering her voice once more, Cienna continued. "I can be of assistance."

"Your Highness, again, if I may be frank. There is nothing that you can do that either myself or one of my own can't. Your being here will accomplish nothing." Cienna opened her mouth to respond, but Urthro held up his hand. "Go. Pharn needs you to do whatever it is to keep us safe. If you were the least bit worried, you would not have come to us like this. You would've been at her side the entire time." Cienna's eyes dropped in shame. "Your people need you," Urthro said softly. "Your mother *needs* you. We'll take good care of her. I promise."

Cienna's voice caught in her throat once more. "I – she – you -"

"I understand," Urthro said gently. "The Headmistress asked that I take especially good care of you before she left. Besides," he said with a wink. "If my lord and his family were to pass on too quickly, I would be out of a position. People would say I'm a cursed healer. No, it would be bad for everyone involved if I didn't do my job properly."

"Thank you," Cienna whispered.

"Master," one of the healers called out hurriedly. "She's opening her eyes again."

"Her beat is getting stronger," another one reported. "Her breathing too."

"Excellent," Urthro said, turning away from Cienna and returning to the queen's bedside. "Felio, prepare another dose of Eidmann's root. We'll mix it with penny thistle. Her beat should stabilize once we get the thistle in her. Petre, count the time between the beats," he began clapping his hands slowly, "like this. If there's more than two hits between each beat, we'll need to try something else."

Cienna began backing away during the commotion. The knot in her stomach from earlier loosened as she saw that her mother was in capable hands. *She's always been safe,* she thought. *It's just my guilt that's been worrying me. I've been too hard on mother. I need to trust her now. She trusted my decisions even when I didn't.*

With a soft *thump,* the princess shut the door to her mother's room. The guards stood at attention as she passed by. Cienna felt herself walking with a lighter step than she had earlier that day as the tension she had been carrying slowly melted away.

"Thank Aria, everything's going to be all right," she breathed. "Master Urthro is right. I need to do what I can to keep Pharn, and all of Zanir, safe."

"Hey, Waterbug," Caitlyn called out from the hall. "We're getting ready to leave soon." Cienna sped up, catching up to the redhead. The two fell in step as they walked through the hallway and out of the caer. "Is everything okay? Have you found someone to act in your stead?"

The princess nodded her head. "Yes, I spoke to my caregiver, Yalla, and she is sending word to my uncle down in Cre-shaw in the south asking that he come up and take charge while Mother is healing."

"Is he your mother's brother?"

"No. Uncle Jaes is Father's younger brother. He watches the borders and part of the coast. Mother's family is out on the Isles and Aunt Tynni is up at the northern borders. Uncle Jaes is the closest, and probably the best prepared, to help."

The pair raised their hands to block their eyes as they were greeted by surprisingly bright sunlight in the late afternoon. Cienna squinted her eyes as she held her hand up higher, unused to the lack of usual flowing sleeve hanging down by her wrists. Outside was less chaotic than inside, but not by much. Thol stood off to the side of the entrance instructing the soldiers who were staying behind. Cienna recognized some familiar faces from her father's guard among the dozen or so new recruits.

"Hopefully those boys will be enough," Caitlyn said. "I'd hate for a major siege to be their introduction to life as a soldier. Look at them. Younger than that Cory kid."

"I think his name is Cody."

Caitlyn waved her hand dismissively. "Point is, that poor boy is too young to be in the battle that felled the king. He shouldn't have come out alive. Lucky bastard; the gods really must've been watching over him. I doubt those boys will be as lucky. It'll be a bloodbath."

Cienna felt the knot in her stomach tighten once more. *Am I making the right decision? Everything felt right just a moment ago. Now, I'm not sure.* The princess brought her hands into her body, wringing them.

The redhead glanced over and took note of the princess' nervous tic. Reaching over, she gently grabbed Cienna's hands to stop the young woman from outwardly displaying her unease. "Calm yourself, Waterbug," she said softly. "You can't let your people see that you're insecure. Whatever affairs you've set up, I'm sure they'll be fine. Trust yourself."

A weak smile played on Cienna's lips. "You sound like my master."

"We're in no position to be second guessing ourselves. We must take decisive actions to keep those we love safe."

"That's all I want," Cienna mumbled. "I don't want to let everyone down."

Caitlyn laid her hand on the princess' shoulder. "No one does."

As they rounded the corner, they spied Brody and Alverick organizing the forces. Oldar stood off to the side, speaking with Ronan. Cienna watched the group, noting pockets of men fidgeting nervously. They were seasoned soldiers, but the tension in their face showed their unease. Dez and Zemé also stood away from the main force, talking.

"Looks like everyone's a bit nervous," Caitlyn noted. "Must be the prospect of going up against evil or something."

"How can you take this so lightly?" Cienna asked incredulously. "Gods are coming to Corinth. A huge war is imminent, and you're so relaxed about everything?"

"What do you want me to do? I'm terrified. Al is probably as much of a danger to us and he is to everyone else, the clans are warring, a possible rebellion may take place, and the gods have decided that they want to join in. I'm doing what I can to keep everyone from panicking. If I can keep a straight face along with Brody and the officers, then I'm doing my part to help the army from falling apart."

"I'm sorry, Caitlyn," Cienna said. "I didn't mean it. I appreciate you thinking about how you present yourself. Gods know I need to change how I present myself."

"It's okay, Waterbug. We're all a bit uptight right now. Keep your spirits up. We'll weather this storm."

YRD SAT alone in the back of the tavern shrouded in the shadows as people dined and drank in the low light. Near the bar, a man sat on a stool under a red-lit lamp playing an oud while a young woman danced around the floor. His hands moved nimbly over the strings on the pear-shaped body, stopping occasionally to accent the woman's moves with a flourish of beats on a nearby drum. Wyrd watched her body undulate, her exposed midriff keeping time with the beat while coins jingled around her hips from a scarf. He licked his lips as his eyes followed her.

At the table next to him, a group of men broke out into raucous laughter, their tankards clanking on the table, sloshing spirits on the floor. One of the men shoved his chair backwards, pushing against the table with his boot. The legs scraped across the floor and the man slammed into Wyrd's table, spilling some of his ale on the table and his lap.

The man turned to face Wyrd, his eyes glazed over from imbibing too many spirits, and laughed. Wyrd felt a surge of anger as his eyes were torn from the dancing woman to address the drunkard. The man slapped Wyrd's arm, slurring out something as he continued to laugh, his hot breath washing over Wyrd and smelling of anise and curry. Wyrd narrowed his eyes.

"Leave me," he hissed.

The man slurred out something unintelligible, possibly an apology, before staggering off to rejoin his table. His friends broke into laughter once more, the noise punctuated with a shout as they mocked their friend. Wyrd glowered at the group before searching for the dancer. It didn't take long before he found her once more.

His eyes followed her hungrily, taking in every move of her dancing body. He'd never lusted after a woman so hard before, but as he watched her, he felt every fiber of his being consumed with desire. The group next to him erupted into a drunken cheer as she moved closer to them, her hips swinging in time with the music. Wyrd fought the urge to shoot them a glare, instead keeping her within his sights.

Once everyone leaves, it should be easy, he told himself.

I WANT TO DEVOUR HER, the voice in his head said. **SOFT. DELICATE. PURE. DELICIOUS.**

Wyrd tried to ignore the voices in his head, but ever since he was hit with Alazi's flame, this new voice joined the jumble. Unlike the others, however, this one was much more compelling. It drowned the others out to the point where it had been a while since the other voices in his head spoke to him. This one became dominant, pushing the others into the shadows. And it was strong.

His fingers drummed on the table in frantic taps. He fought the urge to pull his knife from his pocket, but he could feel himself losing control. In an effort to distract himself, he took a drink from his glass and laid his palms flat against the worn wooden table. His hands twitched as he forced himself to keep them in place.

YOU COULD DO IT NOW, the voice said. **IT WOULD BE EASY. NO ONE HAS POWER LIKE YOU. YOU ARE A GOD. SHOW THEM WHY THEY SHOULD FEAR YOU.**

Wyrd's gaze never left the dancing woman. Her movements mesmerized him, kept him focused, like fire. However, they also fanned the flames of desire. His body ached to pull her close to his and squeeze the life from her slender frame. If she was a man, he'd probably slip into the shadows and just wait for the show to be over before slitting his throat. However, she deserved more than an unceremonious death. It was the least he could do for her.

As she moved around the room, she stopped behind one of the tables with a large candle burning brightly. The glow of the flame engulfed her body, leaving only the upper part of her exposed. The tip of the flame curled around her as the smoke drifted up and blended in with her hair.

IT'D BE SO EASY. JUST ENGULF HER IN FLAME AND WE CAN BECOME ONE.

"No," Wyrd snapped. "She is too delicate for that. My people do not deserve that fate."

LOOK AGAIN, the voice hissed. **IS SHE REALLY ONE OF YOUR OWN?**

Wyrd took a closer look as she moved closer to the torches that provided light to the tavern. He scanned her features and her body, trying to see what he missed. Drops of sweat beaded on her body from her exertions, the few that ran down creating little trails of paler flesh underneath the dark. Her face was not as soft as the Qu'ari women, but just a bit sharper.

Then he saw it. How could he have missed it? Her eyes. The blue eyes of the north.

A smile twisted on his lips as he watched his prey with renewed interest.

The song ended with a flurry of her hips, creating a rapid clinking of the coins tied to her scarves, and the couple took a bow amid the cheers of the tavern patron. A handful of coins were flung from all over the room towards the two, landing around them with a *thud*. The young woman flashed an alluring smile as she called out her thanks to the generous patrons. Her voice stirred something inside Wyrd. The tone was rich and buttery, a perfect match for her beautiful face.

"Weren't they wonderful," a large man said as he walked over to the two of them. "I want to thank the talented Tek and the lovely Jytte for joining us this evening. They'll be performing every fifth day starting at dusk. Now let's see if we can't get one last song out of them?"

The crowd broke out into a loud roar. Several fists pounded on the table as voices shouted for more dancing from Jytte. The pair looked at each other before returning their attention back to the tavern patrons. Tek clapped his hand three times. With each clap, Jytte shot her hip to the side, her coins jangling with the sudden, forceful movement.

Wyrd settled back into his chair once more as Jytte began dancing around the tables. He felt a smile tug at his lips as he watched her move. It was almost too perfect. The object of his desires was also the woman he'd been trying to find for months.

He'd heard there was a spy living in Xan. He assumed it would be a man, since the barbarians favored open shows of physical strength instead of subtle nuances like Wyrd preferred. But for it to be a woman, he admired their foresight.

They're smarter than I gave them credit for. Let's see how this plays out, for now.

IV

Birds chirped in the warm morning air as Pram walked through the streets of Fa'Tinh. Despite the early hour, they were crowded with bustling bodies heading out to the market. Children chased dogs, weaving between the slowly moving adults, calling out as they ran. Women walked in small groups, carrying woven baskets to the market for their daily shopping. Occasionally, their laughter punctuated the avian choir.

Pram found himself smiling as he moved among the people. The last week had been difficult as Wyrd amassed his followers. More moved to join his cause than Pram liked. Tension hung in the air now that their leader was gone. He could still see it in the actions of his people.

He kept the hood of his cloak up and made sure to cover his face as best he could. For the most part, he was able to travel through his home without too much trouble, but he could feel stares as he went by. Even the women on their way to the market gazed; they got quiet while their eyes followed him as he moved in the opposite direction towards the market.

At his side, Hroth walked in silence. The man had dyed his hair a dark brown to try and better fit in with the people of Xan, but it didn't seem to be doing much good. Eyes glared at the pale-skinned man with the tattoos on his arm wherever he went. Even Pram's familial markings that he'd gotten when he was young aroused suspicion. With a heavy heart, Pram had begun covering up his non-magic tattoos.

"Things are too tense," Hroth noted, his gravelly voice edged with concern. "If you ask me, I would seriously consider getting those you love out of here. I don't mean to overstep my bounds, but with all I've been hearing, coupled with the distrust in the streets, it's only a matter of time before chaos erupts. Fire never is predictable."

"I appreciate your candor, Hroth, but I don't know where we can safely take them," Pram replied. "Zaa'ni had her baby yesterday, and is in no shape to travel. We should be able to wait it out."

"We don't know when the Great Heart will return," Hroth countered. "Pram, uh, sir, Fa'Tinh needs to be cleared. At a minimum. I would honestly say that all innocents in Xan should leave, but I don't know if that's even possible."

"Speak freely, Hroth. Now's not the time for you to question yourself."

"Is there a cave or something where we can hide Len's family and yours? Just for a few days even. The flames speak of something big coming soon."

"I don't know," Pram replied slowly. "There might be something up north in Ro'thre, but I don't know if it'd be safe for us, let alone a large group."

"Ro'thre would be perfect," Hroth said.

"No, we are... not on the best of terms with Ka'lev."

"Why?"

"Well, there's the failed attack at Zanir's northern border. And Wyrraji's actions with your Flame companion. Not to mention the other Flame and Illoth have also died. Then, there's you. You haven't exactly gone back to her after the mission failed. I don't imagine she'd be too pleased knowing that five of her men are dead."

"True," Hroth said. "That'll definitely slow down her business. I'm sure she'll come for her due soon though."

"One issue at a time," Pram replied. "By the gods, that's all we can handle."

The two walked in silence for a while, ignoring the uneasy stares they received. Whispers usually followed. The tension was only broken by the bark of a stray or shout of a child. As the pair walked further away from the market square, they encountered fewer interruptions.

"Maybe you're right," Pram finally said after some of the men who were finally making their way to the market glared at them. "I fear that Len will not be returning soon. His family needs protection, as does Honorable Mother."

"Yours too," Hroth said. "Pram, don't ignore your duty to your family."

"All I do, I do to protect the Great Heart and the interests of Xan. My family... my family must –"

"Your family must be protected, Pram. You can't sell them short just because you've pledged your life to your leader," Hroth said more forcefully.

Pram stared at the Flame, his eyes wide, incredulous.

"Did you ever wonder why I abandoned my old life to follow you?" Hroth asked. "You are a good man. It's evident in how you try and keep peace in your land. Don't sacrifice your life for someone else's dream."

The pair walked in silence for a while. Pram kept his eyes down, an uncharacteristic action for the usually composed general. He felt his stomach knot as he tried to think of a way to respond to Hroth. The general found himself opening and closing his hands, placing his thumb on his middle or index finger in an attempt to crack them. He forced himself to relax, giving his hands a shake and making them hang limply at his sides.

After some time had passed, Pram couldn't take the silence anymore. Despite the writhing in his stomach, he managed to raise his eyes. To his surprise, he noticed that there weren't a lot of people walking around. They'd covered a decent stretch of ground and were nearing the edge of the village. It wouldn't be too long before they were in the woods by Mother Intan's home.

"You don't know what I've done to keep the peace in Xan," Pram finally said, his voice resolute.

"What do you mean?" Hroth asked. The inflection in his gravelly voice rising slower and higher than usual.

"I'm not happy about it," Pram replied. "I helped Len gain power by throwing a coup. I was part of the former Great Heart's personal guard, and I passed information to Len that allowed for him to overthrow the regime. What makes it worse, is that the man was Zaa'ni's uncle. I never told her, but I buried Ras' body outside of Fa'Tinh. He had a proper ceremony and I performed the burial rituals, but I never told her that Len killed him. I told everyone that I smuggled him out of Xan and that he is living in hiding." Pram's voice cracked a little as he spoke. "Ras was a good man. He didn't deserve what happened to him. He brought us peace, united the clans in a way that no other had. That's how our current system came to be. But it had to be done, for the future of our people."

Pram's eyes dropped once more and his fingers began tapping on his thighs. Though he knew he did what he believed to be right, he still struggled to accept his role in the uprising. The general and Ras had been close, and it hurt to betray a friend. Deep down, Pram knew that this was why he fought so hard for Len to succeed. If Len failed, then Ras' death was in vain.

"You've done no worse than I," Hroth said, interrupting the general's thoughts. "It's the risk we take. If you truly believe in your cause and acted in Xan's best interests, you need to keep moving forward. Don't be a martyr. We're getting your family out."

Pram's eyes popped up and he glanced at the Flame. The man stared ahead as they walked off the path and made their way into the woods. He walked with such ease. Hroth moved with a casual step. There was nothing to indicate that he was troubled by his past. Normally Pram wasn't either.

"You know, I don't think I've talked about this since the night it happened. I justified everything as doing what needed to be done."

"What's happening now doesn't change anything," Hroth said. "Just because your plans are changing, that doesn't mean that what you did was wrong."

Pram felt his spirits lift. The heaviness that settled in his stomach moments before unknotted and disappeared. "I think I know a little cave off the border of Ro'thre and Xan where we can hide everyone."

Hroth grunted in approval.

The trees around them grew thicker, blocking out the sky the closer they got to the Honorable Mother's. The sweet scent of peat moss mixed with the earthy soil created a pleasant aroma as they walked in the warm morning. Birds occasionally chirped in the trees, sending out trills in the otherwise soundless forest. Their feet fell silently on the thick moss, deadening the sound of their footsteps. The air was heavy with the perfume of the flora. No breeze blew through, keeping the air thick all around.

"How many people actually know about this place?" Hroth asked. "It seems pretty far from the main part of the village. I can't imagine that Len's mother would be in danger."

"Honorable Mother is known for some of her shaman work to help women struggling to conceive. She makes teas and says prayers to help bring about fertility. Enough know about this place that it could become problematic."

Hroth sighed. "What a shame. It's beautiful out here. If I lived in a place like this, I wouldn't be killing people for money."

Pram shot the man a look.

"Before I moved to Ro'thre, I lived out on the Bone Coast. My parents died in a fire when one of the pirate groups got a little too drunk and decided to burn the nearby houses. There was a lot of death that day." Hroth stopped talking and the two walked in silence once more. After a lengthy pause, he continued. "I killed my first man too. I was twelve. He was drunk, stumbling around. I watched as he tried to push himself onto a girl, not much older than myself. I'd just pulled myself out of our burning home as it collapsed on my parents and little brothers. I picked up a rock and began smashing him over the head. Blood was everywhere, and her eyes were terrified. Eventually, she ran away, but I kept hitting him. I don't know when he died. I just felt empty, disconnected from everything around me."

"I've heard of the destruction the pirates can bring. I don't blame you. If Wyr-raji were to target my family, I would kill him without hesitation."

"You wouldn't hold back because he's your leader's friend?" Hroth asked.

"Not at all," Pram said. There was a finality in his tone that took even him by surprise.

Hroth let out a snort. "Then I'll continue to keep an eye on him."

Off in the distance, the dark wood of Intan's house came into view. Smoke curled out of the chimney, drifting lazily into the forest and disappearing into the white clouds dotting the sapphire sky.

V

OLDAR STRETCHED his arms and felt his back crack. After sleeping on the hard ground last night, his body felt like he'd been kicked by a mule. Those last couple weeks at home were enough to make his body forget what it was like to sleep outdoors. The pebbles dotting the uneven ground didn't seem like a big problem at the time, but now he regretted not sweeping them away.

A large yawn escaped him as he traveled with the troops. Yesterday had been a long day. Brody sent out a handful of riders to various parts of Zanir requesting aid to meet them at the gorge in three days' time. With his permission, Oldar sent one of the messengers to Madden to have soldiers meet them as well. It was the least he could do since the poisoning. The king was actually surprised that he hadn't been thrown into the dungeons before they left. Alverick's and the goddess' appearance really complicated things.

Standing nearby, a soldier kept an eye on the Alocaran king, distrust lining his face. The man's jaw was set and his arms were crossed as he followed Oldar's movements. Catching the soldier's eye, the young king felt a twinge of disappointment as the man shook his head almost imperceptibly. With just the slightest of movements, he knew the truth: he was not out of the woods yet.

Looking ahead, Oldar spied the small form of Zemé walking by herself. Her long, green hair lay against her back like a patch of moss, and at her feet, small tufts sprung up from the dirt. Her hands waved in the air in front of her as she appeared to chat to herself. Occasionally, a butterfly or bird would fly around her and perch on her hand. Zemé would say something to the creature before it flew away.

"I can't believe she's real," Cienna said, surprising Oldar. "I mean, I always knew we had the Siblings, but I never would've imagined that one of the old gods actually existed."

Oldar glanced at the princess. She had been removed from most of the proceedings, letting Brody handle all of the assignments. The king's stomach knotted as he looked at her. It was his fault that her mother was fighting for her life.

"If my aunt knew that I was walking with Zemé she would probably faint," Oldar replied. "The last time we spoke, she kept praising her. I didn't think Zemé was real either. I thought she was an old relic."

"What else is out there?" Cienna asked. "We've seen a demon, a wyrm, and now a goddess. This can't be good."

"Honestly," Oldar said as he ran his hand through his hair. "I don't want to know." Cienna looked over at him questioningly. "With all we've been through, I'm starting to think there's much more out there just waiting to be seen. What if they want to get involved in whatever shite we're about to have?"

The princess groaned. Oldar's lips twitched into a faint smile and his stomach unknotted a bit as he walked next to her. Having a conversation like this was more than he could've hoped for. Perhaps, he hoped, he would be able to smooth things over and begin to repair the damage between Alocar and Zanir.

"Me neither," she agreed softly.

The two walked quietly together in the warm morning. Oldar felt eyes boring onto him wherever he went. Glancing around as they traveled, he noted the angry glares of soldiers following him and the princess. As with the man from earlier in the morning, each one locked gaze with the king and shook their head, their jaws set as he passed by. Cienna seemed oblivious to the scrutiny, her body relaxed as she walked with him.

Forcing himself to ignore the watchful gaze of the royal army, the young king let his eyes wander, taking in the surrounding scenery. A flash of gold to his left caught the king's attention. Turning towards the movement, Oldar was surprised to see a fawn standing frozen in fear next to a couple ash trees. Her ears were perked forward and her body tense, ready to run at any moment. The king noted that no one else seemed to notice the fawn, and smiled. Though he'd probably regret it later, he didn't have any intentions of alerting one of the soldiers to the prospect of fresh meat. Oldar locked gaze with the fawn. Her large, brown eyes were wide in panic. A moment later, she turned and bolted into the trees and disappeared from sight.

Why couldn't we have shared a moment like this when we first met? Oldar wondered. *If our relationship started like this, things could have been much more different.*

"The queen," he broached tentatively. "How is she doing?"

He heard the princess choke back a sob, but she remained quiet. Oldar felt his stomach drop once more as he tried to figure out what to say next. Things were going so well between the two of them, albeit strained, but it was an improvement from their relationship previously.

"I'm sorry," he continued. "I never would have allowed for anything to leave Alocar if I knew he was even thinking of doing that. He'll definitely have to pay for his actions." The king stopped awkwardly as he found himself about to begin babbling. "Please say something," he finished lamely.

"It took everything I had to leave her," Cienna said. Her voice started out soft and shaky, but grew stronger as she continued. "I hated you, more than I would've thought possible. I wanted to hurt you when I first saw you in the Hall. Now, now, I'm just numb. I can't process my emotions."

"I'm sorry," he replied softly. "I never wanted you to be hurt because of me. You mean so much to me."

"Stop," she said firmly. "How can you say that? We don't really know each other, and I haven't even been that nice to you."

"But I *do* know you," Oldar insisted. "You are strong, stubborn, and care deeply about your people. You wear your passion out in the open. And I admire you for all that you are. You make me want to be better."

"Don't," Cienna pleaded. "There's too much going on right now. I can't think about anything now unless it's related to Mom or what we're about to do."

"Please, tell me we can talk when this is all over. All I want is a chance."

Cienna looked over at the young king. His eyes were earnest, his mouth pulled in a tight line. Oldar watched as she searched his face, studying him. Almost imperceptibly, she nodded. He felt hope blossom in his chest as she looked away.

"I'll talk to you, but you have to earn it," she said.

"Anything," he said quickly. "Name it."

The princess looked off to the side and scrunched up her nose as she sucked in her mouth while she thought. After a few seconds, she turned back to him with a glint in her eye. "Protect me and Caitlyn, keep us safe in the upcoming battle, and we'll talk."

Oldar felt his hope disappear. He was no soldier, not even mildly agile. It would be difficult to keep the two women safe against an army of seasoned warriors. Maybe his soldiers' protection would suffice. He needed to find a way to join his forces with Zanir's; it was his only hope. With a deep breath, Oldar closed his eyes and forced himself to push away his doubt.

Opening his mouth to speak, he saw a slight smile play at the corner of the princess' lips and her eyes sparkle. He felt his anxiety deflate as he dared to hope a little once more. Oldar allowed for his body to relax and felt the tension leave him in a welcome wave.

"I will let you know when the time is right," the princess said. "For now, let's focus on fighting the gods."

"Of course, milady," Oldar said with a nod of his head. "I truly appreciate your generosity. I hope to be able to earn your forgiveness and your trust. I still have great hope for our two lands to unite and do great things."

A voice called out to the princess beckoning her over. With a wave, Cienna took off at a jog, her wavy hair bouncing down her back as she moved. Oldar couldn't help but smile as he watched her retreat off into the distance. He finally had something that he hadn't felt in a long time: hope. Closing his eyes and taking a deep breath, the young king promised himself he wouldn't lose his focus. With his newfound hope, he finally had something to hold on to, something to bring him happiness once more.

VI

BRODY WALKED at the head of the army. Turning to look at his retinue, he felt a sense of pride in what he'd accomplished. He never imagined that in such a short period of time, he'd be leading the king's army into battle. Despite his excitement, a sense of foreboding hovered in the background.

I did it, Bannen. I wish you could see me right now.

To his side, Alverick rode atop the late king's prized warhorse. The Avalanche gazed straight ahead with glazed over eyes. Uncertainty still showed on the man's face.

I can't imagine what he's going through. I wonder if he'll ever be the same.

"Al?" Brody asked tentatively. "What's going on? You seem distracted."

Alverick blinked deeply several times. Brody could almost see him mentally shaking his head to clear whatever thoughts were troubling him.

"Oh, nothing," Alverick replied. The answer came out as airy, but there was an underlying tone of concern that couldn't be hidden from Brody. "You know, just wondering if we're going to stand a chance in ending this before a bunch of gods decide to join the fight."

"Do you really think the gods are going to bother with joining in our petty human squabbles? Surely they have better things to do." Brody tried to keep his tone light, but like Alverick, he failed.

"Well, we have one traveling with us already," Alverick said motioning to the earth goddess. "It can't be good if she's decided to come to Corinth." Brody grudgingly nodded in agreement. "And then there's her," Alverick said, jutting his chin towards Dez. "I still don't know what to make of her."

Brody couldn't help but agree. "She is a mystery."

The two continued on in silence. Brody kept the pace leisurely, helping the army conserve their energy and giving time for any reinforcements to arrive. The young soldier found himself biting his lip while deep in thought.

How am I going to hold us together? What would Bannen do?

Brody forced himself to take a deep breath before following that line of thought. He knew that by second guessing himself he was only opening himself up to doubt and failure. If he wanted to follow in his brother's footsteps, Brody had to be decisive.

I have to plan for the worst, Brody told himself. If the gods are going to join the battle, we have to ally ourselves with as many powerful people as we can. We have a couple magi, and one god. Both Dez and Al are unbelievably strong, and who knows how strong Zemé is. Caitlyn and the princess are good to have in a pinch, especially Cait's skill with a bow. If we get the rest of Zanir to join us, along with Oldar's forces, we could have something.

The enemy has Swordbane, his general, and that guy who was a devil on the field in the siege against Pharn. They have one Flame left. We sent Vahnyre into the abyss. What could they possibly have that would bring the rest of the gods out? What are we missing?

Brody sighed as he walked deep in thought. There had been no news of any goings on in the other countries, nothing other than Dez's ramblings when they saw her in the Hoary Oak. Everything he'd been focusing on had been between Cienna and Oldar and their crumbling alliance.

"Do you remember the dream I had?" Alverick asked. "The one right after we returned from the other realm? Aramaine?"

Brody nodded. It was hard to forget how broken his friend was and how he'd woken up the next day babbling about the darkness. Alverick's actions put him on edge that day. It had been hard to pretend that things were back to normal after all that had happened.

"Well, there was someone stronger than the aethren. Something that even Vahnyre held in deference. I think *he* is going to be the problem."

"Al, didn't you say that was all a hallucination brought on by exhaustion and your almost Snapping?" Brody asked.

"I think it was a warning," he replied. "When I'd Snapped, everything came all at once, but I was unable to focus on anything. Images, voices, words, it all came at the same time. However, one thing was constant: there was a darkness coming that threatened to engulf all of Corinth. I don't remember the dream too much, honestly. I remember it happened, but I don't remember what was said. I do remember the feeling of it all, and that, that..." Alverick cut off, unable to finish his thought.

"Bannen," Brody said softly. "That's the one thing I remember clearly. But Bannen is dead, Al. It was just your memory of him."

"Bannen is *with* me," Alverick said forcefully. He looked around quickly to see if anyone noticed his outburst. "Bannen is with me," he continued quietly. "He was with me in the gorge when we fought Alazi and the aethren. He was with me in Aramaine." Gazing around, Alverick got a soft look on his face. "He's with me when I travel, Brody. He's keeping me safe. Sane."

"He's your Anchor. It's only natural that you'd be so strongly attached to him," Brody said gently.

Alverick mumbled something that Brody couldn't make out, but didn't push the issue further. Brody felt a twinge of regret as he saw the Avalanche's jaw clench and a vein throb in his friend's temple. The two went back to traveling in silence once more. Small clouds of dirt kicked up under the warhorse's hooves. Brody coughed as the dust swirled higher. Alverick's hand came into view with a water skin. Taking the skin, Brody gratefully took a mouthful of cool water. Swirling the liquid around in his mouth, Brody let it refresh him and clear out the dust.

"Thank you," he said, handing the skin back to Alverick.

Alverick nodded as he took it back. In short while, the Avalanche appeared to be lost in thought staring straight ahead as he rode Styx.

Brody took this time to take in their environment. One of Bannen's first rules was to always be alert and aware of one's surroundings. Brody had taken that to heart, especially since his brother was killed in an ambush.

He slowed his pace and let others pass him until he was surrounded by soldiers. Many of his comrades walked with a tense, uneasy gait. Their conversations amongst each other appeared normal, but there was no levity in the group. Any laughter was stilted and ended abruptly. Their hands were by their sides, but when they walked, their weapon arm did not stray too far from the hilt.

Turning his attention back to his friend, Brody watched as Alverick sat straight-backed in his saddle. Styx walked with a smooth, fluid motion, barely disturbing the man atop. Occasionally, Alverick would bring his hands up, moving them in a way like he was either talking to someone or measuring out something. Brody wasn't quite sure. Whatever it was, he kept an eye on his troubled friend.

To the side, Caitlyn walked past him. She alone seemed to be relaxed out of all he'd seen in the last few minutes. Her bow lay slung across her back by her quiver. Her hands hung loosely by her sides and her eyes darted side to side while taking in the scenery. A small grin played on her lips as she watched the birds flying about overhead. For a while, Brody watched the redhead enjoying the graceful arcs of the birds as they rode the eddies and air currents above.

How can she be so relaxed? Brody wondered. *Is it because she's just as bad as Al?*

As if sensing his thoughts, Caitlyn tugged on the glove on her left hand, pulling it over the jagged tattoos that Brody knew marked her as a Spark. He still had not gotten her to tell him when or how she got ahold of any holy blood. All of the holy rituals were performed in the Mageri by the headmistress. There was no way to get the blood.

Unless, she killed a mage and tried to draught him. Brody gasped as the full weight of his thought hit him. *There's no other way to explain it.*

Brody glanced over at the redhead as she wandered mindlessly among the troops. The woman looked around before calling the princess over to her. With a flounce of her wavy hair, Cienna was by her side within moments. The two talked animatedly, one of the few conversations Brody had seen day. A laugh erupted from them, the high-pitched sound ringing over the general chatter and sounds of the large moving army. If he wasn't so distracted, the sound would have caused a smile to break out on his face. It was much needed to break the tension.

Alverick rode on Styx, thankful for her patience as he tried to navigate his thoughts. When he returned to Pharn with Caitlyn and Brody, the warhorse did not try and force a run, but traveled at a moderate pace. He could feel the horse straining to run, her muscles tense as she fought the urge. Alverick noted the eagerness in Styx and was surprised that he could sense something like that.

"I guess it's an expansion of my powers, like how I can sense movement in the grounds. I've never felt something like this before though."

Styx's ears twitched at the sound of his voice. The movements caught the Avalanche's attention, and he reached out to scratch her behind the ears.

"Thank you for being so understanding with me," he said as he ran his fingers through her mane. "There's too much going on right now, and I'm glad you're not making extra work for me."

As if in response to his words, Styx whickered as she walked, her ears twitching to shake off a fly that landed on them. She threw her head back as she walked and let out a small neigh, her feet dancing as she traveled. Alverick gripped the reins as he pulled back on them. Styx's dark eye turned to glance back at the man on her back and the two shared a moment. There was an understanding that passed between the two, and she calmed down at once. She returned her attention to the road in front of her, the tension leaving her body. She wanted to run, but accepted that she couldn't.

Several minutes of uneventful riding found Alverick's mind wandering. Whatever Zemé did produced fantastic results. He struggled to remember the last few days, but eventually gave up whenever he got to his time in Aramaine. It was like there was some sort of barrier between his mind and his memories. Everything was clouded in a haze of red.

"Why can't I remember anything? What happened?" Alverick lamented.

"*Do you really want to know?*" Bannen asked. "*If your mind is trying to keep you from knowing, maybe it's for the best.*"

Alverick turned to find his friend walking beside Styx. Reaching out to touch Bannen's sword, Alverick found it still strapped to his back. When his hand touched the cold steel, Alverick felt a warmth fill him, a peace that pushed away the red haze and replaced it with a fuzzy light.

"Am I going crazy, Bannen?" Alverick asked.

"*You've grappled with your sanity for years,*" Bannen replied. "*Why are you wondering now?*"

The words caught him by surprise, but Alverick did not deny them. He'd felt himself losing touch with reality after draughting.

"I thought I managed to stave off any ill effects," Alverick mumbled to himself. "I did what needed to be done, but at what cost?"

"*It's our duty. We pay the ultimate sacrifice to keep our king and kingdom safe.*" Bannen motioned to himself for effect. "*We chose this life, and all that comes with it.*" Bannen turned to gaze at his little brother, a look of longing on his face. "*Sometimes, it comes too soon and we lose what's most important to us.*" Bannen turned his attention to Caitlyn before giving his friend a knowing look. "*But we knew that when we signed up.*"

Alverick followed his friend's gaze.

She was beautiful. Caitlyn's red hair shone in the sun. A luster reflecting the brilliance caught his attention as her head bobbed with each step. A smile played on her lips as she spoke to the princess, her eyes twinkling like they used to in the old days. She was happy.

Alverick felt his stomach knot as he looked at her. His desire was as strong as it was years ago.

"I should've asked her when I had the chance," he said. Disappointment hung on his every word.

"*It's not too late,*" Bannen replied. "*Don't wait until it is.*"

"But what if –" Alverick's question cut off unexpectedly as he turned to face his friend, only to find that he had disappeared. The knot in his stomach tightened as his throat constricted. He felt his face flush as his eyes began to blur from tears. "Not again," he told himself. "I'm not losing her too."

VII

LEN RESTED his elbows on the worn wood of *Graak's Fury*. The cool salt spray against his face in combination with the tang of the air did little to alleviate his mood. Three days of travel on the open sea should have been his chance to sit and gather his thoughts, yet he found himself reflecting on his failures. The bones had been in his favor; he should have succeeded in his conquest against Pharn. Everything was perfect. He had the power, he had surprise, he had determination. He couldn't dream of a better scenario. And yet, it all came crumbling down around him.

How could I lose to that Avalanche and his men? My people have literally trained for lifetimes to hone our skills, and those undisciplined soldiers manage to go toe to toe with us. I even planned for other magi among their ranks, but they manage to best me there too.

And then Wyr-raji betrays me. The young general found it difficult to finally admit that his childhood friend had sabotaged him. *He'll face his justice when I get back.*

"You ready for battle?" Kayna asked, dropping her hand heavily onto his shoulder.

Len glared at the woman out of the corner of his eyes. "Gods' mercy, you are insufferable, woman. Leave me be."

"Do you really inspire people with that attitude?" she asked. "Relax. Let the sea calm you."

The general returned his gaze to the waters. The waves rocking the ship were a brilliant blue. White foam caps broke the blanket of azure as the waves crested. Gentle motions pushed *Graak's Fury* as winds filled the sails. He hated to admit it, but their travels on the Eastern Seas had comforted him a little despite his frustrations.

"See," Kayna continued. Len glanced over once more and noticed a relaxed smile playing on her lips. The breeze played with her hair, causing smalls strands to blow across her freckled face. "Just let the waters take your worries and enjoy the moment. We'll be back to more serious matters before you know it."

"How do you live so carefree?" Len asked. "Big things have been set into motion, at least back home."

Kayna closed her eyes and breathed in the tang of the salty sea air with a content sigh. "I learned long ago that I can't worry about things I have no control over. All I can do is pray that Graak is in good spirits whenever I'm out on the sea."

Reaching into her trousers, the redhead pulled out a smoothed stone and held it out for Len to see. He stared at the rock, trying to understand the significance it, but couldn't. Kayna ran her thumb over the stone, her finger sliding easily over its slick surface.

"This is like a talisman for me," she explained. "As long as I've had it, I've had fair seas and good winds. Graak has favored me and my crew, blessed us with his mercy. You, you've dabbled in things that Man should not meddle with." Len opened his mouth to interject, but Kayna held up a hand. "You told the Scourge that you summoned a demon, one that turned on you and made your friend god-blessed. We are not meant to casually call on the gods. Any misfortune you've brought onto your people is your own doing."

Len opened his mouth once more, but closed it on his own. It all made sense. Ever since his defeat at Pharn, he'd been desperate for anything to bring him victory, even if it sacrificed his honor. Consumed by his pride, Len had let his judgement become clouded by Wyrd.

"I should have seen that Wyr-raji was leading me astray." He stood in silence for a while, the cool spray of the ocean misting his face once more. "I knew he was," Len finally admitted. "But I believed in my gods to keep me safe. The Windstrider watches over me and my family."

Kayna gasped. "Freyna has chosen you? But how?"

Len shrugged. "The wind is ever fickle."

The pirate leaned once more on the side of the ship. Her thumb ran over the stone once more as she stood deep in thought. Len returned his gaze back to the open ocean. Overhead, gulls squawked as they rode the air currents. The ship crested a high wave, slamming down as she landed back on the surface. The resulting splash caused the cool waters to soak the crew on the lower deck. Cries of surprise rang out as a few of the men shook their hands to try and rid themselves of excess water.

"When this is over," Kayna said, a smile of her face as she stared out into the horizon, "I'll help you with your problems. We are both protected by gods, despite your poor decisions. I will give you the numbers you need to bring peace back to your home. In return, I ask one thing."

"Your debt is already being paid with this trip," Len interjected.

"My *father's* wish is being fulfilled," Kayna corrected.

"Then my debt is to your father," he replied flatly.

Ignoring his statement, Kayna continued on. "In return for my help, I ask for one thing: remember that my father saw something in you. It is in your best interest to not disappoint him. He may be just, but he is not always merciful." She paused for a moment as Len could feel his eyes widening involuntarily in surprise. "Don't worry though," she added. "I saw something in you too. If you are what I believe you to be, I will do everything in my power to help you. Just don't anger the Scourge."

Shoving her stone back into her pocket, the pirate gave Len a pat on the back before walking off, leaving him alone with his thoughts once more. He watched her saunter away, confidence radiating from her relaxed gait. Her crew cleared out of her way as she went by, issuing orders to some of them, which they promptly rushed off to fulfill.

Freyna's mercy, he bristled, *what did I get myself into? I've got two people I apparently owe a debt to, yet they both offer to help reclaim my honor as the Great Heart.*

A cry from one of the crewmen gave him pause. Turning towards the commotion, the young general noticed a familiar figure walking across the deck. Dark hair and olive skin, Dez casually walked towards the side of the ship. She ignored the man's call, as usual, and pulled herself onto the ledge, dangling her bare feet over the side. Occasionally, a spray from the ocean misted her, causing her to lean back.

"And then there's this one," he muttered. "I still have no clue what to make of her."

Len thought back to when he first saw the woman in the Bone Coast. He'd been waiting for Angh to give his next orders, when all of a sudden, she showed up accompanied by a group of pirates. The pirate lord had some revelation when he spoke with her, or whatever he did, because he'd been sequestered in his room for the last three days.

I wish I knew more about her, Len mused. *All I know is that she's a powerful Tempest, and Shadow. It would really help me figure her out. I'm going to need to know her disposition if I'm going to try and bring her with me. Her skills would give us the advantage against Wyr-raji.*

"She's an interesting one," Maya said, startling the general. "It's nice having another woman on board though."

Len grunted in response.

"Kayna is really excited to have you on this trip," Maya continued. "She wants to see what you can do. It's been a while since she's been this excited. I'll admit, I'm intrigued."

"You can't have been in many battles if my presence excites you," Len replied, his voice curt.

"You'd be surprised what we've been through," she retorted. "The Scourge's interest is what's intriguing. Kayna loves the thrill of battle. I, on the other hand, am more interested in you."

Len raised a questioning eyebrow, skepticism plain on his face.

"I've traveled further than most of my cohorts," Maya said. "I have not seen a person who exudes an aura like you do. There's something about you I can't really explain."

Len turned away from Maya and looked back out at the sea. His eyes glanced over to Dez several times as he tried to ignore the woman next to him. He didn't want to admit it, but a part of him was captivated by the two women. Back in Xan, women were not as likely to be fighters. They were more likely to engage in espionage and strike from the shadows. His wife's cousin was a perfect example. Seeing these two in action was something he very much wanted to experience.

"We'll see after this if I still fascinate you."

Maya smirked as she caught his eye. "I hope we don't disappoint." Without another word, she turned and walked off in the same direction as Kayna.

Exhaling, Len took a moment to clear his head before returning back to the calming waves. *These women are harder to read than I imagined. I don't know if I will be able to pull this off.* Closing his eyes, Len let the gentle rocking of the sea help him focus his thoughts.

Taking three deep breathes, the general breathed out slowly on the last one and opened his eyes. A chilly breeze rustled his hair and tugged at his clothes. There was something familiar that washed over him as the wind moved around him. A reassuring calm he'd felt before.

"The bones are still in my favor."

VIII

Zemé sat under the shade of a maple tree on the outskirts of the camp. There were plenty of small pockets of soldiers around that she wasn't too concerned with missing any important announcements. The tree pulsed with life against her back. She savored the energy flowing through her and that she shared with nature as she tilted her head back and closed her eyes. Her mossy hair rested lightly on her back and began to grow onto the bark of the tree.

Heaving a sigh, the goddess let the weight of the day dissipate and started regenerating her energies. In the distance, she could her the chatter and laughter of camp blending with the chirping of the birds. A frog croaked a little way off, welcoming the evening. Resting her fingers on the earth, she could tap into the life of every person in the group. They maintained a high level of energy despite the day's march.

Everyone appears to be in good spirits, she mused. *This bodes well considering the trials ahead.*

More laughter broke out from the groups. It seemed that the heaviness hanging over the retinue due to the queen's poisoning was starting to fade. The princess mentioned before they left Pharn that her mother was not in grave danger, but she also was not out of the woods yet. Perhaps they were hopeful, or maybe they just needed to enjoy themselves after all they'd been through.

The hearty scent of stew wafted her direction. Although she did not need to eat the food of mortals, the aroma was welcome and caused her mouth to water. Cheers broke out as men rushed to line up for dinner. Zemé cracked open an eye and watched as a long queue of men holding tin bowls formed by the camp's chef. A few of them jostled each other, ribbing their friend and cracking a joke.

Her eyes scanned the group, looking for the Avalanche. Every time she thought about him and what she saw when she touched his mind, it caused her stomach to knot. He'd seen so much, and if what he saw was true, the land was in dire straits.

Things were already bad, she reminded herself. *Otherwise, I would not be on the mortal realm. I can't let myself be tricked into thinking that it's all the nonsense of a Snapped mage. To do so would be foolhardy.*

She continued to look among the soldiers for him. Leaning against a tree on the outskirts opposite to her, Zemé spied Caitlyn. The redhead tugged on her gloved hand as she talked to the princess. Cienna was engrossed in an animated story, her hands moving wildly as she recounted her narrative. The archer's arms crossed and her eyes scanned the camp, much like Zemé's were.

Something caught the princess' eye and she said something briefly to Caitlyn before darting off. Zemé's gaze lingered on Cienna as she made her way to Brody, who stood talking to the Alocaran king. Once the princess caught up with them, the goddess returned her attentions to the redhead.

Caitlyn's eyes were drawn to one spot in the camp. Turning her head slightly, Zemé saw that the archer was watching Alverick as he fed Styx some travel pellets. Returning to Caitlyn once more, the goddess noticed a deep longing in the redhead's demeanor. Her body faced the man, much as her gaze honed in on him. Uncrossing her arms, Caitlyn returned to tugging on her glove. She also began chewing on her cheek.

What an unusual way to soothe oneself, Zemé noted. *It's almost as though she's self-conscious about that hand.*

A moment later, Zemé let out a gasp as Caitlyn took off her left glove. The jagged tattoos of a Spark covered the entirety of her hand. However, unlike Alverick's tattoos, hers had large sections where the markings were broken up, revealing her naked flesh where the tattoo should have been.

Tainted, the goddess marveled. *I never would have imagined that she would be so collected with her condition. But what does that mean for their mission? There's two now who are unpredictable. I'll have to keep an eye on them both.*

Her eyes darted back to Alverick. The Avalanche had left the horse and was talking to Brody while in line for some food. She could see his face break into a smile, but noticed that it did not extend to his eyes.

There's uncertainty with that one, she noted. *I did what I could, but I don't know if it was enough.*

Brody made some comment in response, and he and the men nearby broke into laughter. Zemé watched as Alverick attempted to join in the joviality but his reactions seemed forced. His mirth came out in a short bark and the corners of his mouth did not turn up, but it was most evident in his eyes. They were hollow and unsure.

Zemé felt her stomach knot as the Avalanche struggled to engage with his peers. Many seemed oblivious to his efforts as they joked after their long day's travel. The goddess noticed that both Brody and Caitlyn, as she walked over to join the group, kept shooting furtive glances at the man. At one point, the two appeared to share a look after Alverick stumbled over a joke.

Those two, they will be his strength. I wonder if the Avalanche is her Anchor, and he hers? It would answer several questions. Do others know her secret?

A moment later, the princess walked over with a small bowl of stew and a chunk of bread. With a smile, she offered the meal to the goddess.

"I hope this is enough for you," Cienna said as she placed the bowl on the ground. "I wasn't sure how hungry you were, but I wanted to make sure you got something to eat before it was all gone."

"Thank you, Princess," Zemé replied, nodding her head as she picked up the bowl. "Your generosity is much appreciated."

Cienna lingered by the goddess, picking at the top of her boots before pushing on her knees to stand up.

"You seem distracted, Princess," the goddess said. Though it was a statement, the question hung in the air.

Cienna nodded and began to sniffle. Her eyes gradually turned red as tears leaked out of the corners. Taking a large, shuddering breath, the princess forced herself to regain her composure. "My mother," she said briefly before fighting back another sob. "I know she's fine, well, at least as fine as she can be, but I am so worried about her."

"You worry for her health," the goddess replied. "That you made the wrong decision coming on this quest."

The princess nodded, wiping her eyes as she sniffled.

"Do you think your people would be better served if you stayed home?"

Cienna shook her head.

"Then what do you worry about? You know you made the right decision for your people. You left her in the most capable hands you could. You can't let fear guide your actions, child. Only failure can come from such decisions."

The princess sniffled once more and wiped her face. Cupping her hands, she focused on her Stream energies and filled them with cool water with a thought. Cienna dipped her face into the small puddle in her hands and cleaned off the grime and tears. When she pulled away, water running down her face and onto her blouse, her eyes were a little less puffy.

"Thank you," she said softly. "I know that I shouldn't be dividing my attention, but I can't seem to shake the feeling that I shouldn't be here. I know I'm doing the right thing, but still, something eats at me."

"It's doubt," the goddess said sagely. "You doubt yourself, your skills, and that guides your actions. It's okay to be unsure, but you must act as though you are absolutely correct with each move you make."

"But I can't always be certain, even if I pretend to be so."

"Then you will not maintain the respect you deserve," Zemé said flatly. "If you think you're wrong, act with confidence until you find out otherwise. It is okay to be flexible. Showing you can change your will as the situation around you changes you is the sign of a great ruler. Trust yourself. You'll find that it will help you find the answers to your questions."

Without another word, the princess dipped into a curtsey and walked away. Zemé could see the confusion in the girl's face. She only hoped that the princess would heed the advice.

IX

THE LAST COUPLE OF NIGHTS had been long. Zaa'ni cradled Heru in her arms as she laid in her bed. The babe suckled at her breast making little grunting noises as he fed. Sunlight poured through the window, beams breaking through the cracks in the sheets that were placed over them to provide her with a measure of darkness. In another part of the house, she could hear Bermet and Berkah playing, their hushed giggles occasionally turning into shrieks of laughter.

Zaa'ni sighed as she heard Altansari's voice softly remind the girls to be quiet. The girls broke into whispered exclamations of joy before Zaa'ni could hear their feet pattering off to another part of the house. Kemala's voice could be heard over the running asking her mother to make some lunch for her and Elok.

Heru stopped suckling while she was lost in thought as she listened to the children play. He began snoring as his mouth moved away from her breast. His lips moved occasionally as he nursed in his sleep. Zaa'ni gave a content sigh as she smiled down on her little boy.

Len, when are you coming home? There's so much going on right now.

A light knock on her door pulled her from her thoughts.

"Come in," she said.

The door opened a crack and the Honorable Mother poked her head in. The small woman's round face beamed at her daughter-in-law and grandson, wrinkles crinkling deeply around her eyes. Her long silver hair was tied up in a high bun.

"Are you up to some food, dear?" Mother Intan's voice was soft and steady despite her fragile appearance. "Altansari has made some flatbread and lamb for the children."

Although she was exhausted, Zaa'ni pushed herself up off of her bed mat. "That sounds wonderful," she replied. Placing the sleeping Heru in his little nest of blankets and pillows, she stretched her back before walking out of the room with the Honorable Mother.

"He looks just like my son, but there's something about him," Intan said as they walked towards the kitchen table. "You can tell that he's not on his first life here."

Zaa'ni sat down gingerly on the cushion on her chair. Altansari quickly brought over a bowl of lamb and a piece of flatbread, which Zaa'ni eagerly bit into. Fighting back a yawn, she dipped the bread into the bowl, soaking up the lamb's juices.

"You've said this before, Honorable Mother," Altansari said as she corralled the four children into their chairs so they could eat. Berkah and Bermet shot each other knowing looks as they bit into their lamb before devolving into silent giggles.

"Many years ago, back when my grandmother mother was just a girl, Xan had a great hero. His name was Heru, and he protected us from a great darkness. Whatever it was, the elders forbade our people to speak of it and it was forgotten over time. By the time I was a little girl, Heru's sacrifice was lost to time. However, there are still some among us who remember that he gave his life to protect his people."

"And you think my little boy holds the soul of Xan's champion?" Zaa'ni asked.

The children stared at the old woman as they ate. Elok and Kemala's mouths hung open like fish as she told her story.

"Honorable Mother, do you really believe in such things?" Altansari asked. "Isn't he just a myth, like the Faceless?"

The children's eyes moved from one adult to another. Berkah chewed with wide eyes, her mouth moving slowly.

"It is not for us to question the past," Intan said, her voice stern. "The elders hid our knowledge from us for fear that we would misuse it. But for those of us who remember, it is our duty to share it and make sure we prevent history from repeating itself."

"But aren't the stories told to teach us lessons, Didi?" Bermet asked.

All of the children turned their gaze to her as she dared to interrupt the adults' conversation. Kemala sat with wide eyes and her hands over her mouth, while Elok mouthed "no" and shook his head. Berkah gave a small nod as she struggled to smile at the young girl.

"Of course, they are," Zaa'ni broke in. "Didi was just saying that the elders want us to remember the lessons in the stories, but to not be afraid." She shot a look to the other women.

Intan gave Zaa'ni a disappointed look, but did not push the matter further. Zaa'ni shot Altansari another look and gave a slight shake of her head. Altansari nodded and the three went about their lunch as though the conversation never happened. The children looked around at each other, confusion etched on their faces.

"Eat up, my dears," Intan told the children. "When we're done, we can go out in the back and pick some berries for dessert. Your mothers were going to make jam later today, but I'm sure they won't have a problem if we snack on some." She smiled warmly at the children, the wrinkles on her face deepening.

"Yeah!" Kemala said enthusiastically.

"Shhh," Altansari chided. "The baby is sleeping and we don't want to wake him up."

"Sorry, Mommy," she whispered.

"It's okay, baby," her mother said, stroking her daughter's hair. "We just want to make sure that he gets enough sleep. Babies need a lot of sleep."

"I need a lot of sleep," Elok said with a smirk. "A lot of food too."

"Yeah, we know you eat a lot," Berkah teased. "Soon you'll be fat like Zhafir."

Elok put down his food and dropped his eyes. Altansari shot her eldest daughter an angry glare before turning to her son.

"Don't listen to your sister," she said, reaching out and rubbing his arm comfortingly. "She's just being rude. Of course, you need more food. You're a growing boy and if you're going to be a warrior you need to make sure you get enough energy to keep you strong. And you," Altansari turned to Berkah, "you know better."

Elok looked up and stuck out his tongue at his sister from behind his mother's back. As she turned to face the whole table, he brought his face back to a neutral look and began nibbling on his food once more.

Zaa'ni held back a chuckle as she watched the spirited little boy and his sister. Both kids were strong-willed like their father. They also shared their mother's stubbornness. She hoped that when Bermet and Heru were older, they'd both express hers and Len's personality along with their own.

A cry from her room caught her attention. Heru was up. Taking a final bite of her lunch, Zaa'ni left to go take care of her son. As she sat on her mat cradling the infant, she heard chairs scrape on the floor and the children take off to the berry bushes behind the house with the Honorable Mother. Altansari crept into the room, sitting down next to the woman as she breastfed her baby.

"What do you think Honorable Mother meant?" she asked Zaa'ni.

"I don't know," Zaa'ni replied. "It's not like her to tell tall tales like that."

Altansari chewed her lip as she furrowed her brow. "I didn't think so. Pram has always said that Honorable Mother has been a reliable source of information. Not to mention, she's one of our most knowledgeable elders. I can't imagine her making things up like that either."

"And that worries me," Zaa'ni said as her lips delicately brushed against Heru's head. "I don't want him to have some predetermined destiny full of darkness."

Laughter floated through the window from the back, punctuated with squeals. Kemala's giggles could be heard running by the house, disappearing as she moved further away towards the berry bushes. Altansari smiled softly at the window as the voices moved away until they disappeared.

Zaa'ni pulled Heru from her and began gently patting his lower back to help him with gas. His little eyes were closed and his mouth hung open as she held him. With a burp, Zaa'ni offered herself once more. When he didn't take it, she began rocking him in her arms as he cooed happily, his chubby arms waving in the air towards her face. She smiled down at him and babbled at him in a high-pitched voice.

The baby opened his mouth and eyes wide and grunted, his hands reaching for her face. Zaa'ni felt her stomach fill with butterflies of happiness as she played with her little boy. He would be smiling and giggling before she knew it. She sighed at the thought, a small twinge of sorrow trying to sneak in, but nothing could disrupt the butterflies she had flying around inside her. It was the same feeling she had when she first held her daughter. It was pure bliss.

She didn't even realize how long she was staring at Heru's face until she felt Altansari's hand grab hers. Zaa'ni looked up at the woman sitting next to her and saw her face had paled. Her friend's hand gripped hers tightly, Altansari's knuckles turning white against Zaa'ni's flesh.

Zaa'ni turned to ask her what was wrong, but Altansari brought her finger to her lips, telling her to be quiet. With a nod of her head, Altansari motioned towards the window. Zaa'ni craned her neck a bit to try and look out, but the makeshift curtains blocked her view. Warm sunlight still streamed inside, but there was something strange that she could not put her finger on. It took a moment, but then it hit her – there was no birdsong in the air like there usually was. Everything had gone quiet.

A strange chill ran down her spine. Forcing herself to mentally shake off the sensation, Zaa'ni realized that her breath came out in little puffs. She turned to look at her friend once more, but something else made Zaa'ni's blood run cold. Outside the window, just underneath the glass, she heard a low, rumbling growl followed by a series of grunts and heavy sniffing. Zaa'ni felt her stomach drop and she cradled her son closer to her. Her eyes darted over to Altansari's and the woman looked paralyzed on the mat. Eyes wide, her friend mouthed two words and pointed at her. Zaa'ni shook her head in confusion. Altansari repeated the motion, but as she mouthed the words, she let out a breathy "the baby" as she pointed to Heru.

Zaa'ni's eyes flew to her son, who was staring curiously at the two women. His mouth opened and closed as his tongue poked around in search of food. With trembling hands, Zaa'ni brough the babe to her chest once more and stuck her nipple in his mouth. She closed her eyes and prayed that he would latch.

At that moment, whatever was outside began scratching on the wall of Intan's home. The noise made her and Altansari jump, startling the baby. Zaa'ni's mouth dropped open as he pulled away from her and let out a little sound. With shaking hands, she tried to get him to eat again, whispering frantically to her son to not cry. Mercifully, he latched onto her once more and began feeding, but he stared at her with wide, curious eyes.

Tears began to fall down Zaa'ni's cheeks as she struggled to keep her breath from coming out ragged. Altansari was frantically mouthing something, her fingers interlocked as though she was praying. The creature stopped scratching and returning to sniffing.

Sweet merciful Freyna, she prayed and an unnatural wave of dread washed over her, *keep my baby and the others safe.*

The room went dark as a shadow blocked the window. A large, indistinct form appeared against the makeshift curtain. Almost humanlike in shape, a hand reached up and the sound of a claw scratching against the window made her blood run cold. Altansari gripped Zaa'ni's hand in a death grip, her mouth still moving in soundless prayer.

Taps on the glass were punctuated with heavy breathing. Zaa'ni couldn't believe that she could hear everything so clearly. Sweat rolled down her back, making her silks cling to her despite the chill. After several agonizing seconds, the creature let out an ear-piercing shriek that touched Zaa'ni to her soul before darting off.

Warm sunlight entered the room once more, but Zaa'ni couldn't seem to get warm. Looking down at Heru, she heaved a sigh of relief as she saw that he was sleeping peacefully at her breast once more. Tiny baby snores filled the silent room. The sound of ragged breathing came once more and made her heart stop. It took a moment before Zaa'ni realized that it was her own.

With a forced laugh, Zaa'ni felt tears of relief run down her face as she tried to calm her racing heart. Looking over at her friend, she saw that Altansari was praying once more, her eyes closed and tears streaming down her face as well.

"Thank blessed Freyna that we are safe," Altansari finally breathed. "By the gods, what was that?"

"I don't know," Zaa'ni said slowly. "Should one of us go out and look for the children?"

Altansari nodded.

Zaa'ni tried to choke back a sob, but couldn't. Her breaths came out in ragged gasps and tears flowed freely. Altansari put a comforting arm around the young woman's shoulders and rested her head next to Zaa'ni's as she ran her fingers through her hair. She made soft soothing noises as she tried to calm the young mother.

"Calm yourself, Zaa'ni," Altansari whispered. "Be strong for your little one. I'll go and bring our babies back safely."

Planting a kiss on Zaa'ni's head, Altansari got off the mat and headed towards the door. As her hand touched the wood to push the door open, Zaa'ni finally found her voice.

"Thank you."

Altansari turned and gave her a warm smile. It would've filled Zaa'ni with relief, had her friend not still looked petrified, her body standing stiffly by the door.

The sound of the front door opening startled both women. The children's voices filled the house with their laughter. As quickly as she dared, Zaa'ni got up from her bed and followed Altansari out of her room and into the main part of the home. Pram and the Flame were helping the Honorable Mother bring in a bucket full of berries as the children ran circles around them.

"Pram!" Altansari cried, running over to her husband and flinging her arms around his neck.

The general took a step back, startled at his wife's sudden movement. His arms encircled her and held her tightly as she cried into his chest. Zaa'ni couldn't help but feel a twinge of jealousy as the two held each other closely. A sudden touch at her waist made her jump. She looked down and saw Bermet smiling at her as she hugged her mother. Behind her, the blue-haired girl leaned against the table in the room, staring at Zaa'ni with knowing obsidian eyes.

With a nod, Freyna disappeared from the room. Unseen by the others.

X

THE SILENCE WAS BROKEN and birds began singing once more, bringing life to the forest. Pram and Hroth shared a glance before picking up their pace. Not a moment earlier, the pair had been engulfed in a bubble, the forest and all of its life blanketed in a stillness that left the two feeling unsettled. And then, the blood-curdling shriek rent the air before everything returned to normal. The cry lingered around, echoing all around them.

"What was that?" Hroth asked. "You felt it, right?"

"Everything was quiet," Pram said. "Are you cold?"

Hroth nodded.

"This does not bode well," Pram said. "I hope we are not too late."

The two abandoned their caution as they moved through the forest with a hurried pace. They no longer tried to avoid snapping twigs and hiding their tracks as Pram led them towards the Honorable Mother's house, praying that they weren't too late for whatever just happened.

A pit settled in the general's stomach as they neared the home. The sound he'd heard was nothing like he'd ever heard before. It wasn't a wolf or a dying rabbit, but it sounded like something much larger. He raced ahead of the Flame, his feet pulling him closer to the home, when something caught his attention. Holding up his hand to stop their advance, Pram crouched down and crept towards a nearby tree, Hroth following suit.

Peering around the trunk, the general looked around for the source of the noise. A moment later, Intan rounded the corner with the children in tow. She mumbled under her breath her wizened hand clutching at a pendant around her neck. The younger ones raced around, circling the Honorable Mother, laughing as they popped a few berries into their mouths. Excited chatter filled the air. Trailing behind, Berkah lugged a pail full of dark berries. The children seemed completely oblivious to the strange phenomenon only moments before.

Pram felt the tension in his chest disappear as he straightened up. Glancing over, he saw Hroth lounging against the tree he'd been hiding behind a moment earlier. He felt a smile tug at the corner of his lips as he watched the Flame casually surveying their surroundings. The man was always alert.

Damn Flame, Pram mused, *he's always one step ahead of us. Is it because of his blood magic?*

As he stepped out from behind his tree, three giant thumps pounded into his body with cries of "Papa!" Burying his head in his eldest's hair, Pram held his children tightly. He felt his chest tighten as the image of the three of them disappearing popped into his mind. The general's voice caught in his throat for a moment before he managed to speak.

"Is everything okay?" he asked.

They trio broke the hug and began babbling animatedly about their adventures berry picking. Kemala kept trying to speak over her brother and sister to tell her father about the butterfly she saw while Elok kept flexing his arm and bragging about how strong he was getting. Pram shot a glance over at the Honorable Mother and watched as she ushered Bermet to the front door. The old woman caught her eye as she slipped the circular pendant back under her top. Marking herself and the house with a holy symbol, she then did the same to her granddaughter.

"My little ones," Intan called out, "it is time to go inside. Your mothers are going to want these berries as soon as possible, and we need to separate some for later. Give your father a minute to relax."

"It's all right, Honorable Mother," Pram said, nodding his head in thanks to the matriarch. "But Honorable Mother is right." He pushed his children towards the door as well. "We must be getting inside. It'll be dark soon and we don't want your mother to worry." Turning towards Intan, he offered his hand. "Do you need any help, Honorable Mother?"

"No, no. I can manage, thank you." Intan's wrinkles deepened as she smiled at the general.

Whistling for Hroth to follow, the group entered the home.

～⌇～

Altansari's arms squeezed Pram tightly, her head buried into his chest. The general held his wife gently, feeling her slight frame shaking against him. He whispered soothing words to her as he looked around. The children were running around, babbling and laughing before following Intan into the kitchen. Hroth trailed behind, carrying the bucket of berries. Pram caught his eye, and the Flame shrugged his shoulders before helping the matriarch carry the food.

Glancing over at Zaa'ni, he watched as the young woman's eyes lingered on where her daughter had stood just moments before. She seemed to be looking at something, lost in her own world. Her mouth moved, but she didn't actually say anything. This went on for several seconds before she suddenly looked away. When their eyes met, she quickly looked away.

"Is everything okay?" Pram asked softly.

Zaa'ni looked away, unable to meet his gaze. Pram couldn't help but notice that she appeared distracted. Altansari finally released her grip on him, taking a few steps back and wiping her eyes. Both women had a haunted look about them. It was the same one that Hroth and he shared just outside of the home.

"No," she replied. "I'm just missing Len and feeling a little vulnerable. But having Altansari and Len's mother here have been a godsend."

Pram looked over at his wife. Her eyes were red and puffy from crying, and she kept rubbing them. Whatever made that noise earlier, she heard it. Altansari was a strong woman. This was out of character for her.

"Sari," he broached gently. Pram watched as she flinched when he addressed her. She did not want to talk. Time to try another tactic. "Sari, did you notice it getting colder earlier?" The two women's eyes widened momentarily as they were caught off guard by the question. "As Hroth and I were coming back, we noticed an unusual chill in the air. Maybe the howl of the wind in the distance? I couldn't really tell."

"It wasn't the wind," Altansari said quickly. "But you already knew that, didn't you?"

"Did you see anything?" Pram asked. "All we heard was the cry and felt the chill. If a Flame is feeling cold, that gives me pause. Intan and the children seemed to have not noticed whatever that creature was."

Zaa'ni breathed a sigh of relief, her hand going to her chest. "Thank the gods above."

Pram remembered the matriarch muttering to herself as she rubbed the pendant around her neck. Had she been praying to the gods, seeking their protection in their vulnerable state?

Intan believes in the old ways, he reflected. *No doubt she carries charms and other forms of protection passed down from her ancestors. And if Len is as blessed as he is, it stands to reason that she would also be in the gods' favor. There's no way the children did not hear that screech or feel the cold.* Pram's musings were broken as his wife began speaking.

"We saw something," Altansari said. "A shadow, in the window. It scratched the glass with its claws."

"And that scream," Zaa'ni added. "It was like nothing I've heard before. It terrified me to the essence of my being. I'm just glad Heru wasn't disturbed."

"The gods were watching over us all," Altansari said. "The babe was quiet as can be. As though he knew something was going on. I've never experienced anything like this. It's a miracle the children were kept safe."

"Damn," Pram swore. "This is worse than I could have imagined."

"What do you mean?" Zaa'ni asked.

Running his hand through his hair, the general let out a sigh. "Hroth and I were going to try and sneak you all out of the house and into some caves in Ro'thre. Things in Fa'Tinh are getting too unpredictable, and with Even-hand still out, I would rather you all be somewhere safe. With this *thing* prowling around, I don't know if I feel safe leaving you and the children in a cave with no protection."

No physical protection, he wanted to say.

"It can't be that bad," Altansari said.

"I'm afraid it is," he replied.

"We are better off here," Zaa'ni said. "Here we have shelter. Besides, Mother Intan's home is sacred. No one would dare defile an elder."

"Wyrd's actions are becoming quite erratic," Hroth said, stepping into the room. "He preaches discord and sows doubt into the minds of those who are weak-willed or greedy. He promises a new era, all while speaking of devouring Xan."

Altansari gasped, her hand going to her chest. Zaa'ni's mouth dropped open.

"Surely, he can't be thinking of destroying our home. His home." Zaa'ni exclaimed.

Before Pram could respond, Hroth answered. "He's under the influence of Fyre. It is very difficult to keep from watching everything burn."

"What about you?" Zaa'ni asked, her eyes narrowed. "You're of Fyre. What makes you different from Wyr-raji?"

"Those of us who are chosen to walk the path of destruction know that we must tread lightly. Flames usually make good military men, or in my case, muscle for hire. Killing keeps us content, for the most part. There are some who have more bloodlust than others. And then we have Wyrd. He was touched by the gods directly. He didn't undergo the trials I did. I risked my sanity and life to acquire this gift from the priests in the mountain. Wyrd did not. He does not understand or appreciate the power he now has. He has not trained himself for when the urges first hit. Instead, Wyrd leaves himself open to Fyre's influence, devouring whatever gets in his way."

"But what makes you think he's going to destroy Xan?" Zaa'ni asked again.

"From what I've seen, Wyrd wants nothing more than to consume. He's unstable, and he thinks that by controlling others he'll be seen as strong. Your Swordbane is in a dangerous position. If he can't stop Wyrd, he'll be killed. You all will."

Zaa'ni's mouth dropped open for a moment before closing it tightly, creating a thin line. Altansari slumped into the nearest chair, her hands bunching the silks around her hips. Pram just nodded. He'd expected as much. Hroth's information proved to be invaluable, confirming the general's fears. If they were going to take action, it would have to be soon.

But dare they flee the home with that *thing* roaming about? Pram's duty to his home required him to make sure that all of his kin stayed safe. It was a vow he'd taken as a boy very seriously. Now? Now he struggled to keep his people from revolting and returning to a life of chaos that the younger generation did not know. Pram felt a pressure behind his eyes start to build that would undoubtedly become a headache.

I have one duty, and that is to Xan, he told himself. *Do I transport Len's family to safety, putting them above the safety of my brothers, or do I keep them here and pray they'll be safe while I juggle the rest of Xan's people?*

Pram glanced over at Hroth. The Flame leaned against a wall, stretching languidly as the general worked frantically to determine the fate of his brothers. Nothing bothered the man. Perhaps Pram could take his family and go with Hroth back to the Woods of Lingora, offer his services to Ka'lev and serve as a mercenary. He didn't have any blood magic, but he still had a considerable amount of skill he could put to use. His resolve from earlier was breaking.

"Hroth," the general finally said. "Come with me outside. We need to talk."

The Flame pushed off from the wall and followed Pram as he walked outside of the house, leaving Zaa'ni and Altansari in the room, confused.

XI

GRUMBLES OF INDIGNATION FILLED the camp as the soldiers of Pharn continued on their march. Orange, pink and purple tinged the sky as the sun's rays began peeking over the horizon. Birdsong filled the air, the finches chirping only to be answered by the trills of warblers. Alverick rubbed his eyes, trying to get the sleep out of them as he stifled a yawn. His body ached from sleeping on the ground. Somehow, he managed to find the only cluster of pebbles during the night.

Another yawn broke free as he stretched his arms up high in hopes of cracking his back. With a satisfying pop, he felt the tension release a bit. The soreness was still there, but at least he managed to do that much. He twisted side to side in hopes of loosening up. The crisp morning air rustled his hair as he turned, helping to wake him.

Off a way, Alverick's eyes caught Caitlyn struggling to wake up. The redhead stretched as well, her hands on her hips as her back arched, as her mouth opened in a huge yawn. A moment later, Caitlyn finished stretching and moved on to alternating between slapping her face and rubbing her hands for warmth. Occasionally, she brought them to her mouth and breathed on her hands for extra warmth.

He watched as she slowly began packing up her camp. Caitlyn crouched as she rolled up her pack. The sun's rays made her hair shine like silk in the early morning light. Straightening up, she picked up her bow and quiver. The archer plucked at the catgut string several times, testing its strength, before she was satisfied and slung the weapons over her back. Looking around, she spied a wain and tossed her sleeping gear into it with a dull thump. No sooner had she cleared her camp did the princess walk over, striking up a conversation with Caitlyn. The redhead's face was relaxed, a smile filling her freckled face, as she spoke with the young girl.

Alverick felt a deep longing as he stared at the woman. His memories reminded him of the old days, despite the damage he'd done. All he wanted was to go back to those days, back when he, Caitlyn, and Bannen would travel the city in peace. Alverick yearned for peace. However, that would have to wait for now. Now, he must pack.

The skies were brighter, the sun comfortably risen above the horizon by the time the camp had broken up. Alverick stood by Styx, her reins hanging loosely in his hands as she munched on some travel pellets. The atmosphere in the camp seemed generally lighter than it had the day before. Men talked and joked as they waited for orders. Those who had a mount leisurely scratched their horses behind the ear as they spoke with their neighbor, the occasional knicker or whinny breaking the din of human voices.

Brody walked up to the tree in the center of the camp and clapped his hands to get everyone's attention. The group quickly quieted as all eyes turned to the young captain. Alverick let his gaze wander. He noticed the young Alocaran king move closer to Brody. The princess and Caitlyn also inched their way closer to Brody.

"Good morrow, everyone!" Brody called out.

Voices rang out in greeting to the young captain. Alverick returned the greeting, his dry voice scratching his throat as he shouted. He removed the water skin from Styx's travel bags and took a long drink of cool water. The cold liquid soothed his throat as it ran down, helping him wake up further. Shaking the skin, Alverick noted that it was getting close to empty.

Shit. I'll need to fill it soon.

"Today we continue forward to the land of Xan," Brody continued. "We will fight to help our allies, and prevent the darkness from spreading."

Shouts of anger broke out from the group. Cries of "Death to Sword-bane!" and "Damn the Xan" could be heard over the general yells. Alverick looked around and watched as the mood in the camp started to turn. His eyes returned to his friend as he struggled to regain control of his soldiers. Styx pawed the ground nervously.

"Please!" Brody called out. "We have a responsibility to our allies to protect them. The Great Heart pledged his support to us when we fought at the gorge. Now we must return the gesture."

"He caused the problem to begin with!" someone called out.

"Let him rot!" another added.

Alverick watched in dismay as the energy in the camp turned against Brody. Handing his reins to the man next to him, Alverick began walking over to Brody.

I have to do something, he thought.

"Silence!" Brody shouted.

Alverick looked around in shock as the outbursts from the camp stilled. He could feel the anger in the air, but it had been replaced by tension. Men stood anxiously, shifting ever so slightly as they bit their tongues, waiting to hear what Brody had to say. Their eyes stared at the young captain with uncertainty, their mouths drawn in tight lines and their jaws clenched. Turning to look back at his friend, Alverick saw a leader.

Brody stood in front of them with his back straight and his expression confident. His eyes shone with a determination that Alverick usually only saw during training. Though his jaw was set, it was not clenched like the other soldiers. He faced his comrades with a calm authority.

Bannen... you'd be proud.

Alverick found himself smiling at the young captain. Returning to Styx, he took her reins back from the man who still looked bewildered at receiving the king's horse's reins and held them loosely in his hand once more. Patting the horse on the muzzle with his free hand, Alverick began tickling her under the chin, his fingers moving through her whiskers. Styx knickered and pawed the ground with her foot. Her tail swished as she leaned into him.

"I know that we've had nothing but trouble since they attacked," Brody continued. "However, King Jaste believed in keeping your word, even if it was to your enemy." Men shifted on their feet as he spoke. "We may not like it, but we have an alliance, and we will use this alliance to strengthen both of our lands. But right now, they need our help." At this, Alverick noticed that Brody's gaze dropped momentarily and he dragged his foot across the ground. He hesitated before taking a deep breath and continuing. "Just like at the gorge, we will be facing a foe unlike any we've ever faced before. One with the strength of the gods without their markings."

Startled gasps broke out in the group. Alverick felt more shifting in the camp through the vibrations in the earth. He felt himself wanting to disappear into the ground. He knew what was ahead. He'd gotten a glimpse of it when his mind Snapped. Only he knew the dangers that they were all walking into. Him, and the goddess who walked with them.

"We will hold their people to justice for the murder of our king. For the deaths of our people, and for the people of Alocar." At this, Brody motioned to Oldar who stood off to the side listening. "All I ask is that you trust me as much as I trust all of you. We are in this together, and we shall succeed, together."

The camp broke into a thunderous roar as men raised their fists into the air. Alverick noticed that the tension had not fully left the camp, but that was overshadowed by their pride. The shouting continued for several minutes while Brody stood in front of them all, smiling. His boyish sparkle danced in his eyes, but there was still the determination that had been there when he gave his speech.

Alverick felt his chest swell with pride for his friend. Brody had struggled for years to distinguish himself from his big brother. It appeared that after everything they'd been through, he finally managed to do so.

XII

Hroth walked through the streets, a hood covering his face. He slid through the crowd easily, no one paying attention to the Flame as he blended in with those around him. People chatted freely, the tensions that had been blanketing the capital over the last couple weeks lifting since neither Wyrd and his followers, nor the Great Heart or Pram were around. Hroth liked working alone. It was easier to get information that way.

Clusters of women dressed in cream, orange, and yellow dresses gossiped about how nice it was for things to be back to normal now that their husbands were back. A few of the younger ones beamed over their brothers returning safely. Their concern for Fa'Tinh and the turmoil she faced overshadowed their desire for normalcy. Not even out of earshot, a woman covered in black mourning garb trudged on, her head down. Next to her, three young children no older than seven walked by her side.

Hroth watched as the woman pulled out a few coins from a nearly empty pouch and handed it to her family telling them to go and pick up some honey cakes. The little ones' eyes lit up as they took the money and dashed ahead of their mom. The woman, who Hroth realized couldn't be older than Zaa'ni, kept her head down as tears rolled off her cheeks. Ahead, the colorful, happy women prattled on without a second thought for whoever may be around them.

The Flame felt a twinge as the sight of the mourning woman pulled at his emotions. He'd seen people like her far too often. Too many families were destroyed from raids, fires, and disease, not to mention those affected by his own hand. He always lingered a few days after one of his jobs. He never knew why, but he always felt the need to see the aftermath of his handiwork. And they were always the same.

Reaching into his pocket, Hroth felt the cloth he stuffed in there to mute the jingle of his coins. Pulling out a gold piece, he palmed the coin and picked up his pace. The mourning woman moved slowly, trying to put distance between herself and the oblivious groups ahead of her. It didn't take long before the loud chatter died down and more mundane conversations could be heard.

Hroth maneuvered until he was in front of the woman and slightly to her left. He slowed his pace until it matched the general flow of the crowd. Once satisfied that he wouldn't outstrip her, Hroth returned his attentions to those around him. As he observed, he gradually brought his hand in front of him against his stomach, the coin resting on his body.

Shops were open, their doors and windows flung wide in hopes of drawing in customers. Bright silks shone in the sun, catching the eye as one walked past. Other shops had fragrant oils or bottles of wine, the glass reflecting the light and sparkling in the window. Every now and again, Hroth watched a young woman drag her partner into a shop to get a better look.

Pretending to be distracted by a bottle of oil, the Flame waited until the mourning woman was nearby before dropping the coin in front of himself and deftly pushing it into her oncoming line of sight. The woman approached, her gait still slow and her head down. Hroth watched her out of the corner of his eye, making sure to step forward to look at the bottle while exposing the coin now off to his side. He was rewarded with a gasp. He focused his attentions on a different bottle of oil as the sound of shuffling feet approached.

A gentle tap on his shoulder caught him by surprise. Turning to face the mourning woman, he came face to face with a pair of deep brown eyes. They were so dark that her whites were a pale shade of blue. He felt his breath catch in his chest. She was lovelier than he expected.

"Did you drop this?" she asked. Her husky voice sent a shiver through the back of his head and down his spine. She proffered the gold coin to him.

It took a moment, but Hroth managed to find his voice. She was over a head shorter than him, and underneath her black clothes, he could see that she was slight of frame.

"No," his gravelly voice sounded far away to him as he shook his head. "Looks like the gods have blessed you with great fortune."

The woman dropped her arm and gaze. "The gods have not blessed me," she replied softly. "They have taken my father, my brother, and my husband from me these last few days." Hroth raised an eyebrow in surprise. "My brother was killed in the battle at Pharn, while my husband was killed at the gorge. My father was wounded, but succumbed to his injuries a few days ago. All I have left are my children."

"I'm sorry that you've suffered so much in the name of war," Hroth said. "I can appreciate what you've gone through." Reaching into his pouch, Hroth pulled out several coins. Placing them into her hand, he closed her fingers over the collection of gold, silver, and bronze. "Here, take these to help you feed your family. At least fortune will smile on you today."

Turning away from the fragrant oil bottle, Hroth started walking down the street. A knot twisted in his stomach as he left her. He didn't get far before he heard her husky voice cry out to him. Moving to face her, Hroth saw the young woman racing to catch up with him. She gripped his arm as she held her chest and caught her breath. He felt a tingle in his arm at her touch.

"You left before I could say thank you," she said. "Please, if there is anything I can do to repay you, I will do what I can."

"Take care of yourself and your children," Hroth said simply.

Tears welled in the corners of her doe-like eyes, the droplets catching in her long eyelashes. "Thank you," she said. She paused, a question hanging at the end of her words.

"Hroth."

"Thank you, Hroth. Please, at least let me treat you to a meal. It's the least I can do to repay you for your generosity."

Hroth mulled over the offer. It had been a long time since he'd had a home-cooked meal. He usually kept to himself when he ate. The idea of having company intrigued him.

"I would like that," he replied.

The young woman beamed through tear-filled eyes. She clasped her hands together in front of her and exclaimed, "Excellent! Are you free tonight? I can meet you in front of the Wolf."

The Dancing Wolf? he wondered.

"Just outside of the main square?" he asked.

"Yes, the one by the fountain," she confirmed. "I work nearby, so if you get lost ask for Maen."

Maen, huh?

Movement to the left caught Hroth's eye. Maen's voice sounded distant as he turned his head towards the source of movement. A few shops over, Wyrd traveled down the street. Hroth noted that his movements were predatory, almost as though he was stalking something. The man's gaze was fixated on something in front of him. Hroth scanned the people in the street and noticed a slender woman with light hair weaving around people.

The woman seemed unaware that she was being followed as she moved casually in between everyone else in the street. She stopped in front of a store and gazed through the window, her hands unconsciously grabbing her hair and moving it from her back to over her shoulder. The woman's fingers played with it, running through her hair as she admired whatever she was looking at. When she stopped, Wyrd did too. He always kept some distance between them, allowing for him to remain unnoticed.

Maen's voice suddenly came back into focus as he returned to their conversation, his eyes never leaving the god-cursed man.

"I didn't realize that you had someone else."

"Wha-?" Hroth turned to face Maen, her doe-like eyes unable to meet his.

"The girl over there," Maen replied, pointing to the light-haired woman. "You've been watching her intensely."

"No, it's not that," Hroth said.

His explanation was cut short as the woman began moving again, only to be followed by Wyrd. Hroth noticed that the man's hand went to his hip, rubbing the sheath resting gently on his side. The Flame watched as Wyrd's eyes darted around momentarily before pulling up his hood and continuing after her.

"Come," Hroth said, grabbing Maen's wrist. "But stay quiet."

"What's going on?" Maen gasped as she tried to pull her arm free from his grip. "Let go!"

Adrenaline coursed through the Flame, a combination of fear and desire that he'd never felt before. He wanted to hunt Wyrd like he hunted the woman, but his stomach twisted in knots as he thought about the primordial power the man possessed. And then there was Maen.

Turning to face her, Hroth stared into her deep brown eyes. He read the uncertainty, the fear that filled her at his erratic actions.

"Listen to me," he said quickly, his eyes darting back to his left, trying to keep Wyrd in view. "That man, I have business with him. The woman I was looking at, she's in danger."

"Why are you telling me this?"

"Because, if you would still like to invite me to dinner, you need to know that you could be endangering yourself. I would love to join you, but my work keeps me from getting close to others." Releasing her arm, Hroth took a deep breath to try and calm the both of them. If he could control himself, she would begin to relax. "I'll be at the Dancing Wolf tonight. I will wait until the sun has set. Do not feel obligated to join me, I know your children's safety comes first. I will understand. It was nice meeting you, Maen."

Without another word, Hroth turned and began following Wyrd.

~~⌇~~

The sun crept closer to the horizon as Hroth made his way to the Dancing Wolf. Lamplighters made their way through the streets, placing their flames in the lamp and filling the area with brightness. Bright oranges, pinks, and purples painted the skies as stars began to pop out. Their tiny pinpricks twinkled in the heavens as the inky darkness spread.

It had been a long afternoon chasing after Wyrd, and the Flame was tired. He sat down on the ledge of the fountain to rest his feet. The gentle sound of water running into the bottom of the basin soothed him. Resting his palms against the edge, Hroth leaned back and closed his eyes as he exhaled. He felt his body melt as he sat.

Wyrd turned out to be surprisingly tricky to follow. The man moved with a stealth that Hroth hadn't anticipated, keeping to shadows and making sure that he stayed far enough away, surrounded by others in the streets, that even if the woman had turned around, she would not be able to pick him out among the crowd easily. Even Hroth had trouble keeping an eye on him at all times.

What Hroth did notice was that the woman appeared to be traveling as though she feared being followed. Several times, she would double around a street, cutting through an alley or side street, only to re-emerge on the main road. Wyrd must have been following her for a while, because every time she ducked down a quieter street, he continued on, waiting for her to pop back out so he could pursue her once more.

There was something about the woman that made Hroth uneasy. She didn't appear to have any tattoos, but she carried herself with the air of someone who'd seen trouble a few times in her life. She knew how to stay alert without appearing paranoid, whether it was the way she kept her path erratic or how she found subtle ways to look over her shoulder casually. The woman knew how to listen to her instincts.

Darkness surrounded the square, broken up by the flickering lights from the lamps and the brilliant moon. Families finished their business for the day and made their way home, while men roamed the streets on their way to the tavern after a long day's work. Checking his surroundings, Hroth pushed himself up and pulled his hood off of his head. His dusty hair lay matted to his head after a day of sweating under his hood. He made his way to the Dancing Wolf, the main tavern in Fa'Tinh, the warm glow of her bright lights flooding the darkness as the door opened.

The Dancing Wolf bustled with life as Hroth made his way to a table. Lamps lined the walls, filling the tavern with their light and creating long, flickering shadows on the walls. Loud chatter filled the room, broken up by shouts and the clank of tankards being slammed against the tables. At his table, Hroth ordered an ale and a plate of food from the bar maid. Once she left, he leaned back into his chair and began watching the other patrons.

In what seemed like no time, the maid brought back a steaming plate of spiced lamb and vegetables as well as his drink. Hroth took a long draught of his ale, keeping his eyes on the rest of the tavern. Everyone around him appeared to be in good spirits, their conversations lively even if they looked a little tired. Viir's call to action against Len for Liir's death didn't seem to have gained much momentum. Wyrd's actions appeared to not have affected these people either. Hroth felt himself relax a bit. At least there was a bit of good news tonight. He took another bite of food and let himself take his eyes off of his surroundings. As he tucked into his meal, he used the flames on the wall to listen in to the conversations on the other side of the tavern.

They came to him in a jumble of words fast and furious. Closing his eyes, he managed to focus his mind on key words he was looking for, and realized that there was nothing of interest for him at this time. Plenty of talk about a young woman named Pek, but nothing other than bawdy talk from a bunch of drunk young men. Nothing he hadn't heard before in the taverns.

His observations were interrupted by someone softly clearing their throat. Pushing the voices from his mind, Hroth opened his eyes and felt them widen in surprise. In front of him, a young woman with thick, wavy dark hair and large, brown eyes stood looking at him. Once they made eye contact, she averted her gaze, staring down at the table.

"I didn't think you would come," Hroth said, his gravelly voice catching in his throat. "Not that I would blame you. Take a seat," he said, motioning for her to join him as he took another long drink from his tankard.

Maen's eyes darted up and a slight smile played on her lips. She'd changed out of her mourning attire and wore a simple silk dress of pale pink. A matching shawl covered her bare shoulders. Pulling her hair over one shoulder, Maen sat down across from Hroth.

"I'm sorry," she said. "I almost didn't come, but I promised you a meal, and I didn't want to go back on my word after your generosity."

Waving down a bar maid, Hroth ordered another plate of food. Maen asked for a glass of wine, and the two sat in silence as they waited for her food. Like before, it wasn't long before the bar maid returned and set down her meal.

"That's what I love about the Dancing Wolf," Maen said as she took a bite of her dinner. "The service is great. Besides, they've recently gotten some great entertainment."

The room erupted into cheers as the owner of the tavern walked over to the stage. He held up his hands and as quickly as the cheering broke out, the tavern went silent.

"It is my pleasure to bring you our talented performers from the other night," he said, a large smile on his face as he motioned towards the main stage. "Please give a warm, Dancing Wolf welcome to Tek and Jytte."

The room broke into thunderous applause once more and men began whistling as a young woman with light hair walked up to the stage in loose fitting pants and a low-cut top that stopped just above her navel. Behind her, Tek sat on the ground and positioned his drum between his legs. With a one, two, three, he began beating out a high-energy rhythm. Jytte began shaking her hips in time with the music, the high clang of finger cymbals accompanying Tek's beat.

Hroth's jaw dropped as he watched the woman from earlier in the day start dancing around the tavern. All eyes were on her as her hips shook and swayed.

"Isn't that the girl from this morning?" Maen asked.

Hroth forced himself to look away from the woman for a moment, his eyes feverishly scanning the room. Within seconds, he found his target sitting almost opposite him in the shadows of the tavern. He watched as Wyrd's eyes hungrily followed the woman from the darkness.

XIII

THE MORNING SUN BEAT DOWN on Alverick's face as he rode at the front of the group. Brody's speech the day before not only inspired the soldiers, but Alverick noted how even Brody himself seemed changed by the power his words had. He'd known only too well how the young man felt overshadowed by his brother.

People truly grow with adversity, Alverick mused with a smile. *I don't think he'd be where he is right now if he hadn't had to take over. Maybe I should've stepped down sooner.* He glanced over at Caitlyn walking with the princess and Brody. The three looked to be genuinely happy as they spoke. Even Caitlyn, who seemed preoccupied ever since she and Brody rescued him from Aramaine, had a relaxed smile on her face.

"Maybe I could've fixed everything," he muttered to himself. Styx knickered in response, her ears twitching as she walked. "At least I still have one special lady in my life," Alverick said with a smirk as he pat the onyx warhorse on the side of her neck.

He sat in silence for a bit as they traveled on. The closest person to him was one of the newer recruits talking to a friend. Alverick let his mind wander, trying to remember the now clouded bits of his memory before Zemé healed him, or at least afforded him a temporary solution to his problem. Red haze still clouded his periphery if he did not get enough sleep. The last few days traveling had been difficult.

Closing his eyes, Alverick forced himself to try and push the fogginess away. Counting to three under his breath, he slowly opened his eyes once more. Alverick let out a sigh of relief as the haze lessened and wasn't as noticeable as before. Hopefully it would stay that way.

As the morning wore on, Alverick found himself becoming sleepy. The rhythmic motion of Styx plodding along the dirt road in combination with the monotonous scenery passing by and the heat of the day soothed the Avalanche's exhausted body. The fog around his periphery faded into the background and became replaced with darkness. Several times, Alverick found himself nodding off, his chin dipping onto his chest. With a start, his eyes fluttered open and his head shot up.

"You doin' all right there?" the man nearby drawled.

Alverick glanced over at the person next to him. The stocky man with scraggly hair that fell just below his shoulders stared at Alverick with a bored expression, his friend next to him stifling a chuckle. Alverick shook his head for a couple seconds trying to push back his fatigue.

"Maybe ya shouldn't be ridin'," the man continued. "It's dangerous to fall asleep on a horse." His eyes widened as he took a good look at Styx. The warhorse shook her head and gave a whiny before snorting. Her muscles twitching under her shining coat spoke of her strength and lineage. Styx was a noble beast, and she knew it. "By the gods," he swore as his friend's eyes widened. "It's the King's horse. I – I'm sorry, sir," he said suddenly as he stuttered an apology. "I didn't realize. I – I-"

Alverick held up a weary hand and stopped the stammering man. "It's all right. I know the dangers well enough." Patting the horse on the neck, he gave a wan smile. "Styx is a good girl. She knows to not speed up unexpectedly, unless absolute necessary. I appreciate your concern though."

The scraggly man and his friend dropped back in embarrassment, giving Alverick space as he continued on. Alverick could hear them talking hurriedly in low voices. He could almost feel their eyes shooting furtive looks in his direction. Doing his best to ignore them, Alverick focused on the ride.

In what felt like next to no time, his chin started dipping onto his chest once more. A dragonfly buzzed by his ear, momentarily startling him, but quickly lulling him into an almost trance-like state. Feeling quite comfortable, Alverick decided to close his eyes for a moment.

It really is a lovely day. I wish this could last forever.

Alverick opened his eyes and was greeted with darkness. The faint red haze that tinged his periphery was no longer there. It was as if night had fallen in a matter of seconds. Looking around, he couldn't find anyone. His pulse began racing as he realized that he was no longer riding atop Styx. Around him, sparse trees grew out of the springy soil. A bright, full moon hung overhead in the clear sky. In the distance, a long owl hooted once.

"What's happened?" he muttered, running his hand through is hair. "Where am I?"

A slight breeze rustled the branches of the nearby trees. They cast eerie shadows on the ground in the moonlight, their thin branches reaching towards him like gnarled fingers. Alverick spun around, trying to find shelter or a landmark that he recognized to give him an idea of where he was. Beyond the trees, he could see a mountain range.

"Mountains? I wasn't anywhere near the mountains. Am I up north?"

Spinning around, he saw a large structure that looked like the open-sided temples he'd seen on the Isles of Corin. Large pillars towered towards the heavens, the roof of the building having fallen off long ago. Several of the pillars were cracked, the stone piling at the base of the columns. He turned his head from side to side several times before making up his mind. With a deep breath, Alverick made his way towards the temple.

The Avalanche covered the distance to the ruins in short order. The tall grasses rustled in his wake as he moved through them. He tried be stealthy, but there was an unsettling feeling of being watched. The hairs on the back of his neck stood on end and he felt a shiver run down his spine as he approached the entrance to the temple. An energy, almost electrical, seemed to surround him. His heart raced and he spun around, facing the way he came, as he felt a pair of eyes on him.

Nothing was there.

By Aria's grace, I need to calm down. But Ghan's mercy, I have never felt like this, he thought. *What is this?*

Forcing himself to slow down, Alverick took a deep, steadying breath and approached the first pillar. The fallen stone greeted him, as the remnant of the pillar pointed into the sky. Placing his hand on the rubble, he ran it across the smooth surface. Occasionally, he found a dip in the stone where the decorative grooves had been chiseled into the shaft.

His eyes never left the open space in front of him. Despite the light of the moon, he thought he could see shadows moving around in the darkness. Unable to see anything in front of him, Alverick stepped onto the first step. A shock ran through his body sending tingles down him. He gasped. A moment later, it felt as though someone cracked an egg over his head as a cool sensation traveled from the top of his head all the way down. Once it reached his toes, the heaviness around him dissipated.

Alverick got off the step, returning both feet to the soft ground. Everything felt the same. His body was cool and the static energy he'd been feeling around the ruins was still gone. With an apprehensive step, he put his foot back on the step. When nothing changed, he pushed himself forward and entered the ruins.

The Avalanche found himself walking through the open temple. An unanticipated breeze came through the large pillars, causing him to shiver. The moon hung high in the heavens, a wispy cloud floating lazily over the half moon. Tiny pinpricks dotted the sky as the stars shone as brightly as the moon. Despite the beautiful evening, Alverick was unnerved; there was no other sound. Through the open hall, Alverick could see the tall grasses and trees in the distance, but he couldn't hear anything. No owls hooted. No chorus of crickets or cicadas filled the air. Only the gently rustling of the grasses and leaves in the breeze.

His body on high alert, Alverick moved cautiously through the ruins. He strained his ears as he tried to pick up any sound nearby. A low moan off to the side caught Alverick's attention. Dropping into a crouch, Alverick pulled his sword out of its sheath as quietly as possible. Once the weapon was drawn, he pressed his free hand to the ground.

Holding his breath, Alverick tried to sense any movement approaching through vibrations in a patch of exposed soil he found where the stone had crumbled away. He held his position for a long time, reaching out through the earth to try and find the source of the sound. A cloud moved over the moon, casting everything into darkness. Alverick felt the muscles in his body go taut.

Nothing.

I could've sworn there was something, he wondered as he slowly got back up. *It sounded like a voice. What's going on?*

Moving cautiously, Alverick gradually made his way through the open temple in the moonlight. He tried to keep to the shadows made by the pillars because, though he couldn't see anyone, on several occasions he heard the moan once more. With each sigh, he would get more and more tense.

I don't understand, he fumed after dropping to the ground in a crouch for a third time to check for anyone approaching. *I hear something. There's someone out there.*

The leaves rustled in the wind once more. With a sigh, Alverick put his hands on his knees and pushed himself upright. Sheathing his sword, he prepared to turn back, but something caused him to pause.

Music.

This time, he was sure of it; the haunting melody of a lute playing a festive tune in the distance. Taking a deep breath, Alverick worked to calm his nerves before cautiously heading towards the sound. It didn't take long after exiting the back of the ruined temple before a large wooden building appeared. Alverick carefully crept up until he could hear chatter and revelry along with the music. Crouching down, he placed his hand on the ground, searching for the vibrations that would tell him how many people to expect inside.

Alverick nearly stumbled back as he felt the movement from the hall. There were hundreds, if not thousands, of people inside. His heart raced as his body tensed, sword half-drawn.

How are there so many people in there? There's no way it can hold so many.

As he pondered his next move, the door opened and a warm light spilled out into the darkness. Alverick dropped to his belly, pressing himself against the earth as he held his breath. He tried to follow the person's movement as he pressed his hand and cheek to the ground. It was difficult since there were so many nearby. Closing his eyes, Alverick held his breath and concentrated.

The figure walked away from the hall and down the same path towards Alverick. Another cloud moved in front of the moon, blocking the light and providing Alverick with the chance he needed. Pushing himself up to his feet, the Avalanche darted into the tall grasses and over to an isolated tree. He quickly straightened up, pressing his back to the trunk. In those precious few seconds, he managed to make it to safety. As the cloud left and the moonlight returned, he watched the lone figure continue on. With the light shining on the man's back, the figure's features were shadowed, making it difficult for Alverick to see anything.

Shit. Do I stay and hope he doesn't see me, or do I go back? Alverick clenched his teeth and pulled his sword out. *Where would I go? There's no way I can escape without being seen. Maybe if I can sneak up on him I can –*

Alverick's heart stopped as he realized he could no longer sense the lone figure.

Shit!

He looked around wildly, trying to see where the figure went.

No way he just disappeared.

"Al, is that you?"

Alverick felt his jaw drop as the lone figure stepped into the moonlight.

XIV

ALVERICK NEARLY jumped as the figure stepped out of the shadows. Sword held in front of him, Alverick slowly moved away from the trunk of the tree and into the moonlight. It couldn't be him. Forcing himself to be on guard, Alverick inched away from the familiar voice he'd longed to hear once more. In the warm glow of the fires inside the hall behind the figure, a shadow moved, blocking some of the radiance that spilled out into the darkness. Ignoring the brightness, Alverick forced himself to stare at the glow until his eyes adjusted. In the light of the moon, he saw Bannen approaching.

"Ghan's mercy, Bannen!" Alverick swore. "What are you doing here? Where in the hells am I?"

Bannen shifted nervously, his eyes darting side to side. "You shouldn't be here, Al."

"I know. I don't even know how I got here though, wherever here is."

Ushering his friend away from the building he just exited, Bannen shot furtive glances behind him as they traveled through the darkened ruins.

"Bannen, what's going on here?" Alverick asked, surprised at his friend's uncharacteristic actions. "Stop, stop. Tell me, what's going on? Where am I?"

Bannen dropped his head, but stopped pushing Alverick. "Al, you're at *the* Halls. You're in Themba."

"Themba," he gasped. "Land of the warriors." Looking over Bannen's shoulders Alverick stared at the building. "The Halls of the Fallen. Final home of my brothers."

"Al," Bannen said, trying to catch the man's attention. "It's not what you think."

Alverick wasn't listening as he made his way back toward the hall. "Is Jaste there?" he called out. "I have so much I want to talk to him about. And Yuth? I'd love to see him too."

"Al!" Bannen said, grabbing the Avalanche's arm. "It's not like that. You can't just walk in and talk to the dead."

"Why not?"

"Not everyone remembers everything," he said with a sigh. "Some of them, they blocked it out. Seeing you could really confuse them." Bannen ran his hand through his hair. Alverick smiled at the small gesture his friend used to do when he was alive.

"Then I can explain it to them," Alverick offered.

Banned shook his head. "Some don't know they're dead, Al. Their minds can't comprehend it."

Alverick paused, and slowly turned to face Bannen. "Who?"

Bannen hung his head. "Yuth. He still asks about everyone, but his memory is fading. Soon he'll forget. He may not even remember you when you guys join us."

"What about Jaste?" Alverick asked slowly.

"He still remembers."

"I have to speak with Jaste, Bannen. It's an emergency," Alverick pleaded. "Please, guide me through."

Bannen looked towards the hall and back at his friend. With a resigned sigh, he nodded his head and let go of Alverick. "Wear your hood."

Alverick nodded and the two of them made their way back to the Hall. The moon shone brightly overhead. Though he was with Bannen, Alverick felt a strange sense of foreboding. His friend walked stiffly, glancing off to the sides as if he was keeping an eye out for someone, or something.

It's not like him to be so nervous. Not even when we fought the pirates. What's inside?

Alverick found his eyes darting around, looking to the shadows for any sign of movement. As he walked, he tried reaching out into the earth to see if he could sense any other vibrations nearby. His trepidation grew and he became confused as he still couldn't sense anything.

It doesn't make sense that me just being here would put him so on edge, Alverick thought. *But there's nothing out here, not even a mouse. I wonder if my last group from the mines will be there, or if it's just those who have earned the King's favor?*

Bannen motioned for Alverick to be quiet as he walked through the door of the Hall. The darkness vanished instantly as the glow of countless lamps lined the walls. A roaring hearth blazed on the far end of the building. Chatter and laughter filled the room. A young boy played the fiddle while a woman sat nearby with her lute in her lap. Somehow, the lively tune sounded over the din. Alverick watched in amusement as the boy danced around in time with his music, weaving in and out between the wanderers of the Hall deftly without interrupting their conversations.

Alverick could not believe that he was walking among the greatest people in Corinth's history so casually. Despite Bannen's insistence that they leave quickly, he found himself wanting to stay and explore the hall.

On the wall opposite the fiddler, a long table laden with a king's feast sat ready for consumption. Men and women walked by, grabbing a bite to take with them as they moved about. Alverick's mouth watered as he stared at the succulent pigs, roasted pheasants, plates of fruit, and mountains of pastries that lay upon the table. Glasses of wine, tankards of ale, and decanters of rum seemed never-ending. As one was picked up, a young page wearing a cloak was quick to replace it.

"How is no one piss drunk?" Alverick asked, leaning forward to speak directly into his friend's ear.

"You haven't seen anything yet," Bannen replied with a soft chuckle. "If you stay a little longer, you'll be in for a treat. But we don't have the time."

Alverick opened his mouth to respond, but closed it quickly. He started paying attention to those around him, and realized that he recognized some of them. Standing by the fire, a massive man with muscles to rival the gods stood in a loose-fitting white tunic. His thighs bulged against his brown breeches, and his boots barely seemed to contain his calves. Bright red hair flowed down his back and a large scar ran down his face.

"By the gods," he breathed. "Is that *the* Hrothgar Ghreysson?"

"You see the resemblance to Jaste too, huh?" Banned asked. "The first time I saw him, I nearly ran into one of the beams. He's loud too, if you haven't noticed." As if on cue, the beast of a man let out a roar of laughter that caused those nearby to stop talking and look at him. "But he's pretty nice. The only problem is that he speaks the old language and most of us can't understand him. He's got a nasty temper though, so I'd not catch his eye."

The barbarian king took a long drink from his tankard before slamming it down on the table, causing some of the amber liquid to spill out onto the smooth wood of the surface. Without looking, he reached out and grabbed a handful of grapes off of a nearby plate and shoved them into his mouth. The ancient king spoke animatedly as he chewed, the juices dribbling from his mouth. Wiping his face with the back of his hand, the man gestured to the people he was speaking to and they all broke out into laughter.

"Look left," Bannen said.

Alverick's head snapped to the left, his body tensing and his hand reaching for his sword.

"King Iloth is over with some of the kings who came after him. I think Vialle is somewhere among them."

The king stood regally among his contemporaries. Though there were centuries between them, his similarities to the great barbarian king could be seen. Alverick was surprised to see that only Iloth bore any resemblance to his king, Jaste. Iloth's long auburn hair was streaked with grey. His body was not a warrior's body like Jaste's, but slight. The other kings were built more like Iloth, though a couple were on the softer side.

Alverick's gaze lingered on the group before landing on a head with thick, wavy hair a few heads below the others. The head bobbed around for a bit before walking out from the group and standing next to Iloth. Alverick's mouth dropped open a little as he stared at Vialle, the first mage in Corinth. Her whole right arm was covered in the graceful curving tattoos of a Stream. Her hair was tied back in a low tail and rested down the middle of her back.

Despite royal decorum, her arms were bare, exposing the tattoos. Alverick was surprised, not only to see her bare arms, but because Vialle appeared to be more toned than her father. She looked about with a bored expression, her eyes scanning the sea of bodies. A thin stream of water formed in her hand and encircled her forearm. Alverick held back a chuckle as he watched the woman absentmindedly play with the water, moving it from hand to hand as her father spoke to his audience unaware of it all.

Vialle's eyes lit up and the water around her disappeared. Alverick watched as, with a quick word with her father, Vialle darted off from the group and made her way over to a group of women who were, as best as Alverick could guess based on their clothing styles, younger than her. The women talked animatedly, their tattooed hands punctuating their conversation.

"It's a shame the princess died so young," Bannen said as he looked at the group of women. "From what I've gathered, she was the favorite in her family. You'll notice that her brother is much less popular. King Iloth was devastated when she was killed during the fight with the barbarians."

"How old is she?"

"Younger than you," Bannen replied. "How old are you again?"

"Twenty-seven."

"Yes, that's right. She's twenty-six."

"When did she get her power?" Alverick asked.

"I think she was sixteen or so. I haven't had a chance to speak with her yet, but I'm building up my status. The social circles are surprisingly tight-knit for a bunch of dead people. You'd think they'd want to talk to everyone since they have an eternity here."

"Unbelievable," Alverick breathed. "I can't believe she became so strong so quickly."

"What do you mean?" Bannen asked.

"Look at her arm," Alverick replied, trying to discreetly point at the princess. "It took me a long time to get my tattoos to cover my arms. And that's with me draughting. I can't imagine they did that back in her day."

Alverick quickly dropped his head as Vialle looked his direction and made eye contact with him. He heard Bannen swear quietly in front of him.

"She's coming over," he told Alverick. "Don't let this become a spectacle."

Glancing up, Alverick saw that she was rapidly approaching and tugged on his hood in an attempt to hide his face tattoos. In next to no time, she stood in front of him, searching his face.

"You're new here." It was a statement, not a question. "We don't get many like you here," she added as she lifted his hood slightly to see the extent of his tattoos. "How long have you had them? Do they go all over?" Her eyes dropped down, scanning his chest and the rest of his body with a critical eye.

"I've had them for twelve years, your majesty," Alverick replied hesitantly. "And just this side. My arm, neck, and face. Maybe a little down onto my chest, but I haven't checked in a while."

"Hmmm, impressive," Vialle muttered as she studied him. "I haven't seen combinations like this before. How'd you get such a variety?"

"I used a technique called draughting, mixing my blood with another mage's, to grow my power faster."

Vialle gasped. "How? That seems like such an abomination to blessed Aria's sacrifice."

Alverick hesitated, unsure if he would be amiss to tell the truth. After a second, he decided that lying would be worse than the truth. "It's not uncommon among some circles. It would be a waste to let the magic die, especially with as rare as it is for one to be chosen by the gods."

The princess nodded her head, muttering something to herself. Suddenly, a ribbon of water encircled her hand once more. Holding it up to his chest, Vialle lightly pressed her hand against his clothes and closed her eyes as she spoke to herself.

Alverick felt a surge of energy as her energies somehow connected with his. All of his pains vanished and he felt stronger again. The sensation felt cool, like a drink of water on a hot day, and it traveled all over. When it reached his head, it stopped, as if blocked by some unknown force. As quickly as it came, it all disappeared.

"Interesting," she said slowly.

"What did you do?" Alverick asked.

"I touched your magic, and healed you a bit. I'm surprised I could do that considering," she paused, trying to tactfully finish her sentence, "you do not seem to be one of us. You've got a lot of guilt and anger mixed in with you. It's helped you grow, but it's also hindered you. Explains a lot."

"What does it explain?" he asked.

Vialle tapped her finger against her cheek as she studied him. "How you could grow in power. I've never seen anything like it."

"Well, I haven't seen someone as strong and young as you before," Alverick replied. "For our purposes, draughting is a great way for some," Alverick explained. "For others, it's not very effective."

"My guess is because Blessed Aria's blood was pure, it was stronger. My father filled up many vials of blood and kept them safe for generations. My guess is that as the blood ages, the magical properties within weaken, making it harder for people to gain power." Vialle gestured towards the group of women behind her. Their tattoos were not as advanced as the princess'.

"Are all who are accepted like you?" she asked.

"Like me?" Alverick asked, puzzled.

"Able to use several styles," she replied as she motioned to his tattoos.

"Oh, yes. Most of the people I know who use blood magic have at least two styles, but I think it's because I've met some strange people in my life. Most people I know aren't able to use more than one though. And the draughting is primarily used by those of us in the royal armies or those who've gone rogue. Our current princess, King Jaste's daughter, is turning into quite the capable Stream." Alverick dipped his head in reverence to the princess. "Although, I doubt she's ever going to get anywhere near as powerful as you, your majesty."

Vialle's lips turned up in a small smile.

"Milady," Bannen cut in. Alverick noted that his voice was surprisingly timid for the usually confident soldier. "If it is not too much trouble, I must take him to see our king. I hate to interrupt, but this is kind of important."

"It's not like you have anywhere you need to be," Vialle replied, her tone sharp in annoyance.

"Please, milady," Bannen said. "I don't know how much time we have. My friend here, his time has not yet come. He's not supposed to be in Themba right now."

Vialle's eyes widened in surprise as her suspicions were confirmed. "How did you get here?" she asked, her voice lowered, making it difficult to hear above the raucous din.

Alverick shook his head. "I wish I knew."

"Well, I am sad to see you go. I'm quite intrigued by you, I must say. Until next time," she paused, waiting for him to reply.

"Alverick."

"Until next time, Alverick the God Blessed." Vialle gave them both a nod before turning around and returning to her group who had been waiting patiently off to the side.

"By the gods," Bannen said after the princess was out of earshot. "She is intense."

"You know, part of me wishes I didn't have to leave here. I'd love to be able to talk to her more," Alverick lamented.

"Come on," Bannen said, giving his friend a little tug. "You wanted to see Jaste."

XV

Jaste stood off to the side, surrounded by a group of men, a tankard full of mead in his hand. Alverick could see Yuth among the crowd standing with the late king of Zanir. He was surprised to see the king in his royal robes instead of the chainmail and leathers that he wore when he died. Unlike Bannen, both Jaste and Yuth dressed as they normally would. His former comrade wore a simple uniform with the crest of Pharn emblazoned across his chest, while Bannen wore his leathers and a light layer of chainmail.

Alverick felt a warmth in his chest as he looked at the two. They both seemed happy despite their untimely demise. The king practically beamed as he spoke with the group, the mead threatening to slosh out of his tankard as he shook with mirth. Alverick was relieved that they weren't wandering around in the afterlife a mere shadow of their former selves.

"Hey, Bannen, why are you the only one wearing what you died in?" Alverick asked as he continued to watch the group.

Bannen walked on in silence. After a while, he replied, "I chose to return to my death clothes. Most do not seek what they wore at the time of death. It lets them forget easier." Bannen glanced at his friend with heavy eyes. "Or, at least it's easier for them to pretend."

Alverick felt a twang of regret as he walked with his friend. "I'm sorry, Bannen."

"There's nothing to apologize for."

As the two approached, Jaste threw his head back in laughter, his mead sloshing about once more and spilling onto the floor.

"Damn. I hate wasting good mead," Jaste exclaimed as he sucked the amber colored liquid off of his hand.

"Evening, Jaste," Bannen called out, waving to the king. "How goes it?" Nodding to Yuth and the others in the group, Bannen broke through the crowd. "If it's okay with you, I have someone who'd like to talk to you and Yuth. Would it be possible for some privacy?"

"Of course," Jaste said, motioning for everyone else to disperse. "Who is it?"

As the group broke up, Bannen signaled for Alverick to come over. Yuth stood next to Bannen, a puzzled look on his face. Alverick made his way over to the three, making sure to keep his hood up and his tattoos covered. The lack of tattooed people in the Hall unnerved him for some reason.

I would've thought that there would be more magi here in the Halls. There has to be someone else besides Vialle and her group of friends.

Bannen moved the group closer to the wall to afford them a measure of privacy. Once they were secluded, they waited until the little fiddler passed by before Alverick lowered his hood.

Jaste gasped as he saw the Avalanche, while Yuth looked confused.

"Alverick! What are you doing here? Don't tell me..."

"No, no," Alverick said, holding his hands up. "Not yet, at least. Although, before all's said and done, I may be joining you in short while."

"I don't understand," Jaste said.

"Neither do I."

"Al wanted to talk to you," Bannen explained. "It seems urgent."

"Of course," Jaste replied. "What is it?"

"Wait," Yuth cut in. "I don't mean to be rude, but what's going on? Al, where have you been?"

Alverick looked uncomfortably from each person, before speaking. He dropped his eyes, unable to look at the others. "Things have been hard since you two and Garv have died," he said slowly. "We've gone through a lot. We really need some leadership."

Struck by Garv's absence with the group, Alverick suddenly began searching the Hall for him. Bannen gently placed his hand on the Avalanche's arm and shook his head. Turning to the king, Jaste repeated the motion. Garv was not in the Halls. Alverick swallowed hard, trying to push down the lump that appeared in his throat. There was no time to dwell on it.

Yuth stared at Alverick, his mouth hanging open and eyes wide. The officer opened and closed his mouth like a fish gasping for air. "W-what do you mean? Died?" Turning to Jaste and Bannen, Yuth's eyes implored the two to say otherwise. "We're not dead, Al. We're enjoying a break at one of King Jaste's mead halls while we're on the hunt."

Bannen placed his hand on his comrade's shoulder and gave it a squeeze.

"They have you, Alverick," Jaste said, ignoring Yuth's outburst. "And the others are there to help you. With your skill and experience, I doubt you're in trouble. You know you've always been your own enemy. Believe in yourself."

"It's not the usual problems though," Alverick replied, urgency seeping into his voice. "There's so much more going on."

"Your Majesty," Yuth begged. "Why are you playing with him? We're not dead." Speaking slowly, Yuth wracked his brain. "Alverick came back from his trip at the spice mines, and then we all prepared for the Great Hunt with King Storm." He pointed vaguely towards the guests of the Hall. The rest of the dead.

Jaste raised an eyebrow as Yuth tried to piece together the last moments of his life. Yuth's eyes dropped as he tried to remember what happened. His hands came together and he interlaced his fingers together as he thought.

"And Bannen... Bannen..." Yuth's eyes got wide for a moment. Turning to face his friend, Yuth stared long and hard into Bannen's eyes. For the briefest of moments, recognition flashed in his eyes before disappearing. Without warning, Yuth walked away, muttering under his breath and shaking his head.

As he passed Alverick, the Avalanche heard his friend mumble, "Can't be dead. Ridiculous," under his breath.

Alverick watched as Yuth rubbed his hands together as he stalked off to the other side of the Hall. He noticed that the man's eyes began to lose focus as he started talking to someone else before returning to their previously empty look.

"He's forgetting everything, isn't he?" Alverick asked, his voice pained.

"The body heals, but the mind is lost," Bannen explained. "He hasn't been able to process the trauma. It's not uncommon. I don't even know what happened to Garv."

"Did anyone see how he died?" Alverick asked.

Jaste shook his head sadly. "There was so much going on, I don't think anyone ever found out. I know I didn't see him."

"So, no one's been able to explain it to him then," Alverick muttered. "But, how do you still have your memories?"

"I don't really know," he said. "When I woke up, I was alone in the woods and I felt a pain in my chest. As I walked towards the Hall, I tried figuring out where I was and why I wasn't on the battlefield. Everything was just so vivid that I guess it stuck. The closer I got to the Halls, the more I remembered. Hera, my little Cienna, and that bastard who killed me's face. I'll never forget his face as long as I live... either in Corinth or in Themba. It'll take me going to the seven hells before I forget."

Alverick shook his head. He knew he would never forget Jaste's death either: Swordbane's sword sticking out from the king's chest, his hungry smile as he watched the life leave Jaste's body. It was one of the most devastating losses he'd experienced in his life.

"Your Majesty," he broached. "I need your experience. How would you save a fractured nation?"

"What do you mean?"

"Brody created an alliance with Swordbane. Now, the clans are warring within."

"He what?" Jaste asked. "With my killer?"

"Please, your majesty," Alverick tried to pacify the king. "You don't understand. After your death, we followed Swordbane back to his home to avenge you. They sequestered themselves in the gorge and summoned a demon. It went on a rampage. No one was safe and we were all fighting for our lives. It made the most sense at the time. Or so I've been led to believe. I wasn't actually around when the deal was struck."

The king shook his head, but didn't argue further. "Desperate times make us all do things we wouldn't normally do. I won't say I agree with your choice, but it's too late now. Are you taking responsibility for the consequences of your decision?"

Alverick nodded his head. "I have to."

"Then you must honor your word. Pharn will pledge her support to Xan, and you will be responsible for the fall out. Just remember, our interests must still protect Zanir."

"I feared as much. I don't trust Swordbane, but Zanir is an honorable land and she will protect her allies."

Jaste clapped Alverick on the shoulder. "It's a tough position, but I know you'll be fine. Take care of yourself, Alverick."

"You too, your majesty," he replied, gripping the king's arm.

"Will you be staying long?" Jaste asked.

"I want to talk to Bannen a little more, but I should be going shortly after."

"Then I have some more advice for you," the king said. "Watch out for the Grey Man. He's not who he appears to be."

"The Grey Man?" Alverick asked.

The king nodded. "Take care. May you find your way to the Halls someday."

Alverick's breath caught in his chest as his king walked off to another part of the hall. He hadn't expected their meeting to end so emotionally.

"Come on, Al," Bannen said. "We should probably head out."

"But I wanted to talk to you a little more. We haven't had a chance to truly talk since you died."

"Jaste is right. The Grey Man is not someone you want to meet. We should go. We've stayed long enough."

Alverick watched his friend's eyes as they narrowed when he spoke of the Grey Man. Whoever he was, he was a figure of authority and power if he could scare Bannen and the king. Against his better judgement, Alverick shook his head.

"Please," he begged. "Five more minutes. I just need some closure."

Bannen scanned the room, his eyes darting about wildly. After several long seconds, he nodded. "No longer."

A smile tugged at the corners of Alverick's lips as he felt himself become giddy with anticipation. Bannen had always been there for him when he needed his friend most. Even in death, Bannen was around when things were dark for Alverick. Now, he could finally find out how.

"Bannen, how is it you've managed to stay by my side for so long? Surely in death you have more pleasurable things you could be doing."

Bannen's eyes dropped as he was unable to meet his friend's gaze. He looked off into the distance as he spoke. "Alverick, I gave my life for my country. It's everything I was. Everything that I am, is for Pharn. What do I have in death? Nothing. I wander Themba, searching for meaning to my life. But that's it. Everything else... you've lost your Anchor."

"What?" Alverick asked softly. "What are you talking about?"

"It's in your eyes, Al. You're a shell."

"Oh gods," Alverick whispered. His head dropped into his hand as his body slumped against the wall.

Bannen pat his friend on the shoulder. "But you're still here," he tried to soothe. "You just need to find your focus once more. I know you can do it; you've done it before. But right now, there's much going on and we need to figure out what it all means."

"You're right," Alverick sighed. "I just need to keep everything in perspective." Rubbing his face, Alverick looked down at his hands. His eyes were drawn to the tattoos on his right hand. Thick and winding, they moved steadily up his arm. Small jagged branches jutted out on his arm and mixed with thin, delicate swirls. The pattern was beautiful to him, and he let himself take a moment to remember his journey. "Thank you, Bannen."

"Any time, Al," Bannen replied with a smile.

It'd been a long time since Alverick had seen his friend smile. The simple act released a stream of emotions, allowing him to shed the weight of his worries that he'd been carrying since his friend died. The two began talking like they had in the old days. Alverick finally felt himself feeling like his old self. All that was missing was a bowl of Fren's stew and a nice pint.

As Alverick stood talking to Bannen, he noticed a man make eye contact with him and come over. There was an energy about him that made Alverick uncomfortable. He felt himself both reach for his sword, and check the earth around him to see if there was anything he could pull on should he need to make a quick escape.

Picking up on his friend's distress, Bannen tried to catch Alverick's eye. "Stay calm," he said softly. "Trust me. You don't want to get on his bad side."

Bodies parted as the man made his way over to the two. The man was a good head taller than Alverick, and built like a warrior. Alverick could tell that he'd spent a lifetime training. As he neared, Alverick noticed that there was something off about the figure. His skin appeared to be a faint grey, and his hair seemed to taper off in grey wisps. The man's eyes were a dark charcoal that filled his entire eye.

"What are you doing here?" the man asked. His voice rolled over Alverick, causing him to take a step back.

"I, I don't know."

"Leave," the man said.

Alverick felt himself bristle at the man's brusque affect. "I'm obviously here for a reason. Just let me figure out why."

The man's brow knotted as he set his jaw. His hair rustled gently, the wispy ends swirling around his head. Alverick could almost feel a static energy surrounding the two of them. Lowering his voice, the man gave one final warning. "Leave Themba, Alverick, favored son of Zemé. There is nothing for you here."

"Alverick," Bannen said, grabbing his friend's arm, "I think we should leave. I'm sure you'll find what you seek elsewhere."

"No," Alverick replied. His hand tightened around the grip of his sword.

I've survived aethren and Aramaine. No dead man is going to stop me from completing my mission. Obviously, there's something here that I need to learn. Something that will either prepare us for what's to come, or help us succeed. I can't just back down.

His adversary shook his head. Alverick almost thought that he saw disappointment flicker in the man's dark eyes. Throwing his arms out to either side, he sent all nearby flying into the walls of the hall. Alverick braced himself, creating an immovable base by pulling on the earth beneath him. Cries of surprise and pain filled the room as bodies hit the walls.

"Ayr!" Alverick cried in surprise.

But how? There's no tattoos on him. He doesn't even have the silver ones Dez has.

"Who are you?" Alverick asked.

"Thuul," his foe replied. Tendrils of thick smoke radiated from his body, darkening as they intensified. Small sparks streaked across them, flashing like blinding spiderwebs.

Is he a Spark too? A Tempest Spark combination could be very dangerous. It doesn't seem like he's Snapped though.

Alverick's thoughts were cut short as Thuul created a ball of lightning between his hands, the sparks dancing around on his palms. Reaching down into the earth, Alverick searched for anything he could use to his advantage. With a gasp, he had to throw himself to the side as Thuul released his ball of energy in Alverick's direction, barely missing him. The earth's plates could not be moved. They were deeper than any he'd ever pulled on before.

Rolling on his shoulder, Alverick spun around to face his attacker. Focusing on the earth, he began to pull. In his hand, Alverick reached within himself and formed a ball of electric energy. Thuul circled his arms around his body, creating mighty wind, and throwing them towards Alverick. The gust slammed into Alverick, causing him to stumble backwards several steps and the ball of electricity in his hand to dissipate.

Alverick grunted as he struggled to maintain his balance. Reaching down as far as he could, Alverick finally felt himself touch the plates deep within the earth of Themba. Pulling on them, he attempted to wiggle them a bit.

Another blast of wind struck Alverick in the chest. Gasping for breath, Alverick managed to not lose his hold on the tectonic plates. His chest ached as the force of the blast bruised his ribs. Wincing, Alverick succeeded in creating another small ball of energy while he cajoled the earth to move. He threw the ball in Thuul's direction. Instead of dodging the ball of electricity, Thuul reached out his hand and absorbed the energy into himself.

Alverick felt his stomach knot as Thuul stood unfazed from his attack.

How?

"Things will only end badly for you," he said. "Forget what you've seen here."

The ground below Alverick began to buckle. His eyes widened as he felt the movement that no one else could. He was almost there.

"Why can't I get what I need?" Alverick asked, trying to buy himself some time. "I'm not hurting anyone. This is important."

"What could be so important that you disturb the land of the fallen. They've already lost so much. Let them have the rest they deserve."

"But there's something here I'm supposed to find," Alverick said. "I wouldn't be here if there wasn't. Maybe you could help me. Then I could leave right after."

"No," Thuul replied. "The living are not allowed to be here. You must leave."

"Please! Whatever is here could affect the fate of thousands. Possibly nations."

Thuul lowered his hands and tilted his head. "What do you mean?"

Feeling the earth below him firmly in his hold, Alverick decided to see where their conversation was going before unleashing his power. The plates hummed underground, not moving enough to create any damage, but poised to move if nudged.

Placing his hands on the ground, Alverick stayed kneeled where he was. "The world is in turmoil."

"Take your hands off of the ground," Thuul interrupted.

Lifting his hands into the air, open palms facing the man, Alverick cocked his head to the side in question. When the man nodded, Alverick continued.

"The gods are among us. There is a darkness that threatens Corinth, and I don't know how to stop it."

Thuul arched an eyebrow as he stared silently at the Avalanche. Seeing the man was willing to listen, Alverick decided to take a chance and reveal everything.

"I've seen visions. A darkness creeping over the land, and burning. Death is everywhere. And creatures called the Faceless."

"Well, I'll be damned," Thuul said. "Stop pulling on the earth," he snapped. "The last thing we need right now is you damaging the sacred hall."

Alverick flinched at the statement. *How did he know?*

"Stand up," Thuul ordered. Once Alverick was on his feet, Thuul continued. "Who have you seen?"

"A… a young girl with green hair, like moss. But also, Alazi, or whatever was left of him when Czand died."

Thuul held up his had to silence Alverick. The darkness that had surrounded him had disappeared, leaving his hair like wispy clouds once more. Rubbing his hands together, he began muttering to himself.

"Zemé walks among them."

Turning to face Alverick, Thuul placed both hands on either side of his temple. Alverick felt a pressure against his head, as though someone was squeezing it. Images flashed through his mind at a blinding speed. He couldn't even focus on them, but he could feel the emotions that came with them. Pain, confusion, desperation.

By the time Thuul found what he'd wanted, Alverick was drained. Every emotion he'd experienced in the last couple weeks had been amplified. He didn't realize it, but he was gasping as though he'd run a long distance as Thuul pulled away and began rubbing his hands together.

"There's much going on," Thuul said at last.

Alverick struggled to focus on what was being said as he tried to pull himself together. He pictured Caitlyn, her green eyes deep and full of understanding, as he used her as his Anchor. Her voice called out to him, smoothing his frayed nerves and providing a balm for his soul. A heavy hand landed on his shoulder, jarring him and erasing Caitlyn from his mind. He blinked rapidly as he tried to bring himself back to the present.

"Avalanche, there is much resting on your shoulders," Thuul said. Alverick managed to finally get himself to focus and stop his vision from fuzzing. "It seems as though you've been thrown into a battle you know little about, and little deserve. When Vahnyre's bond to the Third Brother was broken, it destroyed the balance that had been created and tipped things in favor of Apophos."

"Apophos?" Alverick asked. He turned to Bannen and was met with confusion.

A loud shout came from the corner by the feast table as Hrothgar stormed over to Alverick and the Grey Man. The barbarian king spoke quickly and loudly to Thuul, his fist shaking and his other hand moving to the war axe on his back. "Apophos" could be heard several times as the man gestured towards Alverick and Bannen. The king's eyes darted over to the Avalanche, glancing at his tattoos before returning his gaze to Thuul. The Grey Man listened intently to the redheaded king before surprising Alverick by responding in the ancient tongue. The barbarian looked to his kin before shaking his head as he backed up. His eyes never left Alverick.

"Tell me, favored son of Zemé, what do you know about us?" Thuul asked.

"Us?" Alverick asked slowly.

"Surely you know about the gods? The source of your powers."

Alverick paused as he pondered the words. His mind moved sluggishly as he tried to think about all that he knew, but he found that after the Siblings, his mind ran blank. The Avalanche's brow furrowed as he tried to re-call anything else about the other gods.

"Just think about it," Thuul said, breaking Alverick's concentration. "We are of the four, and, like the blood magic, can be traced back to Aria's sacri-fice. But, have you wondered why there are other types of magic other than the main ones? Some have found a way to tap into the power of those we call the Ancients. And two of them fought to maintain balance in the world." Motioning to King Hrothgar, he continued, "Apophos, the one we've struggled against, and his brother, Re'nukh."

A blaring horn sounded in the distance, startling Alverick. Thuul's head spun toward the direction of the noise, as did almost every other soul in the room. Bannen squeezed Alverick's shoulder and began pulling him towards the door of the Hall.

"We have to go," Bannen whispered. "You've been here too long."

Alverick turned to his friend, a question dying on his lips as he saw the panic in the man's face. His eyes were wide, his eyebrows threatening to dis-appear into his bangs, and his face a deathly white. Alverick could almost feel the man shaking as Bannen gripped his shoulder.

"Think about these things," Thuul said, returning his attention to the Avalanche. "The way to reset the balance is in Aria's gift. I believe we will meet again. Farewell, favored son of Zemé."

Thuul made his way to the back of the Hall and exited out of the other door. Everyone inside stood around for a while, uneasy at the strange turn of events. Finally, the lutist began playing a sweet song and hushed chatter broke out in pockets before the noise picked up. Alverick turned to face Bannen, but looked around for Jaste. The king shook his head and nodded towards the door.

"Now," Bannen said.

Without argument, Alverick followed his friend out of the Hall and into the darkness once more. The two traveled in silence. As Alverick walked out the entrance of the temple, he felt the initial cooling sensation from when when he first entered the ruins leave; all that remained was the chill of the wind as it picked up.

Bannen did not leave the top step of the temple as Alverick stepped down onto the earth.

"Take care, Al," he said as he gazed at his friend. "Don't forget to hold on to your Anchor. I don't want to see you for a long time." Bannen sighed as he gave Alverick a wan smile. "Keep an eye on Brody for me, will you? I may have failed him, but you're as good as family. I know you'll treat him right."

Alverick felt his face flush as tears welled in the corners of his eyes. Their warmth quickly disappeared as the wind blew around him. A lump formed in his throat, but he managed to push it down as he swallowed hard.

"He's turning into a fine leader, Bannen. When his time finally comes, I know you'll be proud."

Bannen nodded once before turning to walk away.

XVI

A SUDDEN JOLT STARTLED Alverick, his head popping up and frantically twisting in the saddle. Styx pulled against her reins, prancing her feet as his unexpected movement surprised her. Loud snorts accompanied her actions. Getting the horse under control, Alverick leaned over to pat her neck while whispering soothing words. She calmed down in short order, giving Alverick time to get his bearings.

The sun hung low in the sky, inching towards the horizon. Color started to tinge the sky, staining the bottom of the clouds. Nearby, soldiers conversed light-heartedly, despite the long day's travel. Sweat sheened on their faces and left their shirts soaked. The men from the morning seemed oblivious to their surroundings. No one seemed to be concerned.

What just happened?

"You awake now, Al?" Caitlyn asked.

Alverick looked over and saw the redhead walking leisurely by Styx's side. Sliding off the horse mid-stride, Alverick landed between the two and fell into step with Caitlyn, the horse's reins held loosely in his hand. He glanced over at the woman and noticed that her lips were turned up as her eyes sparkled mischievously.

"How long was I out?" he asked.

"I noticed as we were passing out the water skins. I knew you had your own, but I thought I'd see if you wanted to share a bite for a bit. We haven't talked much since we came back from Aramaine... for obvious reasons." Caitlyn's eyes dropped and she tugged on her leather riding gloves.

Alverick watched her nervous tic and wondered when she picked up the habit. She was a strong woman who broke wild horses; nothing intimidated her.

"I've been having trouble sleeping. It's been making things difficult. Even with what Zemé did for me, I don't know if I'm in any shape to fight." Alverick was surprised to hear the despair in his own voice.

"That's why Brody's taking the lead," Caitlyn said. "Because we know that you aren't." She tugged on her left glove once more. "Many of us aren't."

Her statement caught him off guard. Alverick studied her face, trying to figure out what was bothering her. Caitlyn was right. Ever since they returned from Aramaine, they hadn't had much of a chance to talk. There was so much for them to catch up on, and now that she was back in his life, he didn't want to let her go.

Alverick noticed that the glint he'd seen just moments before had disappeared. It'd been replaced with an emptiness. The corner of her lips were turned down and there was a hardness under her eyes. He looked at her hands, watching as she rubbed her forearm and noticed something poking out from the top of the glove. With a gasp, he stopped and grabbed her arm.

"What's this?" he whispered as he tried to pull off her glove. "Cait?"

Caitlyn yanked her arm back, covering her left hand with her right, but the damage had been done. Jagged spikes of her mark were visible. The large breaks between them, keeping them from being one continuous tattoo, could also be seen.

Tugging on her glove to cover the tattoos, she glowered at Alverick. "You told me I would never understand after you draughted your first Spark. Well, now I do."

Turning to leave, Alverick grabbed her arm once more and spun her back around. His grip relaxed as he let go of her arm and clasped her hand in his, their fingers interlacing. "How? Why?" He shook his head, trying to make sense of everything. "This was so stupid," he moaned. "You shouldn't even be able to function."

The redhead's green eyes hardened as she stared Alverick in the face, squeezing his hand as she sought to match his gaze. "Tell me something I don't know," she hissed. "I live every day in fear I'm going to go mad. I was so angry at you. You'd just lain with the pirate and that bar maid. I wanted to show you that you were wrong. That you were just making it all up." Her eyes softened as she remembered the process so many years ago. "I found a Spark. He was drunk, and I brought him home with me. I knew that you mixed the blood, so I thought if I cut him, I could take some and then throw him outside.

"There was so much more than I realized. I panicked and left him in the woods. When I mixed his blood with mine..." Her voice broke as she swallowed hard. "Everything went black for a moment. It was like I fell asleep, but I was awake and staring at... at something, I don't remember what. But my mind was completely blank. Then it was like everything came rushing back at once and I could barely filter it. All I could think about was you, and that is what saved me."

"By the gods, Cait," Alverick swore. "I don't know how you did it, but you're a miracle. Then again, we always knew that you were focused. How else could you put up with me otherwise?" he flashed a weak smile, hoping it would lighten the tension between the two. Alverick was rewarded with a small grin.

"You know, I never believed you when you said it was not often that a mage was born. I don't doubt anything you've said now. I'm just lucky I managed to maintain my Anchor and can function most of the time without much difficulty. That's why I busied myself with working my way to becoming the king's horse breaker. You need to always be alert."

"I'm sorry all this happened because of me. I really wish I'd never messed up like I did. No wonder you could never forgive me." Alverick's hand hung loosely in Caitlyn's.

Caitlyn gave him a small, reassuring squeeze before flashing him a small smile once more. The hardness was gone from her eyes and replaced with a tenderness as the tension also disappeared from around her mouth. She shook her head, struggling for words as tears rolled down her cheeks.

"It's not your fault. You couldn't help it," she whispered. "I understand."

"I shouldn't have done it," he insisted.

"It's not important now. Let's just move forward."

Alverick felt a lump in his throat as he struggled to speak. For the second time that day, he felt his face become warm as he began crying. Wiping his eyes and nose with the back of his arm, Alverick gave Caitlyn's hand a squeeze. The two walked hand-in-hand, ignoring the noise of the world around them as tears rolled down their faces.

~~~

Brody's call for the group to stop couldn't come fast enough. Oldar's body ached from poor sleep, long rides, and all the walking. Before they left, he tried finding a spare pair of boots to borrow because he didn't think his riding boots would be suitable for travel. Now, he regretted that decision. The boots he'd borrowed were tight around his feet, squishing his toes at the tips. While they were fine for riding, all the walking left him in agony. Luckily, he'd kept his personal boots tied to Bells' saddle. As soon as they stopped, he was going to switch them out.

It also didn't help that he had a headache and was drenched in sweat. No one else around him seemed to be losing as much fluid as he was, and that unnerved him. His hands shook as he held his horse's reins and his stomach twisted with nausea. Several times during their march, he had to rush off to the side to hide his body rejecting what little he consumed.
~~~

"Come on. Come on. Come on," he murmured as the army started to set up camp. "Let me just get to my damn spot."

They all hung around aimlessly for several minutes until Brody gave the all clear for them to set up camp. Oldar's stomach turned, causing him to spit out a bit of bile that came up. His body trembled as he shifted where he stood. Bells pranced anxiously next to him, tossing her head and giving a small cry as she sensed her master's discomfort.

"Let's set up!" Brody shouted to the group.

"Finally!" Oldar groaned as he set off for the nearest tree with his horse. "Excuse me! Make way!" he called out to the slower soldiers who were ambling over in the direction he desired. At the sight of the king, the men stopped and turned to find another spot to set up their bed rolls.

After hastily tying Bells to a protruding tree root that arched out of the soil, Oldar plopped onto the ground and ripped off his boots. As the leather slipped off his feet, he let out a sigh as his toes once again had room to breathe. A moan escaped his lips as he rubbed the bottoms of his feet to help soothe them.

"You seem a little anxious," a soft voice said.

Oldar's head shot up and he saw Cienna approaching him. His stomach clenched, but he forced himself to keep from throwing up.

"Are you okay?" she asked as she sat down next to him. Her brows scrunched together as she watched the young king's hands shaking. "You don't seem to be well. You look pale and you've been sick all day."

"I'm okay," Oldar said, wiping his brow with his sleeve. "I'm just a little warm. Maybe that's why my color is off."

Cienna let out a small "oh" and dropped her eyes. She picked up a fallen leaf and began shredding it absentmindedly. Oldar watched as she tore up one leaf and then another. Her gaze was troubled, as though she wanted to say something, but was afraid. The muscles around her mouth tightened as she clenched her jaw.

"What's wrong?" he asked.

"I, I'm just wondering if there is something else. Something you're not telling us."

It was now Oldar's turn to drop his eyes. Keeping them low, he stared at a spot behind the princess, a single yellow flower sticking out of a tuft green grass. He watched as a caterpillar climbed up the stem of the flower, causing it to bend under the weight. As the caterpillar reached the base, it ended up upside down and fell off. With a sigh, the young king turned to face the princess. Their eyes met and Oldar felt that he could no longer afford to hide things from her, let alone himself.

"I'm sure you've heard the rumors about me," he began. "How I am fond of the drink." Cienna nodded as she listened. "Well, after our last discussion, I spent a lot of time trying to mask my emotions. So, I broke my word to myself and drank for almost a whole day." The princess' eyes narrowed. "By the time I regained control of myself, I decided to be proactive and turn myself around. That's when I penned the letter to you and your mother. Anyway, it's been what, four days since I've had anything to drink, and I'm struggling. My body is turning against me."

"I thought you gave up all of that," she whispered, her tone a little icy.

"I tried," he replied lamely. "It's harder than I thought."

Cienna opened her mouth to respond, but closed it as she fought to keep the anger out of her voice. Oldar noticed that she was shaking a bit and her eyes hardened as she looked at him. The princess refused to meet his gaze, instead looking at his forehead. Despite the nausea he was feeling, his stomach dropped as disappointment crept in. He thought they had been making progress in mending their relationship. Perhaps he was mistaken.

"Were you drunk when you met with me and my mother?" she asked stiffly. Her eyes shot over to his, trying to read him.

"No," he replied with a shake of the head. "I'd enjoyed a drink in the days leading up, but I hadn't gotten drunk since the day I returned home and enjoyed an evening with a friend. I would never insult you or the queen by showing up drunk when hosting you."

Cienna's eyes bored into him, trying to discern the truth. He met her gaze and held it for several long seconds. Oldar felt his stomach twist once more, but he didn't have to fight back any heaving. Maybe the end was in sight. The discomfort he felt physically was replaced as the silence stretched on. Finally, Cienna looked away.

"No, you wouldn't," she said. "You wouldn't disrespect your father like that."

"Or yours. Your father was my father's best friend. I met him many times growing up. He did not deserve what happened to him, and I would never disrespect his good name."

"So, how are we going to fix everything?" Cienna asked. Her bluntness caught him off guard. "Once Mother's fully recovered, we're going to have a lot to talk about."

"Well, I, I think we should sit down and have a long conversation. There's a lot we need to talk about."

"Obviously."

Oldar wiped the sweat off of his brow. Glancing off to the side, he watched as the rest of the camp set up their spots and began preparation for dinner that night. He noticed that although most people talked and joked, both Alverick and Caitlyn sat off to the side, secluded from the main camp activities much like he and Cienna were. Brody walked around, checking on the rest of the camp. He smiled as he spoke to people, acting every part the leader.

"Are you confident in the way you've begun your reign?" Oldar asked.

Cienna opened her mouth in surprise, her eyes widening. "What do you mean?"

"We're both young, yet we've had to step up and assume roles that we shouldn't have for a long time. The death of our parents has thrown everything into chaos. Haven't you felt the pressure to live up to your father's name?"

"Yes," she said softly.

"Imagine having to live up to two strong leaders, how much is expected of you, especially when people don't take you seriously to begin with."

"There's so much on your head."

"And that's just the start of it," he sighed. "Top it off with a narcissistic uncle who wants to steal the crown, and then throw in a bit of heartache." Oldar glanced over at Cienna, catching her eye. "Even if it was all in my head, I thought you would be the one person who could understand me. When everything came crashing down, I was more than a bit depressed. I turned to the bottle, and I took it out on you. I'm sorry. It wasn't your fault, and I shouldn't have placed it on you."

"I could have been more diplomatic," Cienna said. "I treated you horribly because I didn't want to see you as anything else. If you were even remotely likeable, it would make it next to impossible to tell Father that I would not marry you. But he's a good judge of character. I'm sorry for not giving you the chance you deserved."

"Looks like we've both disappointed our fathers," Oldar said with a small smirk. "Too bad it's too late to change the past. Maybe we can at least salvage the future?" Hope hung in his words as he stared deeply into the princess' eyes.

"It would make the most sense," she said slowly. "And it is probably in our land's best interests to keep open the pragmatic option."

Oldar felt his chest tighten as his stomach turned with excitement. Despite his body feeling like it was going to shut down at any moment, hope filled him, giving him renewed energy. His lips turned up as a weak smile played on his face. The king was rewarded when Cienna returned the gesture, a glint of compassion in her eyes. This was the princess he'd imagined before he first stepped foot in Pharn.

Her attention was suddenly pulled from him and the corners of her mouth turned down as her eyes quickly dropped to the ground. Turning around, Oldar saw Brody walking nearby. The young man smiled as he waved at the two before walking to check on a group of men a little way over. The elation the young king had been feeling moments before began to deflate as he realized that there was still one big issue to address before the two nations could move forward.

XVII

WYRD SLIPPED out of the Dancing Wolf and into the darkness. His eyes struggled to adjust to the moonlight after the brightness from the many lamps inside the tavern moments before. The silence outside was deafening after the rowdy din he'd suffered through for the last few hours as the men cheered and whistled at the dancing Jytte. None of them noticed her pale skin under the cocoa powder and cinnamon she'd rubbed onto her skin despite the little rivulets of sweat that ran down her stomach and face.

His surveillance from earlier in the day showed him what he needed to know. He watched as she bought large quantities of cocoa powder, cinnamon, and even coffee from the local merchants before moving on to buy her other necessities that afternoon. Wyrd had to back off once Tek arrived. His skin crawled and his insides burned as he watched the man plant a kiss on Jytte's lips, the musician's arms snaking around the northerner's lithe hips.

Did he know what Wyrd did? Or did the barbarian manage to fool him just as she fooled the rest of Xan?

As his eyes adjusted to the dim light of the sparse lamp flame, Wyrd found himself leaning in the doorframe of a nearby establishment, watching the exits of the Dancing Wolf. Patrons dribbled out of the tavern in drips and drabs as the night dragged on. Each time the door opened, the cacophony of drunken men and the sounds of the sitar and drums spilled out into the quietness of Fa'Tinh, their laughter ringing out as they staggered off to their homes.

YOU'VE SPENT TOO MUCH TIME FOLLOWING THIS ONE, Fyre's voice hissed. YOU NEED TO STOKE THE FIRES OF REBELLION. THE GENERAL AND YOUR LEADER HAVE FAILED. YOU SHOULD TAKE OVER AND SHOW THE REST OF CORINTH THE GREATNESS OF XAN. BUT TO SUCCEED, YOU MUST BURN DOWN EVERYTHING AND START FROM THE BEGINNING. START FRESH.

"This is important," Wyrd snapped. "If I can figure out what those barbarians are up to, I can expand my influence."

YOU ARE LOOKING TOO BIG. START SMALL AND ESTABLISH YOUR REIGN. IF YOU BECOME TOO AMBITIOUS, YOU WILL FAIL.

"Shut up. I am doing this my way."

Laughter filled his head as Fyre broke into uncontrollable hysterics. It echoed all around, seeming to come from all angles around him despite the fact that he knew it was all in his head. Wyrd shook his head like a horse trying to get a fly off of its ear.

DO YOU ACTUALLY THINK THAT YOU HAVE ANY SAY IN HOW THIS IS GOING TO PLAY OUT? I HAVE CLAIMED YOUR SOUL AND WILL FOLLOW YOU TO THE SEVEN HELLS.

"I survived your attack and welcomed you into my body. I was the one who summoned you and brought you to our world. You will respect me."

Wyrd's words were met with more laughter.

WE SHALL SEE.

When the voice stopped speaking, the silence around him intensified. It was too late for anyone to be out. Even the strays slept. Only the chirping cicadas broke the stillness. Fireflies floated in the sky, bright dots against the clear, starry night. Wyrd leaned against the smooth wooden door and closed his eyes, admiring the beauty around him.

It had been too long since he'd stopped and taken in his surroundings. Many years had passed since the voices in his head were quiet. With a sigh, he sank down into the doorframe and wrapped his arms around his knees. He was at peace.

A cool breeze ruffled his hair. Wyrd flinched, opening his eyes and placing his hands on the ground on either side of him. His muscles tensed briefly before he relaxed, wrapping his arms around himself once more. The breeze was unnaturally cold, but nothing that should have triggered that kind of reaction from him.

The door to the Dancing Wolf opened once more and the warm light inside spilled out into the darkness. Jytte and Tek passed through the entrance, the tavern owner right behind them. The man gave the pair heartfelt thanks for filling in for the originally scheduled act and told them they were welcome anytime. The other musicians followed close behind, also receiving thanks from the establishment owner. Wyrd moved into a standing position, moving casually so as to not draw attention to himself.

He watched as the group of musicians stood and talked for a while, his adrenaline pumping and the soft hum of Fyre's whispers in the back of his head. Taking advantage of their distraction, he leaned against the door once more, reaching into his boot to pull out his dagger. As the blade cleared the sheath, Wyrd thought better of it and returned the weapon to its original spot. It was better to wait.

Soon, the groups said their goodbyes and split off. Jytte and Tek began walking towards the street opposite the Dancing Wolf. Checking his surroundings, Wyrd slipped into the darkness and followed quietly, like a shadow. The two spoke eagerly about their earnings for the night, Tek praising his luck that he'd found her as a partner.

"Before you joined me, I was barely scraping enough to feed myself. I was playing almost every night, but I couldn't get the extra coin. You've been a godsend," Wyrd overheard Tek saying as the man wrapped his arm around the woman's shoulder and planting a kiss on the top of her head. "Never leave me."

"I could never manage on my own," Jytte laughed. Wyrd noticed the slight accent to her voice. She had done her research and almost mimicked the Qu'ari accent perfectly. "We're a team, you and I... unless I found myself a traveling troupe to perform with."

Tek let out a mock howl of anguish as he gave her a little shove. "You would leave me for the likes of them? I'll be ruined, ruined!"

The two broke into giggles as they continued down the dark, quiet street. Wyrd felt an anger building within him. The way that Tek shared this moment with her so easily, how the woman could act so casually even though she was performing her own espionage, he wanted to see the terror in her eyes before he could get any satisfaction.

The three walked down several streets in relative silence. After leaving the business sector and entering the residential district, the pair stopped outside of a home. Wyrd slipped into the shadows of a nearby home, flattening himself against the wall. Peeking his head around the corner, he managed to get a clear view of the two.

Tek and Jytte spoke for a lengthy period of time before the woman moved to leave. Wyrd felt a rush of excitement. He was finally going to find out where the northerner was staying. He licked his lips as he watched his prey take a step away from Tek's home. The musician reached out and grabbed her arm, pulling her close and saying something too softly for Wyrd to hear. Wyrd's excitement turned into rage as Jytte followed Tek into his home.

Once the door closed behind them, Wyrd let out a growl of anger as he slammed his fist into the wall. He emerged from the shadows and walked up to the home the two musicians disappeared into. Peering through the windows, he looked into the darkness. Down the hall, he saw a faint flicker, as if from the light of a candle, flash in the emptiness.

Wyrd let out a primal cry of rage, sending out a pillar of flame into the sky, before stalking off towards his home.

Hroth pushed Maen against the wall, keeping her out of sight as Wyrd stormed off into the night. Once the man was out of sight, the Flame let her know it was safe to come out.

"What was that all about?" she breathed.

Hroth heard the terror in her voice and pulled her into him. Her body trembled in the warm mid-night air.

"There's not much time," Hroth murmured. Turning to Maen, he made eye contact and said, "Now is the time to decide. How involved to you want to become?"

XVIII

SOLVEIG PACED around, her dire wolf Tyr watching her movements as he lay on a pelt in the corner. A roaring fire filled the room with heat and elongated their shadows against the walls. Hegvaldr and Eivind stood off to the side of her doorway, with her advisor, Henrik, standing opposite the duo. The chieftainess' hands were clasped behind her back as she moved, keeping her from playing with her war axe.

"So," Solveig said without turning to face the men standing before her. "We've been betrayed, and you thought it would be in your best interest to keep this information from me?"

Hegvaldr kept his eyes low, but shot a glare at Eivind. The man ignored Hegvaldr's rage and stood calmly.

"Yes, Konugrr," Henrik said, speaking up when the other two would not. "It seems as though they would have us go to battle unprepared."

"And how did you hear about this, Henrik?" Solveig asked, finally ceasing her pacing.

"I overheard the two of them arguing in the mead hall about what to tell you." He shot Hegvaldr and Eivind a knowing look before returning his gaze to Solveig once more. "After all you've done for him," Henrik nodded towards Hegvaldr, "and this is how he repays you."

"Konugrr," Hegvaldr interjected. "We were not going to set you up for failure. Mighty Re'nukh watches over us, and when we learned that Wyrd bears the mark of Apophos, we knew we must act carefully."

Solveig turned, walked over to the two, and motioned for her advisor to join them. Signaling to the men to follow, she led them over to a group of chairs over by the fire. Slipping into the chair, the chieftainess whistled for Tyr to come over. The wolf trotted over to his master, plopping onto the floor between her and the hearth. A low growl rumbled from the beast as he faced the three men.

"Tell me, Hegvaldr, what happened," Solveig said, ignoring the two other men. Her fingers played on her lap, tapping impatiently.

"We met with Wyrd at a pub in their capital. There was something off about him, but we didn't know at first what it was because he bore the mark of Apophos." Hegvaldr kept his palms flat on his thighs, hands cupping his knees. He kept his eyes locked on Solveig, ignoring Tyr's amber stare. The dire wolf's tail twitched as he issued another low growl. "I would have argued for Grimmrheimr more, but once I saw his power, I knew it was best to return quietly. If not only for our safety," Hegvaldr motioned to himself and Eivind, "but for Jytte."

Solveig leaned back in her chair, bringing her hands up to her chin and tenting her fingers so that just the tips grazed it. Hegvaldr sat in silence, waiting for his leader to speak. Next to him, he saw Henrik fidget in his seat. The older man laced his fingers together and shuffled in the chair, earning him a growl from the dire wolf.

The fire crackled, a bit of wood snapping loudly in the stillness. The chieftainess stared into space as she weighed the information. Tyr got up and repositioned himself until he touched her deerskin boots, his grey fur covering the tan of her shoes. The wolf rested his head once more in the direction of the three men, his amber eyes watching them closely as they waited. As the silence drew on, Henrik gave a little cough.

"What is it, Henrik?" Solveig asked turning her attention to the older man.

"Konugrr," Henrik began, his voice cracking a bit, "I think we need to call a full council to determine how to handle this. I don't think it is worth the risk to continue offering our services, especially if we are not getting anything out of the deal anymore."

Solveig's eyes narrowed at the news. "What do you mean we won't get anything?"

"Hegvaldr's omission that they were not going to fulfill their end of the bargain isn't the only betrayal you've suffered," Henrik said. "We must weigh the options of our next steps."

"It's not that we casually chose to withhold that information," Hegvaldr interjected. "We were at the Bear Claw trying to figure out the best way to tell you. He seems to have connections. He said he would come after you directly."

Henrik closed his mouth, his argument dying on his lips as he took in the man's words. Solveig brought her hands under her chin and leaned forward, resting her elbows on her thighs. Eivind watched Hegvaldr with interest, leaning back in his chair as everything fell into place.

"That's impossible," Henrik sputtered. "Grimmrheimr is impregnable. No one would stand a chance against us; the Almighty Re'nukh protects us. No son of Apophos would dare to come here."

"It's not entirely out of the realm of possibility," Solveig said slowly. "A lone man could come up and deal some heavy damage if the timing was right." She leaned back in her chair and pulled her war axe off her hip, laying it across her lap. "And then we have to think about Jytte. Her skillset makes her too valuable to lose. Besides, I won't stand to lose one of our own to those gutless men."

Solveig quickly got up, startling Tyr. The dire wolf jumped up and circled his master a few times, looping around to also include her chair in his orbit, before settling back down in front of the fire. The entire time, the chieftainess paced a short distance from the group, rubbing her hands together as her weapon lay forgotten on her chair. The three men watched their leader as she formulated a plan. Her eyes stared straight ahead, unblinking, unseeing, as she lost herself in her thoughts. Finally, she turned to the men.

"Before we do anything, I want to hear from you, Eivind," she said. "What do you have to say about all of this?"

"It's what they've already said," the large man said. "Hegvaldr and I were sitting in the Bear talking about that little man and how he's trying to blackmail you. Personally, I wouldn't get involved. We're better off just calling Jytte back and going about our lives. But I also know that's not the way of the Silver Wolf." Solveig nodded. "So, we might as well call the council and go to war."

The chieftainess nodded again. "Well said, Eivind. We uphold the Silver Wolf. With Re'nukh on our side, we will be victorious." Turning to Henrik and Hegvaldr, she said, "Go, gather the council. We'll meet at the Bear Claw before we reach mid-night."

Henrik leapt out of his chair and hurried out of the room, earning a growl from Tyr as he was disturbed once more. Solveig gathered her war axe and began circling the room as she prepared her speech for the council. Hegvaldr made eye contact with Eivind and motioned for the man to join him as they left the room.

Solveig noticed the two and called out to them. "Join me in my chambers. There is much we still need to discuss, and I'm afraid it is much too cold out here to think properly."

"Yes, Konugrr," the men said in unison.

It was never wise to displease Solveig.

XIX

S CHAED STARED out the window of his home above his wine shop. Stars dotted the sky, covered by the occasional cloud lazily drifting past. Sipping a glass of Hanzo wine, Schaed closed his eyes as a light breeze played through the open window. It'd been four days since he sent the bottle of wine to Pharn. Three since Oldar had left. He had expected there to be news of the queen and princess' death. Instead, he was greeted with nothing.

"He should be back by now," he mumbled, opening his eyes once more. "They can't keep Oldar. He's a damn king. There's no way they would touch him... unless." Schaed eyed his collection of fine wines. Nearby, a mortar and pestle sat amongst the remnants of the crushed daffodils, foxglove, and opium. "I don't think I used too much daffodil and foxglove. The opium should've just dulled their senses and helped them fall asleep faster. They shouldn't have been found until the morning."

Schaed leaned back in his chair once more and ran his hands through his hair. He didn't know how much was needed, as he was no herbalist. The thought of the women just dropping dead where they stood had been flashing in his mind for the last few days. If he miscalculated, he just made things much more complicated.

"There's no way it'll be tied to him," he told himself for the hundredth time.

Unable to contain the anxious energy inside him, Schaed got out of his chair, scraping the floor with the legs as it slid back. He began pacing around the room, always returning to the window to glance out into the darkness, hoping against hope that he'd see the king returning. Every time, he would be disappointed as he saw just the brilliance of the moon and the myriad of shining stars.

The light from the lamps across from his shop began to flicker as they ran low on oil. The windows of the residences around him were dark. It appeared that he was the only one up at this late hour. With a sigh, Schaed sank into his chair once more and took up his glass of wine. He downed the glass in seconds, placing it roughly on the table and wiping his mouth with the back of his hand. Cupping his face in his hands, Schaed slumped over with a groan. He couldn't even enjoy the warmth his wine brought him.

"Such a waste," he groaned. "Damn."

Returning the glass to the table, Schaed got up once more and made his way over to clean up his mortar and pestle. Sweeping the remnants of the ground herbs into the pestle, the lanky man gathered the powdered herbs in his hand and dumped them into a cup. He then poured a little water from the pitcher on his kitchen table into the cup. Swirling the powder, he made sure to dissolve all of the herbal residue before heading back to the window and dumping the contents into the street below.

Schaed was surprised at how little that did to ease his anxiety.

"Shit."

Unable to relax, Schaed forced himself to sit down in a chair and bury his face in his hands. He inhaled deeply, his palms pressing against his mouth and making it difficult for him to exhale. Warm air washed over him as he focused on his breathing. The earthy scent of the wine he'd been drinking earlier carried an undertone of sweetness that helped calm him. Schaed sat like this for several long moments, just breathing into his hands, and letting his mind wander. Though he wanted to think of anything other than what he'd done, he found that his mind was empty.

As the night dragged on, Schaed found himself finally drifting off. His breathing became more rhythmic and his head drooped several times, startling him as he almost fell over. After three scares, Schaed leaned over and lay down on the table, his arms cradling his head. He felt his eyes become heavy once more and began drifting off when he began to shiver. Stirring a bit, the lanky man curled up on himself to try and keep warm.

Minutes crept by and Schaed could not get comfortable. The air was getting colder, and he couldn't fall asleep anymore. Sitting up, Schaed looked around to see if he left a window open. Rubbing his eyes, he walked over to the window, but found that it was closed and locked.

"What the hell?" he murmured. "It's not supposed to be cold out."

Touching the window with the tips of his fingers, he recoiled quickly, all traces of exhaustion disappearing, as he rubbed his hands together. The tip of his finger that touched the pane stung a little as he ripped it from the icy surface. Bending over to better inspect the glass, he saw frost slowly creeping onto the glass. It seeped into his home, making him shiver as he watched in awe as his breath sent a puff into the air.

"By the seven hells," he whispered, backing up from the window. "What is this?"

Movement across the street caught his attention. Schaed raced to the candles he had burning in his room, his heart beating frantically, and blew out the flames. The room was quickly plunged into darkness, the only light coming from the moon or the dimly burning street lamps. Dropping to his knees, Schaed crawled towards the window. Pulling himself up, he peered out into the night.

Long black shadows, darker than the darkest night, stretched onto the walls of the buildings across the street. They were human-like in form, but tapered off into nothingness at the top, and the fingers ended in curved claws. Schaed gasped as he tried to find the source of the shadows. Cracking open his window as much as he dared, he fought back the desire to slam it shut once more as the icy chill from outside greeted him. Straining his ears, he tried to hear the sound of footsteps as the figures walked on the cobblestones to try and gauge how far away they were.

Nothing. Everything around him was dead silent. Even the normal hum from the bugs or the hoot of the owls was muted. The emptiness unsettled Schaed and sent his heart racing. His breaths came out in puffs as the heat left his body. He hugged his body in a vain attempt to provide some warmth and stop the shivering, hands moving up and down his arms quickly.

"By the gods!" Schaed found himself swearing. It had been a long time since he turned to the gods for anything. His breath came out in a constant stream, the windows completely frosted over.

Glancing at the table, he saw that his wine glass froze over as well. The last dregs of wine that remained looked like a dark jewel against the now opaque glass. In the corner of the room, Schaed's messenger hawk could be heard shuffling on its perch, a small cry of distress coming from his corner before going quiet.

Even Erth knows this isn't natural. What's going on?

A bone-chilling screech rang through the night, causing Schaed to jump and cover his ears. It echoed both out into the night and in his head. His body doubled over, his head touching the floor, as he tried to keep the sound out. A whimper escaped Schaed's lips and tears began to run down his cheeks as he squeezed his eyes closed as tight as he could. His heart raced and a chill set into his body, one that was different from the coldness seeping into his home.

"Blessed Aria, Eldest of the Three, please watch over me and protect me from whatever has entered Madden." Schaed's whispered prayer came out fervently and he repeated it endlessly. His body rocked back and forth on the floor long after the shriek finally died out.

"Blessed Aria, Eldest of the..." Finally daring to look up, Schaed moved his hands and crawled over to the window. His whispered prayers died on his lips as he looked through the frozen window once more.

The shadowed bodies were no longer moving. Instead, they stood motionless, except for the waving on the top of their heads. Some of them flexed their hands, their claws rubbing together. Schaed managed to hear a rasping hiss in the street below his window. Peeking over the sill, he saw their dark figures milling about, waiting for something.

And then he saw *him.*

Schaed's breath caught in his chest as he saw two figures walking down the street, their boots clacking against the cobblestones in the silent night. The shadowed figures turned to face the approaching couple. A few of them hissed, the noise echoing loudly.

"Oh, stop your nonsense," one of the figures said. Schaed thought the voice sounded familiar. "We're here now, and you'll get your chance to feed."

Stepping into the light, Schaed gasped once more as he saw Oldar's uncle, Alastaire, and his wife, Constance, walk among the shadows. The man stood proudly, back straight and capelet rustling in an invisible breeze. On his hip, a muted silver glow illuminated the area around him, keeping the creatures at bay.

In the wan light, Schaed could begin to make out some of the shadowed figures. His blood ran cold as he stared at the creatures. Tall and humanesque, the black forms ended in indistinct, smoky wisps. Their mouths were elongated with thin, sharp teeth sticking out even when the mouths were closed. The eyes were white with no other color, and the tops of the heads disappeared into the heavens.

"Listen up," Alastaire barked. "We will head to the castle. Anyone you see on the way there, you're free to feast. If you see the king, my dear nephew, you'll bring him to me. Alive."

Turning to one of the figures, Alastaire pulled out a dagger that was sheathed on his hip. As the blade left the sheath, the muted glow Schaed had seen earlier exploded, nearly blinding Schaed with its brilliance as it burned brightly in the night. The creatures closest to Alastaire and the blade withdrew with a hiss, their arms flying to shield their face with blinding speed. Alastaire smiled at the creatures' pain. Holding the dagger loosely in his hand, he let the blade wobble around in his hand as he casually pointed at each of the figures one by one.

"I think you would be best suited for this job, Cassius," he said as he pointed the dagger at creature to his right. The monster brought up its hands and let out a wail as the dagger light flickered, oscillating in intensity. "I'm sure my dear nephew would recognize his old friend, even if you are Faceless now."

Schaed dropped to the ground, his head resting right below the window sill as the creature let out a shriek. His body shook and his heart raced as he tried to process what he'd just seen.

"Oh gods," he muttered. "Cassius."

Tears rolled down his cheeks as he forced himself to peek over the sill and out the window once more. Pulling himself up, he watched as Alastaire waved his hand, dismissing the Faceless into the night. The monsters darted into the shadows one by one. The wavering light from the oil lamp was snuffed out as one of the creatures moved near it as they passed, plunging the street below into darkness, aside from the light of the blade.

Alastaire chuckled to himself as he resheathed the dagger. "Well, Oldar, let's see how you fare against them."

XX

S CHAED'S HEART BEAT in his ears, deafening him, as he slumped to the ground once more. His breaths were ragged, as though he'd run a long distance, and sweat covered his brow despite the freezing temperatures in his home and the ambient air outside. The lanky man's hands shook as they rested on the wooden floor. Bringing them to his chest, Schaed tried to rubbing them together in a weak attempt to both soothe himself and bring a little warmth to his body.

"Oh gods. Oh gods. Oh gods," he muttered over and over. "Blessed Aria, protect me from these hellish beasts. Oh gods. Oh gods. Oh gods. Shit!"

Schaed resumed his previous prayer from earlier in the night, as he rubbed his hands together. After several long minutes, he finally found the strength to peek out the window once more. Darkness below. With a deep breath and shaking hands, he tried to gently close the window. His hands shook so hard that he couldn't budge the frost-covered glass.

"I need to tell someone," he murmured. "Oldar. He needs to be warned."

Abandoning the window, he crawled on his hands and knees towards the small table in his bedroom. Erth ruffled his feathers and let out a low cry as Schaed passed by. Shushing his hawk with a violent hiss, Schaed entered his room and moved to a crouch. Time moved agonizingly slow as he made his way to the table. After what felt like an eternity, he reached the table and pulled a sheet of paper and his quill down to the floor as he plopped down, his back against the wall.

With a shaking hand, Schaed struggled to draft a letter to his friend. The quill scratched furiously on the paper, blotting several times in his haste. Schaed cursed as he finally stopped writing and forced himself to take three deep breaths in hopes of calming his body enough to complete the letter. Leaning his head against the smooth wood of his bedroom wall, Schaed closed his eyes and filled his lungs. Holding his breath for a count of ten, he slowly released the air. He repeated these actions two more times. With each breath, he found himself becoming a little more stable.

Upon finishing his third breath, Schaed opened his eyes and picked up his quill once more. His hand was steady enough that he managed to compose a message to his friend on a fresh sheet of paper. With a soft whistle, Schaed called over Erth as he rolled up the parchment. The hawk landed softly beside him and held out his leg. Schaed scrambled around, looking for a piece of string to tie the note to the bird's leg. After a moment, he found some. Letter secured, Schaed picked up Erth and left the room in a crouch, shoving the first attempt at his note into his pocket.

His home was still freezing, but he managed to make his way to the partially opened window. Running his fingers down the bird's back, he spoke soothingly to Erth.

"Okay, Erth. You need to find Oldar. Get this to him. Quickly." His words came out in a rushed whisper, cracking a little since it was so dry. "Go!"

Raising up from his crouch, he pushed the window open far enough for Erth to fly out. With a grunt, he managed to crack it open enough, breaking off a bit of the ice that had now gathered on the hinges. The force resulted in a loud *pop* that rang in the night. Schaed froze, praying that nothing heard it. He sat for several long seconds, his ears straining to hear a hiss or Alastaire's boots upon the cobblestones.

"Go, Erth," he whispered, sound barely escaping his lips. "Find Oldar. Be safe."

With a soft chirp, Erth puffed out his feathers before taking off. Quiet as a cloud, the hawk flew out of the window and into the darkness, his form becoming nothing more than a shadow in the night. Schaed brought his arm back into his home, feeling hopeful now that warmth was returning. Closing the window, he held his breath as he pulled on the pane. Mercifully, there was no noise as he closed it.

Once again, Schaed slumped onto the ground, his body drained as the adrenaline finally left him and exhaustion took over. He sighed as he ran his hands through his blonde hair. They shook as he pulled his legs into his chest.

"Oh gods," he breathed. "What am I going to do? This is unbelievable."

He shook his head and pressed his palms into his eyes, causing stars to pop into his vision as he tried to clear his mind. Schaed sat in the darkness for a long time, only his deep, rhythmic breathing keeping him from breaking down into sobs of terror. Moon light filtered through the windows, shining a bright light onto the dark wooden floors. His body no longer shook, the warmth having returned to his home and his body finally calming down after the night's events.

With a sigh, Schaed released his legs and pushed himself off of the ground. Yawning, he crawled into bed, still dressed. He pulled his quilt tight under his chin and rolled towards the window. The moon light shone at the foot of his bed, illuminating his deep green blanket. Schaed took a deep breath and let it out slowly, forcing his body to release all of his stress.

He shot one final glance at the window before closing his eyes and letting sleep take him. His mind wandered as images of the Faceless, Oldar, and Cassius came unbidden to the surface. Schaed struggled to empty his mind so he could fall asleep, but failed. Rolling over, Schaed noticed that something was wrong. His feet were cold.

Without opening his eyes, he reached down to throw his comforter over his feet. They were already covered.

His eyes shot open as he realized that the room was becoming cold once more. He let out a gasp and it came out as a puff. A shiver ran down his spine and his breath caught in his throat. With his breath coming out in ragged gasps, Schaed slowly turned towards the window. As soon as he could twist his head enough to see out of his window, he felt his stomach drop.

Outlined in the light of the moon, one of the Faceless peered into his room. A large, clawed hand reached up and delicately ran a claw down the pane. A thin scratch trailed down in the glass. Schaed gasped, holding his breath to avoid making any movement. The creature seemed to be looking off to one side of his room, not having noticed Schaed as he laid in his bed.

Schaed tried exhale in a tiny stream, hoping to not draw any attention to his trembling body. He closed his eyes as the breath came out as a noisy woosh. Squeezing his eyes, he began praying once more, his lips moving soundlessly as he sought out protection from gods that he only recently placed any faith in. His fervent silent prayer became whispered as he opened his eyes when he heard the claw run down his window once more.

The creature fixated on something in the corner of Schaed's room; its claw stopped mid-scratch as it looked at whatever caught its interest. Schaed stopped praying and stared at the Faceless. The top of the monster's head moved gently by some unseen force. It reminded him of smoke blowing in the breeze while the fire smoldered beneath. It undulated slowly in the still night. Schaed also observed small ripples on the Facelss' body, like tiny wisps of steam evaporating into the night.

Is it more solid or more smoke-like? he wondered. *The way they move...*

Schaed's heart dropped as the Faceless' head turned towards him. The creature's white eyes locked onto his as he lay bundled up in his bed, the elongated mouth breaking out into a wide smile exposing a myriad of saber-like teeth. Schaed's eyes widened in fear as the monster opened its mouth and let out an ear-piercing shriek that froze him to the core as it echoed into the night.

Schaed's brain screamed at him to move, but his body would not respond. Instead, he trembled in his bed, wrapped in his dark green comforter as the creature narrowed its eyes at him. The Faceless pulled back its hand and struck the window. The glass cracked under the force of the blow, the pane bending inward.

Adrenaline coursed through his body, sweat beading on his brow and body, making his hands and feet clammy. His heart raced and his breathing became ragged. The creature's smile turned into a grimace, baring its teeth in what Schaed could only describe as a bloodthirsty look. As it brought back its hand once more, Schaed finally managed to unfreeze himself.

"Go!" he shouted, forcing his body to break whatever stupor it was in.

As if released from a Shadow's grasp, Schaed leapt out of bed and took off down the hall. A moment later, he heard a loud slam and the sound of shattering glass. The Faceless let out a howl of delight as the glass fell to the floor. Schaed's breath came out in gasps as he raced to the door. He grabbed onto the short wooden wall by his door, pulling himself around as he slid barefoot on the floor.

He heard a thump in the hallway as the Faceless scrambled soundlessly behind him. Schaed's heart pounded in his ears, not even noticing that the monster didn't make a sound as it pursued him. His hand fumbled with the door for a few agonizing moments before he managed to open the latch and race out of his home and down the stairs towards the main floor of his shop. The door slammed behind him, the sound ringing in his empty building.

Schaed scrambled down the stairs, taking them two and three at a time, and landed on the floor in what seemed to be almost no time. His eyes quickly scanned his shop, looking for somewhere to hide. The door was not too far away. He began making his way towards the front door when he paused. Behind him, he heard the creature hiss as it made its way down the stairs.

They were fast. He'd seen that when they first dispersed at Alastaire's command. He would stand no chance if he ran into the streets of Madden in the dark of night. Not to mention, there were many more wandering around.

I'm dead if I go outside, he told himself. *I need to hide.*

Looking around his store, he noticed the semi-hidden door to his wine cellar that was behind the stairs. Without another thought, Schaed darted behind the stairs, banging his head on them in the process and causing stars to blossom before his eyes as he tried to open the door. His hands shook as he fumbled with the latch.

Gods, come on! he panicked.

With a thunderous explosion, Schaed heard the door to his home burst open. The sound of wood shards falling down the stairs, hitting the landing above his head. His eyes widened as he looked up towards the sound. With a rush of relief, he managed to open the door and dart inside as the Faceless let out another howl as it pursued its prey. Schaed shut the door as quietly as possible and locked the door from the inside.

Glancing around, Schaed saw a small space in the corner between a wine rack and a few barrels. Darting over to the corner, he crouched down and squeezed himself in, bringing his knees up to his chest. His breaths came out in ragged gasps as he struggled to remain quiet while his heart pounded in his ears.

Outside in the shop, Schaed heard the creature moving around, its claws scraping on surfaces as it moved. Loud, rasping hisses echoed in the store. Holding his breath, Schaed hoped that the monster wouldn't be able to smell him amongst the earthy wines in his cellar. His ears strained for any sound, hoping to discern if the creature could sniff him out. He didn't hear anything to indicate it could smell him.

Holy Aria, Eldest of the Three, please protect me from this hellish beast. Merciful Ghan, Middle Brother, watch over me in my time of need. Almighty Czand, Youngest of the Three, please shield me from this monster of death.

Schaed repeated his fevered prayer over and over, tears rolling down his cheeks as he sat cramped in the corner. Adrenaline coursed through his veins, keeping him alert as he strained for any sound to let him know the beast's actions.

XXI

Hera's eyes fluttered open. The room was dim, only a few lamps providing any light. She wasn't in her room; the bed was too firm and her family's tapestry was not hanging nearby. Instead, she was in a bare room along with a few other people. Low chatter could be heard as they talked to each other. Hera tried to move her head, but her body didn't want to. It felt as though something was pressing down on her, keeping her from making any movement.

The queen let out a faint groan as she struggled to move. She was startled to hear a few voices pick up and the sound of feet quickly approaching her.

"Your majesty," a familiar voice called out. She couldn't see who spoke. "How are you feeling? Are you in pain?"

As her vision gradually returned, Hera saw one of the healers from the Magicerium bending over her. He was a soft man with Stream tattoos covering almost half of his forearm. He looked familiar, but she couldn't quite place his name.

She tried to shake her head, but he quickly placed his hand on her shoulder, preventing her from moving. "Please, your majesty, don't move yet. We're still waiting to make sure that the poison is far enough along that there's no threat to you. Can you blink your eyes?"

Hera tried to speak, but it came out more like a moan. She quickly blinked to answer his question.

"Good, good," he said excitedly, rubbing his hands. "The lighting is bad, I apologize, your majesty. My name is Urthro. Your daughter is one of my students. I am the in charge of both the Mageri and the Magicerium while Headmistress Vashe is out. You've been asleep for almost four days. Your daughter has been very worried. Do you understand?"

Hera blinked.

"Excellent. Would you please blink once for yes, and two times for no?"

Hera blinked.

"I appreciate that very much, your majesty." Urthro bustled out of sight for a moment before returning with a small wooden cup. "Are you thirsty, your majesty? I have some water here, if you would like any."

Hera blinked. Urthro motioned to the other healers in the room and had them help prop the queen up enough so he could pour a small amount of water into her mouth without fear of her choking. The cool water felt wonderful against her parched throat. Four days was too long to be going without water.

As they laid her back down, Urthro asked: "Are you in any pain?"

She blinked twice.

"That's wonderful," Urthro said, his chubby cheeks stretching as he beamed at her. "You had a fever and heart palpitations the first couple days. It's only this last day or so that you've gotten color back to your cheeks and your heart felt normal. Do you require anything?"

Hera blinked twice. She paused for a moment, and then blinked once.

"You *do* need something?" he asked slowly.

She blinked once. Hera then looked towards the door, hoping they would understand that she would want them to leave so she could have some privacy. Urthro followed her eyes and his landed on the door.

"Do you want us to leave?" he asked.

The queen blinked.

"I'm sorry, your majesty, but for your safety, we cannot leave. I promised the princess that you would have someone in the room with you at all times until we were sure of your safety. We also have one of the younger members of the guard outside the door, but I would feel more comfortable knowing that you have at least one healer in here with you in case things go bad."

Hera blinked and groaned as she tried to shift her body. She hoped he would take the hint and leave her to her thoughts. As if he could read her mind, Urthro dismissed a couple of the others and took the remaining few to the other side of the room. The two who left shared a look of relief as they rubbed the bags under their eyes.

I wonder if they've been awake the entire time? Hera mused. *I really owe them a debt of gratitude for all they've done. Thank Freyna that Cienna has been spared.*

Despite Urthro's words, she tried once more to turn her head. When she found that it was too much effort to do so, she resigned herself to stare at the ceiling. Glancing out the corner of her eyes in Urthro's direction, she saw that it was late at night. There was a bit of moonlight bleeding into the room, but not enough to see by.

That explains all the lamps. I wonder where Cienna is? Probably trying to figure out what's going on. I can't believe Oldar would do this to us. Such a waste that our alliance has been thrown out just because he couldn't get his way. Looks like we'll need to draft new alliances with the Mountain Tribes and the others.

Hera let her eyes wander for a bit, giving herself more of an opportunity to let her mind wake up. It felt like just a short while ago that she'd been scolding her daughter's lack of trust in their neighbor and lifetime ally. The taste of the wine still lingered in her mouth. It was pleasantly earthy with a hint of sweetness, a delicious wine that she would love to have again. Hanzo wine was known for being the best in all of Corinth. What could have happened to her bottle?

Was the seal still intact? she wondered. *How did no one try and inspect the bottle before it was brought to us?*

Her thoughts raced as she tried to figure out what happened. A number of different scenarios played in her head, none of which answered her questions. It felt like next to no time before her eyelids began to droop. The queen struggled to stay awake, trying to find answers, but she soon found herself asleep.

The queen found herself looking down on her resting body. She knew she was asleep, and yet, she felt wide awake at the same time. Hera was surprised to see how frail she looked. Four days of nothing but whatever herbs the healers had given her was not enough for her to live on. She'd lost weight, and since she was already slim, the change was apparent.

Hera walked away from her body and towards Urthro and the other three healers. They sat down in chairs, trying to relax while they waited. One of the young men curled up in his chair, his head resting on his arm, in an attempt to nap while the others either snacked on some grapes and bread, or took down notes of the queen's progress.

She watched as Urthro got up and stood over the healer as she wrote, making a soft comment on one of the woman's lines as she worked. Hera looked over on the table and noticed that there was a thick stack of papers, all, presumably, of her and her condition. The queen found herself tearing up as she tried to imagine what she'd put her daughter through.

"Do you think the princess will return soon?" the young female healer asked. "Or even the Headmistress?"

Urthro shook his head. "I don't think we're in need of the Headmistress anymore. However, I think if the princess returned, that would be beneficial to the queen. Her majesty is still weak. The next hours should help us determine her course. If we can get her to start eating and drinking, I think we'll be in good shape." The healer pulled up a paper and scanned its contents. "The princess, we have no idea when she'll return. It sounded like they were all going to Xan, not Alocar. Xan is almost seven days from Pharn. We probably shouldn't expect to see her in less than a span."

"Xan?" Hera asked as she brought her hand to her mouth. "What could she be doing out there again?"

"Do you think we'll have a bunch of injured or dying like last time?" the woman asked.

"There's no way to know," Urthro replied. "I hope not though."

"Okay, what is going on?" Hera asked. "This makes no sense."

Moving away, Hera shook her head. She couldn't understand what was going on. How was she able to see herself and listen in on their conversation, but still be asleep? Was she even asleep? Nothing made sense. Making her way back to her body, something caught her eye. A shock of periwinkle blue that seemed very out of place for dimly lit room. With a thud, the blue disappeared out the door, which Hera didn't even notice was open. Turning to give herself one last look, Hera decided to follow whatever just left the room.

Passing through the door, Hera saw a tall, lanky kid with a spear. He was very young. On the other side of the door, another, older boy stood. The two chatted lazily, sharing a joke as they tried to stay awake.

"Are you sad Master Thol didn't take you with them, Cody?" the older looking kid asked.

"I am a little, but I'm also not," Cody replied. "I need more training than what they can give me in such a short period of time. To be honest, I'm surprised I survived both the attack here and in the gorge. I probably should've died."

"You're probably right," the older boy said with a laugh. "Don't worry though. You're here for a reason. Besides, now you can pull weight over some of the others as one of the few Master Thol has taught. Not everyone gets personal training by him. And you even have been given some important duties." The boy motioned towards the queen's door, narrowly avoiding hitting Hera with his spear as he did so. "Not everyone is chosen to guard the queen. They like you. I bet you'll make captain before your career is over."

"Captain," Cody muttered, his eyes drifting off to some faraway place. "That would be nice. But realistically, Efan, you can't possibly see me as captain material. More like one of the trusted officers than a captain."

"You never know," Efan replied.

Hera spun around in the hall, trying to find the blue thing she'd seen earlier. To her right, she saw a little girl in a white dress with periwinkle hair and obsidian eyes. The little girl smiled at Hera and beckoned her forward. Her dress swirled around her and her hair played in a breeze that was only around her.

"Freyna," Hera gasped.

Hera couldn't believe it. The goddess had come to her several times now in the last few days. Reaching towards her bodice, Hera tried to touch the petals she'd carried in a pouch tied around her neck. She panicked for a moment before breathing a sigh of relief as she felt the aged leather bag against her skin. The contents inside brought her warmth and a sense of peace.

The queen looked back up at the goddess and noticed that the two of them stood on a grassy knoll. It was dark out, but not as dark as it had been in Hera's room. The night was still young. A breeze rustled her hair, blowing the grass and flowers on the hill. At the top stood a lone tree.

It looked ancient with its bark burned and aged almost to the point of petrification. Gnarled branches lay bare, their twigs reaching up to the sky like an old woman's fingers. The area around the base of the tree was barren, only dirt and a few small stones and pebbles covered the ground. As Hera approached the tree, she felt a heaviness that threatened to dispel the warmth and peace brought on by the holy petals in her bodice.

With tentative steps, Hera approached the tree. Freyna stood near the tree, but well outside the circle of dirt. Her toes curled as her bare feet rested on the grass. Making her way to the goddess, Hera noticed that her feeling of protection was returning as she neared the small girl.

Hera looked out into the horizon, facing the same direction as the goddess. Her breath caught in her chest. A group of large, unnatural-looking stones stood in a circle. Taller than a grown man and perfectly smooth, they were evenly spaced between each other. Twelve, Hera counted. Twelve stones ringing a single golden flower in the center of the circle.

Despite been far away, a heaviness radiated from the circle all the way to the queen. The goddess reached out and lightly touched Hera's hand. As though a bubble engulfed her, the queen looked down at Freyna, startled at the sudden disappearance of the sense of dread she'd been feeling from both the tree and the stones a moment before. Grabbing the goddess' hand in her own, the queen squeezed Freyna's small hand.

With a flash, Hera was hit with the image of hundreds of dead around the perimeter of the stone circle, the ground now blackened as if a fire raged in the distance. Banners and livery for the nations of Corinth dotted the ground between the fallen bodies. Hera gasped as the force of the vision knocked her back a step. Freyna's grip tightened in the queen's hand.

A long figure stood among the group, an orange glow outlining his body and partially illuminating his face. In his hand, a ball of fire sat casually, waiting to be released. Behind him, two of the stones glowed. The others were cracked or lay crumbled on the ground. In the distance, a bone chilling shriek rang out, only to be answered by several other calls.

"By the gods," Hera swore as she brought her free hand to her breast. "What is going on?" Turning to Freyna, she said, "This is different from the last thing you've shown me."

Freyna nodded.

Hera returned her attention to the field and felt her heart drop. Among the dead, she spotted the curly blonde hair of her daughter. Cienna lay face down in the grass, her face turned towards the dead tree behind the queen. Blood ran down her forehead and dribbled from her slightly parted lips. The princess' eyes were open and glassed over.

A sob escaped the queen's throat and she tried to bring her other hand to her mouth, but Freyna would not let go. Hera shook her head, moaning as tears ran down her face.

"No, no, no, no, no," she wailed. "This cannot be. Tell me it's not true." Hera turned to face the goddess, her eyes wide as she implored the small figure to ease her pain.

Another cry rang out in the distance, only, it didn't sound as far away.

Freyna opened her mouth, but closed it without a word. Her brow furrowed as she struggled internally with something. The two stood in silence, Hera weeping as she looked down on her dead daughter. Finally, Freyna broke the silence.

"This is what will come if balance is not restored," she said. Her voice had a strange undertone to it. Hera thought she could hear the ocean waves and wind mixed in with the goddess' human words. "Look at the land," Freyna continued. "Do you recognize it?"

"No," Hera replied.

Freyna's grip on the queen's hand lessened. "I'm sorry," she said. "This is how I see it. The stones, they are monuments to our power. The tree," she motioned to the tree behind them. "This is the tree planted by my father. Both are filled with the old energy. Find this place. Restore the balance to your world, and prevent what you see before you."

"But how? I don't even know where to begin," the queen stammered. "I don't even know if I'm fit to travel."

Freyna met the queen's gaze. Her obsidian eyes looked heavy as the child goddess faced Hera. Her head drooped and her hand finally broke contact with the queen's. As soon as the contact was broken, the protective bubble that kept the overbearing energy at bay and the vision below disappeared. Hera gasped as the weight of the two ancient markers hit her at once.

"You must find the balance."

"Hmmm." Hera looked out onto the field. Rich, green grass blew gently in the breeze. Leaves on the trees in the distance rustled. Squinting her eyes, Hera tried to find something she could recognize.

Like the previous visions, there were mountains in the distance. How far away, she could not tell. The hard part was not having any man-made landmarks she could reference. If only there was a house or a bit of livestock.

"It has to be close by," the queen murmured. "Southern Zanir? Maybe the Res Mountains?"

Her eyes landed on the golden flower once more. It was mesmerizing. The golden lily stood out amongst everything else like a jewel on a crown. All else looked dull compared to this flower. The grasses around it rustled and moved in the breeze, but the flower did not bend.

Behind it, something caught the queen's eye. Focusing on the stones behind the golden lily, Hera saw a thin strip of blue.

"A stream?" she wondered out loud. "But that could be anywhere."

"Do not forget the balance," Freyna cut in.

Hera jumped, startled at the goddess' words. She'd forgotten that Freyna was there for a moment.

"What does that mean?" Hera murmured. "The balance." Tapping her hand against her chin, she began muttering to herself. "The balance. The balance. Is it balance I need in my life?" she asked.

Freyna paused, unsure of how to respond. "We all need balance in our life."

"But, if it is on this scale, then surely it is more than just my personal harmony." Hera looked to the little girl for confirmation. Freyna did not respond.

Maybe I'm on the right path. I wonder why she just can't tell me outright.

A dark shadow caught Hera's attention on the other side of the dead tree. A large figure leaned out from behind the tree. The queen felt her stomach knot and her chest tighten as she watched the figure observing them.

She can't tell me.

"So," Hera said out loud, breaking the silence between her and Freyna and hopefully not arousing the suspicion of whatever stalked them. "There is something large that needs to be fixed. Something that is out of balance... or harmony. The alliance. Oh gods, I know where this is."

Movement out of the corner of her eye caught Hera's attention again. The dark figure moved out from behind the tree and began walking over to her and Freyna. As he neared, the shadows began to disappear and his form became more corporeal. She could see that he was a man, tall and lean with dark hair.

Before she could make out any more, Freyna gave Hera a push. The queen stumbled back and found herself looking up at a smooth stone ceiling as she lay on a bed. Turning her head, Hera saw Urthro leaning back in his chair with a book on his lap. The other healers lay with their heads on the table sound asleep. A solitary candle burned low, its flickering light barely illuminating the room.

Hera's heart raced as she thought of everything she just witnessed. Somehow, she knew that she had to get a message to her daughter and to the king of Alocar.

With effort, Hera managed to move her hand and touch the leather pouch around her neck. Her arm was so heavy. *Thank Freyna they did not take this off*, she thought as she felt the warmth and comfort fill her like usual.

Urthro stirred at the sound of her sheets rustling. Looking at the queen, Hera watched as a wave of relief washed over his face. "Your majesty, I'm pleased to see you moving. Do you think you can speak?"

Hera opened her mouth. With extreme effort, she managed to choke out a few words: "Bring me any dream reader you can find. We must act quickly. There isn't much time."

XXII

Hᴇɢᴠᴀʟᴅʀ ᴀɴᴅ Eɪᴠɪɴᴅ ᴡᴀʟᴋᴇᴅ behind Solveig in the blackness of night. Green lights in the heavens, their thin lines blowing in the wind, shone brightly in the sky against the dark backdrop and twinkling stars. Hegvaldr sighed, his breath coming out in a puff of smoke. Having spent an hour with her, his spirits were higher than they had been earlier that evening. Eivind whistled a jaunty tune as he walked alongside them. Ahead, Solveig walked with a casual gait despite her exertions earlier.

They passed several members of their tribe as on their way to the meeting hall. Greetings and calls of respect to their leader broke the otherwise quiet night. Solveig returned the salutations with a wave of her hand or the nod of her head.

The thick wooden frame of their meeting hall came into sight, its windows flooding the darkness with a warm glow and coloring the snow orange whenever the door opened. Hegvaldr followed the chieftainess into the building and into the warmth. The heat from the roaring hearth blasted Hegvaldr, the bite of the cold outside quickly disappearing as he moved further into the room. Beside him, Eivind let out a sigh of contentment as he warmed up as well.

"I hate traveling in the dead of night," Eivind muttered. "Damn colder than the wenches at the Bear."

Hegvaldr chuckled. "I'm sure you wouldn't say that about Konugrr," he said to the large man. The noise from the general chatter in the hall covered his statement, keeping it from Solveig's ears. It would not do to have her hear that.

"You know Solveig knows how to keep the nights warm," Eivind replied, a grin spreading from ear to ear.

The two shared a short laugh before making their way to the long table with the other members of the council. Lining the perimeter of the oaken table, a collection of elders and warriors sat around, chatting casually while they waited for their leader to call the council to order.

Raising her hands, Solveig stood at the head of the table and waited for the noise to die down. She didn't have to wait long. In a matter of moments, the group quieted. With a smile, the chieftainess addressed the group.

"Praise be to Re'nukh and all of his glory that we have been able to gather here tonight," she began with a smile as she raised her glass.

Tankards were lifted as the council responded with their adulations to the gods. Everyone took a long draught of the mead that splashed in their mugs.

"I come to you tonight seeking your council. I have received word that someone who we thought was an ally is actually an asp." Gasps and mutterings of dismay broke out among the table. Solveig held up her hand to silence the group. "And on top of it, he is one who bears the mark of Apophos."

"Death to the monster!" one of the elders cried out. "He has betrayed us!"

"Treachery!" another shouted.

"Bring him to justice!"

Solveig held her hands up once more. "I ask our elders what their thoughts are. I have received guidance from the Almighty Re'nukh, but I seek the benefit of your experience before I pass judgement."

A small woman, hunched over by age, stood. The top of her head barely cleared the backing of her chair. The council fell silent immediately, as all eyes turned to the woman. Her long, grey hair was braided and tied together, creating a loop. A thick teal string was woven into the braid.

"This is a blessing from the Almighty," her frail voice cracked out. "Grimmrheimr has long sought guidance from the gods, and we would be foolish to ignore such a strong sign."

"What do you mean, Elderma Kajsa?" Solveig asked.

Placing her hand on the table to steady herself, the old woman took a deep breath before continuing. "I have seen many things in my life," Kajsa began. "My father looked for reasons to leave Grimmrheimr and bring her people with him. Ever since the great king Hrothgar was killed, our people have struggled to find a way to regain our glory. Our last Konugrr, Arild, closed Grimmrheimr to all who do not follow the will of Re'nukh or the way of the Silver Wolf. Our mighty Konugrr's father," Kajsa bowed her head in respect to Solveig, "has done a wonderful job training our warriors and building up trust between Grimmrheimr and the other lands despite our people not venturing past her borders.

"Our informants are without equal. My own granddaughter is working in Fa'Tinh. Everything pointed to a union with other nations and only good for our people. Now, we find out that we've been betrayed, by one of Apophos no less. We would be fools to ignore this warning from the Almighty. My vote is to withdraw from whatever agreement you have and bring Jytte back. She is in grave danger."

A spark popped in the hearth as the council sat in silence. Kajsa's words were not to be taken lightly.

"And do you all believe the same as our venerable elder?" Solveig asked the other four.

The men sat uncomfortably in their seats. Solveig made eye contact with her advisor, Henrik, and bore through him. The man shifted in his seat before clearing his throat.

"Konugrr," he began, "I know that you want to show off the might of Grimmrheimr, especially at this blatant act of disrespect directed at yourself, but I think Elderma Kajsa has a point." The man flinched as Solveig narrowed her eyes. "We've been looking for a clear message from the gods, and I think that there is nothing clearer than what we have received."

"But just earlier tonight you were advocating for a different outcome," Solveig countered. "What brings about this change?"

Henrik cleared his throat. His eyes turned to Hegvaldr, an intensity returning to him as he spoke. "I let my judgement become clouded by the actions of others. I have no doubt in your decision making, but Hegvaldr's behaviors are not suitable for one of his position."

Several chairs shifted against the wooden floor at this comment. A couple of the council took a sip of their mead as the hall went uncomfortably quiet. Hegvaldr watched as Solveig's eyes darted from Henrik to him, her fingers laced together with her index fingers lightly touching her lips. It was a bold accusation to make of her mate. The silence drew on. The chieftainess' personal advisor sat smugly at the table, casually drinking his mead as he eyed Hegvaldr.

Henrik did not expect Hegvaldr to question him outright, Hegvaldr could see that. The elder believed in the old ways, in following the path of the Silver Wolf and not questioning those of higher rank. The warrior felt anger welling in his chest as he watched the man attempted to tarnish his name. Hegvaldr clenched his fist and ground his teeth as he bit his tongue.

"Tell me," Eivind spoke up, "what would the harm be in going down to Fa'Tinh and bringing Jytte back with us? We could disguise it as a trade caravan, we haven't left the wastes in ages so it wouldn't be unreasonable for us to bring a guard as our Konugrr negotiates, and use that opportunity to secrete her back with us. The Silver Wolf requires us to act bravely, but with honor. If the little man threatens us, we have a reason to fight back. Our show of force should be enough to let him know that we are not afraid."

Hegvaldr turned to Henrik and was rewarded with seeing the elder glowering at the large man. The rage died within the warrior as a smirk played on his lips. Scanning the rest of the table, Hegvaldr was surprised to see so many nods of agreement at Eivind's suggestion.

"We can't trust him either," Henrik sputtered. Hegvaldr watched as eyes darted back to the elder. "Everyone knows that Eivind is an oaf, only motivated by food and bedding women. He worked in consort with Hegvaldr to deceive our Konugrr. We should heed the advice of the gods and stay out of it."

"But in effect, we are," Hegvaldr finally interrupted. "We're just delivering our message in person instead of running away with our tail between our legs."

"Have you no respect for what the Elderma has said?" the old man spat.

"Elderma Kajsa has made some good points, but Eivind's will allow for us to remain dignified," the deep voice of one of the warriors cut in. The man, Fenris, placed his hands flat on the table in a sign of respect. His voice was even and he maintained eye contact with Henrik as he spoke to the council. "It is unfair to dismiss Eivind's contribution like that. I have spent years training with him and going on expeditions, and he has been nothing but a true brother. He follows the Silver Wolf completely, and I would not doubt him."

The remaining two warriors nodded in agreement at Fenris' words. Hegvaldr was pleased to see that Halden, one of the elders, also expressed his support for Eivind. Glancing over at the large man, Hegvaldr bit back a laugh as Eivind leaned back in his chair and downed his mead in one massive gulp. Wiping his mouth with the back of his hand, Eivind winked at his brothers in battle.

"I won't deny that I enjoy company of women or good food, Elder Henrik," Eivind said. "I think that we all deserve to indulge in our vices after earning our due."

Fenris and the other warriors let out a bark of laughter, Einer raising his tankard in salute to Eivind before taking a long draught. Even Solveig cracked a smile as she watched the interaction with hungry eyes.

"I too agree with Elderma Kajsa and Eivind's point of following the Silver Wolf," Halden added. "If we can follow Eivind's plan and keep to ourselves, not only would we be displaying our power, but we would still be heeding the word of the gods. The Almighty Re'nukh would not send us this opportunity if we were to just ignore the signs. My vote is to go through with Eivind's plan, but return quickly to Grimmrheimr. I would even go a step further to suggest that we go to the caves up north to wait out this threat until after the winter. We can survive for months in those caverns."

"After winter?" Henrik sputtered. "We would leave our homes unprotected until Toron disappeared from the heavens."

"It is the smartest plan," Fenris said. "I agree with Elder Halden."

Einer and Tormund voiced their agreement. Hegvaldr turned to check the rest of the table. The two remaining elders, who had until then been quiet, sat uncomfortably in silence. His eyes then went to the Elderma.

Kajsa sat with her eyes closed, listening to all the arguments. When no one else spoke, she opened her eyes and stood up once more. Her tiny frame trembled as she struggled to support herself at the table.

"Konugrr," the Elderma said, her soft voice cracking as she spoke. "You have received good advice this night. At the start of this meeting, it was my impression that you wanted to lead Grimmrheimr to war against a servant of Apophos. Though your word is law, I find some of your actions to be rash." Hegvaldr's eyes darted to Solveig's face, trying to read her emotions. The chieftainess sat in silence, her fingers interlaced with her index fingers touching her lips once more.

"Although, you have never been known to go against the will of the council. You have heard my choice. My vote is to stay in Grimmrheimr. But I agree with Elder Halden. We should retreat to the caverns and stay until after winter. If what you said is true, we should expect that the servant of Apophos would not hesitate to come up here to exact any revenge he felt he was owed if we do not uphold our end of the old bargain." The Elderma's eyes softened as she dropped her gaze. "I hate to say it, but I am afraid that my granddaughter may have to wait for the time being."

"No, Elderma," Solveig said gently. "We will get Jytte home as soon as possible."

Kajsa sat down at the table, offering her thanks to Solveig. Hegvaldr watched as the elderly woman's hands trembled as she placed them on the table, just as Fenris had. A twinkle flashed in her eye as she turned to speak to an elder next to her. Hegvaldr could tell that the thought of bringing her granddaughter home excited her.

Henrik looked worried as the Elderma smiled while she spoke to her neighbor. Hegvaldr couldn't help but feel smug at the older man's predicament. The warrior knew that the elder didn't care for him, especially since he'd risen through the ranks and became Solveig's favorite so quickly. Coupled with his intense dislike of Eivind, Hegvaldr couldn't blame the man for his emotions. Earning Solveig's favor had its benefits.

"Thank you, everyone, for your input," Solveig said at last. "You have given me a lot to think about, and a lot to consider about my previous position. I think you all speak rightly, but one suggestion speaks to me more than the other. I believe we should heed the word of the gods. The Almighty Re'nukh would not give us such a clear message if he didn't want us to listen. However, Eivind brings up a good point. We must follow the way of the Silver Wolf. As such, a display of power masked as a trade trip would be perfect. We could make some good coin selling scrimshaw, and it would be nice to pick up some stuff that Grimmrheimr cannot provide.

"Jytte is my most versatile informant. Even if we pull her out early, whatever she's gathered will be invaluable. But, once we extract Jytte, we return home and go to the caves. The snows brought on during the winter will provide us with enough cover to keep us save. Hopefully, the terrain and time will deter him. If it doesn't, we will be waiting. Attacking us in our home, seemingly unprovoked, will draw backlash from the tribes. If he's smart, it won't be worth it."

Hegvaldr watched as, one by one, each member of the council nodded in agreement. By the time they reached the Elderma and Henrik, no one had dissented. When Halden called out Kajsa for her vote, she placed her hands back onto the table, palms down. With a soft voice, the Elderma cast her vote. Agreement.

Henrik's jaw clenched at the decision, but made no other sign that he was displeased. As Halden called out his name for his vote, Henrik sat quietly for a moment. Hegvaldr observed the elder cast a quick glance in Solveig's direction before nodding silently before voicing his agreement.

It was unanimous.

Solveig beamed at the council. Clapping her hands, the chieftainess dismissed the group. Those with mead left in their tankards drained whatever remained, slamming the mugs on the table as one. It did not do to displease her. The few who finished their mead before the end of the meeting joined in with the unified slamming of the mug. Chairs scraped against the floor as the moved to leave. Einer walked over to help the Elderma home, proffering his arm to her trembling body.

"Hegvaldr," Solveig said in a low voice, "wait here."

Taking his time, Hegvaldr hung back as the rest of the council left the hall one by one until only he, the chieftainess, and Eivind were left. The warrior watched as the large man pulled out a piece of seal jerky and ripped off a piece. Eivind chewed slowly, unaware of the other two standing around.

"Eivind," Solveig called out. The large man glanced over at the two. "What are you doing?"

Holding up his jerky, the man mumbled through a full mouth, "Eating."

"Dammit, Eivind," Hegvaldr said, exasperated. "Why don't you just go home?"

"No," Solveig said, holding up her hand.

"Konugrr?" Hegvaldr asked.

"This is your punishment for not telling me the truth when you first returned. When we arrive in Fa'Tinh, you'll give Wyrd my message. I won't be made a fool. I trust you'll deliver the message effectively."

"Yes, Konugrr," the two said unison.

"Now, go," Solveig said, waving Eivind away. "I need you to be well rested for this task."

Shoving the rest of the jerky in his mouth, Eivind lumbered out of the hall and into the darkness and cold. Turning to Hegvaldr once Eivind left, Solveig flashed an alluring smile.

"Come, I'm cold. Join me in my bed."

The two walked out into the night, Solveig leading the way to her home, Hegvaldr right behind. It didn't do well to displease her.

XXIII

OLDAR WOKE UP, his body aching and his head pounding after another long night. The sticks and small stones that he thought he'd cleared away the night before had somehow magically reappeared, poking him in the back. With a groan, the young king rubbed his eyes, hoping to clear away the grogginess. His stomach churned, causing him to flip onto his hands and knees as his body threatened to reject the meager dinner he managed to get down the night before.

Wiping the spit from his mouth with the back of his hand, Oldar looked for his water skin. After a long draught of cool water, he felt better. His headache began to lessen as he hydrated, and he noticed that his hands were no longer shaking. With a sigh, he cleared up his bedroll and made his way to the camp chef in hopes of grabbing a bite to eat.

"Finally deciding to join us?" Brody asked, clapping the king on the back as he lined up behind him. "You were looking pretty rough last night. Everything okay?"

Oldar rubbed his eyes once more and nodded. "Yeah. Yeah, I'm fine. I picked a hell of a time to stop drinking." He flashed a feeble smile. "Last time I quit it wasn't nearly this bad. I don't think I can take much more of this."

"It'll get better. I knew someone who was sick for a week after he gave up the drink. He was a raging drunk though, so I'm sure you won't be ill much longer."

"Let us hope, my friend," Oldar said, flashing a wan smile. "If it goes on much longer, I probably would be more of a hindrance than a help in the coming days."

Brody smirked and clapped the king on the back once more. Oldar found himself losing his anger at the bodyguard, the negative emotion being replaced with respect and even a fondness.

He's just like me, Oldar realized. *We're both struggling to adjust to our new duties that were suddenly thrown upon us. It's a shame we both fell in love with the same girl.*

The king and Brody stood in line, sharing a pleasant conversation while they waited for their breakfast. Men walked by, waving or calling a greeting out to the two. Most went by with a smile, but some still shot the young king a look, their eyes reflecting their distrust.

"Don't mind them," Brody said, catching the king's eye. "Some of them will look at you like Ronan does Dez, but most of them are willing to turn a blind eye about what happened until we get an official word from the princess." Seeing Oldar shift from foot to foot, Brody continued. Lowering his voice, he said, "Look, Oldar. What happened was pretty bad. The queen may be dead for all we know, and all we have to go by is a letter that was supposedly written by you."

"But I didn't do it," Oldar insisted. "I would never do something like that."

"Things didn't end too well with you guys the last time you met," Brody said. "The timing is suspicious."

Oldar's jaw dropped. "You don't believe me."

"To be honest," Brody replied, hesitation in his voice, "I'm not entirely sure."

"Damn."

"Everything moved too quickly. I just came back with Al, who, let's be honest, is a shadow of his former self. Caitlyn hasn't been having an easy time either." He paused, his eyes looking inward as he remembered his time in the abyss. "Aramaine wasn't kind to her. It can change people in there." The young man's gaze dropped.

Oldar watched as Brody withdrew into himself. The young soldier's face paled as he relived the horrors he'd seen when he went to rescue his friend. The king noted that Aramaine wasn't kind to Brody either, despite his statement. The look was fleeting. A moment later, Brody shook his head and blinked, clearing away his thoughts. If Oldar hadn't been paying attention, he would've missed it.

"And Cienna," Brody continued. "Well, she has been struggling with things ever since her father died. All I can say, is that you may want to pray that the queen hasn't either."

"What should I do?" Oldar asked. "How do I prove myself?"

Before Brody could answer, the two grabbed their breakfast and walked back towards Brody's resting spot. The two noticed Alverick and Caitlyn waiting nearby. Both looked to be in much better spirits than they were yesterday. Alverick especially. His face was more relaxed than they had been since he returned from the abyss.

"Remember your oaths," Brody finally answered.

As they approached Alverick and Caitlyn, they saw Cienna walk over. Oldar took a bite of his meal, a piece of dried meat and a slice of bread, and enjoyed the combination of the two together. Deer were not as common in Alocar as they were in Zanir, but he'd had fresh deer on multiple occasions in the past. Oxen and cattle were more common back home.

Taking another bite, Oldar made eye contact with Cienna and shot her a smile. To his delight, the princess returned the gesture. Oldar glanced over at Brody to see if she was actually looking at him, and was pleased to see that she was looking directly at the king.

Seems like our talks the last couple days have been productive, he smiled to himself. *If I keep talking to her, maybe we can fix the damage I did from the last time they visited.*

Oldar stood for looking at the princess for a while, unable to absorb what was being said by the others. In his mind, he worked on a thousand different ways to reignite the old alliance after all he'd done.

The fact that we haven't had a messenger come riding to find us bodes well, he thought. *Those left behind knew we are making our way to Xan. It's not like they can't find us. As long as the queen doesn't die, there's a chance that we can go back to the way things were.*

Shaking his head, Oldar chided himself for being so naïve. After what had happened, things couldn't go back to the way they had been.

I only hope I can mend the wrongs I've caused. Without them, I have no one. Life will be pretty lonely if I don't even have allies I can turn to. I want that relationship like our parents had. As long as we don't get any bad news on this trip, I should be able to make things work.

"But do you really think that we can do this without Vashe?" Caitlyn asked.

Her tone caught Oldar by surprise, pulling him from his thoughts and back to the conversation in front of him. Alverick's brow was furrowed, his eyes troubled as they spoke. Brody paced back and forth, his hands behind his back as he tried to come up with an answer. The princess stood with wide eyes, her hands covering her mouth.

"You said there was darkness and stuff, Al," Caitlyn continued. "Even that little girl saw something bad. Vashe is strong. She showed that when she helped us out in Aramaine. We need her for this."

"But we don't even know where she is," Brody replied. "She could be any-where. Besides, that necklace you had that connected the two of you hasn't glowed like it did when you two were bonded. What if we used up all of the magic?"

"Even if we knew where she was, who is to say that we can get to her in time?" Cienna asked.

"We know where she is," Caitlyn insisted. "Scrymme."

Alverick's head popped up, his eyes going hard. "No," he said flatly. "We are not going to Scrymme. I will not allow it."

Caitlyn tried to sputter a response, but couldn't form any words.

"I have to agree with Alverick," Cienna said, stepping forward. "As your princess, I forbid anyone from heading to Scrymme. Their people are not known for being kind to outsiders. I will not tempt another attack on my people."

Caitlyn frowned, but didn't push the matter further. She pulled at her leather gloves for a moment before deciding to pull them off. With a sudden jerk, the redhead ripped off both gloves and shoved them into her pocket. Cienna gasped and Older had to bite back an exclamation of surprise as he saw her tattoo covered hand. The jagged tattoos were not continuous. There were large breaks in between, exposing her bare flesh.

"By the gods," Oldar swore, the words tumbling out of his mouth. "How?"

"You're... tainted," Cienna breathed.

Caitlyn took a deep breath. Her hands began to tremble and her eyes started to water, but she did not break down. She took a couple more deep breaths and ran her hands through her hair.

"Maybe the gods decided to spare me," she said simply.

"You knew?" Cienna asked Brody and Alverick.

The two men nodded. The Avalanche walked over and wrapped his arm around her shoulder. Kissing her on the top of her head, he nodded once more.

"There is much to discuss when all is said and done," Alverick said. "Right now, we must figure out how to proceed. We need the little girl."

"Zemé," Brody said. "I spoke to her earlier, after we'd left Pharn. Al, I think at least you and I should have a discussion with her. I think there's some stuff you need to know before we go on."

The group looked at Brody questioningly.

"She fixed his mind, but what more can she do?" Oldar asked. "She's just a little girl."

"She's not," Brody said, shaking his head.

Caitlyn opened her mouth to speak, but a shout from the camp startled the group. They turned towards the direction of the commotion and saw a man pointing at a hawk as it sat in a nearby tree. The bird ruffled its feathers as it screeched. He held out his leg, showing off the attached message and crying out again.

"Communications!" the nearest man called out.

"Anyone have experience with hawks?" another called out.

A man walked over, a leather pouch turned inside out and covering his arm. Holding his hand up towards the bird, he whistled. The hawk eyed the man, its head tilting as it stared at the makeshift leather glove, before flying down and landing on his hand. The man ran the back of his hand down the bird's back a couple times before reaching down to untie the string holding the letter to its leg.

The bird ruffled its feathers once more and chirped as he pulled off the message. Once the letter had been detached, the bird flew to the tree once more and waited. The man looked at the parchment in confusion, scratching his head as he tried to figure out who it was for. Noting the seal, he looked at it for a moment before asking:

"Anybody know someone with a wine bottle and the letter "S" on their seal?"

The group grumbled, no one able to recall anyone with that signet.

"I think I do," Oldar said, raising his hand as he walked over to the man holding the parchment.

The man handed the king the rolled parchment and moved away to afford the king some privacy. Oldar ran his fingers over the red wax, tracing the "S" in the middle of the wine bottle. He broke the seal and unrolled the parchment. Reading the message, his eyes widened with each line. His stomach dropped as he read one word over and over.

"Oh gods," he muttered once he finished the message. "I, I have to go." Turning to Brody and Cienna, Oldar began shoving his belongings into his bag. "I have to go. Now." Once he finished packing, Oldar began looking for his horse. "Where's Bells?"

A soldier walked over with the horse. "I just took her out with the others so she could eat some grass." He offered the mare's reins to the king.

"Wait," Cienna called out. "What's going on?"

"My uncle is trying to overthrow Alocar. He marched into Madden with a small force of, I couldn't read what was written, but something scared Schaed and I need to get back to protect my people."

"Take one of our faster horses," the princess offered. "It'll take you too long to get home if you use yours. We'll watch her until you can come back."

Oldar strode over to Cienna and took the reins of a dun stallion from her hands. "Thank you," he said as he stared deeply into her eyes. "This gift, I won't forget your kindness. I'll return him as soon as possible."

"Be safe," she replied softly.

Tying his bags to the horse, Oldar climbed on and adjusted his grip on the reins while he sat in the saddle. Turning to Cienna, Brody, and the others behind them, he gave a curt nod before digging his heels into horseflesh. The stallion took off in the direction of Alocar, kicking up dust as he ran.

When Zemé and Alverick spoke, they mentioned something called the Faceless. Oldar had dismissed it as the ramblings of someone Snapped. Now, seeing it in Schaed's missive, he knew that things had gotten serious.

XXIV

OLDAR FOUND HIMSELF WANDERING through a heavily wooded area. The dense canopies blocked out some of the midday sun, providing the young king with enough shade to keep him pleasantly cool as he traveled. He walked alongside his mount, the horse's reins dangling limply in his hand as he tried to make headway of his surroundings.

The dun stallion Cienna gave him was a marvelous beast, lean and strong. He was surprised to find that the horse's temperament was so relaxed. One of the horses Caitlyn had trained, Cienna told him. Whatever the situation, he could not have asked for such a gift.

"I think we're really making some headway," he said as he pat the horse on the flank. "Too bad I had to leave Bells back with them. She would've loved to come home, but could never match your pace." He sighed as he thought of his horse. "You know," he said to the dun stallion, "I don't even know why I'm talking to you about Bells like you even understand. I know they say you warhorses are smart, but it's not like you can keep up a conversation."

The stallion snorted and twitched his ears, drawing a surprised chuckle from the king.

"I suppose, maybe you can."

The two walked in silence for a while as they enjoyed the cooler temperatures. A dragonfly buzzed around Oldar's head, startling him and causing him to duck. It hovered around his head for a moment before flying off towards the horse. The stallion twitched his ears once more and bobbed his head in an effort to keep the dragonfly away.

The sun had reached its midday arc and Oldar was beginning to regret his decision to try and take a shortcut. Going northwest instead of backtracking the way he'd come seemed like a good idea. Schaed's hawk, Oldar believed his name was Erth, took off that direction. What better idea than to follow the bird with his innate ability to find his way home? As it turned out, horrible.

"The last thing I need right now is to be lost when some mythical monster like the Faceless is wandering about." The king chuckled to himself. "Who would've thought that I would even believe in something like this? Not even a month ago I was worried about politics and idealistic nonsense, and now I've got gods and demons walking around. Dammit." Running his free hand through his hair, Oldar shook his head, trying to make it all go away.

"What do you think, Aelthur?"

The horse nickered and bumped his head into Oldar's arm. He decided to name the beast Aelthur after the legendary king of Ro'thre. The horse held an air of majesty and dignity about him. Bells was more peaceful, but Aelthur, he was a different beast.

"Gods, it must be my body reacting to me cutting out the drink, but here I am treating horses like they're people." Oldar shook his head once more as he laughed. "I must out of my mind."

Looking around, Oldar tried to find a source of water. The two stopped for a moment and listened. All he could hear was birds chirping and animals calling out to each other. Aelthur swished his tail and pawed the ground impatiently, but did not make another sound. After waiting several long moments, Oldar realized that he couldn't hear anything to lead him to believe that water was nearby.

Pulling the water skin off of Aelthur, the king poured a little in his hands and rubbed it onto his face. The water, warmed by the heat of the day, left him feeling refreshed. Drops of dirty water dripped from his face and onto the ground.

"I didn't realize I was this dirty already," the king muttered.

Replacing the skin, Oldar and Aelthur resumed their travel. Taking the opportunity to relax and enjoy the scenery, Oldar found himself feeling much better than he had in his travels with Brody and the soldiers. His hands no longer shook and the nausea was gone. He felt like his old self again. A smile tugged on the corners of his mouth until he found himself smiling ear to ear.

"We must be going the right way," he said after a lengthy period of time. "We must be near the forest on the outskirts of Ånchal." Aelthur shook his head. "You weren't with us last time, but that city has a direct underground route to the capital."

They walked in silence for a while longer. Oldar scanned his surroundings, trying to figure out when the outpost should be popping into view. "It was night when I last saw her though," he mumbled. "Maybe I'm not as close as I thought I was."

Overhead, a hawk screeched, causing the rest of the birds in the area to fall silent. Oldar looked up into the canopy and saw the outline of the predatory bird flash. With a sudden whinny, Aelthur stopped walking and pranced back a few steps. Startled, Oldar looked around and saw a snake crossing in front of them. The horse threw his head back, but did not try to bolt.

"Shhh, shhh," Oldar soothed the horse, patting him on the neck. "It's all right. Calm. Calm."

Aelthur stopped pawing at the ground, snorting as the snake's tail disappeared into the tall grasses on the other side of their path. Patting the horse's snout once more, Oldar tried to keep the beast calm.

"See? It's nothing a great horse like you should be afraid of. You're fine."

The sound of a snapping twig caught Oldar's attention. His head spun towards the sound, his hand reaching for the dagger on his hip. Scanning the forest around him, the king tried to find the source of the noise. He hadn't seen anything big enough to make that sound. Not even deer.

Is it the Faceless? What do they even look like?

"Let's go," he whispered to his horse. After a quick scan of his surroundings, Oldar clambered onto Aelthur and settled himself into the saddle. Lightly tapping the horse with the heels of his boots, Aelthur took off at a light trot. Oldar cursed the way the hoof beats echoed in the forest.

We may as well be shouting, 'Here we are!' How is this so loud?

A moment later, Oldar's heart sank. Behind him, the sound of approaching hoof beats and rustling grass to his sides announced oncoming riders. His heart began to race. Kicking his heels into horseflesh, Oldar urged Aelthur into a run as the others neared. Shouting to the horse, he leaned down low on Aelthur as he rode. Around him, the others picked up their pace, matching his speed. Calls from the riders rang out in the air, getting lost in the thunderous sound of hooves. Dust kicked up all around him.

To the side, Oldar saw a slim figure with their face covered by a white cloth. Their bare midriff and arms were the only bits of exposed flesh. With a sudden cry, Aelthur turned sharply as another figure on a white horse charged in front of them in an effort to cut them off. Oldar let out a cry of surprise, yanking on the reins to direct the horse.

On his left, the third rider came into sight. Smaller, the rider flashed a feral grin as they cut their angle, trying to box Oldar and Aelthur in. A sizzling ball of bright energy flew past Oldar's right ear. Crying out in fear, the king spun his head and saw the rider behind him charging up another ball of crackling electric energy in their hand.

"Stop running and you won't be killed," the voice in front of him called out.

Oldar's head quickly turned back to face the rider who bore down on him from the front. This one was shorter than the other and also quite slim. He was surprised to hear that the voice was feminine. The owner didn't sound much older than Cienna. As the other three pursuing him closed in, Oldar realized that he had no choice. Pulling on Aelthur's reins, the horse slowed to a stop. Oldar kept his hands in the air, hoping that the mage behind him would not attack again.

The four horses quickly closed the space between them and the king, circling him. Aelthur pawed at the ground, his tail swishing wildly as the pursuer to their right worked to slip a rope around his neck. Shaking his head, Aelthur whinnied and tried pulling away. The person holding the rope grunted, his voice deep, as he tugged on the rope. Swearing in another language, Oldar tried to place him.

As his assailants tied Aelthur to their mounts preparing to take him away, Oldar tried to figure out who they were. The one tying Aelthur's rope to his saddle was tall and slim, his bits of exposed flesh revealing his pale skin. Oldar was surprised at how fair the man was. The reflection of the sun off of his exposed midriff nearly blinded the king. Loose fabric covered his arms and legs, in the style of the Eastern Coast, the design being neither masculine nor feminine. Under the fabric, Oldar thought he saw the markings of tattoos.

Next to the pale man, the shorter figure with the feral grin rode up to the slim man and began talking. Oldar couldn't hear what they were saying, but he could hear the timbres of their voices, doing a double take as he heard a rich bass coming from the shorter one. Unwrapping his head covering, Oldar saw the man looked like one of the members of the Mountain Tribes. His petite stature accentuated his lithe frame. His hair, comprised of long braids, was tied back in a high tail and twisted up in a type of bun. Gold wraps adorned his braids, several of the gold pieces fitted around turquoise stones.

Before riding off, the shorter man said something to his companion that Oldar couldn't understand. The man's accent was thick and his speech cadence choppy. The rider who was behind them during the pursuit called out to the short man. Oldar didn't get a chance to further examine him before his gaze was directed to the Spark who attacked him earlier.

The Spark's tattoos went all the way up to his elbow, the jagged lines poking up towards the rest of his arm. He also spoke with an accent as he conversed with the shorter man. Oldar was surprised to see someone from Xan with magical tattoos. Normally, the only markings on their body were familial ones. He hadn't heard of many making the pilgrimage to Pharn to test their fate.

The unrest before Ras probably didn't help, Oldar conceded.

"All right," the leader on the white stallion called out. Oldar was surprised to find it belonged to a woman. "Let's head back." Her eyes narrowed onto Oldar and took him in. They quickly moved over his face, taking in his features, before traveling down his body. She stopped and stared his hand for a moment before studying his face once more. With a giddy smile, she rode over and grabbed his face.

"I don't believe it," she said softly as she held his chin. Raising her voice, she addressed her crew. "Looks like we have someone special, boys. We got ourself here royalty."

"Zanir?" the pale man asked.

"Looks like Loran's boy," she replied.

The shorter man chuckled as the Spark came in for a closer look.

"You're right," the Spark said. "Chol really gave us some good information."

"Ka'lev," the pale man called out. The woman turned to him.

"You think we'll get anything from Zanir? If they're holding our guys hostage, we could get an equal exchange with the prince here."

"I'm not worried about them right now," Ka'lev said. Motioning to the group, they began traveling back out into the forest. "They can wait a little longer. I need to get everyone from the young Xanan leader before I try and deal with Zanir. They're strong. They can handle it."

She's got agents all over, Oldar panicked. *Who is in Alocar? Damn, I wish I could warn Cienna.* His mind raced as images of rogue magi running loose in Pharn flashed through his head. After a moment, he paused. *I'm pretty sure I would've heard of Pharn taking prisoners. Other than Xan, I mean. With the queen at death's door, they wouldn't leave her so vulnerable. They must be dead.*

The thought that Ka'lev's men were not a threat at the moment calmed him, gave him a chance to observe his surroundings and try to come up with a plan. Ka'lev led them through dense forest. The trees here had thicker trunks than he'd ever seen.

Are we going north?

The temperature also cooled a little. Searching his mind, Oldar tried to remember his maps that his father used to try and teach him to read. North of Xan was the heavily forested nation of Ro'thre. His father did not deal with their king very much. King Xichuan wasn't known for being overly hospitable, so the late King Storm was hesitant to send anyone other than his wife to deal with the northern king.

Oldar's mind wandered as he began staring at Ka'lev. She had the same dark skin and delicate nose like the women of Thurl, but her hair was not in the traditional hairstyle. Thick tattoos wound up her arm and onto her shoulder, occasionally spiraling into thinner ones as they radiated out from the main part.

Stream, Oldar realized. *There's a Stream and a Spark. I'm in trouble.*

As he continued to look on, he realized that at least two of his captors were very powerful. Turning back to the pale man and the short man, Oldar tried to see if they bore any tattoos. The shorter man moved constantly, fidgeting on his horse even as they rode. A bit of bare flesh was exposed on his hands, and the king thought he could spy the mark of the Flame on his hand.

Three.

His eyes darted to the pale man. It was difficult to tell because his clothes covered so much of his body. He remembered seeing something on the man earlier. Just then, the group hit a spot where the sun shone through the canopy. The rays hit the thin, white fabric, and underneath Oldar could see the hazy markings of a Shadow. The contrast was startling.

Shit! Four skilled hunters, and they all can use blood magic.

Oldar suddenly realized that he could no longer see everyone. Scanning the area, he tried to make sure he kept them all in view. He didn't want to die with a sword in his back.

Ka'lev is point. Twitchy is behind her. The pale man is to my right. Where is the Spark?

Swiveling his head, he felt his heart begin to beat heavily against his chest as he came to the realization that the Spark was not behind him or to his left. Panic set in and his breathing became rapid and shallow.

Maybe he's broken off from them to go home, he tried to reassure himself. *One less person to worry about.*

A moment later, a powerful force hit him on the back of his head and he fell into blackness.

～～

Oldar woke up with his head throbbing. He tried to rub his temples, but found that his hands were bound behind his back. A little way away, he saw the four sitting by a fire and sharing a meal. They laughed as the Flame told some story while they ate. Oldar's stomach rumbled. It had been hours since his last meal, and a paltry one at that.

He felt a chill on his feet and realized that his shoes and socks had been stripped off, leaving his feet exposed. His outerwear had also been removed, leaving him with just his breeches and a thin shirt. A shiver ran through him as a breeze kicked up in their little glen.

There was a pressure on his back, most likely from a stone that dug into his flesh through his thin shirt, making him uncomfortable. Shifting his weight a little, the king managed to find a spot where nothing was sticking nor poking him. Aelthur noted his shuffling and let out a small nicker. The noise caught the attention of the group and drew them over.

"Well, I see you've finally woken up," Ka'lev said. "I'm surprised you were out so long. Was afraid Blo'u killed you."

Oldar's eyes shot to the Xanan man. He still couldn't figure out which tribe he was from. The Spark's features looked like a blend of several of the clans. The king found himself staring at the man and forced himself to look back at the woman. A powerful energy radiated from her, and he didn't want to lose sight of her like he did Blo'u.

"So, tell me young princeling, what brings you to Ro'thre's borders? You're far from home, and with a Zanirian warhorse no less." Her tone was casual, but in the shadow of the firelight, her eyes looked hungry. "Did you kill someone and steal their horse? I thought you were allies."

Oldar knew he had to think quickly if he was going to talk his way out of his predicament. Trying to keep his face neutral, he said: "The horse was given to me by the princess." He was disappointed to see that this did not elicit a reaction from her. "I wanted to go for a ride through the woods and must've lost track of time."

"Cut the bullshit," Ka'lev said sharply. "Tell me the truth."

"I am," he replied hurriedly. Her eyes narrowed as she stared deeply into his eyes. "I didn't realize that I'd traveled into Ro'thre. My apologies to His Highness. Please, let me go and I will make it up to you and yours quite handsomely."

"Xichaun does not control us," the pale man said.

Ka'lev shot him a withering look, silencing him instantly. "The Woods do not belong to the king," she said simply. "Lingora has been my home for longer than he's been married. He knows not to travel into my land."

The Woods of Lingora? The Woods? Oh gods, I'm in trouble. Oldar's mind ran wild as scenario after scenario of his death at the hands of the mercenary magi played in his head.

"How much are you worth?" Ka'lev's question caught him off guard. "I don't want to repeat myself," she said after some time had passed. "Frankly, that's the only thing that's keeping you alive. Nothing you had on you was worth anything."

Nothing? Did she not find Schaed's note? Looking at the mercenaries' faces, he realized that they hadn't found everything when they searched him while he was unconscious. Surely, they would have recognized Schaed's wine seal if they had. *I have one advantage. As long as they think they can get money from my family, they'll keep me alive. Not like Uncle would pay a ransom for me.* The thought made the young king's heart sink a little.

"I should just kill you," Ka'lev said. Oldar's heart began racing once more at the nonchalant way she said that. "But I have a better idea. I know a Tempest who can probably spare a little blood. Let's see if it runs in your family."

Oldar's blood ran cold. Attempting to receive magical gifts was extremely dangerous. In fact, he chose to pass when his father offered to take him to the Mageri when he was twelve to test his luck with the ceremony. The thought of losing his sanity for a bit of power was not enough to sway young Oldar. It was even less appealing now.

Caitlyn was lucky. I'm never lucky. Mom's bad days were bad.

The short man, the Flame, began laughing at Oldar's turmoil. The king stared at the mercenary leader as she smirked at him. Butterflies flew in his stomach, making him feel nauseous once more. Sweat beaded on his hands, and even his feet, leaving them feeling clammy. With what he hoped was an imperceptible gulp, Oldar struggled to maintain his composure in from of this intimidating woman.

All she wants is to see me squirm, he told himself. *If I give her the satisfaction of my discomfort, she'll keep going. I need to keep my expression neutral and not give in to whatever she says. This is the only way I stand a chance of getting out alive.*

"What do you say, my little princeling?" Ka'lev taunted. "Want to see if you're special like your mommy?"

"It would be a shame to waste such precious blood on one such as myself," Oldar replied. "Whether I Snap from the blood or become Tainted, there is not much to gain by this."

"There is plenty to be gained," Ka'lev replied. "We've been bored up here waiting for our brother to return. If your body accepts the blood, we'll keep you to grow our ranks. I'd rather save our Tempest's blood and use yours on others. However..."

"But I have no combat training," Oldar blurted out. "I would be a complete waste of resources." He immediately regretted his choice of words. Labelling himself as useless would be a surefire way to getting himself killed.

"What if we ransom him like we planned?" Blo'u asked.

"Blo'u has a point," the pale man said.

"Dzerik, I would think that you more than anyone would understand that there is always a value to something," Ka'lev snapped. "We have never had a Tempest in our group. Imagine the money we could make just with the threat alone. They don't need to know that he's being used for his blood."

"But they're so unpredictable," the short man said.

"Yes, but also useful, Bikal."

"How so?" Blo'u asked. Oldar noted that he seemed to be the only person who could talk back to her. Even Dzerik, whom the king thought was higher ranking, seemed to defer to the Xanan man. "We threaten people with him, but if we can't back it up, we have nothing. We operate from the shadows. Besides, Teok would charge an arm and a leg for this."

Ka'lev shot daggers at the Xanan man. "We are low in numbers as it is. Teok would not be so foolish as to try and extort money from me to keep the Myrani going." When the others expressed their surprise, she continued. "Two have been captured by the Zanirians, else they would be back by now. And that smooth talking fat man talked me out of three of my Flames, and my other Shadow. Hroth is one of them. There is no reason for him to take this long to come back. You know how I feel about him."

Blo'u and the others shared a glance. Even Dzerik looked concerned. For some reason, that man's expression made him uncomfortable. Dzerik seemed like the type who would be hard to read.

"Now, Dzerik, Bikal. Go get some water for us. We're on the low side. Blo'u, come with me to find Teok. He shouldn't be too hard to find."

The men dispersed quickly at Ka'lev's orders. Oldar was amazed at how fast the camp emptied. The king laid on his side in the quiet night. The crackling of the fire and the chirping of the cicadas provided the only noise. He lay in silence a little longer before a thought struck him.

Bringing his knees to his chest, Oldar rolled himself onto his knees. With effort, he managed to stand up from that position. Sticks and stones jabbed into his soft feet, but Oldar forced himself to ignore it. His adrenaline was pumping as he made his way to Aelthur. The horse was tied to a tree. Sensing the importance of what was going on, Aelthur stood still.

Twisting his hands in an attempt to loosen his bindings, he managed to slip one of his hands free from the tie, rubbing the flesh off of his hand in the process. He winced as he pulled the rope off of his other hand. Blood ran down his hand as his heart raced, numbing the pain. Glancing around one last time, Oldar grabbed Aelthur's reins, pulled himself into the saddle, and took off into the night.

XXV

THE SUN BEGAN TO RISE, painting the sky a beautiful orange as the soft purples faded away. Birdsong filled the air, welcoming the gorgeous day that was dawning. Oldar trudged through the trees, Aelthur trailing behind. His body was exhausted and his eyes ached from trying to keep them open all night. He'd managed to wrap his bloody hand while he rode and stopped the bleeding. A dull ache was all that remained from his injury. He'd traveled straight through the night primarily on horse, but gave Aelthur a few breaks.

Those breaks were short, however.

All night, the king looked over his shoulder, praying that the mercenaries did not catch him. He knew he was damn lucky to have escaped as easily as he did. Ka'lev leaving him unattended was a miscalculation. If she caught him, there would be no second chance.

Now, he wandered through the woods in his thin shirt and breeches, his clothes in one of the saddle bags. He hadn't dared to stop and get dressed as he pushed Aelthur. He didn't want to risk stopping and being caught once more. However, Oldar had no idea where he was. He was hopelessly lost.

"We are in trouble, Aelthur, my friend," Oldar managed to get out while he yawned. "I have no clue where we are. Who knows if we're even out of Ro'thre?"

His feet dragged as he walked. Shaking his head, he rubbed his eyes before pulling himself up into Aelthur's saddle. Taking a quick bite of an apple and dried meat to give himself some energy, Oldar then nudged the dun stallion on the sides with his heels, sending Aelthur into a spirited trot. The bouncing gait of the horse helped Oldar shake himself awake.

Though his eyelids were heavy, the cool breeze as he raced through the early morning refreshed him as well as the little snack he'd had. With every clop of the hooves, he heaved a sigh of relief as he did not hear a second set following behind.

The morning dragged on, the sun reaching its zenith, when suddenly, his eyes caught a glimmer of blue in the distance. His heart leapt into his chest as he dared to hope.

"Ånchal."

With renewed energy, Oldar urged Aelthur on. The horse seemed to appreciate the young king's urgency and began racing towards the outpost. Sweat beaded on his brow and his breathing came out in gasps as he surged forward. The gates of Ånchal quickly came into view.

"Come on! Come on!" he breathed.

Aelthur wheezed, his lungs working like the bellows, sweat running down his neck in rivulets. His black hair was matted against his dun coat, getting darker as it dampened. Foam frothed at his mouth. His teeth chomped down on the bit, the metal keeping the stallion from biting down on himself as he ran.

Shouts rang out from the wall walk as Oldar rapidly approached. Men scrambled to get into position as the king and stallion bore down upon them. Archers drew their bow, aiming their sights on the king.

"Stop or we'll shoot!" a man called out on the wall.

Oldar pulled sharply on the reins. Aelthur slowed down so quickly that Oldar was almost thrown off. His hands gripped the pommel of the saddle, hoping to keep himself seated.

"Don't shoot!" Oldar shouted. "Oldar!"

Men lowered their bows, a lone archer keeping the king in his sights with his long bow. Some of the soldiers ran down to the gates. The man who addressed Oldar earlier held up a spear. Shouts of "Don't shoot!" and "It's the king!" could be heard above the commotion on the wallwalk.

"Hold!" the man with the spear cried. As Oldar stopped and sat in front of the gates of Ånchal, Aelthur struggling to breathe after his exertions. "We need confirmation that you're truly King of Alocar." The man slammed the butt of the spear against the stone.

"When in solitude, nature's beauty calls loudly to those who look," Oldar said, reciting his father's favorite phrase. Several of the men on the wall looked confused. Young men scratched their heads, conferring with their neighbor. "Oh, dammit guys! Let me in. I'm tired as hell and I just escaped from the Myrani." Oldar gestured to his lack of clothing. "Let me in."

The wallwalk burst into movement as men rushed to open the gates at the mention of the Iron Fist. Oldar glanced around, scanning the tree lines for any sign of pursuit. The thought of Ka'lev or another member of the Myrani catching him still weighed heavily on his mind. Within moments, the gate was opened and Oldar ushered Aelthur through them. The gates could not close fast enough for the exhausted king. Only when they finally closed with an almighty *thump*, Oldar found a measure of relief that he hadn't felt in a long time.

"Forgive me," the soldier with the spear said. "We did not recognize you, or your horse, from so far away."

Oldar waved a hand, dismissing the man. "You did what you needed to do. You were right to question. This is a Grey horse, loaned to me in my time of need by the princess. Zanir has also graciously offered to watch Bells while I am conducting my business back at home."

"Will you be in Ånchal long, your majesty?" the man asked.

"No. I am leaving through the tunnels now. Take care of Aelthur, he's had a long, hard trip. We've covered much ground in the last two days."

Oldar handed over the reins to one of the other soldiers, who fumbled with them as they were passed off.

Heading towards the underground tunnels, Oldar felt a surge of fear. If he somehow managed to find his way to the outpost this easily, there was no reason that a band of mercenaries couldn't either.

What if they followed me from the shadows? he panicked. *There's nothing stopping them from taking Ånchal. I don't doubt that the Myrani are seasoned warriors. We would be in big trouble if they attacked.*

Turning towards the soldiers once more, Oldar asked, "Who here is in charge?"

The man with the spear raised his hand. "I am, your majesty."

"Who are your best watchmen?" Oldar asked.

"Eirik and Mendelson," the man replied, a slight question to his tone. "What is this all about, your majesty?"

Do I tell them? Oldar wondered.

"I ran into some rogue magi late yesterday. The Myrani," he decided. "There were four of them, and they had a taste for blood. They brought me to the Woods of Lingora and planned to ransom or kill me, but I managed to escape. I don't know if they followed me though. I didn't hear or see them, but they're stealthy. I want to make sure that we stay on guard for the next few days. Ånchal can't be overrun. Her tunnels to the capital must be guarded at all costs."

As one, the soldiers all snapped to attention and let out a call of affirmation before saluting the king. Satisfied that he'd done what he needed to, Oldar made his way to the tunnels. His body ached and his eyes burned, but he knew that he could not rest. Not yet. As he descended the stairs, he stopped and sat on the bottom step for a moment. Leaning against the walls, Oldar closed his eyes. He only needed to rest for a moment. After a few minutes, he would be recharged and ready to speak with his uncle.

It wasn't until hours later when the evening guard came to light the torches in the sconces of the tunnel that he noticed the sleeping king at the bottom of the stairs. Unsure what to do, he quietly retreated and stood guard at the top of the stairs.

XXVI

M EN SCRAMBLED on deck as they prepared for battle. Kayna made her way amongst the ranks shouting out orders to her crew. Len pulled out his scimitar and warhammer, his battle axe being left back at home, and stood ready along the rail. The young general bounced on the balls of his feet, keeping his muscles warm and ready.

"How did I get myself roped into this?" he asked himself. Len watched as three men scurried up the ratlines into the nest, one carrying his short sword in his mouth.

"You seem nervous, young general."

Len turned to see Dez saunter over to him. Her dark hair was tied in a high tail and her shirt was tied back, exposing her midriff. On her hip, a short sword sat in a simple black leather sheath. Dez's usually aloof demeanor was replaced with a solemn one as she gazed out into the sea. Jylla's ship, *Silver Maiden*, approached, her flags rustling in the breeze. A large vessel, her prow crested the clear blue waves, leaving a spray of white foam in her wake.

"How did we get pulled into this?" Len asked as he returned his attention to the incoming ship. "Neither of us owe these people any allegiance. I never even got to discuss the matter further."

"He just sort of took over, didn't he?" Dez finished. "He has a way about him, that pirate lord."

"So, is it true?" Len asked. "He's your brother?"

Dez fell uncharacteristically silent. Len glanced over and noticed a tear rolling down her cheek. It surprised him to see any emotion from the woman other her usual detachment. Her hands gripped the smooth, worn wood of the ship so hard her knuckles turned white.

"It's complicated," she said finally. "But it gives me answers I never had. Or never wanted to hear. I never worried about death before. I just never aged past my thirtieth year. It was always a mystery why others grew old, but I did not. One by one, those around me died; everyone I ever became close with. I told myself that after little Vashe, I would never open my heart to anyone again. Now, I know why. I cannot die. The spirit of Aria lives within me."

"Like Alzai being two separate gods," Len replied.

Dez nodded.

"So, your power comes from the goddess?"

"No. Well, to an extent. Aria's presence is the reason I've never Snapped. I've done more than anyone should ever be able to do. Pushed my body and mind past their limit, yet I've been lucky to keep my sanity. She's hinted at her being the cause of me never Snapping, but I never understood why. I just thought it was the playful banter we always shared."

"Why are you here?" Len asked again. "You have no reason to be here."

"Why are you?" she asked, turning to face him for the first time since they began talking.

"I'm here to get aid for my people," he replied, his tone sharp despite his incredulity. "There's no reason for me to be here otherwise. I suppose I am paying my debt up front."

Dez flashed a smile at the young general. "Then I suppose we've both been pulled in by something greater than us. We both play a crucial role in this, otherwise the gods would not be directing us as they are."

"Do you think that we're being maneuvered by the gods?" he asked. Len's mind flashed to Freyna's visits and their increased frequency. Her presence afforded him and his family with protections others didn't have. Len remembered how Freyna seemed to favor his daughter especially.

Dez touched his elbow gently as though she could read his mind. "It's a possibility."

Len turned away from her and focused on the horizon. Men still shouted and raced about on deck, but it was less chaotic than it had been moments earlier. A man to Len's right stood ready, his sword drawn and jaw set. Looking down the line, he saw that each man was ready for battle. Len felt a swell of confidence as each person he glanced at stood strong. It was like he was looking at his own brothers of the Qu'ari elite.

"Stand strong," Kayna called out. "With Graak's will, we will be victorious. Jylla must pay for his actions, and we are the ones to hold him accountable. The Scourge will not let us flounder!"

A roar rose up from the ship as the crew brandished their weapons or shook their fists. Len felt his adrenaline begin to pump in anticipation of the upcoming battle. He couldn't die now. He had too much to do.

"Ready?" Maya asked as she slipped in between Len and the man on his right. In her hand, a slender-bladed sword was at the ready.

"Why wouldn't I be?" he asked. "This isn't my first fight."

"I assume it is on the sea."

Len shot her a withering glare before turning away. With a mighty splash, the *Silver Maiden* crested a large wave and came within range of *Graak's Fury*. Kayna's voice rang out and a hail of arrows took flight from the nest and the back of the far side of the ship. Len watched as they rained down on Jylla's crew with deadly accuracy.

I thought pirates could only brawl, he mused.

Cries from the *Maiden* filled the air as men were struck. Bodies hit the deck, blood staining their clothes. Len struggled to maintain his balance as the ship rode a high wave. His hand slammed on the side of the ship in an effort to stay on his feet. A splash of sea spray hit him in the face, stinging his eyes, before he stumbled into the side as the two ships crashed into each other.

"Hang on," Dez shouted, her arms beginning to glow silver. "It's about to get bumpy."

Raising her glowing arms, Dez began to draw on the surrounding winds and focusing their currents. As another wave surged towards the two ships, she used the wind to turn the *Fury* slightly, avoiding another violent clash like before.

A mighty roar from the *Maiden* caught Len's attention. Jylla's crew climbed onto ropes, preparing to board the *Fury*. To his left, men shouted out, some in shock, as Dez's winds whipped around her in frantic fashion. Several of the onboarding pirates turned their attentions to the Tempest as she stood on deck summoning the wind.

"Protect her!" Len called out to those nearby. "Don't let them disrupt her!"

Those near Dez looked over at the young general, uncertain if they should comply. A moment later, they watched in awe as she threw her hand in the direction of the ship. A powerful gust of wind slammed into the vessel, pushing the sails inward and creating some space between the two. The men who were about to board screamed in shock as their ropes suddenly took them over the choppy, open sea instead of over the *Fury*. A cheer broke out among Kayna's crew as five men raced over to create a protective circle around Dez.

Feeling confident in his decision, Len glanced to his right and noticed Maya staring at him, a smirk on her lips. "You've done this before."

Heavy footsteps fell on the deck, causing Len to spin around. Angh made his way through the ranks weaving between his crew as they scrambled to regroup. The pirate lord exuded an air of calm despite the chaos going on. His sword lay sheathed on his hip, untouched as the invading pirates threatened to breach his ship.

The gale created from Dez's winds turned the previously calm seas into a roiling battlefield. The sails whipped about, the *Fury's* flags threatening to rip off and blow away. Waves crashed into the side of the ship, spilling over the railings and soaking men with its icy waters. Dez stood, her eyes closed, as she focused on controlling her tempest. Those around her looked around, unsure of how close to get to her, but fear shone in their eyes as the periphery gusts pushed and pulled them.

Angh made his way to the Tempest. He ignored the strength of the wind and walked right through to her. Silver lines glowed on her dark skin, wrapping up her arms and intertwining with her other tattoos. Dez's arms were raised over her head, manipulating the air around her. The pirate lord walked up behind her and placed his hands on her shoulders.

Dez did not open her eyes at his touch. She kept her energies focused inward as she built up her tempest. Len watched as the large man braced himself behind Dez and closed his eyes with her. The two of them were then engulfed in a brilliant silver glow, just like they had been in the cave when Dez was first brought to him. Len raised his arm to shield his eyes from their blinding light. Men from the attacking ship paused as they saw the pillar of light illuminating the *Graak's Fury*.

Len stood in awe of the power the radiated from the pair next to him. He felt the same primal fear that filled him when he first met the man. His gut twisted in knots and his hands became clammy, making it difficult to keep a firm grip on his scimitar. Len's clothes and hair whipped around him, the force of the gusts pushing him back. Widening his stance, the young general worked to keep his balance in the chaos that blew around him.

This is the power of gods, he realized. *By Freyna, she was right. I'm in the middle of something so much more than I could ever have imagined. I don't think that we've even scratched the surface of it all.*

Hurried footsteps raced up the stairs and onto the main deck. Try as he might, Len could not get his body to respond to his mind telling him to turn his head. He found that his hands were shaking at the raw power that he was experiencing to his left. It reminded him of the young warriors he'd encountered in battle; just like the boy he faced in the battle at Pharn.

"This is what separates the soldiers from the men," he breathed. "So help me, Freyna, I will not fail."

"Hold!" Kayna's voice rang out somewhere behind him. Though she couldn't be more than a couple arms' lengths away, she sounded as though she was far from him. "We prepare for boarding. Maya! Len! Join me and my team as we cross over. We'll take Jylla's ship and end this."

Kayna's words snapped Len out of his paralysis. Though the winds tugged at him, he felt a warmth that he had begun to associate with Freyna's presence. Turning away from the two gods engulfed in shining silver, he commanded himself to meet Kayna and her special crew. As he quickly approached her, he sheathed his scimitar and hammer, wiping his hands on his tunic to remove some of the moisture.

"Grab a rope," she instructed Len and the other eight around her. "We find Jylla and we end this. Let's get this done quickly."

Another crash sent Len stumbling forward into Maya and another man. Spinning around he saw the two ships had slammed into each other.

"Dammit!" Kayna shouted. "The *Fury* can't take much more."

XXVII

WAVES COLLIDED with the ship, sending water over the sides of both ships. Men cried out in shock as the cold sea soaked them, the water threatening to pull them off the ship and into its depths or crush them between the boats. White foam sprayed into the air as the turmoil churned the waters. The bodies of the two ships cracked as they slammed into each other, the force throwing men to their feet.

Len struggled to remain upright as another jolt almost toppled him. His heart raced as he wrapped a length of rope around his hand once more. On more than one occasion, he cursed himself for what he was about to do. The young general quickly realized that the sea life wasn't for him. He preferred to do battle on more stable ground.

"When I give the signal, we jump," Kayna said to Len and the others. "You'll want to unwrap your hand, Len," she warned. "When you hit the apex of your arc, you'll want to let go right away so you land on the ship. If you're not careful, you'll either fall into the sea or land back on the ship. I've seen more than one person crash into a ship too. Not a fun way to go."

The young general grit his teeth but grudgingly unwound the rope from around his hand. His body tensed as he waited for the redheaded pirate to say the word. Without realizing it, his gaze drifted back to the silver pillar that was Dez and Angh. The two stood engulfed in her silver glow, her hair flying about having snapped the tie that previously held it up, as her tempest grew. The men standing nearby, offering protection to the woman as she tapped into her energy reserves, had long left the area. The pirate lord's arrival made it near pointless for them to be there.

Kayna's voice calling out brought Len back to the events at hand. He heard her shout for them to go. Taking in a deep breath and holding it, Len pushed off the side of the ship.

His heart stopped beating as he soared over the roiling blue water. Salt spray spewed all around him, soaking him as he flew in between the two ships. The water made it difficult for him to maintain his grip on the rope. He felt his heart fall to the pit of his stomach as his hands began to slip.

Mighty Freyna, this is not the end. It can't be!

A moment later, the dark brown of the *Maiden's* wooden deck came into focus. Around him, Len watched as the other pirates let go of their ropes, landing onto the deck and pulling out their weapons. In a panic, he quickly let go of the rope and felt his body continue its arc as he was propelled forward. With a *thump*, Len felt his feet hit the solid ground. His momentum carrying him and forcing the young general to drop into a roll to avoid stutter stepping and falling onto his face. With practiced grace, Len emerged out of his roll with his weapons drawn, ready to face his advancing foes.

Jylla's crew balked at the Qu'ari elite as he stood up with his weapons ready in a defensive position. Now that he was on the wooden deck of a ship once more, Len found himself much more at ease as he advanced with his blades spinning in dizzying patterns. A smirk tugged at the corners of his mouth. Maybe this life wasn't so bad after all.

One of Jylla's men took a step forward, his sword raised in his hands, but Len managed to deftly slap the blade out of his opponent's hand. The man, now disarmed, shot his comrades a fearful glance before making a hasty retreat. The remaining three shared a glance before charging him as one with a mighty bellow.

Len wove in between the blades, his body, scimitar, and hammer dancing around the strikes with relative ease. The straightforward style of the pirates could not keep up with the intricate motions of the Qu'ari elite. Within moments, the three dropped to the ground, their weapons clattering against the wood, with non-lethal wounds. The young general made sure to cut them in places that would not heal easily. With another smirk, Len glanced at the fallen men behind him one last time before advancing forward once more.

Jumping down the stairs to the main deck, Len landed next to Maya. The woman fought off two men on her own, and one of Kayna's men was down. A pool of blood forming around his neck told Len that he would not be getting back up. With a shout, Len charged one of the men, distracting both enough for Maya to hamstring one of them with her blade.

The wounded man cried out, dropping his weapon, as he fell to his knees. Seizing the opportunity, Len struck at the remaining man and scored a hit to the stomach. The man let out a scream of agony and dropped to the deck. Blood pooled around him as he tried to staunch the flow of blood with his hands.

Ignoring the wounded men, Len glanced over at Maya. Blood soaked through her shirt from a cut to her arm.

"You need to wrap that," he said.

"I'm fine," she replied, wincing as she spoke.

"No. You need to wrap it now or you'll risk infection." Pointing to his own arm, Len lifted his sleeve a bit to show off the cloth that encircled his arm. "Trust me."

With a scoff, Maya ripped a piece of cloth from her dead partner's shirt and quickly tied a knot around her wound. Using her teeth, Maya managed to wrap it tightly. Nodding at Len, she moved her arm a bit to show that she was fine.

"Where's Kayna?" he asked.

"She must be deeper into the ship. Jylla won't be on the deck if he thought that Angh was here, even on his best day. I'm sure our beacon of silver over there has kept him sequestered in his cabin. We'll have to be quick if we want to keep her from being overrun. Most of his men aren't as easily downed like these two here."

The boat rocked again, throwing the two off-balance. Len stutter stepped to the side to avoid running into Maya or the fallen men. His hands quickly wrapped around her waist to keep her from falling backwards.

"Thanks," she said. As the ship leveled again, she pushed him away and smoothed the bit of her shirt sticking out from her bodice. "Let's go."

Without another word, the two took off, heading towards the heart of the ship.

~~

Trails of sweat ran down Dez's temples and beaded on her forehead. Her breath came in ragged gasps as the whipping winds surrounding her made it more difficult to breathe. The Tempest's hair flew around her, moving with the gusts she manipulated. Feeling a disturbance in her squall that finally encompassed both ships, she opened her eyes, turning her head to the right. Three members of Jylla's crew managed to cross the sea to land on the *Fury*. A cry from the quarter deck startled her as the invaders took advantage of the empty area to push their attack forward.

Two men broke off and raced down the steps towards the main deck, the third maintaining his position on the quarter deck. The two engaged a couple of Kayna's crew, their swords clashing in the bright sun. A second group of pirates landed on the main deck moments later, swords drawn. They quickly moved on the lone defender with a vicious flurry of slashing swords. In moments, the poor man was cut down.

Angh let out a cry of rage as Dez threw a blast of wind at the second group of attackers, knocking them to the ground. Several of them were thrown into part of the ship, all rendered unconscious by her strike. Angh's hands left her shoulders as he went to battle. The silver light that had engulfed the two only moments before dissipated until only the tattoos on her arms glowed from her exertions.

With quick strides, the Scourge approached the unconscious men, effortlessly picked them up one by one, and threw them over the side of the ship. Dez flinched as the two boats crashed into each other once more, right where the unconscious men had landed. Turning her attention to the *Silver Maiden*, she tried to ignore the screams that suddenly filled the air to her right. Glancing over, she saw that Angh had reached the first group of invaders.

Closing her eyes once more, Dez felt confident that she'd created a storm she could control, before focusing on the sea. Using her Stream energies, she began pulling on the roiling waters, her hands moving in a large circle in front of her. Bit by bit, a funnel began forming in the choppy waters, growing out of the ocean.

Exhaustion suddenly set in as her energy levels dipped drastically. Dez almost fell to her knees as her vision swam. The voice in her head that would usually provide her with the encouragement she needed to push forward was surprisingly silent.

"Where are you?" Dez gasped. "I need you."

Len stepped over the fallen man at his feet. Blood stained the man's shirt as a large slash from Len's sword cut him open at the ribs. Taking a deep breath, he tried to still his breathing as he started running once more through the lower levels of the *Maiden*. Another jolt sent him lurching into the side of the ship. Len tried to brace the impact with his arm, but his head slammed into the wood. His legs buckled as stars burst in front of his eyes.

"Are you all right?" Maya asked as she straightened up. She managed to not lose her balance too badly as the ship rocked.

Rubbing his temple, Len waited for the stars to disappear and the blackness to recede. "I'll be fine."

A cry down the hall caught their attention. It was a woman's voice.

"Jylla doesn't have any women in his crew," Maya said, an edge of panic in her voice. "We need to hurry."

Taking off down the hall, Maya rammed her body, shoulder first, into the closest man. The man was thrown into the wall with a cry of surprise. Shaking his head to clear it, Len ignored the blackness that threatened to consume him and followed Maya towards the sound of Kayna's voice. As the man Maya hit moved to stop him, Len paused to kick the man's leg, causing him to buckle, before slamming his fist into the man's temple, dropping him instantly.

The ship rocked violently, the sound of waves crashing against the ship left the young general feeling more than a little concerned. He and Maya ran deeper into the heart of the ship in their search for Jylla and Kayna. If anything were to happen to the *Silver Maiden,* they would join her as she sank to the bottom of the sea. Len's heart raced from both adrenaline and an emotion he never thought he would acknowledge: fear.

Images of his wife and daughter flashed in his mind, threatening to distract him as he fought his way to the heart of the ship. A loud shout ahead was quickly followed up with the clang of clashing swords. Maya and Kayna came into view. The two women dueled a tall man with dark hair tied in a low tail. His muscular body danced around in the cramped space with a litheness that Len would not have guessed. They finally found Jylla.

Jylla side-stepped a strike from Maya, only to be kicked in the thigh by Kayna. The redhead's cheek bled from a cut under her eye. Dried blood stained her hand, presumably from when she tried to wipe her face after the strike. Her green eyes were hard as she moved her sword deftly in an attempt to disarm Jylla. Despite what Maya had said, the pirate did not seem to have any problem showing his fighting prowess against the two women. And he was skilled, no doubt about that. There was a reason he commanded a crew.

The ship lurched once more, sending the three combatants tumbling into a wall, and almost knocking Len off of his feet. He felt unsettled as he tried to calm the churning around and within him. Without warning, Len hunched over and heaved, emptying his stomach in the cramped quarters. Wiping the bile with the back of his hand, the young general straightened up, trying to keep the three in sight.

"What in the hells is going on?" Jylla cried, his voice trembling. "This is not natural. Graak must be furious."

Bringing her sword arm up a bit to eliminate any opening in her stance, Kayna shot him a withering glare. "It's not the Ayr, Jylla," she spat. "It's the Scourge's sister."

"The Scourge has a sister?" he asked, fear evident in his voice as his eyes widened. "But no one knows anything about him. The Scourge has been around for time immemorial. Not even Fiern knew about him. And his sister controls this storm?

"She's a Tempest," Len said. He was surprised at how calm his voice sounded despite his nausea. "I've encountered her once before and seen her banish a demon to the abyss."

The three shared a look of incredulity, their weapons lowering slightly.

"She's taken on a demon?" Maya asked. "But she seems to be nothing more than a woman touched."

Len locked eyes with Maya. The news clearly shocked the woman. She hadn't been there to see the Scourge embrace Dez's tiny form in his large arms as tears ran down the pirate's face. Dez shared his emotion as she closed her eyes in relief. The two left the moment unexplained between them before leaving the cave to track down Jylla.

Another jarring heave sent the four staggering. Jylla barely managed to brace himself against the wall as Maya bumped into Kayna.

"Look, we need to get out of here now," Len said. "We can continue this later, but we're going to die if we stay down here. The water's getting more and more violent."

Jylla clenched the pommel of his sword, his knuckles turning white as a vein in his temple throbbed. The pirate did not want to get up.

"Look," Len snapped, "we don't have time for you to keep wasting time. You can either die down here, or you can face judgement later." When Jylla didn't move, Len let out an exasperated sigh and kicked the man's leg, dropping him to one knee before managing to disarm him. The pirate let out a strangled cry as his sword left his hand. "Now will you go, or must I kill you myself?"

Kayna's mouth hung open as she watched the exchange. Grabbing Jylla roughly by the collar, Len began pulling him down the hall.

"Let's go!" he growled.

The two women sprinted past him, their weapons still drawn. Jylla yanked himself free of Len's grip and grudgingly began following them. As they encountered members of his crew, Jylla shouted for them to get to the main deck and prepare to abandon ship.

～～

Dez held her hands out in front of her, a large funnel of water sticking out of the sea and moving towards the *Silver Maiden*. The fighting on the *Fury* had ceased as all aboard both ships watched the cyclone approach in fear. Men on the *Maiden* shouted in terror as the outermost waters slammed into the ship. Several men were almost torn from the bow of the boat and tossed into the sea. Only a few loose pieces of rope flapping in the wind managed to save them from a watery grave.

A grunt of exertion escaped the Tempest's lips as she struggled to command both storms. The wind threatened to get away from her, the gale surrounding the two ships ripping the sails and tearing flags from the mizzenmast. Bits of wood splintered away from the *Maiden* from the force of the winds. Men ducked for cover, clinging to anything they could in a futile attempt to weather the storm.

From behind her, Dez heard a deep voice. It triggered a sense of longing within, awakening the previously silent Aria. Tears rolled down Dez's cheeks once more as she finally felt the familiar comfort she'd known for so long. In her mind, a shining image of Aria engulfed in silver stood out, filling her every pore with holy energy. The goddess' long silver hair flowed freely down her back, just as her tears.

"That's enough," the deep voice said again. "You can stop now."

With a shuddering gasp, Dez dropped her arms. The silver tattoos stopped glowing and returned to their normal color. Around them, the winds died down and the cyclone crashed into the sea with a monstrous splash. Both the *Fury* and the *Maiden* rocked wildly as the waves churned around them. A light shower of sea spray rained down on both ships as everything began to calm.

Turning to face the voice, Dez saw Angh standing behind her once more. A look of serenity filled his face as he looked down on her. The comfort she felt moments before from Aria's return intensified as she looked at the man. Though he was ageless, the lines and weathered features he'd had when she first met him was slowly melting away. The grey in his dark hair was turning back to its lustrous silver.

"Ghan," she said to him, "do you think you'll stay down here now that you know Aria is okay?" Dez held her breath as she waited for his answer.

"I don't know," he replied. "You told me Czand is dead, but I know that he is not truly gone. Splitting from Vahnyre was not enough to kill him. He'll be back soon. Well, what I would call soon. But Man, he needs guidance more than ever. I've found a way to maintain some order with these people. I don't know if I could leave them so easily." He smiled as he watched Kayna and the remaining members of her attack force escort Jylla and his crew onto the *Fury*. "What about you? Surely you would like to rest."

Dez gulped. "I'll be coming home soon," she said, relaying Aria's message. After a pause, she added, "I hope you don't punish yourself forever, brother. None of this was your fault."

Angh squeezed Dez's shoulder, a gentle smile on his worn face. "You too, dear sister. You've sacrificed so much. You deserve rest."

The two stood side by side as the last members of Jylla's crew crossed over onto the *Fury*. Soon, the trial was about to start, and she knew that it wouldn't be the captured pirate who would be facing judgement.

XXVIII

JYLLA STOOD before the Scourge, his head high and his expression smug. While in the heart of the ship, Len would not have believed that the rogue pirate had been willing to sink to the bottom of the sea instead of facing the pirate lord. Len leaned against the side of the *Fury*, the waters finally calm once more now that Dez's magic no longer commanded the elements, with his arms crossed against his chest. His weapons sat sheathed on his hips. The blood had been wiped off of the blades with one of his victims' shirts, as there were several dead who were no longer needing their clothes on the *Maiden*.

Angh sat on top of a cluster of wine barrels, his hands on his knees. The pirate lord stared at the rogue pirate, his penetrating stare making several of Jylla's crew shuffle uncomfortably. Jylla tried to meet the imposing gaze, but broke contact multiple times. Angh narrowed his eyes at the man. He was rewarded a moment later by Jylla taking an involuntary step back.

"You are here today in front of me and my crew for breaking the Law of the Seas," Angh called out. "You extort the people of the Bone Coast for your protection, yet you and yours torment them at the same time. It is known that only one option is open to you."

"I can't control my crew when they're drunk!" Jylla protested.

"As captain, you are responsible for your men. You have been pushing the boundaries of what I'll allow for at least ten years now. I have been merciful with you up until this point, but no more." Angh stood up and walked over to where Jylla stood.

The pirate tried to maintain the distance between the two of them, but Kayna grabbed him by the arm to prevent him from fleeing. Her other hand held him tightly on the back of the neck.

"Let go of me, woman!" Jylla hissed as he tried to break free.

Kayna gave him a swift kick in the leg, causing it to buckle. All the while, she watched him with a bemused expression. "Now, now," she said. "You want to pretend that you're the king of the Eastern Isles? Then you get to enjoy it all, the benefits and the consequences." As she spoke, Kayna used her knee to push down on his weakened leg, dropping Jylla to his knees.

"Damn you, woman!" he snarled as he tried to push himself onto his feet.

Angh's massive hand shot out and forced Jylla back to his knees. The pirate let out a shout of surprise as the larger man handled him roughly. As quickly as he pushed Jylla down, the pirate lord grabbed the pirate by the collar of his shirt and shook him violently. Angh's eyes flashed dangerously as he glared at the man.

"If you want to remain captain of your ship, you will honor the Law of the Seas and also those on the council who are your equals. And if you want to live, you will want to be on your best behavior. Do you understand?"

Jylla whimpered as he nodded his head. The motion was hindered by Angh's hand balling up the fabric of his collar. The pirate lord gripped the shirt so tightly that his hand shook lightly in his rage. To the side, Kayna stood with her arms crossed against her chest a look of concern on her face. Her eyes darted from the pirate captain on the deck to her father as he glowered at the man at his feet. Len noted her discomfort as she chewed her bottom lip.

This seems very unlike her, Len mused. *I wonder if this is out of character for Angh. He did seem much more mellow when I first met him. But that energy I felt that day. It's different from what I feel now. It's much heavier now.*

Primordial rage radiated from Angh. It covered everyone on the ship like a thick blanket. Len glanced around and saw that one by one, members of both Jylla's crew and Kayna's crew fidgeted as they looked around for the source of their discomfort. More than one turned away from the interaction, rubbing their arm awkwardly as they tried to distance themselves from what was going on.

His eyes landed on Maya. She sat lightly on the barrels that Angh had been sitting on moments before. Her legs were crossed and her left foot jiggled as she watched the exchange, her lips pursed. Maya caught his eye and shook her head. The motion was barely perceptible. Right after, she nodded to Dez standing next to her. Tears rolled silently down Dez's cheeks as she watched her brother pass judgement on the trembling pirate. A silver aura glowed faintly around her, visible to Len's eye. Those around her did not seem to notice the strange occurrence.

"So, Jylla," Angh continued. "What is your decision?"

"I – I want to remain on the council," Jylla stammered.

"And what will you do to ensure you remain on the council?" Angh prompted.

"I'll change. We won't extort and raid more than the laws allow." The captain stared at Angh eagerly, seeking confirmation that he was saying the right things.

"That sounds acceptable," Angh said after a moment's silence.

Jylla breathed a sigh of relief. All around, the heaviness that had previously been smothering all on the ship began lightening. Men stopped fidgeting and people no longer felt uncomfortable watching the interaction. Averted eyes once more found their way to the pirate lord as he towered over the pirate captain as he still sat kneeled on the deck.

With a visible sigh of relief, Jylla closed his eyes and the corners of his mouth turned up in a faint smile. His shoulders, which had previously been raised and tense were now relaxed. He no longer appeared hunched over as the Scourge gripped his shirt and pulled him up. Angh noticed Jylla's change in posture and smiled down on the man. His hand loosened up on Jylla's collar, giving him a little slack so he could move.

A moment later, a spray of red splashed onto the deck as Angh's hand shot out with a dagger and slashed Jylla's right eye. Jylla screamed in pain as the blade bit into his flesh and moved from his cheek to partway through his forehead. Angh released his grip on the pirate captain and shook the dagger, a shower of blood droplets hitting the deck. The pirate lord grabbed the back of Jylla's shirt to wipe off the remaining blood as Jylla hunched over in a ball, his hands pressed against his face as he cried in agony.

Sheathing his dagger, Angh turned and walked towards his cabin. "Consider this a warning," he called out over his shoulder. "Next time I will not be as merciful."

Men parted as Angh walked by. No one wanted to be around the man. Len felt his stomach twist as he saw the power the pirate lord commanded. Dez followed the Scourge, the group parting for her the same way they parted for him.

"Take him away," Kayna said to the pirates, nudging Jylla with her foot. "May we meet on better winds."

Members of Jylla's crew scooped up their captain and one by one they left the ship and reboarded the *Silver Maiden*. Kayna's crew set about preparing the ship to return to the Bone Coast. Bits of wood and rope needed to be repaired, but nothing that would jeopardize the *Fury* on her voyage home.

Len took one last look at the *Silver Maiden*, her tattered black flags waving gently in the breeze, before walking to the other side of the main deck to stare out at the open waters. The warmth of the sun had returned now that Dez's winds were no longer whipping around. Puddles of water still sat on the deck from her cyclone and the violent waves. Men called out to each other, trying to make sure no one was unaccounted for. The Scourge's judgement afforded no time to count the dead.

Life on the seas wasn't much different than life in Xan.

XXIX

Dzvareliah rested in the shade of a tree as her husband spoke with some soldiers. She took a bite of the large red apple in her hand, the sweet juice exploding in her mouth, and watched the interaction intently. It was a small group that traveled: Dzvareliah, her husband, and seven other soldiers, one of whom was the young boy her daughter seemed to have favored. The boy stood tensely as his king addressed them. Dzvorth waved his arms as he spoke. His son's death still angered him.

Taking another bite of her apple, Dzvareliah sighed as her husband jabbed at a spot on the map in one of the soldiers' hand several times. The king was not happy. The queen closed her heavily lidded eyes and leaned her head back against the tree. A light breeze ruffled her hair, which she kept tied in a high tail, and a few strands tickled her face. Her daughter's antics the previous week created quite a bit of chaos, the extent of which most didn't even know.

Dzvri's death was not the only pain Vashe had inflicted on the Ari family. The theft of the holy artifacts from Queen Dzvareliah's room made her blood boil. Her husband's rage flashed in her mind as she watched the men converse off to the side.

"Dzvri's death is a tragedy, but not completely unexpected," she had told her uncontrollable husband days after he found his son's body in the darkened hallway. Dzvareliah could still see Dzvorth's blood-stained hands from when he cradled Dzvri in his arms. *"Dzvri would have gotten himself killed one way or another."*

Dzvorth howled in rage and moved to slap his wife, but stopped just short of her face. Dzvareliah held her position as she stared him down with a cool face. He wouldn't hit her. He never did.

"We have no heir to the Ari throne," he had spat. *"What of my legacy?"*

"I am not yet barren," she had replied coolly. *"I can still bear you children. Besides, we both know that I'm not the only one you bed."* Her eyes narrowed as she glared at him, causing his eyes to drop for the briefest of seconds. *"Right now, we must focus on what's important. My store of holy blood, as well as the ceremonial dagger and Blessed Aria's stone, are all gone. Without them, we cannot continue our legacy. We must get it back from her, no matter the cost."*

The stone, the queen could live without. It was the only reminder of Aria's sacrifice — a piece of her final resting spot. But the blood, that was a different matter. Without that, Scrymme would have to find other ways to create magi through blood magic. She shook with rage at the thought of the holy blood becoming diluted by draughting until it was practically useless.

Dammit Dzvaresh, she seethed. *You knew what would hurt each of us the most. What else did you do while you were here?*

Opening her eyes and lifting her head off of the tree trunk, Dzvareliah watched as Dzvorth moved his finger along the map. *He's still at this?*

The king turned his head in her direction and pointed to something off in the distance. The soldiers all followed where he was pointing, several nodding in understanding as he spoke to them. Dzvareliah felt her stomach knot as she looked closely at the young soldier. Dzvorath shared the high cheekbones of the Scrymmen people, but there was something about the way his slender face and silver eyes that looked familiar.

The youth said something and the king roared in response. The young soldier flinched, causing one of the more seasoned soldiers to apologize for him.

"Dzvorath is still a bit unsure of himself after being attacked by one of his own," the older soldier said, patting the younger one on the shoulder. "But we'll make sure he mans up before nightfall."

Dzvorath? Dzvareliah wondered if she heard correctly. *I wasn't wrong about Dzvorth after all.*

The queen shook her head. She had been taken by the king when she was only thirteen; he was already twice her age when he chose her to be his wife and bedded her for the first time. He expressed his disappointment as she was only able to bear him two living children, a son and daughter. His rage used to make her shake, but she'd learned quickly to manipulate him. To trick him into taking out his anger on the staff. To Dzvorth, as long as he could act out his frustrations, he didn't care who the victim was.

As time went on, he became less observant, his attentions focusing elsewhere. His obsession with purging Corinth of the unworthy passed down to their children, giving Dzvareliah time to herself.

I'm surprised he was so confident as to give Dzvorath a royal name. Really, she chuckled to herself. *He should have been more clever. I know I was.*

Tossing the core, Dzvareliah stood up and wiped her hands on her riding pants before making her way to the group. When the others saw her approach, they quieted down. All except the king.

"Have we decided where we will strike first?" she asked. "If our information is correct, Dzvaresh is somewhere in Pharn, right?"

"We have decided to first try and take the ore mines in Xan before heading to Zanir like originally planned," one of the men replied. "We've never left Scrymme before. Now is the perfect opportunity to strike and take what we can before those heathens can build up a proper response. Your daughter," the man flinched as the queen gave him a withering glare. "I mean, the traitor, probably is expecting us to come for her. We would lose out on a valuable opportunity if we don't go for the mine first. She can wait."

Dzvareliah nodded her head, studying the map still in the soldier's hands. Thick black circles were made in three strategic spots in Xan. Two of them were near the periphery closer to Ro'thre, but one was deeper into the heart of the land.

"Fa'Tinh isn't far from one of those," she noted. "Is that an ore or spice mine by the capital?"

"Ore," the first soldier replied. "The king, our blessed ruler from the gods, suggested that we split into two groups. Two of us heading for the spice mines on the periphery, while the rest of the group heads to the heart of Xan to take the ore. The two who head towards the spice mines can create a diversion and draw away their troops, leaving the ore mine more accessible."

"And you really think that'll work?" Dzvareliah asked.

The man looked to the king and then back to the queen. His previously calm demeanor faltered as he tried to find an alternative meaning to her words. Dzvareliah smiled at his predicament. Who would he choose, the king or the queen?

"Oh, dammit woman," Dzvorth sighed. "Can't you give it a break? I've worked long and hard preparing for this siege. Dzvri and I have studied maps, seasonal harvesting patterns, and damn trade patterns for close to ten years. Of course, it'll work."

Got him.

"I just wanted to be sure. If Dzvaresh is expecting us, she may have sent out messages to Zanir's neighbors warning them of us."

"He didn't mean that," Dzvorth said. "She has no reason to believe we would be going anywhere but to her."

"Do we know she didn't see anything?" the queen asked. "We don't know how long she was in Caicyne Ari."

"It can't have been long, your holiness," the man quickly interjected. "Prince Dzvri had spoken to a member of staff not long before he was found dead. There wasn't enough time for her to go sneaking around for information."

Dzvareliah stood quietly. She was impressed with the man. Her eyes drifted lazily over the rest of the soldiers. The other five met her gaze, their heads giving a slight involuntary nod to back up the first man's statement. When her eyes landed on Dzvorath, the youth met her gaze. Determination shone in his eyes. She admired that about the boy. While Dzvorth could be violent, she was the one most feared. It filled her with warmth to see his resolve standing firm.

Finally, her eyes darted over to the king. Dzvorth huffed, his arms crossed over his chest, and shifted his weight from foot to foot. Dzvri's death really unhinged him. The king was starting to slip into dangerous territory with his rash behavior.

I'll have to bring him back, Dzvareliah noted. *A few words can fix some of the damage right now. The rest will take time. Probably not until Dzvaresh is dead.* The queen fought back a sigh of annoyance as she continued to stare at her husband. *I hope he doesn't do anything stupid. If Scrymme becomes a joke because of our first time out of our homeland he'll be the first to go.*

"That's reassuring," she finally said. The queen noted an almost collective sigh of relief from the soldiers, the action only standing out because she'd seen it so many times from her own staff when her anger subsided. "Is there a plan for dealing with Dzvaresh?"

"Nothing more than what was previously discussed, your holiness," a soldier replied.

A smile tugged on the corners of the queen's mouth. It had been a long time since she'd seen her daughter. She wanted to make sure that they had a nice chat before she killed Dzvaresh herself.

XXX

Vashe gasped for breath as she cut through the thick vines, slowly heading eastward through the foliage. The stale air and rich smell of earth created a musty scent that hung deeply in the air. But there was something else. She could feel a heavy blanket over the area, surrounding her, engulfing her. An ancient magic that lay sleeping, untouched through the ages.

She left her horse at the last inn on the border of Ro'thre, traveling by foot the rest of the way. Sweat beaded on her brow and her back. Wiping the sweat with the back of her hand before putting her knife back into its sheath on her arm, Vashe cursed as a vine almost snapped her in the face. The air was deadly quiet. Not even the chirping of birds could be heard. After a while, her foot scraped against a worn stone. Though the thicket had not lessened, she noticed that there were more stones on the ground and the earth was a rich red.

Suddenly, Vashe hit a wall. In front of her, an invisible wall of ancient magic stopped her. Testing the area tentatively with her hands, she found herself perplexed. Though it would give to her touch, she could not push her way through. She stepped away from the wall and took her pack off her back. Pulling out a heavy leather-bound book, Vashe flipped through the pages. After a few minutes of searching, she found what she was looking for.

Vashe looked around for something to draw with. She found a low-hanging branch and walked over. Reaching up, she snapped a small twig off of the branch. Vashe walked back to where her pack was and placed the tome back into it. Twirling the stick around as she looked for the right place to work, she decided to settle for a spot slightly to her left. Taking a deep breath, she collected her energies and got to work.

Crouching down, she stuck the twig into the soft earth and drew a rune. It was an arcane thing, filled with ancient symbols belonging to a dead race. Once she completed the rune, Vashe pulled out the knife once more and pricked the tip of one of her fingers. Watching the crimson bead forming, Vashe walked over to the wall and traced the rune with her blood.

As she drew the rune, she felt her body coursing with magic that was not her own. Thousands of years' worth of magical protection flooded her, threatening to overwhelm her. She struggled to complete the ancient text within the symbol, her face contorted in pain, eyes closed.

"I am Dzvaresh Ari, daughter of Scrymme and Headmistress of the Mageri of Corinth. I've survived assassination, and I'll be damned if I am beaten by the Ancients." Her tattoos began to glow as she pushed back against the invading energy. "By the blood of Her Greatness Aria herself, I. Will. Not. Be. Beaten."

With a scream, Vashe threw all of her magical energies against the wall. The muscles in her arms tightened as she flared her power.

A deep, booming chuckle filled the air.

"Welcome, daughter. We've been waiting."

Vashe's eyes popped open. Darkness surrounded her. The only light came from the glowing silver tattoos on her sleek frame. *What's going on?* she wondered, her eyes studying the strange phenomenon with interest. *My tattoos, they've never shown any signs when I've used them before. This is like what happens to naran.*

The air around her was no longer heavy. In the distance, she heard the chirping of birds once more. The sound was unsettling after the long stretch of silence she'd endured as she made her way through the jungle. Stepping forward, she found that there was no longer a barrier preventing her from moving forward. Picking up her pack and slinging it over her shoulder, Vashe slowly made her way into an abandoned land.

Before she'd gone more than a few paces, an ominous feeling settled in her stomach. Looking behind her, Vashe tried to figure out the source of her discomfort.

"Enlil, what secrets do you hold?" she murmured.

Unable to see any nearby threat, and unable to sense one through the shadows with her magic, Vashe took a deep breath and continued on. No sooner had she taken one step then she stopped. *I can't feel anything with my Shadow magic*, she realized. Closing her eyes, she reached out and searched the nearby shadows for any source of life. The seconds dragged on as she quietly felt her surroundings for any sign of life. The birds sang around her, somewhere in the canopy, but Vashe could not feel anything else.

Vashe's heart began to thump as she couldn't feel any rabbits or deer. It wasn't unusual to not have them nearby, but after the stillness she'd been through, the lack of any life unnerved her. Her hands became clammy as her senses elevated, straining to hear or see anything. With a sigh of relief, Vashe wiped her hands on her pants and continued on her trek as she felt a trail of ants climbing on a tree root that was sticking out of the soil.

The canopy was bright and the air warm. Vibrant birds flew overhead, singing their exotic songs. Everything suddenly felt more pleasant. Despite the beauty around her, her mind returned to the voice she'd heard. It sounded familiar, but she couldn't place where she'd heard it.

Wiping the sweat from her brow, Vashe went to pull out her water skin. She took a seat on the ground and enjoyed a long draught of her water. Swirling it around in the skin, she noted how it was almost empty. With a sigh, she returned it to her bag and pulled out a bit of dried meat. Taking a bite, she slowly chewed the snack while she took in her surroundings.

A dragonfly with shimmering jeweled wings flew overhead, the light of the sun shining through its translucent wings. At her feet, fuchsia, pink, and orange flowers grew out of the emerald grass. Everything beyond the magical barrier was beautiful, more vibrant than anything she'd ever seen. The red-brown soil she could see between the grass blades did not look like the clay that she had encountered in Ro'thre, but appeared to be full of nutrients. A worm wriggled through the grass, trying to escape the heat of the day and bury itself in the earth.

Beams of light shone through the canopy, the sky peeking through. The only thing missing was a cool breeze. Leaning against a nearby tree, Vashe closed her eyes and tried to figure out what the voice welcoming her into Enlil meant when they said they had been waiting.

Waiting for what? Someone to discover Enlil? What lies further in her land?

She sat for a long time, her body alternating between dozing off and startling awake with a question. Images of Aramaine, the mighty Ein, and her time spent back home played through her mind. She'd seen so much in the last couple weeks, so many things that she wanted to take time and explore and study. Giving up the opportunity to spend time in Aramaine with Ein was one of the hardest things she'd ever done. Vashe had spent years studying the wyrm. Years trying to scry him through her special pool.

The beast left her in awe. She'd almost not had the willpower to say no. Knowledge. The experience of a lifetime. He'd offered it to her, but she turned it down.

What did I lose by turning him down? The abyss would've brought me closer to Themba, to the seven hells. There are entities I could've learned about. Creatures I can't even fathom existing. And Ein himself. His blood holds so many secrets. Damn. I would've loved to take something back to study.

She sat in silence a bit longer, but eventually opened her eyes and pushed herself up. "I've wasted too much time just sitting here. I need to move forward."

Vashe continued down her path, working her way to who knew what. All she could hope was that she would find what she was searching for. Time passed without a way for her to measure it. The canopy blocked the sun's movements and the lengthening shadows confused her. They seemed to go in all directions.

As her stomach began to rumble, Vashe determined that she would probably not find the ruins that day and started looking for a place to bed down for the night. Vashe had been tapping into her Shadow energies all day, trying to feel for any other life forms. Apart from the occasional bug, she couldn't even find any small animals like rabbits or mice. Setting up her camp, Vashe realized that she would not be having much for dinner that night.

"Hopefully I can find something tomorrow. I'm running low on everything."

Straining her ears, Vashe hoped to hear running water. If she could find a water source that would be a godsend. With disappointment, she wasn't able to hear anything. Pulling out a piece of dried meat and an apple, Vashe ate her meager meal as slowly as she could. A fire blazed in front of her in the small clearing she had made, warming her hands as the day began to cool.

A chorus of crickets and cicadas began chirping as night came. Vashe pulled her legs into her chest, scooting closer to the fire, as the chill of the evening set in. A shiver ran through her body; Enlil was much colder than she'd expected. Warming her hands by the fire, Vashe tried to figure out the best way to keep herself from freezing while making sure that she got some rest that night.

"I'm not made for this weather," she groused. "I can't imagine how the people of Xan manage. Theirs is the closest to this type of climate."

Huddling by the fire, Vashe rocked towards the heat, the balls of her feet catching her right before the flames. Reaching out into her surroundings, Vashe took advantage of the darkness and tried to find more life with her Shadow magic. Just like earlier that day, there were no small animals or deer anywhere to be found. Though she could hear owls hooting up in the trees, she couldn't seem to find any nests. It was reassuring to her that she could at least find the insects that chirped around her.

"At least I know my abilities have not been diminished upon crossing the border into Enlil," she mused. Vashe didn't want to admit it, but a part of her deep down believed that she would be stripped of her blood magic once she found the ruins, although she didn't know what to expect when she finally reached them.

She sat in silence for a while, her body shivering wherever the heat of the flames did not touch. The rest of her was pleasantly warm as the crackling fire heated her body. Vashe felt her eyelids drooping as exhaustion set in. Her head dropped to her chin and her arms, which were hugging her legs to keeper balled up for warmth, began to loosen and slide down. With a start, she quickly tightened her grip on her legs and tried to keep her head raised.

For some reason she could not explain, Vashe was hesitant to fall asleep. The longer she sat in front of the fire, the stronger a sense of foreboding dread filled her. It pulled at her very core, causing her stomach to begin twisting in knots and her heart to beat faster. The emotion unnerved the Scrymmen woman.

I haven't felt this way since I ran away from home, she observed. *Both times.*

An owl hooted, breaking the otherwise calm night. The crickets and cicadas chirping created an almost hypnotic atmosphere as she sat there in front of the fire. Vashe felt her eyes growing heavy again. She'd traveled for too long with too little rest, and now her exhaustion was catching up with her.

"Maybe a short nap," she yawned. "Just enough to recover a bit. I'll need it for tomorrow."

Laying down on the soft earth, Vashe curled into a ball, her back against the trunk of a tree and her face to the flames. With a sigh, she closed her eyes and let her body sink into a fitful sleep, her hand clenched the hilt of her dagger, just in case.

Vashe crept through the darkness, the brilliant white of the moon shining overhead, exposing her to anyone nearby. Though she reached out with her Shadow skills, she could not feel any life around her. The lack of life unsettled her. Even in a place like Enlil, life should return after a natural disaster. Nothing was abandoned forever.

She stalked forward, her dagger palmed in her hand, resting against her forearm. Ahead of her, the sprawling ruins of Enlil greeted her. Fallen monoliths basked in the moonlit night, a pale shadow of their former splendor. Piles of rubble blocked one of the entryways into the remnants, while chunks of stone partially obstructed other entrances.

Fallen tree trunks dotted the perimeter, but none were close to the actual stone building. Crouching down, she noticed that the ground that was once so soft and lush was now dry and withered. Blades of dried grass crunched under her feet with each step no matter how carefully she moved. Her heart raced and her mouth went dry as one patch of grass sounded in the night like a snapped twig. Dropping to the ground, Vashe reached out with her energies to see if anyone was around.

She waited with bated breath for what felt like an eternity before slowly getting up off the ground. Her head turned rapidly side to side, trying to find the source of her discomfort. Every fiber of her being screamed at her that she was being watched, but there was nothing. Not a soul could be seen nor detected, and it only heightened her panic.

Blessed Aria, I don't know what to do. Please, send me some guidance.

Vashe's foot hit the smooth stone of the first step of the ruins. She breathed a sigh of relief as she no longer had to worry about the dried grass. Her feet traveled quietly on the worn stone, the occasional pebble being kicked, causing it to skip across the floor. Blades of dried grass stuck out between the large crumbling rocks. They tickled her legs as she walked through the ruins.

The large stone structure let the light stream in through the open facing walls. Giant swaths of wall had been destroyed, their stones laying around in a pile of rubble, blocking access to part of the building. As Vashe moved further into the ruins, the air became heavier, making it difficult to breathe. Her heart pounded and she struggled for breath.

A shadow off to her right caught her eye. Crouching down, Vashe moved slowly towards the movement. Mercifully, the pillars afforded her a measure of protection from the moonlight, but not much. She still could not detect anyone in the shadows, which made her heart beat faster.

I saw something, she thought. *How in the seven hells can I not feel them?*

Vashe crept up to the nearest pillars and peeked through them. In the light of the moon, she saw a dark shadowed figure standing in an open room. White light shone down, elongating his shadow on the stones. Vashe brought her hand up, trying to find a way to reach out and touch the figure when a hand clamped over her mouth. Her eyes darted to the side and a man's face stared back at her. His silver eyes stood out in the moonlight. Bringing his free hand to his lips, he motioned for her to be quiet as he shook his head no.

～〜～

With a gasp, Vashe's eyes popped open. Her heart thundered against her chest as she struggled to breathe. Her skin felt clammy and sweat dotted her brow. Bringing her hand to her face, she realized that she was crying. Hiccupping, Vashe pushed herself up and brushed a strand of hair out of her face. The fire burned low, the embers struggling to stay lit from the lack of kindling. Its low glow barely provided any heat against the freezing night.

"Are you okay?" a melodic voice asked.

Vashe jumped, her head spinning toward the sound of the voice. A man sat nearby, his back resting on the trunk of a tree as he stared into the dying fire. In the wan light, the shadows flickered across his face. His eyes were highlighted in the light and they looked so familiar.

Dark skin and silver eyes.

"It's been a while," he said when she didn't say anything. "I'm glad you decided to come to Enlil after all. I promise it'll be worth your while."

"What are you doing here? Did you follow me?" Vashe's voice came out in a hoarse whisper as she gasped out the words. Her heart pounded in her chest. *Why can't I sense him? I couldn't touch him back in Scrymme, and now I can't reach out and sense him.*

The man, Dseti, Vashe remembered, threw a few small sticks into the fire, keeping it alive. "I came to watch you," he said simply. "When I met you in Scrymme, I knew you would be heading out here." Vashe's mouth went dry at this news. "And, knowing who you are, I knew that you would be in danger if you ran into him."

"Him?"

"My brother," he replied. "He's been getting into a lot of trouble lately."

"Who is your brother?" she asked quietly.

"What do you know about Enlil?" he asked, evading her question.

"It's the home of the ancient people of Corinth. It was destroyed generations ago, going further back than I know. Some say it's the home of the gods."

"And?" he prompted.

"And... home of evil," she finished slowly.

Dseti threw a few more sticks into the fire. "Yes," he said with a sigh. "There is much mystery surrounding Enlil. I find myself coming here when I need some time to think." His head leaned back against the tree as he stared into the heavens through the canopy. Dseti plucked a blade of grass and began weaving it between his fingers as he let his mind wander.

Vashe stared at the man, unsure of where he was going with the conversation. Her mind raced as she tried to figure out his next step. "Dseti?" she broached. When the man turned to look at her, she took that as confirmation to move forward. "You said the last time we met that you were a wanderer." He nodded in affirmation. "And you speak of coming to Enlil almost casually, as though you have no difficulty entering through her barrier."

Another nod.

"And you speak of a brother who is dangerous, and would harm me if he knew I was here?" she finished her statement as a question, trying to figure out if that was what he was implying.

Dseti pulled his knees into his chest like Vashe had earlier. "Do you remember what else I told you that night we met?"

Vashe was thrown off by his question. Wracking her mind, she tried to recall their conversation back in Scrymme. His silver eyes watched hers as she struggled to remember.

"I pointed out Maah-res' disappearance," he said gently, giving her the answer to his own question. "It's troubling to see the majestic Maah-res gone from the heavens. She is a great protector, keeping watch over Man from above."

"Does your brother have anything to do with this?" Vashe asked slowly.

Dseti nodded. "Your dream was no normal dream," he said. "He was looking for you. You pose a great threat to him, and he used Maah-res' absence to his advantage. If you would've reached out to him, he would have consumed you."

Vashe's tattooed hand involuntarily went to her throat as shivers went down her spine that had nothing to do with the freezing temperatures. She remembered how she'd been so close to touching the figure with her Shadow abilities. It was said those who were blessed with Shadow skills were given the ability to touch another's soul. Being able to manipulate someone's shadow was akin to manipulating their very essence. Just a little more and she would've alerted some entity to her presence. But had he planted the dream in her mind? And just who was he?

Vashe decided to get more information from him. After some quick thinking, she tried to think of a way to lead the conversation in a direction she could control. "Dseti," she began. She was relieved when the man nodded to her, willing to continue on. "You speak of things that are beyond me, as though you know more than you are alluding to. Please, I already have a *naran* who is an enigma. If you know something, tell me. Dark things appear to be happening. I don't have time to figure this all out when there are so many lives at stake."

Dseti buried his face in his hands and sighed. His fingers ran through his hair. In the moonlight, the man appeared exhausted, the muscles of his back drooping. Vashe could see that he carried the weight of many on his shoulders, and that he was nearing his breaking point. Something was threatening to crush him.

"Do you believe in the gods?" he finally asked. Caught off guard by the question, Vashe sat in silence. "I know you are smart, my daughter," he said. "You've seen things that most cannot even comprehend. Enlil is what you know it to be, deep down. Only the gods can travel here, or at least, that's how it is supposed to be. Ancient magic fills her lands, permeates the halls of the temples. Re-Mara, Atunari, the two major ruins you'll see tomorrow. They're beautiful, and filled with power.

"The temple in Atunari is the one of your dream. It is the shrine to my love, Maeyu'dana, and her guardian, Maah-res. This is where I will take you tomorrow."

"Maeyu'dana?" Vashe gasped. Pulling out her leather tome, she rifled through the pages rapidly until she found what she was looking for. Handing over the book, she pointed to a line for Dseti to see. "Is this about her? I haven't translated the text yet, but one word keeps showing up: Maeyu'dana. I copied it from an old book I took from home when I was younger. It's in an ancient tongue that I haven't figured out."

"And through the years, one thing remained clear. Of the four Ancients who wandered through the realms, one could not be found: Maeyu'dana. Without her

presence, the balance of harmony was ruined. The gods could not maintain their unity. The harmony could not be restored. Maeyu'dana's absence is only the beginning. Darkness will follow." Dseti's reading trailed off as he closed the tome and placed it on his lap. The wanderer rubbed his eyes just above the bridge of his nose as he processed what he just read.

"This is from Re-Mara," he said suddenly. "A text pulled from Enlil herself before Man burned her to the ground. It was a time when Man and their gods, the Ancients, as you would call them, communed easily, receiving visions and guidance. I knew Maeyu'dana when her spirit was mortal. Her death had grave consequences for the people of Enlil. As did mine."

"You were mortal with her?" Vashe asked.

Dseti nodded. "A priest. But that was long ago. I must atone for my sins, for killing myself, and that is why I wander. I was promised that I would be reunited with her once more. Until then, I help my brothers, the two Ancients, maintain balance and harmony."

He handed her back her old leather tome. Vashe took it back and placed it into her bag. She looked back to him as he sat in front of the fire, now practically dead since no one had fed it any more kindling. Dseti stared into the flames, his eyes hollow as he searched for something deep within. Vashe saw his pain, the haunted past he most likely was reliving. In the smoldering embers and a beam of moonlight, she was able to finally take a good look at him.

The man had dark skin like her *naran*, as well as one silver eye, like Scrymme. Her gaze was drawn to a large scar on his chest, the lighter scar tissue tracing a jagged line over his heart.

A priest who committed suicide, she thought. *What horrors has he experienced in his quest to atone for his sins?*

XXXI

The sun had barely started its ascent into the sky by the time Vashe and Dseti began their trek towards Re-Mara and Atunari. Sparrows and finches trilled as they sang in the trees, the heaviness and silence from the previous day apparently forgotten. The deeper they traveled into Enlil, the more life they suddenly found. Vashe found the juxtaposition between the two days unsettling, but carried on. Dseti was not overly concerned, and if one of the Ancients was not worried, she reasoned that she would be okay too.

After their conversation the last night, Dseti's disposition had taken a more light-hearted tone. Much like her *naran*, the wanderer kept much to himself and displayed a cheery exterior. The two traveled in relative silence, but she noticed Dseti humming as they walked. She took comfort in this.

Her eyes still burned with exhaustion. Vashe did not get a good night's sleep. Between her troubling dream and Dseti's revelations, her mind was too full of questions to allow for her to sleep properly. As she laid down in a vain attempt to sleep, ideas bounced around, refusing to let her relax. Stifling a yawn, Vashe stretched her arms as they walked.

"Is there a water source nearby?" she asked. "It's been too long since I last filled my skin. Some food would be nice too. I haven't been able to find so much as a rabbit since I came to Enlil."

"There is a river near Re-Mara that branches off into a stream. There's also a creek by Atunari. At Maeyu'dana's temple, there's a pond inside, and something nearby. I don't remember what, but we will find it. We can stop at her temple."

Mouth dry, Vashe thanked Dseti for his help and continued on. Their path quickly disappeared as thick, knee-high grass made it difficult to walk. The trees disappeared, and the two walked out in the open. Vashe found herself struggling to breathe as she recognized the path they took. It was the same one as her dream. Without warning, Dseti darted off to the right. Startled, Vashe reached out with her Shadow energies to see if anyone was nearby.

Just as quickly, she pulled back, scolding herself for her hasty reaction. Tapping into her Shadow energies had almost gotten her in trouble, albeit in her dreams. If there was an Ancient stalking her, she needed to be careful.

Recalling their conversation the night before, Vashe struggled to accept all that was happening.

"Apophmet has been interested in you for a while," Dseti had said. *"Your knowledge and ingenuity, along with your untapped power, make you the perfect weapon for him to try and utilize."*

"Untapped power?" she had asked. *"It can take a lifetime before one reaches their full potential. What does that even mean?"*

"You'll understand soon," he had replied. *"If he's so concerned about you, I think it's only right that you be as fearsome as he imagines."*

Stepping over something hidden in the tall grass, Dseti gave a little hop. Vashe nearly tripped over the large bit of stone he had evaded a moment earlier. With a stutter step as she widened her legs to go around the rock, the Scrymmen woman barely missed tripping over it. She thought she heard Dseti chuckle in front of her as she let out a curse as she tried to avoid the stone.

"You said last night that the great panther is Maeyu'dana's guardian," Vashe began. Despite being tied in a high tail, her hair was plastered to her body thanks to the sweat. "How does that work? Are you able to travel through the heavens?"

"Ever the curious one," Dseti said, chuckling once more. "I'm not sure how to explain it, but there is a realm that only we can travel to. You wouldn't be able to get there like you did to visit the wyrm, where Maeyu'dana managed to tame the beast. It was quite impressive."

"What's it called?" Vashe asked, excitement bleeding into her voice.

"N'aaru. It translates to Final Paradise in Corinth's common tongue. I think you'd call it *Eleshir Anun*, in Scrymmen."

"*Eleshir Anun*. N'aaru," she mumbled. "Would you let me interview you when this is all over?" she asked. "You would provide so much information about the ancient tongue and the olden days. So much is lost."

"I can make no promises," he said. Vashe thought she detected a hint of disappointment in his voice.

The two walked in silence for a while. Vashe used the time as an opportunity to take in the beauty all around her. Now that the canopies opened up, she was able to take a look at her surroundings. In the trees, she saw beautiful jewel-colored birds like she'd never seen before. Their crimson chests and long tail feathers reflected the sun until they shone like gems. They trilled the most amazing song she'd ever heard; it was unlike anything she'd ever experienced.

Golden flowers dotted the perimeter of the tall grasses, growing close to the trunks of the red-brown trees. They were accompanied by some radiant pink flowers that grew in bunches. Hummingbirds flitted from flower to flower, delicately sipping the nectar from each one before moving on for their next meal. Butterflies flew in the sky, their brilliant orange and black wings flapping delicately.

Vashe turned to face the front and felt her heart jump to her chest as she realized that Dseti was gone. Spinning around, she tried to find where he went. Her mind raced as thoughts of taking the wrong turn or missing a side path rushed in one after the other. Off to her left, she heard the tall grasses rustling. Whipping her head in that direct, she let out a sigh of relief before stifling a gasp as she saw Dseti returning with a pair of rabbits in his hand.

She hadn't been using her Shadow skills since she partnered up with him, and the sight of another mammal, especially one that they could eat, provided a measure of comfort she wasn't expecting. Her mouth watered at the sight of them.

"Let's stop for lunch," Dseti said as he began walking out of the field once more and into the shade of one of the trees. "We're not too far from the temples and I believe you said you could use a snack."

Her stomach growling, Vashe eagerly made her way out of the tall grasses and into the shade.

~~~

The two rabbits were devoured quicker than she would've liked, but Vashe found herself rushing through her meal in an attempt to reach the temples before the sun began to set. A sense of urgency had been tugging at her since her arrival, but the foreboding she'd been feeling overshadowed it. In what felt like no time, the pair were on their way.

They didn't have to travel far before a sprawling stone structure came into view. Vashe let out a gasp of wonder as the ancient city of Atunari came into view. Large stones comprising the Temple of Maeyu stood off to the side, separate from the greys of the wall to the main city. The stones lay strewn about, having fallen centuries ago. In the middle of what would have been a courtyard, a large marble statue stood tall. It was of a beautiful woman. A stream wrapped around the temple, winding into the side and into the heart of the shrine.

The tall grasses disappeared and were replaced with shorter grass. Smaller stones that had crumbled off from the main structures were dotted all around. Vashe bent over and picked up one. It was smooth like marble
~~~

with dark grey veins running through it. She watched as Dseti made his way to the statue in the middle of the courtyard.

As she approached it, she noticed that the woman was even more beautiful up close. Her large eyes and small, flat nose accentuated her high cheekbones. Gold leaf decorated her hair, eyes, and lips, as well as bits of her simple dress. The feet of the statue were bare, her small, delicate feet posed as though she were taking a step forward. In ancient script, there was a little bit of text at the base of the statue. Vashe could only make out one word: Maeyu'dana. Staring at the statue, Vashe noticed that she no longer felt anxious as a sense of serenity washed over her.

"My daughter, we should probably go inside. There isn't much time before evening comes."

The Scrymmen woman looked up and saw Dseti ascending the steps of the temple. He quickly disappeared into the shrine, leaving her standing alone in the courtyard. With the absence of his presence, she noticed that the heaviness she originally felt when she first entered Enlil returning. The peacefulness that had washed over her moments before began dissipating. She raced up the steps, two at a time, after the wandering god.

Cresting the top of the temple, Vashe was greeted with the remnants of a gorgeous shrine to the first goddess. Luck had somehow preserved the inside, protecting it from the ravages of time. In the center of the open-air structure, there was a pond with crystal clear water. Two goldfish swam in lazy circles in the water, creating small ripples as they occasionally brushed the surface. The lily pads and blooms that sat on top of the pond were not overgrown or taken over by algae.

A layer of dust and dirt covered the white marble stones, muting the color of the mosaic on the floor, but it was not enough to mask the pristine stones or destroy the mosaic on the floor. Smooth columns held up the roof, barely a crack marring their surface. Light streamed in, landing on the tiles on the floor and illuminating the design: a dark-skinned woman with long, flowing hair surrounded by pink and red tiles. Her eyes were closed, with her hands held out in a welcoming embrace.

An altar on the far wall was covered in gold leaf and deep orange flowers. The image of Maeyu'dana was painted on the wall and seemed to be the only thing that had truly faded over time. Small trinkets lay at the base, offerings to the goddess from a different time. At the foot of the altar, Dseti stood, staring at the image of the goddess.

Vashe made her way over to him, admiring the beauty of the shrine with each step. Vines wrapped around the columns closest to the main walls of the city of Atunari, while green shrubs grew up untended. A jeweled dragonfly flew through the hall, the glint of the sun sending sparkles from its wings. As she approached the wandering god, she noticed his attention was solely on the image of the goddess. Eyes closed, he held his hands out towards her, tears running down his cheeks.

Her gaze dropped to the scar on his chest. His words from the night before rang in her mind. An eternity of wandering to atone for his sins.

"Give me your hand, my daughter," Dseti said, reaching out to her.

Vashe flinched. She hadn't realized that he knew she was beside him. Holding out her hand, he gently grabbed hers, holding it up towards the image like he did with his right. Taking his lead, Vashe held up her left hand.

"Close your eyes," he said. "Open your mind. I feel something, and I think that together we can push through."

Nodding, she closed her eyes and took a deep breath. As she cleared her mind, pushing all thoughts to the side, she entered the same meditative state that she used when she used her scrying pool. Vashe focused on her breathing, making sure she took slow, steady breathes. Time passed, and she began to feel a tugging in her stomach. In the corner of her mind, she noticed a tiny white spot in the blackness.

Ignoring the speck, she continued to work on her breathing. The dot grew, becoming brighter as it began filling her mind's eye until the darkness was replaced with white brilliance. A dark figure took shape in the distance, approaching slowly. The figure was slight with long, flowing hair. Despite being unable to see her features, Vashe knew that it was the goddess. The feeling of serenity she'd felt outside the temple returned as the figure drew near.

Trust the blood, the goddess said. The rich, husky tone of her voice filled Vashe with peace as Maeyu'dana's arms opened wide, as if to embrace her. *Your power lies there. Dip your vials into the pond before using it. Apophmet fears your strength, dear daughter. In order to defeat the Darkness, you must sacrifice yourself. Trust the blood.*

A pressure on her hand yanked Vashe from her trance. Opening her eyes, she saw Dseti squeezing her hand, his eyes still closed as tears ran down and his mouth moved. He whispered words she could not understand, speaking the ancient language. The serenity still surrounded Vashe as she watched the wanderer speak to his love. Moments later, he slowly opened his eyes.

"Thank you," he said. "Did you get what you needed?"

Nodding, Vashe lowered her left hand and reached into the pouch on her hip. She pulled out one of the vials of blood she took from her mother's holy chambers. "She told me that if I put the vials into the pond, something will happen. Something that would increase their power."

"Go quickly," Dseti replied. "We haven't much time. The Darkness is approaching."

Vashe made her way to the pond, Dseti and Maeyu'dana's warning about the Darkness ringing in her ears. *Both have mentioned Darkness. I must have missed something before I left. I need my horse.*

Pulling out the second vial, Vashe crouched down in front of the pond. The two goldfish stopped swimming in their lazy circles and made their way over to her, surprising Vashe. It was almost as though they were aware of what she was about to do. Closing her eyes and muttering a prayer to both

Aria and Maeyu'dana, Vashe leaned over the waters, trying to find a deep spot to dip the vials of blood into the holy pond.

As soon as the bottles entered the water, the goldfish swam over and began swimming around the two vials. Occasionally, they would create an intricate pattern in the water, almost as though they were drawing a rune. Vashe watched their movements, mesmerized by their symbols. With a gasp, she realized that they were drawing several runes.

Protection.

Power.

Purity.

Over and over, the fish traced the ancient runes around the vials of blood in between circling them. As long as they drew the symbols, Vashe kept the vials in the water. Once they finally stopped, she pulled the vials out and shook them off. Holding the dried bottles up in the light, her eye was drawn to the sunlight refracting off the glass vials and the blood inside.

"Are you going to use it?" Dseti asked as she examined the vials.

"Yes. But I need a way to keep from spilling. I've never draughted before." Pulling her mother's silver dagger from her hip, she handed the vials to Dseti. "Open one of them please. When I tell you to, pour a little on the blood. We need them to mix. Actually," she interrupted herself. Using her teeth, Vashe ripped off part of her sleeve and handed it to him as well. "After you pour it, I'll need you to wrap me too."

"I can do that."

The light from the sun, reflected off the dagger. Vashe studied her arm, trying to find the best spot to make the incision. After a while, she settled on a spot. If she needed to fight later, she needed a place that would let her still use her hands or grip a weapon. Muttering a prayer once more, she took a deep breath and cut the back of her forearm. She heard herself take in a quick breath as pain blossomed in her arm. Blood quickly began running down her arm.

"Now," she told Dseti. Uncorking one of the vials, the god carefully tipped the bottle until a few drops of blood landed on the cut. He then took the strip of cloth and bound her arm, tying a tight knot.

"Thank you," Vashe said. She felt the warmth of the blood from the vial beginning to run up her arm as it mixed with her own.

It had been a long time since Vashe had gotten her first taste of the holy blood. She forgot what it felt like. The fear of being rejected by the holy blood and doomed to live a cursed life, those thoughts came flooding back to her as she waited for the pulsating warmth to subside. But she didn't have time for that.

"Let's go," she said to Dseti. "Time is short. The Darkness is almost upon us."

XXXII

IT HAD BEEN TWO DAYS since Hroth and Maen followed Wyrd after the show at the Dancing Wolf. The man had kept a low profile, staying out of the streets, making it difficult for Hroth to keep tabs on him. However, the damage had been done. Hroth still heard talks of uprising amongst the Pshwani. Viir's group, emboldened by Len's continued absence, began causing more trouble to the people of Fa'Tinh, creating tension and panic.

Fewer and fewer people could be found wandering the streets. They only came out when they absolutely needed something. Hroth noticed that every time Pram tried to address the people of Fa'Tinh, he was met with resistance and fear. No one wanted to go against Wyrd and his newfound powers.

"What are we going to do?" Maen asked.

The two were walking back from the market under the guise of buying vegetables. With Pram and Len's mother's blessing, Hroth began bringing Maen and her children to Intan's home in hopes of keeping them safe. He and Pram still had not figured out what that creature from the other day was, but they figured that it was better to keep them all in the home instead of exposing them.

"Nothing," he replied. "It's been two days and Wyrd's keeping a low profile. He won't be doing so much longer. I wouldn't be surprised if he's actually still keeping an eye on her."

"So, we follow her until he makes his move?" Maen asked.

"The best thing we can do is watch and wait. We'll gather more information this way. Stuff we can use and bring back to Pram."

"Do you think you and the general can do anything though?" she asked. "It's been weeks since the Great Heart disappeared. People are talking about how he deserted us. My neighbors are saying that he ran away in shame, abandoning us all, because of his defeat at the hands of those Zanirian swine. He wouldn't leave us, would he?"

Hroth saw the fear in her eyes. She was beginning to believe the propaganda.

"Swordbane is an honorable man," he replied. "Otherwise, a man like Pram would not follow him with the devotion that he does. Pram is a pragmatic man. He does not blindly follow for the sake of following. Until he is concerned, I have no worry. Trust your leader. He is coming back."

Maen nodded, but her eyes reflected her doubt. Hroth didn't blame her. He'd seen too many people like her over the years. Their lives were destroyed because their lords could not properly protect them, primarily from people like Wyrd.

A woman hurried past the two, bumping into Maen with her shoulder, before flashing a worried glance behind her. She muttered a hurried apology before turning around and dashing off. Hroth glanced around and saw a few people watching the interaction from the cover of their buildings. Shopkeeps quickly averted their eyes, refusing to make eye contact with him, as he caught them watching.

"There she is," Maen whispered. "Her partner is with her."

Returning his attention to the street, Hroth saw that Maen was right. She modified her path so she could keep the two performers in sight. Hroth followed suit. The two followed Jytte and Tek down the street, the dancer carrying a large cloth bag filled with vegetables and other spices, while her partner kept close as he carried a few packages of meat.

Hroth motioned for Maen to fall back a bit to put a little more distance between the two. She did so easily, keeping pace with the Flame. Hroth was impressed with how quickly she picked up his cues, and without question. He found himself glancing at her out of the corner of his eye and smiling. She was quiet and blended into crowds easily.

A subtle change in the air caught his attention. The hairs on his arms stood on end. His eyes darted side to side, frantically trying to find the source of his discomfort. After several tense seconds, he finally found it. Coming towards him from a side street, Wyrd quickly traveled down the road, turning abruptly until he fell into step behind the two performers. His attentions were solely on the young woman as she walked with her companion. Hroth noted that orange lines, almost like veins, were moving up his left arm. Like a blood tattoo.

Strange, he thought. *It's almost as though his power is growing. Like the Fyre is taking control of him.* He motioned for Maen to slow down a little more, putting distance between them and Wyrd. They walked in silence, Maen almost casually. Hroth's mind tried to figure out the significance of the Qu'ari's change.

Alazi.

Hroth stopped in the middle of the street as he made that revelation. Maen, Wyrd, and the two stalked performers quickly began to disappear. Maen happened to glance to her side and noticed that Hroth was no longer walking with her. She spun around until she noticed him behind her. The young woman began walking toward the Flame. Blinking, Hroth finally acknowledged her approach.

"We have to go back," he muttered, an uncharacteristic urgency in his tone.

"But he'll get them," Maen hissed. "We can't just leave them. You saw him shooting fire like a madman the other night."

Hroth glanced at the two, hurrying along, unaware of the threat nearby. His chest tightened and a lump formed in his throat as he tried to push down the unfamiliar emotion that tugged at him. With a gulp, the Flame grabbed her hand.

"Go," he instructed. "Take them and go down a side street." Maen opened her mouth to reply, but he gave her a squeeze and continued on. "Find a place where they can stay, not either of their homes. Once they're safe, head to Intan's house."

"My home is not too far from here. I can hide them there," Maen said. "What are you going to do?"

"Something I probably should've done a while ago," he admitted with a sigh. "I wasn't prepared the first time, but this time I at least know that he's more capable than I anticipated. I can only imagine that he'll be stronger now."

Maen turned to face him before giving him a hug. "Be safe," she whispered into his ear. Breaking apart, she gave his hands a squeeze before darting off to the safety of a side street.

Hroth waited until she was out of sight before using his Flame energies to create a large fireball in his hand. Taking careful aim, he threw the ball, launching it towards Wyrd at great speed. As the ball traveled through the air, it expanded in size until it was the size of a melon. The ball exploded just above Wyrd's head, as anticipated, sending a shower of stone and splintered wood down on him. Wyrd swore as he dove to the side, his arms over his head for protection as others nearby screamed in panic.

Go! Hroth urged Maen, hoping that she would take the opportunity to grab the two performers amidst the screams and falling rubble.

"You dare attack me, Flicker?" Wyrd spat. "Didn't you learn how futile it was the last time?"

Hroth bit back his anger at being called a Flicker once more. He didn't need to prolong the fight too much. He just needed to keep it up until he could find a place to hide. Keeping the plan in his head, Hroth began growing another fireball in his hand.

"I guess I'm a bit slow," he replied, forcing his gravelly voice to remain calm and even. "To be honest, I'm just tired of you and your followers terrorizing these people."

"What do you care?" Wyrd sneered. "All you're here for is money. You mercenaries are no better than Viir or his people."

Hroth watched as Maen spoke rapidly to Jytte and Tek as they took shelter in a doorframe. Grabbing Jytte's hand, she pulled the woman up and took off down the street, Tek following behind. Relief began to wash over him, but the Flame knew that he couldn't let his guard down now that Wyrd was angry. He turned his attention back to Wyrd, the man's orange eye flashing in the sun.

As the ball in his hand reached the size of a grapefruit, Hroth brought it up and motioned to throw it. Wyrd reacted to the ball of flame by bringing up his hands, palms facing out, creating a wall of flame between himself and the approaching ball. Anticipating a defensive maneuver, Hroth pulled on the tail of the fireball, turning it into a whip-like weapon. Snapping his arm, the flame whip snapped in Wyrd's direction, striking the shield.

Wyrd grunted in pain as the heat from the two flames slammed into each other. Hroth struggled to keep the fire whip in a physical form as long as possible before it dissipated. His eyes scanned the streets, looking for a way to escape. A cry of surprise escaped his lips as a ball of fire flew his way, causing him to release the whip and jump to the side to avoid being hit. The heat of the ball went right over his head, crashing into a building behind him. The wooden flowerbed under the window caught fire, the wood crackling as the flames began spreading. Black smoke began rising to the heavens as a second fire ball was launched at Hroth by Wyrd.

Diving to the right, Hroth jammed his elbow into the cobblestones, sending a wave of pain up his arm and into his neck. He attempted to roll onto his side, but only managed to flatten onto his back before a third ball came speeding where his head had been. The heat burned intensely as the god-enhanced flames barely missed him. Fires were popping up everywhere the fireballs hit, sending up plumes of black smoke and screams of panic.

From his time wandering the streets, Hroth knew that if he could just get to his feet, there was a side street close by where he could take a few turns and loop back around, hopefully losing the crazed man. He hoped that he'd bought Maen and the other two enough time. Rocking onto his back, Hroth launched himself onto his feet by pushing with his hands against the stones. As he did so, he engulfed his hands with flames so that as soon as his feet touched the ground, he began throwing ball after ball of fire towards Wyrd.

Wyrd brought his arms in front of him in a defensive posture as he braced himself for the onslaught. Hroth made sure to give his throws a bit of curve to keep Wyrd guessing where the next one would land. With each throw, Hroth gradually made his way to the right. With grunts of exertion accompanying each throw, he inched his way closer to safety. Until finally, with one massive blast, he shot out a pillar of flame from both hands in Wyrd's direction, engulfing the man in fire. He waited several long seconds before dropping his hands and dashing down the side street.

Screams still filled the air as people struggled to put out the fires destroying their shops and homes. As he raced through the streets, turning sharply several times in an effort to confuse his opponent, he heard Wyrd let you a primal yell of rage. A wall of flame towered into the sky. A shiver ran down Hroth's spine as he jumped down from a stone wall.

To Maen's, he thought. *Then to Pram.*

XXXIII

S CHAED SLIPPED into the Gilded Rose, finding a wall covered in sunlight, and sat down with his back against it. He hadn't slept at all since he'd crept out of his wine cellar. He'd spent the entire night cowering in the back corner between the barrels of wine. It had been the longest night of his life. The creature left at some point, but he never figured out exactly when. It was only when he heard bustling in the street that he knew the creature had gone and day had come. He had survived.

Rez'maré began walking over to his table, but paused when she saw the lanky man. With a sigh, she sauntered over, a bored expression on her face. "What do you want?" she asked. Schaed shook his head and motioned for her to lean in closer. A look of disgust crossed her face as she took in his disheveled appearance. "By the gods, Schaed," she exclaimed, "you're a mess. What happened to you?"

"Something bad has happened, Maré," he whispered, his voice frantic. "I saw something last night, and, oh gods, Maré."

"Take a deep breath," she told him. "I can't understand anything you're saying."

Closing his eyes, Schaed forced himself to take several deep breaths. He ran his hands through his hair, his fingers getting caught on snags. Schaed shook his fingers through his hair, trying to free them from the tangles.

"Maré," he said slowly, deliberately. "We have to find Oldar, someone. Alocar is in trouble, and we need to do something."

"What do you mean?" she asked, slipping into a nearby chair.

"Last night, I saw Oldar's uncle bring in a group of monsters, I think he called them the Faceless. I don't remember. These creatures, they can travel through the shadows, but they also have a physical form. I sent a warning to Oldar, but I haven't heard back. Erth hasn't returned. Well, I haven't been home since."

"What?" Rez'maré began.

"One attacked me in my home," Schaed continued. "I somehow managed to hide, but, by the gods, Maré. I don't know what this means, but it can't be good. We need to get out of here. Find somewhere safe."

"Gods, Schaed," Rez'maré whispered, her hand covering her mouth. "You can't be serious?"

"You've heard about the people they've been finding dead this morning. How do you explain that?"

"I can't," she replied, shaking her head. "But Schaed, even if we do leave, what do you think will happen? We can't hide forever, and with Alastaire acting as regent until Oldar comes back, it's not like we can exactly claim sanctuary. Who would believe us?"

Schaed buried his face in his hands as he tried to think. He was exhausted. He hadn't slept more than a few naps in the last few days. Nowhere felt safe, except his cellar where he could hide amongst the earthy wines. Schaed rubbed his eyes with the heel of his palms, trying to force himself to focus.

"It doesn't matter right now," he said after a while. "All that matters is that we get out and find somewhere safe to hide. We can deal with the rest later."

"We need a plan other than hiding," Rez'maré insisted. "Besides, I'm sure there's a logical reason behind all of this. Oldar's uncle probably heard that the king had stepped away, just like last time, and has offered to keep an eye on Alocar until Oldar returns. Maybe you just saw some shadows while you were hallucinating and it all turned into a bad dream. There has to be something more to this."

"Dammit Maré!" he hissed, slamming his hands on the table. The few people in the tavern turned his direction at the sudden noise. Shooting them a wan smile, he returned his attentions to Rez'maré and said in a low voice, "Maré, you know I wouldn't make something like this up. Please, you have to believe me."

Rez'maré bit her bottom lip as she thought about all he said. Her eyes avoided his gaze as she was suddenly unable to look at him. "I'm sorry, Schaed," she said, barely more than a whisper. "I just can't." She stood up and began walking away.

"Maré!" he said, grabbing her hand. Her eyes locked onto his, and he could see the pain behind them. She wanted to believe him, but he knew that she couldn't. He'd messed up one too many times.

"I think you better go," she said, wiping her eyes. "Goodbye, Schaed."

Schaed watched as Rez'maré disappeared to another part of the tavern. He watched her for a few moments before getting up and walking out the door. The Gilded Rose used to be a place where he felt comfortable, but now, his only sanctuary turned him away. For the first time in his life, Schaed was unsure of what the future held.

XXXIV

THE RYDASH GORGE LOOMED in the horizon, the red clay earth and peat moss providing a welcome sight for the forces of Pharn. They were getting closer to the capital of Xan. Alverick's body ached from the days of riding and walking, not to mention sleeping on the hard ground. All of it coupled with his previous adventures left him feeling sore all over. *The life of a soldier*, he'd mused on more than one occasion. *Always the most comfortable accommodations and best of food.* It always brought a chuckle whenever he remembered Bannen's old phrase.

He'd seen Bannen a couple of times since his meeting in Themba. Every time, he'd felt a surge of excitement at seeing his old friend. The prospect of sharing another conversation left him full of hope. However, their last discussion also left him feeling empty. The Avalanche struggled to accept that the Bannen he now saw was all in his mind. After the last few days, he felt more alone than he had in the abyss.

Brody jogged over. Alverick couldn't find it in him to be happy to see his friend. Despite Brody's efforts to engage him, Alverick's trek through the Land of Warriors left him wanting to stay in Themba instead of returning to Corinth. Only Caitlyn's presence seemed to keep him grounded.

"Al, how are you doing?" Brody asked. "I could really use some help figuring out what our next move should be. You know the gorge better than anyone here. Should we be worried of an ambush?"

Alverick looked at Brody, staring through his eyes and into his soul. Brody tried so hard, but Alverick couldn't bring himself to believe him.

You have as much information about the gorge as I do.

"I think we should be fine. I don't think they are expecting us, but we should probably still send in perimeter guards. I think Caitlyn and Cienna would be a good team, and maybe one more pair to take the left flank."

Brody nodded energetically, rubbing his hands together. "That's a good point. With all of the internal chaos, aid from a former enemy is probably the last thing they're thinking about."

You don't need me. You're doing just fine.

"You've really grown," Alverick said. "Bannen would be so proud of you." Brody grinned, his boyish gleam sparkling in his eyes. "Have you thought of how you want to address Swordbane? I can't imagine that he'd be receptive to your help. You'd almost want to make sure you emphasize the fact that we're here to help, not push."

Jaste said to honor our word. Your charisma will get you far.

"You're right, Al," Brody replied. "When we first made the alliance in the gorge, he was not willing to bow. I just need to show him that he can keep his dignity while asking for our help. Do you think we'll be in trouble if a rebellion breaks out while we're there?"

"No. The Qu'ari are their strongest fighters. As long as he can control his clan, the threat shouldn't be too bad."

The edge of the gorge lay ahead. Alverick and Brody stopped. The Avalanche watched as Brody walked up the very edge and scanned the terrain down below. The younger man took in the various ambush points and exit routes, making sure he had an escape plan for any situation.

Brody really has grown. I'm not needed anymore.

As the rest of the force approached the precipice, Brody motioned for them to close in so he didn't have to yell. It took a while, but the remaining soldiers marched up to the waiting group. Alverick observed from the side as Brody found a large rock and jumped on top of it.

"All right everyone," he shouted. "Let's break for lunch and cross the gorge once the sun's passed midday. We should be able to get comfortably through the gorge and find a nice spot on the other side to set up camp. If my calculations are correct, we should be at their capital by tomorrow."

An excited rumble broke out from the tired, hungry crowd. Alverick pulled Styx away from the group and tied her to a tree. Pulling out some rations from his saddlebag, he nibbled on some dried meat as he leaned against the tree. Plopping down, he dropped his water skin at his feet and closed his eyes as he rested.

"Here," Caitlyn's voice sounded in front of him.

Without opening his eyes, Alverick held out his hand and wrapped his fingers around the bowl she proffered. Cracking open his eye, he saw a couple pieces of flatbread and fruit. His mouth watered at the sight of the simple meal. Between his personal rations and the meal in front of him, he was going to be feeling good once he finished.

"Thanks," he mumbled.

"Everything okay?" the redhead asked as she sat down next to him.

Alverick shook his head. "I need to clear my mind."

Closing his eye, Alverick leaned back against the tree once more with a sigh and let his mind wander. His body throbbed, but as he rested, he felt himself melt into the ground. A slight pressure encircled his hand, giving it a squeeze. Alverick could hear Caitlyn breathe deeply as she sat down next to him. Her presence had always been enough to help him relax in the past.

His breathing slowed as darkness filled his mind. Before he knew it, he found himself walking through a field in the middle of the night. The twisted trunk of a dead tree reached out, threatening to snag any who walked by with its spindly twigs. Alverick felt a surge of excitement as he traveled in the darkness. He really wanted to see Bannen again.

I can't keep focusing on Bannen, he told himself for the hundredth time. No matter how hard he tried, however, he knew that he could never push Bannen from his mind.

Alverick moved through the night, the only source of light coming from the sliver of the moon hanging overhead. It was frequently blocked by thick clouds, plunging his surroundings into darkness. His nerves began to get the better of him as he realized that, just like when he was in Themba, there was no sound to herald life nearby. Alverick tapped into his Avalanche energies to see if he could feel anything moving, but again, he could not.

I must be in Themba again.

The prospect excited him. Alverick wanted to see the king. He was surprised to find that he also wanted to speak to Vialle again. There were so many questions he had after their meeting, so many answers only she could provide. Alverick tried to find any landmarks to let him know he was on the right path to the Hall. However, in the minimal light nothing looked familiar. He thought that he was near the ruins at one point, but he ended up not recognizing anything as the gnarled trees closed in on him.

After what felt like hours, Alverick began to give up hope that he would find the Halls of the Fallen or anyone to talk to. A tree stump next to a thick, knotted tree provided Alverick with a respite from his exertions. Even in the Land of the Warriors, his body ached. Burying his face in his hands, the Avalanche tried to clear his mind and figure out where he was.

"What's going on?" Alverick mumbled into his hands. "I thought I was so close. Dammit."

Time passed slowly as Alverick sat by the ancient tree. Several slow-moving clouds passed over the crescent moon, blocking the light and plunging the area in darkness. All of this went unnoticed as the Avalanche sat motionless on his stump. No sound pierced the night. No owls hooted. No insects chirped. Not even the nearby grass so much as rustled. Everything around him was dead.

As the moon reached its zenith, a sense of foreboding fell over the area. Alverick finally lifted his head from his hands as the sinister blanket engulfed him. Cold sweat broke out on his brow and hands as he began looking around for the source of the threat. Reaching out with his Avalanche energies once more, Alverick could not pick up any vibrations in the earth.

What's going on? He asked himself, his voice catching in his throat and unable to come out. *This is the same feeling I had when the Grey Man was nearby. I think Vahnyre and Alazi felt the same way. It's almost as though it's the power of the aethren.*

Alverick cautiously got off of his stump and pressed himself against the thick, gnarled trunk of the tree he was seated next to. Through the tangle of branches, Alverick dared to peek out into the distance. He couldn't see it when he was seated on the stump because of the massive jumble of branches, but standing up, he could see a clearing a little way off.

Moonlight once again kissed the area as a cloud finally passed by. In the light, Alverick could make out the slight form of a little girl. He moved to help her, but something held him back. As he took a closer look at the girl, he noticed that she had periwinkle hair, and that her skin was very fair under her cream-colored dress.

Movement from the clearing caught his attention as the little girl struggled to push herself up. Her obsidian eyes appeared glazed over. A trickle of blood ran down from her forehead, as well as out of the corner of her mouth. Small cuts and bruises covered her arms. With great effort, Alverick watched as the child pushed herself up to her feet, her body swaying as she took a couple staggering steps.

A sudden jolt from his naval pulled at him. His surroundings disappeared in an instant, the body of the little girl becoming a pale dot in the darkness, as he was dragged back to the first twisted tree he saw when he first entered the land. Just as suddenly as it came on, it stopped. Alverick opened his eyes and shut them quickly as the light from the sun nearly blinded him. Tears formed at the corners of his clenched eyes from his pain.

On the side of his temples, Alverick felt a gentle touch. Gradually, he opened one eye, then the other, as he sought to acclimate them to the sun's brilliance. A figure stood in front of him, her moss green hair flowing down her back. Zemé stared deeply into Alverick's eyes, her hands resting gently on either side of his head, just like she had when they first met in the main hall at Caer Grey.

Her hands trembled as she lightly touched his skin, her eyes staring off in the distance. Tears rolled down her cheeks as her lips quivered. Pulling herself from the depths of his mind, the goddess locked eyes with the Avalanche.

"I have to go," Zemé whispered. "Freyna needs me. Something's happened to her and she needs my help. Get to Fa'Tinh before it's too late. I'll join you if I can."

"Wait!" Alverick called out.

He watched in shock as the goddess faded away until there was nothing in front of him. Alverick turned to Caitlyn to see what she thought, but the redhead sat by his side, eating some of her rations as she watched Cienna and Brody talking to the side. She didn't even seem to notice that the goddess was gone.

"Cait!" Alverick cried, trying to shake her shoulder. Caitlyn sat motionless, still watching everything around her. "Cait!" He tried to catch her attention by shaking her. He thought he was touching her shoulder, but to his dismay saw that it actually seemed to go through her body, as though he no longer had any physical form. "What's going on?"

An eerie silence surrounded him, just like it had in Themba. Dead, gnarled trees began appearing around the camp as darkness crept in. The afternoon sun disappeared, replaced by a sliver of moon in the late-night sky. Alverick jumped up, twisting around to see if anyone else noticed what was going on. His fellow soldiers were no longer around. All he could see were Caitlyn, Cienna, and Brody. The princess and her guard looked hazy, as if he were viewing them through a dirty window.

"Brody!" he called out. The young soldier and the princess shared a smile, their bodies almost gone as the haze engulfed them. Turning to the archer, Alverick felt a wave of relief wash over him as she still sat where she had been, her body still in focus.

A circle appeared, clouding everything around her. Like his comrades, it fuzzed her surroundings, but somehow, she still appeared normal. The darkness intensified as a cloud covered the moon once more. In that instance, Alverick was back in Themba. Caitlyn seemed frozen in time as she sat eating her rations.

"What's happening?" he asked the emptiness. Alverick spun around, trying to find something to give him a landmark.

Nothing looked familiar.

Crouching down, Alverick grabbed at his head as he screamed into the night. He knew he should have been quiet, but his emotions pressed against him from every pore until he could not contain the energy swirling around inside. He was spent. His body was exhausted from everything he'd undergone the last month, and his mind was torn, barely holding together by a thread. He just wanted to find a hole and crawl into it.

"I'm done," he whispered. "I just want to die."

A solitary tear rolled down Alverick's cheek. Darkness crept in, quietly blanketing him as he hunched over. The trees loomed over him, threatening to wrap him in their spindly branches.

"Al."

A familiar baritone called out to Alverick in the blackness. The Avalanche ignored him.

"Al."

The voice called again, more insistent.

"Remember your Anchor," the voice said. "Both of us."

Alverick's head snapped up. "Bannen?"

Bannen walked over and placed a hand on Alverick's back. "Al, you need to go back."

A second figure walked out of the darkness. Alverick's jaw dropped as the Grey Man accompanied Bannen, stopping in front of the Avalanche.

"Go back, Avalanche," Thuul commanded. "You've done me a great service, and I won't let you falter. You save my sister, and I owe you a boon. Apophos has tried to break you, but you are strong. Take this gift and return to your world. My brother will be informed of your actions."

The god handed Alverick a small ball of gold that shone brightly in the darkness. As it touched his hand, his body was filled with a warmth that washed away his pain. His mind was still in tatters, but there was a light that filled in some of the dark spaces, bringing him a little clarity, just like Zemé had.

"Al?" Caitlyn's voice broke through the blackness. "Hey, Al."

The golden ball in his hand glowed brighter as her voice became stronger. Alverick stood up. With a surge of brightness, the golden ball melted into his flesh. The light went down his arm until his whole body was engulfed. Once the last of him was covered by the golden light, everything became so blinding that he needed to close his eyes.

He opened them a moment later and found himself sitting under the tree in the middle of the camp. Men bustled around, cleaning up the camp without much urgency. Thol stood by some of the younger recruits, berating them for their lackadaisical attitude to their duties. Some more seasoned soldiers waited off to the side, watching the exchange and laughing. Ronan stood over by Brody and the princess, grinning at the older man as he chastised the younger ones.

"Are you okay?" Caitlyn asked, squeezing Alverick's knee. "You looked a little lost there for a moment."

Alverick's eyes landed on the redhead, concern etched into her face. A light breeze blew by, rustling their hair sending a few leaves dancing across the grass. He could have sworn that he heard Bannen's voice telling him to live as the leaves went by.

"Yes, I think I was just lost in thought."

"Well, Brody called for camp to clear up a little while ago. Why don't you get Styx while I clean up over here?"

Alverick looked down at his plate of practically untouched food. As if she sensed his thoughts, Caitlyn picked it up and began wrapping the food in a cloth to take with them. She hummed a little tune as she packed everything up. Out of the corner of his eye, he noticed Brody weaving his way through the camp. The young man stopped to talk to soldiers occasionally, but most of the time it was to give a few words before continuing on.

Catching his eye, Brody made his way over to Alverick as he still sat on the grass. Though he smiled as he greeted the Avalanche, Alverick noted that Brody's gaze was troubled.

"All right there?" Brody asked, helping Alverick up from the ground.

Alverick took the young man's proffered hand and finally forced himself to get up. The pair walked over to Styx as they made preparations to enter the gorge. He remembered the last time they stood at the edge of the precipice. Down below, an army of skilled warriors were waking up. Among them, a demon. Like last time, Alverick and Brody were bringing the fight to the clansmen. This time, however, they were far fewer in number. He didn't blame the young man for his hesitation.

"It brings back a lot of memories, doesn't it?" Alverick asked, skirting the question.

Brody nodded.

"This time will be different," Alverick said. "We'll be facing a much smaller force. They'll have no choice but to surrender quickly."

"Gods I hope you're right," Brody replied. "If they're as stubborn as that Swordbane, we're going to have our work cut out for us."

Alverick stared out over the gorge. Fa'Tinh was maybe a day's ride. Assuming they didn't have any trouble crossing the valley, of course. Reaching out with his Avalanche energies, he didn't feel anything nearby. It gave him hope that he could still feel his friends and brothers-at-arms, unlike when he was in Themba. It was a small comfort, but it was enough.

A pillar of fire shot into the air a long way off. Both Alverick and Brody shouted in alarm. It was followed shortly after by a bunch of smaller bursts in quick succession. The two shared a glance as they watched this display of power.

"Let's camp here tonight and come up with a plan of attack," Alverick said. "I don't want to go into a Flame war unprepared."

Brody agreed and ran off to spread the word to the rest of the camp. Alverick continued to watch the flames until they abruptly stopped moments later. Big things were going on if the goddess Zemé had to run off. And if the inhabitants of Themba were getting involved, it couldn't be good. The Darkness was closing in quickly, and Alverick had no idea how to stop it. With Oldar and any help he might have brought gone, it wouldn't hurt them to wait a little longer to figure out their next step.

XXXV

L EN STALKED back to his room. His arm ached having not fully recovered from the attack on Pharn. The battle with the *Silver Maiden* the day before had really aggravated his wound, causing him to spend most of his time in his room to avoid anyone seeing him hurt. Slinking down onto his mat, Len took off his shirt and examined his arm. The wound hadn't reopened, but there was dark bruising all over his bicep. With a grunt, he lifted his arm and rotated it, testing his mobility.

At least I can still move it without too much difficulty. I need to rest up before we get back home if I'm going to stand any chance against Wyrd.

He laid back on his mat with his arms behind his head and closed his eyes. The wood from the boards of the boat, though worn down from the bodies who lain there before him, still made it difficult for the young general to relax. They were making great time. Kayna called it riding the wind, but he took it to mean that the wind was pushing them forward instead of them fighting the wind for progress.

His mind wandered to his family. Zaa'ni and Bermet, his wife's large belly peeking through her fine silks, smiled at him. Bermet waved energetically as she giggled silently, calling him over to her. A soft wind blew around them, kicking up pale blue petals. The petals swirled around them, encircling them.

Behind his family, a small blue-haired girl spun around. Len felt his breath catch in his chest as he watched the goddess dance around his wife and daughter. Freyna made eye contact with him and her smile faltered as they locked gaze. Her hair flowed about her as if she were underwater. She held up one finger and shook her head pointedly.

What does it mean?

Freyna pointed up to the sky behind her. Overhead, Toron's moon hung full and bright, a red ring glowing around it.

The blood moon. That's only a cycle away. Not even three days' time. Will Wyrd gain greater power then? I have to get back home.

Len pressed his palms over his eyes as he let out a sigh. "How did I end up here?"

I am the Great Heart, yet these people make demands of me. Well, I suppose one is a god, so that can be overlooked. Len smirked as he wondered how he'd become entangled in the affairs of gods. *I'm destined for more than the seer foretold. The bones have been cast. Now, we wait.*

A soft knock on the door startled him and he snapped his eyes open. A second, louder knock followed. With a grunt, Len pushed himself up onto his elbow. "What do you want?"

The door opened and Maya walked in. "I thought you might need this," she said as she sat down next to him, a jar with cream-colored salve and cloth in her hand.

"I'm fine," Len grumbled as he sat up. "I don't need anything."

"It'll help your arm," she replied.

"I said I don't –"

"You risk infection if you don't treat this," Maya insisted. "You may not be bleeding, but look at the discoloration." Her hand traced over the bruising on his arm. "If this is weeks old, it should be getting lighter. It's not."

"My healers have looked at it."

"Obviously not close enough. Let me use this. It has an herb that you mainlanders haven't discovered. It's great for treating infections."

Len pulled his arm away. "What kind of herb?" he asked as he stared at her.

Maya delicately brought his arm back towards her. With the jar in between her legs, she unscrewed the lid and placed it on the floor. "I'm from out east," she explained. "A place called Tallanun, over the horizon. We have a purple blossom called halothis. Our people aren't god-blessed like your people out here, so our warriors rely on their natural abilities to keep them alive in battle. Since our healers aren't god-blessed, they spent centuries finding ways to treat infection. Up in the mountains, they found the halothis and discovered its ability to treat infection, among other things. We've been cultivating it ever since. I'd almost say it's just as effective as your god gifts."

As she spoke, she gently rubbed the salve onto his arm, making sure to cover up the bruising and closed gash with a thin layer. Len watched as her fingers moved in circles over his arm. A slight tingle shot up his arm and he felt the bruised area become warm.

"It's fast," he noted.

"It's incredible. If the area gets hot and stays that way for a day, you'll want to reapply some more and see a healer. That's usually a bad sign of infection, but as long as you keep using it you should be okay. We didn't have a lot of people lose limbs when they used it. Although, normally we rub the milk of the herb directly on the wound. But I've never had any issues."

"How often have you had to use it?"

Unlacing her bodice, Maya loosened it enough so she could lift up her blouse. Underneath her breasts, a long, thin scar marred her body. "Before I met Kayna, I ran into someone who fancied themselves a member of the pirate council. He was just a piece of shite who terrorized people for money. And pleasure. Jylla actually killed him for his actions." She let out a snort. "Imagine that scum passing judgement on someone for derelict behaviors. But, no one opposed him, and the council even gave Jylla their blessing.

"Anyway, that shite wouldn't take no for an answer and ran me through outside our local tavern. Hurt like hell, too. From what I remember, someone took me to a shaman and they covered me in halothis milk. Never had any infection, but I was in and out for a span because of the blood loss. I think it healed pretty well though. Looked like it does now by the end of the span."

Maya ran Len's hand over the scar. As his fingers traced the thin line, they brushed against her breast. Her hand stopped guiding his and she started screwing the lid back onto the salve jar. The young general's hands lingered where she had been holding him a moment before. A flush of excitement filled him, the thrill and anticipation almost overwhelming him. A moment later, he pulled his hand away and rested them against his thighs.

Once she'd finished tightening the lid, she placed the jar down and laced up her bodice once more. Len watched as her fingers nimbly tied the strings, cinching her waist. His arm was still warm, but it no longer tingled.

I may have to find a way to open trade for this halothis. This would be a great boon to my people.

Len rotated and flexed his arm, distracting himself while Maya finished lacing herself. He found himself pleasantly surprised as his arm no longer ached as much as it had. There was still pain, but it was dulled as the herb's milk worked its magic.

"Maybe you did need my help," she said as she held out the cloth for him.

Len took the proffered cloth and began wrapping his arm with it, pulling it tightly with his teeth as he tied the knot. "Perhaps. Thank you."

"I can leave the jar with you to apply later," Maya offered. Moving to stand up, she placed one of her hands on his leg, high up on his thigh.

The young general grabbed her hand and pulled her back down. "What are you trying to pull?"

Maya flashed a coy smile. "Nothing. I just want to make sure you don't die because of your own arrogance. The Scourge has big plans for you. I might as well do my part to make it worth your while to stay."

"I need to head back. My people need me. We had a deal."

Maya pulled her arm out of his grasp and stood up. "I understand." With another smile, she slunk out of the room.

Len lay back on his mat with a sigh. "Damn, that woman is going to be the death of me."

~~

Up on the deck Dez stood staring out into the great blue sea. Her chocolate hair, tied in a high tail, fluttered about as the wind blew around her. A smile played on her face as she closed her eyes to avoid getting sea spray in them. The sun shone down on her, keeping her pleasantly warm as the cold ocean water splashed up and droplets hit her face.

"This life suits you, Sister," Angh said.

"Yes," Dez replied, her eyes still closed. "I never knew peace like this before. It's a shame we have to head back so quickly."

The Second Brother placed his arm on Dez's shoulder. Dez felt a tranquility within that she knew must come from the goddess inside her. It made her happy to see Aria so at ease after all they'd been through. The two had a long talk in her room while they were making their way to meet Jylla. Aria and Dez spent countless hours in quiet solitude trying to remember the lost parts of their lives. They had yet to discuss the future.

Dez could not bring herself to ask the goddess about what lay in store. She spent most of her life not worrying about what was ahead. Now, she had to find a way to come to terms with whatever the future held.

"Are you happy?" he asked.

Both Dez and Aria were surprised by the question. Dez knew that the goddess was happy. She'd finally reunited with her brother, and she knew that her younger brother would be okay once they'd returned to their home. Aria radiated peace, which spread to Dez. However, Dez could not be sure that she was.

"You ask a loaded question," Dez replied. "One of us is. The other cannot say. Let's not worry about that right now though. Vahnyre has transferred some of his essence over to a mortal, and we must figure out how to draw out that power."

The two fell silent. *Graak's Fury* dipped and bobbed on the open sea, large waves crashing against her hull and sending up spray. Men worked to keep her course steady on the choppy waters. The sails whipped around, their fabric snapping loudly in the afternoon air. Those who did not have anything to do lounged about on the deck drinking ale or eating strips of dried meat. No one seemed bothered that their captain blinded a man the day prior. It was all part of their normal life, one similar to the life that Dez left in Scrymme over a century ago.

Her mind wandered to the young Xanan general. Both Dez and Aria could see how troubled he was; his mind and heart were split in two.

Where is he? Dez wondered.

He can't have gotten far, Aria mused.

Oh, you're terrible, Dez replied with a smile on her lips. *By the powers, I'm going to miss you.*

What do you mean? Aria asked.

Dez did not respond. Instead, she crossed her arms over her chest and stared out at the horizon. The sky was bright, the soft white clouds moving quickly through the heavens. Gulls circled the ship, calling out to each other. Occasionally, she would see one dive into the ocean for a bit of fish. Ahead of the *Fury*, Dez spotted a few dolphins jumping out of the water as they played with the ship. The Tempest smiled in wonder as she watched the foreign creatures interact with the ship.

She watched them for a long time, never losing interest in the dolphins riding the surf. The wind blew in her face, cooling her off from the midday heat. As the day went on, the winds began picking up. In the distance, Dez noticed a patch of darkness growing. The change in weather caught her attention, as well as that of several of the crewmen. Angh also appeared to notice. The pirate lord walked over to the ledge and rested his hands on the railing as he stared out into the distance. Dez noticed the tension in his posture and walked over.

"Rough waters ahead?" she asked.

"No," he murmured. "This is much worse."

Both Dez and Aria perked up at the tone in his voice.

This is bad, Aria said. **Someone is not happy.**

The clouds ahead stretched out along the horizon as the original bunch took on the form of a dark figure. Men on the deck cried out, some shouting about the Dark Man, and raced to their posts in an effort to tie down any loose ropes or move things below deck. The winds picked up, whipping around them, the Scourge's coat tails flapping next to Dez.

"Everyone below deck!" he called out. "We're in for some rough waters."

Dez felt her heart jump to her chest. He just told her that was not the case. Her mind raced as she tried to guess at how wild things were about to become.

"Stay here, Sister," Angh said, his voice softer so the others wouldn't hear. "You're about to be reunited with an old friend."

The ship sailed under the dark expanse, the winds tearing at the sails. Barrels began sliding across the deck as the waves rocked the boat. Dez gripped the railing and tried to widen her stance so she could maintain her balance. The air became cold as the sun disappeared behind the clouds. Angh grabbed her hand and pulled her away from the side of the ship.

The god led her to the forecastle so they could be at the highest point of the ship. Dez looked around, trying to figure out why he was not taking them below the ship. Surely, they couldn't be actually speaking to someone.

The winds howled around them. Dez thought she could hear a multitude of voices whispering around her. Angh stood in the middle of the forecastle, his eyes closed, seemingly untroubled by the rocking of the ship or the strength of the winds. He nodded his head on occasion, as though he was listening to someone speak. Dez followed his lead and closed her eyes, opening herself to the voices she thought she could hear.

The balance is broken. You must head back. Vahnyre has gone too far and the Ancients are coming. Darkness awaits. Follow the Qu'ari and keep him safe. He is favored by Freyna.

Dez gasped, her eyes still closed, as she heard the news.

"So, it's true," she said, her voice being carried away in the gusts. "You were right."

What we heard in Pharn was true, Aria replied. **If Graak says the balance is broken, then things are worse than we could've imagined.**

"Graak?" Dez asked.

Eldest brother of Ayr. He prefers to stay isolated from everything. If he's bringing us a warning, things are dire.

Zemé and Thuul are with Freyna. She got caught by Apophmet speaking with the queen of Zanir, and was punished for meddling with the balance. He disregards Vahnyre's actions. I will not stand by any longer. Re'nukhtet is struggling. We must do our part. The Darkness is coming.

"What can we do?" Angh called out. "We are stuck here in the middle of the sea. Time is almost out."

I will provide you with favorable winds. You should arrive on the shore by nightfall, if you handle the waters, Ghan.

"Thank you, Graak," Angh said. "Take care of Freyna."

The sky began to clear and the winds died down. Angh held out his arms to calm the seas and stop the waves from slamming into the *Fury*. In front of her eyes, Dez watched as the sails were suddenly filled and the boat lurched forward.

"Man the helm," Angh said as he stood with his arms outstretched, parting the water for the ship to pass through. "Let's get her home."

Dez ran over to the giant wheel and gripped it tightly. The helm tried to turn as the rudder caught on underwater currents, but she held on tightly. Graak's form and the rest of his clouds quickly disappeared into the horizon as the *Fury* sped towards Thyllasis.

XXXVI

THE MIDDAY SUN SHONE brightly on the streets of Madden. Oldar shielded his eyes as he stepped out of the underground tunnels of Ånchal and onto the smooth cobbled streets of his home. His body felt invigorated after falling asleep the night before and he walked with a spring to his step. The king whistled a tune as he traveled through the streets towards Castle Storm. His merriment was short-lived, however.

The streets were uncharacteristically empty. The usually-bustling streets only had a handful of people traveling down them despite it being midday, during what should be the height of traffic.

Oldar quickly became uneasy. Those who did walk by kept their heads down, hurrying to their destinations without stopping for casual conversation. Only those who traveled close enough to the king gave a quick nod before hurrying on their way. Oldar tried to find a soldier on duty, but couldn't see anyone in Alocar livery. That didn't help his discomfort.

A tall figure in a brown cloak quickly approached the young king, their head down and a large rucksack slung over their back. A sheet of blonde hair fell out from the hood of the cloak, but the figure tucked it back behind their ear the moment it was exposed. A silver ring with a blood red stone was displayed as the traveler's hand was peeked out from the brown cloak. The sun caught the light of the gem, catching Oldar's eyes. It seemed very familiar.

"Schaed?" Oldar called out tentatively. He hoped his friend lay under the cloak. There was so much he needed to talk about.

The cloaked form slowed down and looked up. Relief and then fear washed over Schaed's face as he saw the king. His mouth dropped and Oldar was pretty sure he saw his friend readjust his grip on the rucksack to keep it from falling as well.

"Oldar," Schaed said in a hushed voice as he pulled Oldar out of the road and into the shade of a building overhang. "What are you doing here?"

"I came back as soon as I got your message," Oldar replied.

"You have to go. We have to leave now." Schaed said. His frenzied voice and panicked expression did nothing to ease the king's earlier unease.

"Why? What's going on? You said something about the Faceless?"

Oldar's question died on his lips as Schaed quickly covered his mouth with a hand, shushing him at the same time. The lanky youth's eyes widened in terror as he looked around them in the street, his head snapping rapidly from side to side. He shushed Oldar once more before pulling he king in closer.

"You mustn't say their name," he hissed. "Your uncle brought a group of those creatures into the city and set them loose. He's taken up in the castle. People are dying, Oldar."

"Do people know he's brought them in?"

Schaed shook his head. "I saw them last night when he entered the city." His eyes were haunted by what he'd seen.

"I have to talk to him," Oldar said, moving towards Castle Storm once more. "Surely, he'll listen to reason."

"No!" Schaed said, a little louder. His eyes frantically scanned the streets once more. "No," he repeated more softly. "He's looking for you, Oldar. He brought them here to kill you. By the gods, it's not good. We have to leave."

"I can't leave my people," Oldar said. "You owe me a favor for trying to set me up to murder the queen. Come with me."

"Murder the queen?" Schaed gasped. "I didn't do that. I just wanted her to be sick."

"Well, she almost died."

"Shit."

Schaed's eyes met Oldar's. The lanky man was terrified, Oldar could clearly see that. They darted around, always watching for something. It broke the king's heart to see his previously carefree friend so paranoid. Oldar looked into Schaed's eyes and saw that he had not been on the poppy. Whatever he saw, he saw while clear-headed.

"I swear, Oldar, I didn't do that," Schaed said softly. "But I will do what I must to repay you for my actions. I'm sorry." His voice trembled; it was such an unsettling sound for him.

Oldar tried to think of a way to focus his friend's mind. The king's own mind raced with questions. Most of them centered around his uncle and what he could do to oust the man once more. But Oldar knew that he was desperate, and that led him to do something dangerous. Instead, he settled on the most pressing question.

"What are the Faceless? I've heard them referenced a couple times before your letter, and no one seems to want to talk about them."

"They're these shadow creatures," Schaed said, agitated excitement building in his hushed tones. "Long, tapering claws, and a mouth full of sharp teeth. You'd think they couldn't do anything being shadows, but they've already killed a couple people." As he spoke, Oldar saw hints of his old friend returning. Schaed was focused and not acting on his adrenaline. "The guards have tried to downplay it, but they're confused. And scared."

"But what about Uncle?" Oldar prompted.

"No one really said anything when he showed up with your aunt," Schaed admitted. "You'd been gone for four days. Rumors were starting to spread that you'd been held captive in Pharn. Although, I'm surprised they just handed over the throne. You would've thought they'd actually put up some resistance. It's not unheard of for kings to be gone for a span, and you hadn't been in battle."

"Something's up. There's no way he got to just march in without something happening. Pru wouldn't allow it." Images of his childhood caretaker flashed in his mind. The elderly woman laying beaten, or worse, on a cold stone floor in their dungeon was one of his biggest fears. Oldar knew that Alastaire wouldn't shy away from anything to get him what he wanted, but he prayed that his uncle would leave his former caretaker alone. "Oh gods, Pru. Schaed, we don't have time. We have to go."

"Oldar, Oldar," Schaed said, now trying to calm the young king down. "Wait a moment. We can't be sure he's hurt Pru. There're many ways he could've gotten in without a big scene. Let's not jump to the worst case."

Oldar took a deep breath, trying to push the images of his beloved caretaker lying injured and scared on the dungeon floor. It was hard, but after a few, he managed to calm down. While Schaed kept watch on the street, now devoid of all life, Oldar tried to figure out the best plan of attack. Alastaire and Constance did not know that he had returned. If their monsters were creatures of shadow, it would probably be best to not stay anywhere where they could suddenly pop out.

"How many have you seen today?" Oldar asked. "Is that why everyone's acting so scared?"

"To be honest, I don't know if they can come out during the day or if they just hunt at night," Schaed replied. "I watched them move quickly from shadow to shadow, snuffing out the lamps as they went by, but one broke into my home. It chased me through my house, and I only lost it in my wine cellar. I was there all night."

Oldar blanched at the thought of being chased by one of the monsters. Forcing the image out of his mind, he asked: "Any signs that they're nearby?"

"It gets unbelievably cold. My windows froze over, and I could see my breath. I've never been so cold."

Oldar stopped. His mind raced as he tried to take in everything and process a plan to move forward. He began copying Schaed's mannerisms, checking his surroundings every few seconds. It wasn't safe for either him or Schaed to confront his uncle. If he went, his uncle would most likely unleash his monsters against him after getting whatever he wanted from him. If Schaed went, he'd probably be killed where he stood.

There had to be some way for Oldar to get information about his uncle and his monsters. The young king racked his brain trying to figure out who he could use to gather intelligence. He hadn't gotten to meet the spies his parents had stationed around Corinth. Oldar kicked himself for focusing too much on his issues with Cienna to not learn about the everyday politics of his land.

He wished Grymme was still there. The stoic man would have known what to do. With a sudden inspiration, Oldar nearly jumped as he whispered excitedly, "Ingmar!"

"What?" Schaed asked.

"Ingmar," the king repeated, pulling his friend in closer. "He can get us the information we need and also check on Pru. He can get places casually without arousing suspicion."

"Perfect! Meet me in my wine cellar. I think that's the only place we're truly safe. I don't think they can find us there."

"Do you think we should find Rez'maré and bring her with us?" Oldar asked.

"No," Schaed said, his eyes dropping. "I tried taking her with me this morning, but she didn't believe me."

Oldar saw his friend's face drop as he remembered the conversation. Schaed's shoulders drooped and his eyes stared down at the worn cobblestones. He'd never seen his friend like that before. Schaed had always been the member of their group with a joke always on his lips and a smile on his face.

"It's okay, Schaed. I'll see you soon."

"No," Schaed said, popping his head up. "You can't go. If anyone were to see you, they'd kill you on the spot. Let me go. I can at least keep a low profile if your uncle has anyone out looking for you. Here," he said handing Oldar a key. "Take this and hide in my cellar. I'll have Ingmar meet us there and we can figure out where to go from there."

"Thank you," Oldar said. "I really appreciate it. Stay safe."

～⌇～

It didn't take long for Schaed to find Ingmar. The soldier was making his rounds outside the castle with some of the younger recruits. They walked around, their movements tense even though there was no one around. Schaed's eyes darted around before he took a risk and raced over to the men. Ingmar and the younger soldiers drew their weapons, startled by the sudden appearance of the lanky man.

"Stop!" one of the younger men cried. He brandished his sword at Schaed. The lanky man would've believed that the younger man would've run him through if it hadn't been for his shaky voice.

"Please," Schaed said, holding his hands up just in case. "I've come to speak with the captain.

Ingmar reached over and placed his hand on the flat of the blade, pushing it down. The younger soldier shot the captain a shocked look, but did not argue as Ingmar sheathed his own blade.

"What do you need?" Ingmar asked.

"I need to talk to you," Schaed said. He eyed the younger recruits for a moment before making eye contact with the captain once more. "Alone. Please."

Ingmar glanced at Schaed, his eyes searching the lanky man up and down before nodding. "I'll be over later for the evening change. I need to go and eat anyway."

The younger recruits snapped to attention and saluted their captain before continuing on their rounds. Ingmar heaved a sigh. Schaed gawked in surprise as he saw how much the man had aged since the late King Storm's death. It unsettled him to see the soldier looking so vulnerable. Scared him, almost.

"What do you know?" Ingmar asked. Even his voice dripped with exhaustion. There was nothing about his demeanor, from his puffy red eyes to his sagging body, that indicated anything good was afoot. "Is it about the murder?"

Schaed was taken aback by the bluntness. "No," he said, shaking his head. As if he almost forgot, he suddenly turned around, taking in everything in their surroundings. "Well, kind of. I need your help, but I cannot say out in the open. Please go to my shop and we can speak more frankly there. It would be so noble if you would join me."

Ingmar's eyes perked up as some of the exhaustion seemed to melt away. "Let's go."

"No," Schaed said quickly. Dropping his voice, he added, "We must go separately. Once you arrive, we can maybe share a fine glass of wine. Please."

The captain nodded and began heading down the road. Schaed felt a wave of relief wash over him as Ingmar made his way towards the wine shop.

Scanning his surroundings, Schaed made his way home taking side streets. He traveled quickly through the streets, keeping to the walls of shops and homes to provide him with coverage from Alastaire or one of his monsters. A sudden movement out of the corner of his eye caught his attention. His head snapped towards shadow, but he couldn't see anything.

"It's okay," he whispered to himself, exhaling to relieve the stress he was feeling. "Almost there."

As Schaed neared his shop, a cloud covered the sun, throwing everything into shadows. His breath caught in his chest and he tried to pick up his pace. So far, he'd been lucky to not see anyone on his way home. Though he was tense, he allowed himself to feel a bit of hope. It was quickly dashed as the temperature around him dropped. Schaed's heart jumped into his throat.

"Sh-shit!" he gasped.

Panic gripped the lanky man as he broke into a cold sweat. His head spun around, trying to find the monster that he knew lurked nearby. A pocket of frozen air blew against his back. His body trembled as he forced himself to turn around. A toothy grin greeted him as one of the Faceless slipped out of the shadows.

A strangled scream ripped from his lips as he began running towards his home. The light from the sun seemed to dim further as the coldness engulfed him.

XXXVII

S UN BEAT DOWN on the traveling group of northerners as they worked their way down the snowy mountain. Solveig wiped sweat off her brow, tempted to take off some of her furs to help cool off, but her leathers would expose too much to the elements and she feared being burned. Tyr padded along beside her, his tongue lolling out as he panted in the heat.

She was happy that she'd left the Elderma and rest of the elders back home. Traveling with Hegvaldr and the other warriors of the council made her feel strong. They were a small group, just the seven of them, but they were her best. No one would be able to intimidate them.

The group traveled light, carrying with them only a few sacks tied to their hip filled with delicately wrapped scrimshaw. Eivind groaned as he snacked on a large chunk of deer meat. With the group consisting of just the soldiers, Solveig was pleased that no one would say anything about his gluttony.

"Do you think they'll have anything good to eat?" Fenris asked. "Did you get a chance to taste anything?"

Eivind nodded with a grunt. Hegvaldr snorted at the large man as he tore another piece of meat from the bone.

"It's not as juicy as what we have, but they've got some good spices coating their meat," Hegvaldr said. "Their ale is just piss though. I wouldn't expect to get good and drunk off their swill."

"Damn," Fenris said as Tormund shook his head. "I was hoping for a nice pint. I'm getting thirsty thanks to this heat."

"It's drinkable, but don't expect something great," Hegvaldr replied.

"They've got some great seasoned meat buns that go well with their wines," Eivind said, finally speaking. "Hegvaldr just doesn't enjoy the simple pleasures of a good wine and meat."

The men laughed as Tormund slapped the other on the shoulder. They joked and jeered amongst each other. Solveig cracked a smile at their raucous banter. Tyr shot the men an annoyed look as a low growl rumbled in his throat.

"Now, when we get there," Solveig said. "We'll need to make our presence known. Once we get there, Eivind and Hegvaldr will break off to look for Jytte. Visit as many pubs as you need to. I'm sure that'll be hard for you, Eivind."

Snickers broke out in the group. Eivind waved them off, taking another bite of his meal. The rate at which the large chunk of meat was disappearing impressed Solveig.

I may have to give him more of a chance, she thought. *Well, two is always better than one.*

"Is it as hot there as it is here?" Einer asked, his face covered in sweat. His long hair was matted on his head and his face slowly turning red. "I can't imagine it getting any worse than this."

"It's horrible," Hegvaldr replied. "The days are unbearable, but the nights are damn cold. You don't have time to adjust to anything."

"Get drunk," Eivind muttered through a full mouth. "'At's how I got through."

"Not everyone can just keep eating and drinking like you," Hegvaldr snapped. "Sometimes we just need to find ways to adjust."

The group continued their banter once more. Tyr repositioned himself between Solveig and the joking warriors. He kept shooting them glances, but didn't growl again. Solveig leaned over and scratched the dire wolf behind the ears. The wolf closed his eyes for a moment as he savored her touch.

"Your time will come," she said softly. "You'll be able to be free in a few days."

XXXVIII

OLDAR SAT in the darkened wine cellar, his body crammed between a pair of oaken barrels in the corner. Schaed's words on the best way to hide rang in his ears. Oldar still wasn't sure if he believed his friend, but he knew that something was dreadfully wrong. He dug a trench in the loamy earth of the cellar, the rich smell filling him with nostalgia.

His father used to take him to the woods outside Madden to pick berries with the local wine merchant. Before Schaed and his father managed to secure the Hanzo wine rights, the local wines were made from blackberries found the capital. Oldar smiled as he remembered the long days picking berries with his father.

A muted thump quickly pulled Oldar from his fond memories. The king's ears strained as he tried to figure out if Schaed had arrived or if it was something worse. Heavy footsteps on the wooden floors echoed in the empty shop as the chink of chainmail rattled in the silence. Oldar crept out from behind the barrels and cautiously made his way to the cellar door. He thanked the dirt floor for muffling his footsteps as he approached the door. The heavy footsteps outside continued to move around, searching for something.

As he reached for the door handle, Oldar noticed a cluster of ancient runes carved in the wood of the doorframe. The king's hand briefly touched the brass handle before moving to the carving. His fingers delicately traced the lines, trying to remember the ancient language as he worked to figure out what it said.

"Forevermore with you shall be, protected by the Great Zemé," he whispered.

"Your majesty?" a voice called out, startling the king as he stared intently at the markings. "Are you here?"

"Ingmar?" Oldar asked tentatively, cracking open the door enough to peer out with one eye. A wave of relief washed over him as he saw the captain striding over to him. "Boy am I happy to see you." Oldar pushed open the door and pulled the soldier into the cellar with him.

"Are you all right, your majesty?" Ingmar asked, concern edging his voice.

For the first time since he'd entered the wine cellar, Oldar realized that his chest was tight and his body tense. His heart slowed its pounding in his chest, until he could no longer feel it any longer. Oldar ran his hand through his hair in a vain attempt to calm his trembling hands. "I'm fine," he muttered. "I guess I've been better, if truth be told."

"Your friend seemed to think that you're in trouble," Ingmar said. The captain's eyes scanned the cellar, moving from the king to all of the corners in an attempt to make sure their surroundings were safe.

"Where is Schaed?" Oldar asked. "How did you know where to go?"

"He's well known because of his wine dealings, among other things" Ingmar muttered tersely as he began circling the floor. "He said something about this being noble, and knowing him, he'd never use that word. Considering everything's that's been going on these last few days, I didn't want to take a chance."

Oldar noted the dark shadows under the soldier's eyes in the candle light. The man looked exhausted. Deep bags circled his eyes, which were red and puffy. A thick layer of stubble covered his chin from the long shift he'd just worked. The look did not suit the normally clean-cut man.

"I should wait for Schaed to come, but there's no time," Oldar said. "My uncle's trying to usurp my throne once more. Schaed says that he's brought an army of dangerous monsters to carry out his plan. I need you to keep an eye on him and find out what exactly he's doing. And keep Pru safe. Please, keep her safe. Or better yet, smuggle her out of the castle and bring her back here if you can."

Ingmar stopped pacing around the wine cellar and turned to face the king. The shadows around his eyes somehow seemed darker, intensifying his gaze. "Please, your majesty," he said as he lowered his voice. "Do not speak about this. Stay hidden. I can't say much, but it's not safe for you here. I can't help you like you want."

"But Ingmar, you've been so honorable in my father's service," Oldar began.

The captain held up his hand to silence the king. "I have too much scrutiny. I might be able to get you something, but if I were to do much more, we would both be in trouble. Strange things have been going on, and I don't know if it's worth your life to confront him. Please, run away. I swore to your father when I first took my oath that I would keep the royal family safe at all costs. I've failed your parents. I wouldn't be able to live with myself if you died on my watch."

Ingmar squatted down, his hands clawing at his head through his short hair. Moments later, he plopped down on the dirty floor, his fingers still clutching at his head. Oldar stood over the man, speechless as the usually unflappable soldier struggled to compose himself. The king felt a twinge of pity for the man who'd given up so much, only to fail.

Crouching down next to the captain, Oldar pat the soldier on the shoulder in what he hoped was a comforting way. It felt strange being so personable with the stoic man. Reaching behind him to sweep at the dirt on the ground, Oldar sat down across from Ingmar.

"I don't know what to do. Where to go." he said simply. "My alliances are tenuous at best. I can't count on my people to protect me, or even my other family to be able to keep me safe. As we speak, Zanir goes to aid the Qu'ari nation with a coup. All of Corinth is falling to shit, Ingmar. What are we going to do?"

"I don't know," Ingmar said quietly. "I really don't know."

"Did you see them?" Oldar asked. "The monsters?" The Faceless?"

The captain shook his head. "I haven't seen anything. The murders are still being investigated. It doesn't look good though. The bodies are torn apart, as if they were ravaged by a wild animal. Wolves haven't been seen in Madden since before your father's time. There's no way it could be wolves. He's got all of my men and the castle staff scared. No one wants to go in, and no one seems to be able to go out. Whatever he brought with him, it's got everyone on edge."

"If not wolves, then what could it be?"

Ingmar shook his head once more. "That's the big question, I'm afraid."

The two sat in silence for a while, waiting for Schaed to return. Oldar tried to take in all that the captain had said. It sounded like things were as bad as Schaed had intimated. The king had hoped his friend was exaggerating, but Ingmar's reluctance to help him frightened him. In fact, the soldier's suggestion that the king flee his homeland had made his blood run cold.

I'll never get to the bottom of this if I can't find out what Uncle is doing. This is my home. I can't let them push me out. But how am I to fight such creatures. If it was just Uncle, or even a human army, I would stand a chance. But these things? Who knows that they're capable of? Obviously, a lot. Damn. This is a fine mess I've gotten myself into.

When Schaed never showed up, Oldar began to worry. It was not like his friend to disappear.

Maybe he decided to run away after bringing Ingmar to me.

"Your majesty," Ingmar said, breaking the silence. "I must go. I would like to eat and take a nap before my next shift starts. I haven't had much of a break since before your uncle came in."

"Oh, of course," the king replied. "Thank you for meeting with me."

"My pleasure," Ingmar replied, saluting his lord once he got to his feet.

Ingmar made his way to the cellar door. As he opened the door, Oldar called out:

"Please don't say anything about our meeting. I'm not ready for my presence to be known yet. I need to decide what I plan to do."

"Of course, your majesty," Ingmar replied, saluting once more. "Take care, your majesty. I hope to see you under better circumstances. Until next time."

"Until next time," Oldar said as the door closed behind the captain.

Ingmar trudged through the streets of Madden. Now that the murders were no longer fresh, the fear had worn off and more people went about their day. Shops were busier and a nearby tavern was filled with music and dancing lights. Despite his exhaustion, Ingmar was pleased to see the populace out and about once more. No children ran around, but at least young couples and older citizens walked about, a few bags in their arms either filled with food or some other purchases.

His mind wandered as he tried to focus on making his way to the castle. A warm bowl of stew and a strong ale kept him on his feet moving forward. If he had time, he could even have a quick wash before he slumped onto his bed. A bit of drool dripped out of the side of his mouth as he thought about the chunks of potato, carrot, and meat swimming in the hot stew. Ingmar could almost taste the full-bodied ale as the aroma of his planned dinner filled his nostrils.

Ingmar's stomach rumbled. It had been almost a day before he'd had a proper meal, and he was famished. The mouth-watering scent of fresh bread caught his attention. The captain's head spun and saliva ran down his chin, which he quickly wiped with the back of his hands, as he walked past the local bakery. In the windows, loaves stared at him, begging him to buy and consume them.

"By the gods," Ingmar swore. "I don't have time, but gods... I can't resist."

Before he knew it, the soldier found himself inside the bakery looking at a display of herb bread. He didn't remember doing it, but he walked out of the shop with a warm loaf of herb bread in his hand. The soft loaf warmed his hands, the delicate aroma filling his mouth with saliva. His stomach rumbled once more before he took a large bite. Thyme and oregano filled his mouth. Ingmar was also surprised to find the subtle taste of tomato in the bread as well.

A groan escaped his lips as he savored the warm meal. He tried to chew slowly, but before long he'd already devoured half of the loaf. Ingmar found he was able to focus a little better after his snack. In order to compensate for the time he'd wasted in the bakery, Ingmar picked up his pace. A passing cloud blocked the sun's light. Several people in the street stopped and looked up, confused at how dark it had suddenly gotten. More than one commented on how it was darker than usual.

Ingmar noted the peculiar darkness with interest. His mind suddenly filled with an image of Schaed and concern washed over him. The young man should've made it to the meeting with the king. Despite his agitation, Ingmar felt confident that he wouldn't have just run off after getting the captain to go to the wine cellar.

Acting on a hunch, Ingmar left the main road and began traveling down side streets. He wound through the alleys, hugging the backs of the shops and keeping out of sight. After passing two streets, he had yet to encounter anything. Feeling a bit foolish, Ingmar decided to return to the main road at the first opportunity. Rounding the corner, Ingmar felt his heart drop as he found a body in the middle of the alley.

With a deep breath, the captain cautiously approached the prone form. Disappointment filled him as he saw deep gashes across the lanky man's chest. Blood soaked his tunic and pooled around him. A single scratch sliced his neck. Schaed's blue eyes stared ahead of him, wide in fright at whatever had found him. Placing his hands over the young man's eyes, Ingmar gently closed them. It was best to let him rest peace.

Ingmar stood up slowly and began looking for a place to hide the body so that no one else found him; Ingmar could get other soldiers to help clear up the scene before anyone noticed. Gripping the body under the armpits, he dragged Schaed and leaned him up against a wall in a sitting position. The pool of blood and accompanying trail would have to wait to be cleaned, as would his uniform.

Time was not in his favor. Making his way to the castle by the main streets, Ingmar abandoned all hope of a warm meal and a nap. Alastaire was up to something, and Ingmar knew that it was his duty to figure out how to help the rightful king.

XXXIX

P RAM SAT in a chair his face buried in his hands. The children played in another part of the house with Intan, the matron watching over the infant as well. Zaa'ni and Altansari sat down on a nearby chaise, while Hroth, Maen, and a pair of musicians sat on the floor in front of them. Tension was building in his temples, the beginning of an ache threatening to form.

"Are you sure you weren't followed?" Pram asked, finally looking up. "He's proven himself to be ruthless time and again. We can't risk him coming to Honorable Mother's home. This is our one safe place."

The male performer wrapped his arms around the young woman, her arms hugging herself as she looked around in fright.

"I managed to bring them all back safely," Hroth replied. "I couldn't risk Maen's children being pulled into this. We doubled around several times before making our way here."

"What's going on?" the woman asked. Pram noticed a heavy accent as she spoke. Though she clamped her arms around her knees, her voice remained steady as she spoke. "I did not think that those marked by Apophos lived among the clans." Her eyes fell on Hroth, distrust evident behind her thick lashes.

"I'm not the one you should fear," Hroth said flatly. "That man, Wyrd, has been stalking you for a while." The woman sneered at the Flame, her lip curling. "His power does not come from divine judgement, but from a curse. It's almost as if it comes directly from the gods themselves."

The woman opened her mouth to argue, but Pram held up his hand and cut her off. The man's mouth gaped open just a bit, his eyes moving rapidly side to side as he followed the conversation. Altansari held her hand to her mouth, her other hand gripping Zaa'ni's. The two women squeezed their hands tightly, their knuckles turning white. Pram glanced over at the young woman Hroth brought with him. Her big brown eyes took in everything.

She's almost as composed as Hroth, Pram noted. *I wonder where he found her. He's done a lot of reconnaissance on his own, huh? I wonder what else he's discovered.*

In another part of the house, a couple of the younger girls began shrieking and the sound of slapping feet on the floor came closer as they ran around. Intan's soft voice called out to the children, muffled.

"Who are you?" Pram asked the woman with the accent. "You're clearly not one of us."

"She is," the man interjected for the first time, his voice a rich tenor. "It's just a combination of Hanzo and Thurlish."

Hroth raised an eyebrow at the response, a smirk playing on his lips. No doubt he noticed the accent too. The woman closed her eyes and let out a sigh. With a gentle motion, she shook off her companion's arm and scooted forward a bit.

"You're perceptive," she said finally. "I was not born here. However, I've been living here for a couple years now, and consider Fa'Tinh my home. I make an honest living here."

"If you were making an honest living, you wouldn't be lying about who you are," Hroth said.

"As if you're being honest?" she snapped. "I know your kind. They're not one to be trusted."

"We still don't know your name," Pram cut in, trying to stave off any more argument. "The sooner we know who you are, the sooner we can figure out Wyr-raji's plan."

Another sigh escaped her. "My name is Jytte. I was born in Stöartgaard and came to Fa'Tinh to gather information." Turning to her partner, she lowered her eyes. "I'm sorry, Tek. I didn't mean to deceive you."

Tek looked as though he'd seen the dead. "Why didn't you tell me?" Jytte flinched at the pain in his voice.

"I can't just come out and say that I'm from the North," Jytte explained. "People would be instantly suspicious about anything I did."

"Well, you weren't coming with pure intentions." Tek couldn't meet her eyes. "But still..."

"Now is not the time to worry about this," Pram said as gently as he could. The young performer met the general's gaze and nodded. "Wyr-raji has been quiet until this morning. Viir and the Pshwani have not been as vocal, but there are still rumblings. Your presence is distracting Wyr-raji from whatever his original plan was."

"I don't think so," Hroth said. "He's been stalking her like prey. I think he needs her for part of his plan."

"What could he be working on?" Zaa'ni asked.

"You said you were gathering intelligence?" Pram asked.

Jytte nodded. "Konugrr sent me a message a few moons ago that she was working with someone to gain new land for our people. Someone who was going to use our strength to overthrow the Great Heart."

Zaa'ni gasped. Altansari brought both hands to her mouth. Pram's eyes narrowed as he leaned forward on his elbows.

"He needed additional power if he was going to complete his plan," the general muttered. "Liir's death was just a lucky coincidence for him to mask his actions."

"But where does Jytte come in?" Tek asked. Pram noted the Flame's bemused expression. "We've been partnered together for maybe six months now. We see each other almost every day."

"Peace," Pram said, raising his hand. "We are not going to pass judgement on her. Right now, we need your help."

"She needs to stay in hiding," Hroth said. "Both of them. Things are getting dangerous. My fight with him earlier proved that. He's not concerned with any destruction he may cause. His mind is consumed with his fixation on Jytte. If either she or Tek were to be found in the streets, I don't think he would hesitate to attack."

"It can't be that bad," Jytte replied.

"It's true," Maen said. Pram had almost forgotten of the young woman's presence.

"What do you mean?" the general asked.

"We followed them to Tek's home and when she went in with him, he let out a blast of fire in rage. If he knows where you live, he won't hesitate to make his move."

"He's unstable," Hroth added.

"Gods," Pram mumbled. The general ran his hands through his hair. "We need a plan. We can't keep hiding like this."

"I agree," Hroth said.

"But can we do?" Zaa'ni asked. "Len's still out, who knows where? His presence kept our people together."

Pram rubbed his hands together. His mind raced as he tried to figure out a plan of attack. In the back of his mind, he found himself praying that Len returned soon. Pram's attempts to gather anyone other than the Qu'ari elite was met with resistance. No one wanted to take a stance with either clan.

"Take them out to the caves," Hroth spoke up. Pram's head snapped up, surprised at the Flame's voice. "If you can get your elite to clear as many people as you can, I can engage with him. The longer we wait, the stronger he becomes. Your Great Heart may not come back and we need to take action now."

"I can't let you do that," Zaa'ni gasped. "You've been such a help to my husband. We should wait for him to come back."

Pram shook his head. "No. Hroth is right. We need to leave as soon as possible. However, you will not fight alone. The elite will join you."

"It would be pointless," Hroth replied.

"What about the creature in the woods?" Altansari asked. "That monster we saw a couple days ago. It's still out there. Honorable Mother's home is the safest place for us."

"That's true." Pram rubbed his temple. Many scenarios ran through his mind, a number of possible variables flashing in combination. They all sat in uncomfortable silence as he thought. "The elite will take our people to safety. We'll head for Thurl first. They stand for peace. I'm sure they'll grant us sanctuary. I agree that homes are probably safer than the elements. However, I will stay with you, Hroth. Maybe together we can reason with him."

Pram glanced over at his wife. Her eyes were ringed red as tears were half-way down her cheeks. She clutched her silks, her body shaking with silent sobs. Altansari met his gaze and shook her head. The general held her eyes and nodded. I have to, his stare told her. Two raking shakes later and Altansari finally nodded. Tears dripped off her cheeks and onto her silks. Zaa'ni reached over and grabbed Altansari's hand. The women shared a squeeze.

Jytte's eyes were hardened. "I can fight too," she said in her thick accent. "My people will be disappointed if I do not follow the Silver Wolf and allow a couple of outsiders to shield me."

"No!" Tek said. "You can't."

The barbarian woman reached out and rubbed her partner's knee. "I'll be fine. Re'nukh will protect me."

The room fell silent as reality set in. The shouts and giggles from the children sounded so far away to Pram. He tented his fingers together and leaned forward, lost in thought. All of his experiences, all of his decisions, led up to this moment. Something big was about to take place, and Pram wasn't sure he'd make it to the end. Closing his eyes, he mouthed a prayer to the ancestors.

XL

L EN WAS GLAD to be back on solid ground once more. After his time at
sea, he had no desire to go back. The young general tapped his foot impatiently as he waited for Angh and his crew to finish packing. True to his
word, Angh pulled as many men as he could to take back to Xan. He crossed
his arms across his chest as he waited outside of the tavern. Maya and several
others waited outside with him, the pirates sharing a lewd joke amongst
themselves.

Maya paid Len no mind. After their encounter on the *Fury*, he did his
best to avoid her. In response, she did not attempt to corner him again. Len
glanced at her out of the corner of his eye. He didn't want to admit it, but
the woman intrigued him. She tempted him more than any other.

The sun was comfortably in the air, its rays beating down on the Bone
Coast, warming Maya. The tangy sea air filled Len with the scent of the
ocean. He was a little disappointed there was no breeze to help cool him off.
He'd grown used to the wind while on the *Fury*.

Shortly thereafter, the pirate lord and the remainder of his crew spilled
out of the tavern. Kayna's hair was tied up, the tip of it playing on her bare
shoulders. Behind her, Dez sidled next to Maya, her hair also tied up in her
now characteristic tail. The two women began speaking softly, Dez shooting
Len a furtive glance or smirk during the conversation.

The young general tried to not concern himself with their conversation,
but any time Dez was involved, Len had learned that he needed to keep his

guard up. The Tempest let out a short laugh before shooting Maya a smile and walking away.

"All right, everyone," the Scourge said. "Our time to show the mainlanders the strength of Pirates of the Western Isles. Len has demonstrated his courage out on the seas and shown us that he's a man of his word. Now, I expect you all to join me so I can keep mine. Our enemy may have the power of gods, but we are not alone."

The group broke out into a loud cheer, many of them raising their weapons to the air and shaking them. Len felt his lips turn up slightly. The pirate lord knew how to command a crew, and not through fear. Len could feel energy radiating from the man just like before. This time, however, Len did not feel uncomfortable tension like on the ship.

Angh turned to Len, his face relaxed and a spark in his eyes. With a nod, he said: "Lead the way, young Son of Xan."

His impatience getting the better of him, Len barely acknowledged the god's gesture as he took off down the road leading out of town.

Vashe pushed her way through the magical barrier protecting Enlil. Dseti's presence made going through the ancient magic easier; she didn't need to make an offering this time. Or maybe it was because she'd already made one to get in. Whatever the reason, Vashe did not care. The two pushed their way through and began making their way to the nearest town so she could retrieve her horse.

Her body still tingled with the pure energy that coursed through her. She made it through the night without Snapping or becoming Tainted, and now she felt reinvigorated. Her Shadow markings moved to her right hand, covering it completely half way up her forearm. The hazy tattoos looked different from her other ones. They almost had a silver sheen to them and their pattern was different. If she believed in her mother's teachings, Vashe knew that she would be the most revered person in Scrymme. The thought brought a smile to her lips.

Dseti led the way, clearing overhanging foliage from their path. The two traveled quickly through the jungle. Though they did not run into anyone as they fled Maeyu'dana's temple, both of them moved with an unspoken urgency. A heavy presence followed them. Even now that they'd cleared the ancient barrier, the two still felt uneasy.

"He's still following us," Dseti said suddenly, startling Vashe. They'd been traveling so long in silence that she'd forgotten what it was like to hear another voice. "I can feel him. There's something he doesn't want us to find out."

"You're a god. Why?"

"I couldn't tell you."

The two continued on in silence. Apart from their heavy breathing, neither spoke. The trees lessened as they exited the jungle and made their way across Ro'thre's border. The sloping hills and verdant fields were a welcomed change from the tangled mess that was Enlil. Wildflowers dotted out from the rich green, providing a splash of color to the hills. Horses ran freely, their manes and tails flying behind them. When they caught the pair's scent, they stopped at the crest of one of the hills to watch for a bit before taking off in the other direction.

Despite being rushed, Vashe enjoyed the beauty of Ro'thre. This part of the realm was less populated than Zanir or Pharn, allowing nature to rule. She remembered reading somewhere that the royal family did not engage in conflict, adopting a pacifist lifestyle, but kept their borders open for trade opportunities. Ro'thre was not a rich land, but they were bountiful.

As they neared the inn she'd stayed at, Vashe noticed the heavy presence that had been following them seemed to have disappeared. She no longer felt an anxious foreboding. She looked to Dseti to see if he noticed it as well. Instead of feeling relaxed like Vashe, the wanderer appeared to be even more so on edge. His head twisted side to side with every few feet. He seemed to be straining to hear or see something. The actions put Vashe back on guard.

"This isn't right," he muttered. "Something's wrong. What is he doing?"

The inn they'd been searching for loomed ahead on the top of a gentle slope. A long fence encircled the building, keeping in the guests' horses as they enjoyed their stay. A thin trail of smoke wafted out of the window and the enticing aroma of warm meat and lentils made her mouth water. It'd been a few days since she'd had a proper meal. Her stomach rumbled, telling her what she already knew.

"Let's go inside for a bite," Vashe said, hoping to distract Dseti. "We can talk a bit about our next plan of action before we head out. My horse can carry us both. We probably should rest. I doubt either of us slept well in Enlil."

Dseti mumbled an answer that she took as agreement, but his eyes continued to look around. Taking the lead, Vashe somehow managed to pick up her pace as they trekked up the hill. The aroma of food was almost unbearable. As they reached the summit, Vashe could hear merry chatter and a fiddle playing an upbeat tune. Even in the afternoon, the room was filled with warm firelight shining through the windows.

～

Sitting at a table with a plate of meat and vegetables in front of her, Vashe tucked into her meal with enthusiasm. The first bite filled her with a wonderful combination of herbs and spices; turmeric, coriander, and cloves were among the ones she could recognize. She took a sip of wine, savoring the fruity flavor, before she turned to the wanderer. Dseti barely touched his food, his fork picking at the vegetables sitting on his plate. His glass of wine was untouched. He stared off into the distance, his silver eye unblinking.

"You don't feel it anymore," she said quietly, touching his hand to get his attention. "That's what's bothering you." The wanderer met her gaze, but didn't say anything. Feeling as though she was on the right path, Vashe continued. "It's almost as though his attention is elsewhere."

"I thought you were his primary target," Dseti explained. "I'm afraid I may have overlooked something."

"So, I may not be what he's looking for?"

"No. He still wants you. Otherwise, he wouldn't have tried to contact you in your dream back in Enlil. I just haven't worked out the rest. Everything feels wrong, like the world is out of balance, but I can't place the source."

Vashe leaned back in her chair and crossed her arms. Things had been strange ever since Alverick returned from the spice mines. The visions in her scrying pool had been clouded, obscuring her efforts. She'd blamed it on the strange silver and orange energies she'd seen down in the Rydash Gorge. Before she left, Vashe felt confident that the two energies were her *naran* and Vahnyre, and attributed the disturbances to their strange powers.

Vashe had never felt sure, but she was pretty confident that there was more to her master than met the eye. The silver light surrounding her in the scrying pool led Vashe to believe that she may even share the protection of the gods. When everything calmed down, she wanted to try and get answers from her *naran*.

"Should we get a room and try and sleep?" Vashe asked. "Even a few hours would be beneficial."

Dseti shook his head. "You can sleep. I need to check something."

"Are we still in danger?"

"I don't know. You finish up and I'll join you shortly. Once I've finished restocking our supplies, I'll come get you. We should leave before Toron's moon reaches her zenith. She should be full enough that we can travel easily in her light."

Dseti finally began digging into his meal, taking small bites to savor it all. A smile of contentment crossed his lips and he let out a faint groan. "I had forgotten how nice the food is here."

"You've been here before?" Vashe was happy that his mood appeared to be lightening.

"Oh, yes," he replied. "When you're as old as I am, you get to know places very well. Growing up in Atunari, I found that her neighbors reminded me the most of home whenever I left. Old King Aelthur really enjoyed the old ways and tried to keep his family in line with that. Their current ruler, however, is nothing like his predecessors. We need to avoid the forested areas if we want to stay out of his sight."

"But almost all of Ro'thre is forest. Should we find another way back?"

"Let's wait until tonight before we make our decision. Go and rest."

The news surprised Vashe. It had been a while since Zanir had received anything new from the country. Ro'thre wasn't a big source of income for Zanir, so Jaste had mainly left them to themselves. If there was a change in the dynamics, it could spell trouble for her future. She lowered her head and took another bite of her food. Vashe didn't think she'd been getting a nap after all.

XLI

THE CASTLE HALLS WERE COLD despite the warm afternoon. Servants hurried about with thick clothes draped over their shoulders. Every hearth in the castle was lit with a roaring fire and there was a serving boy stationed nearby to keep the flames fed. Ingmar wove his way through the halls, watching as women carrying towels or finishing some other chore darted past, their breaths coming out in puffs. He managed to snatch a spare tunic from one of the servants and slipped it over his head to hide his blood-stained clothes.

The soldier fought back a shiver as he moved deeper into Castle Storm. His chainmail and leathers were not enough to keep him warm in the frozen halls. He kept his eyes peeled. On the stone walls, Ingmar noticed that a thin layer of frost was creeping up, covering them. No one spoke. No greetings were called out nor smiles shared. Everyone moved about, keeping to themselves.

Ingmar reached out to the nearest person who wasn't carrying anything, a young woman hugging her shawl tightly against her slim frame. "Where is Lord Alastaire?"

The woman met his gaze for a brief moment before pointing off to the main throne room. In that moment, he saw eyes that were filled with terror. She was trying hard not to show it, but they were wide open. Tension showed clearly around her eyes and mouth. Her hand trembled as she gestured, but Ingmar couldn't be sure if it was from the cold or fear.

"Thank you," the soldier said. The young woman began hurrying off, but Ingmar stopped her once more. "Where is Miss Pruvencia? The dear woman was looking for me earlier while I was on my shift."

The young woman mumbled something that sounded like kitchen, her breath coming out in a wisp of hot air before hugging her shawl closer to her body and hurrying off. A blood-curdling howl echoed in the hallway, causing Ingmar to jump. The young woman let out a whimper. Ingmar's head darted towards the direction of the sound. Turning back to ask the woman about the noise, he saw that he was alone in the hall. She'd ran the remainder of the distance and rounded the corner.

"By the gods," he swore, his breath coming out in a large puff. With a steadying breath, Ingmar continued on.

The soldier picked up his pace as he walked down the hall. He heard echoes of the howl from earlier, but nothing as loud as the one he'd heard with the woman. By the time he made his way to the throne room, Ingmar's hands were freezing. He rubbed his hands together after knocking on the heavy oaken doors. It wasn't long before the door opened just enough for him to squeeze through before shutting quickly behind him.

It was as though the season had changed. The roaring hearth filled the room with a pleasant heat that warmed him to the bones. His hands begun to thaw and he no longer shivered. Ingmar was a little unsettled with the drastic change in temperature. It was a nice day during the planting season, right after the frost. There was no reason it should be that cold.

Alastaire sat on the late king's throne, King Storm's formal crown resting on his head. The man's fingers curled around the armrest, gripping the ornate carving lightly. Across his lap, a dagger rested in a lavish sheath. A faint glow seemed to emanate from the weapon, but the soldier dismissed it as a trick of the light. Snapping to attention, Ingmar saluted the man.

"Lord Alastaire," Ingmar said. "I am glad to see you are well. I've come with a report before I finish my shift."

Alastaire's eyes flashed briefly. "Thank you, captain. I trust it's good news."

Ingmar noted that the question was actually not posed as a question.

"It is indeed, my lord. We've received no word of any trouble either in Madden or the surrounding cities. Everyone seems happy, as I saw many people out shopping. Our younger recruits are currently on duty with some of our more seasoned guards, but they seem to be learning quickly. They'll be shaped up in no time."

"Excellent," Alastaire said, clapping his hands together. "Nothing out of the ordinary."

"Nothing at all, my lord," Ingmar replied. Snapping to attention once more, he asked, "If it is okay with you, I would like to take my leave. I am quite tired and due to return to duty before the sun sets. Is there anything I should be aware of, my lord?"

"Hmm?" Alastaire asked. He thought for a moment. "No. Nothing. You may leave."

"Thank you, my lord."

Ingmar left the throne room and returned to the freezing hall. Instead of heading to his chambers, he turned and made his way to the kitchen.

Pruvencia sat at the servant's table huddled under a bunch of blankets. Her back was to the hearth where a burbling pot cooked the evening dinner. The logs crackled and popped as the flames ate away at them. The heat felt nice against her backside as she nibbled on some grapes and bread. The kitchen was quickly becoming very crowded as more and more members of the castle staff tried to find an excuse to stay.

Every once in a while, she heard a loud screech coming from the castle proper that sent shivers down her spine that had nothing to do with the cold. The older castle staff worked meticulously to bring the younger serving boys and girls into the kitchen, picking up extra duties from them.

Pruvencia worked to keep the children fed and warm. When the shrieks became too loud, as though they were getting closer, she hid them in the pantry. The children huddled together under blankets and anything else Pruvencia could find them. Whimpers and sobs occasionally broke through her protective barrier, but for the most part, Pru was proud at how brave they were acting.

The door slammed open as a young woman raced in. Pruvencia had heard another howl and just finished calming down the youngest children when the young woman entered. The young woman sank into a chair next to the matronly woman and broke down sobbing, her head buried into her arms. Her whole body shook as she cried.

"There there," Pruvencia said gently as she wrapped her arms around the young woman. The woman's little sisters, aged six, four, and one, stared up at the matron through a gap in the blankets. Tears ran down their cheeks as they watched their terrified sister. "You're safe here, Jaella. The little ones are safe, and you've made it back here. Why don't you take a break for a while?"

A couple of the older staff members who found ways to appear busy in the kitchen nodded in agreement. An older steward brought over a mug of hot cider for Jaella, which she gratefully took a long draught from.

"What are they?" Jaella finally asked between gasps. "They're like demons from the seven hells."

"I don't know, dear," an old healer woman said, her voice fragile. The healer looked to Pruvencia and the two shared a worried glance.

"I'm sure it's just a trick that Alastaire brought with him," Pru said softly as she rubbed the young woman's back. "Stay here for a while."

At that moment, a group of young men were ushered in by another steward. The boys were pale and shaking, their lips beginning to turn blue.

"I found 'em cowering in the corner on the western wing," the steward grumbled. His voice was gravelly, like a bunch of rocks. "Said something about the shadows moving."

"They were!" one of the boys cried out.

"Honest!" another added.

"We heard the scream and suddenly it got so cold. Colder than any other part of the castle. Then we saw the shadows move even though no one was moving." The first boy's eyes were wide in fright as he relayed their story.

"There's nuffink in the west wing," the third boy said. "No reasons for them shadows to move like they did."

Pruvencia stopped rubbing Jaella's back as she stared at the boys. Jaella stopped drinking her cider and watched the room.

"We need to get everyone in here now," Pruvencia commanded. "All of the staff. There's nothing important that needs to be done, and if Alastaire needs something, we'll figure it out." Turning to the healer and elderly steward, Pru began barking out orders. "Esthyl, William, find as much kindling and first aid supplies as you can. We'll need to stockpile whatever we can. Greig, you bring in as many people as you can. Jaella, I know you don't want to go out, but I need you to find people too."

Jaella let out a whimper, but nodded.

"Pruvencia, don't you think this'll draw attention to all the staff and put us in danger?" Greig asked.

"I don't think Lord Alastaire has left the throne room," Esthyl's fragile voice said. "He's kept himself and Lady Constance locked up secure in there."

"All he ever does is feed his fires," William added. "I heard him give orders that none of the fires are to go out."

"Do you think they'll keep the demons away?" Jaella asked softly.

"Like monsters from 'ell, they are," the second boy added.

"Let's keep our mouths shut. The longer we can remain unnoticed, the safer we all will be," Pruvencia said.

"Oh," Jaella said suddenly. "There was a soldier looking for you. Said you were supposed to meet with him earlier today."

Pruvencia's brow furrowed in confusion, but she thanked the young woman. With a wave of her hand, she shooed everyone away and got to work preparing the kitchen to house the entire castle staff. She thanked her lucky stars that Alastaire insisted on using the royal guard to man all of the hearths instead of relying on the castle staff.

Pulling together a bunch of ingredients, the matronly woman began creating a list of food for everyone. In ones or twos, members of the staff began trickling in. With each new addition, Pruvencia gave them a task. Soon, bread dough was waiting to be baked while a second pot of stew was placed on the fire to cook.

The door opened once more, but Pru paid it no mind. She continued going around the kitchen, checking on the stews or handing over mugs of hot cider to the younger staff, ale to the older, and tending to the children. Her bones ached. All she wanted was to sit down and take a break. The cold was not good for her old joints.

Someone behind her cleared their throat, but Pru barely paid them any mind. She finished passing out some cookies to the young children when the throat cleared once more.

"If you are feeling a little off, why don't you take a nice ale or hot tea?" Pruvencia said, turning to face the person with an irritated expression. She felt the color leave her face as she stood facing the man, a soldier. "I – I'm sorry. What can I do for you, sir?"

"Pruvencia." The way he said it, she couldn't tell if it was a question or a statement.

"How can I be of service to you?"

The man looked around at the crowded kitchen. Heads turned and untrusting eyes watched his every move. Pru shot him a questioning look, waiting for him to speak.

"Can you follow?" he asked, motioning towards a spot away from the majority of the group. The last of the staff was straggling in, their faces deathly white as they rubbed their hands vigorously for warmth. It was becoming quite crowded in there.

Pru nodded and followed the soldier to an empty section of the kitchen. Children began crawling out of their hiding place, sloughing off the heavy blankets as the added bodies provided more heat to the room. A few of the younger ones cracked smiles as their family finally joined them. The parents and older siblings flashed wan smiles of relief as they felt both the warmth of the kitchen and peace at seeing the rest of their family safe.

"I need you to promise me that you won't repeat anything I tell you," the soldier said, his voice dropping to the point where it was almost impossible to hear over the din of the castle staff.

"What do you want?"

"Please, promise me," he insisted. "Countless lives are at stake."

Pru met his gaze. Behind his exhausted, grizzled visage, the man appeared to be speaking in earnest. She felt she could trust him. At least, she hoped she wasn't about to make a mistake. Too many relied on her to keep them safe.

"Yes, of course," she replied.

A wave of relief washed over his face, momentarily wiping away his exhaustion before it returned. The bags around his eyes deepened in the shadows of the hearth. He looked as bad as Pruvencia felt. Without a word, she waved over William to bring over a mug of hot cider for the soldier. She watched as he stopped rubbing his hands and gratefully took the steaming mug from the elderly steward. He eagerly took a drink, a faint groan of pleasure escaping his lips.

"Thank you," he said. "I have a message for you from the king."

Pruvencia felt her breath catch in her throat. Tears began welling in her eyes. "My Oldar," she whispered. "He's safe?"

"Yes, but probably not for long." He took another drink. "I need you to go speak with him. Get him out of Madden, and to safety."

"I- I can't leave them," she said, turning to the room full of castle staff. "I must protect them."

"He needs you," the soldier insisted. "Please, I know that I ask a lot of you, but your life and all of theirs is in danger no matter what you do. Alastaire is not right. When I spoke to him a little while ago, he seems... off. I can't explain it. I've never met him before, but I don't trust anything about him. The king, he needs you. I will protect your staff as best I can. You have my word."

Pruvencia's lips began to tremble. She turned to look at the rest of the staff, her fingers gripping the shawl around her shoulders. With a shuddering sniff, she nodded her head. "Okay," she whispered. "My little boy needs me, but please. Please keep everyone in the castle safe. As long as they're in here, they're safe. Have you heard the cries?"

As if on cue, a blood-curdling shriek sounded in the distance. The children stopped smiling and ran over to their parents, gripping them tightly around the leg. No one spoke as the responses echoed around the castle. One of them sounded uncomfortably close.

～∽～

Oldar sat huddled in Schaed's wine cellar, his arms circling his knees as he hid in the corner between the barrels. His stomach was in knots. It had been a long time since Schaed had gone to fetch Ingmar. He couldn't imagine why his friend hadn't returned. He had no sense of time in the darkness.

The door to Schaed's shop opened and gently closed. Oldar held his breath as he heard soft footsteps padding on the wooden floors. He wanted to shout out, hoping it was Schaed who finally returned, but he held his tongue. The footsteps neared the wine cellar. The handle started jiggling. Oldar didn't know what to do. Taking a risk, he left the candles lit and pushed his way further into his corner, hoping the tall barrels would keep him hidden. He cursed himself for forgetting to lock the door after Ingmar left.

Slowly, the door opened and a head peeked in. With a rush of emotion, Oldar sprung out from his hiding spot and crossed the length of the cellar in moments. Tears streamed down his face as he threw his arms around his elderly caretaker.

"Pru!" he cried, his body wracked with sobs. "Oh gods, Pru! I'm so happy to see you."

"I'm so happy you're safe, my boy." The woman's voice shook.

Breaking apart, the woman held the king's face in her hands. She gently brushed away the tears that streaked his dirty cheeks, tousling his hair occasionally as she tried to soothe him. Pruvencia stared at Oldar with baleful eyes.

"I've got some bad news, my love. Schaed is dead."

XLII

Brody looked over his camp in the early morning light. The sun was just beginning to rise, her pink fingers stretching through the darkness. Birds started their morning symphony, the warblers, finches, and songbirds singing in perfect harmony. His men slept peacefully despite the heat. The day before had been long, but mercifully uneventful, as they traversed the Rydash Gorge and made their way into Xan.

A couple of men stood guard on the opposite side of the camp, but the rest were undisturbed. Brody had been surprised at the lack of resistance they'd encountered when crossing the gorge. It unsettled him. The warlord nation should've had scouts watching their border, keeping the Great Heart informed. Since there were no keeps or castles, leaving the land open like this seemed to Brody like an invitation for trouble.

Well, they've been fighting themselves up until like fifteen years ago, he figured. *I bet no one wanted to deal with their disputes. Still, it seems wrong not to have run into one person. That display yesterday must be more serious than we thought.*

Brody tried to remember the events from the day before. Pillars of flame interspersed with fireballs and other shows of power flashed in the air. He wasn't sure if it was fighting or a training match. To his knowledge, Xan didn't have many, if any, who were blessed by the gods. The thought of an unaccounted number of magi didn't help ease his concern.

His eyes scanned the slumbering camp once more. It didn't take long before they found the princess. Cienna didn't say much this trip. She didn't seek him out like she used to. Brody felt a twinge of sadness. Normally, she would run and tell him everything. He loved watching her eyes light up and a smile fill her face as she talked. Now, with her mother fighting for survival and Corinth in despair, she suddenly withdrew from him. Instead, he'd caught her talking to Oldar.

It's probably for the best, he thought. *She's a princess. She needs to be with someone of her own station. The wife of a guard is no life for her.*

Brody stared at Cienna as she slept. Her thick, curly hair, slung over her shoulder and tied in a low-hanging tail, moved gently with her body as she breathed. The young man watched her sleeping. She looked serene, her face relaxed and untroubled by bad dreams. Brody sighed as he knew what he must do. A lump caught in his throat as he ripped his gaze away from her.

Goodbye, Cienna. I wish you nothing but happiness.

～～

The morning sun shone in her eyes, waking Cienna up with a groan. Throwing her arm up in a vain attempt to block out the light, the princess rolled over onto her other side before finally giving up and getting up. The birds sang loudly overhead, undisturbed by a man nearby snoring loudly.

"How did I ever manage to sleep through all that noise?" she mumbled as she rubbed her eyes. "It's like trying to sleep through a damn stampede."

"Tch tch," Caitlyn clicked her tongue as she plopped down next to the princess. "When did her highness learn such foul language? Surely, this isn't proper for one of your station." Her tattooed hand, now free of her leather glove, clutched at her breast in mock horror.

"Oh stop," Cienna replied, giving the redhead a shove. "If anything, I picked it up from you."

"That's the beauty of not being a princess," she replied. "I can talk any way I damn well please, and no one will be disappointed in me."

Cienna gave the woman another shove before breaking into giggles. Caitlyn flashed a smile — a genuine one. It made the princess glad to see her friend happy once more. Ever since Caitlyn and Brody had returned to Pharn with Alverick, the redheaded archer seemed off. Withdrawn and moody. Even when she laughed with the princess, Cienna couldn't help but notice that it seemed forced. The last couple days, Caitlyn had spent them solely with Alverick.

Maybe their time together helped her come to terms with whatever she was dealing with. Cienna was happy to see her friend embracing her Tainted status and walking around with her gloves off. She still wore them when she rode, but for their day-to-day minutia, Caitlyn kept them off. Cienna smiled as she remembered how much of a surprise it was when people first noticed them. They'd given the redhead a wider berth than usual. But Caitlyn took it in stride.

"How are you and Alverick doing?" Cienna asked. "You both seem to be feeling better." She pointed towards the Avalanche as he stood by Styx talking to Brody.

Caitlyn turned to face the soldier, a wistful smile on her face. "It was hard, but I think he's doing well. He has his days, but given everything he's been through, I'm just happy that he's managed to find his Anchor."

"That's wonderful."

"How are things with you and Brody?" Caitlyn asked. "I haven't seen you two sneaking away for a little quiet time as much as I thought you would." She gave the princess a wink.

Cienna felt her face flush as she brought her hands up to her cheeks. "How could you imply something like that?" she hissed. "There are people around. They might hear you. What would they think if a rumor like that spread?"

"Relax," Caitlyn said. "I wouldn't do anything like that. I just thought the two of you would have wanted to spend more time to yourself now that you've chosen him."

"We haven't really talked much, actually," Cienna said, her eyes dropping to her lap. She plucked a blade of grass and began shredding it. "I think he's been leaving me to deal with my thoughts on my own." As an afterthought, she added, "Oldar's actually spent more time with me, now that I think about it."

Caitlyn raised an eyebrow. "Really? Did he apologize for how he acted?"

"Yes. We actually had a nice conversation." Caitlyn let out a snort of derision. "He seems to be as troubled as you and Alverick. I... I don't know why, but I feel bad for him. He's gone through so much, yet he's managed to keep his composure, for the most part. I wish I could do the same."

Caitlyn grabbed Cienna's hand and gave it a squeeze. "You're doing fine. You still have your mother, so if you mess up, she can help you fix it."

At that moment, Brody walked over to the two. "Pack up, we're leaving soon," he said.

"Why so quiet?" Caitlyn asked.

"Something's not right," he replied. "I'd rather approach with an abundance of caution instead of letting our guard down. That's how Al and my brother were ambushed. I don't want to repeat their mistake."

Before the women could say another word, he walked off to the next group and began speaking with them quietly. Cienna felt a stab of disappointment that Brody hadn't stayed to talk to her more or ask her how she was feeling. She jumped a bit as she felt Caitlyn's hand rubbing her back. The redhead looked at her with concerned eyes. Cienna tried to flash a reassuring smile, but instead she felt it came out as more of a grimace as tears welled up in the corners of her eyes.

～～

Brody tried not to think about what he'd done as he led Pharn's forces towards Xan. They moved at a snail's pace, making sure to keep to the safety of the sparce trees. The heat of the early morning was already making him sweat. His mouth felt dry, but he didn't want to take a sip from his water skin yet.

"Are you well?" Alverick asked.

The Avalanche's sudden question startled the young captain, pulling him from his efforts to keep his mind empty. He knew he should be paying attention to his surroundings, but he couldn't bring himself to focus.

"I'm fine," he muttered. "We shouldn't be making too much noise. We're bound to run into someone soon."

"The lack of guard unnerves me too," Alverick admitted. "I know what happened. Caitlyn told me. Promise me we'll talk when this is all over."

"Yeah, we'll talk at Fren's."

Alverick gave Brody's shoulder a squeeze and shot the young man a smile as they made plans to meet like the old days. Brody was surprised at how much that simple thought made him feel better. He found he was able to focus a little better.

It's all for the best. Entering a warlord nation as it is on the brink of civil war with a preoccupied mind probably doesn't increase my odds of survival.

Brody led his troops through Xan. As they moved further from the gorge, the weather became more pleasant and the land lusher. Brody was surprised to see that their nation wasn't that much different from Zanir. For some reason, he'd imagined Xan to be a barren land filled with some exotic animals grown for eating. Seeing that wasn't the case left him feeling horrible. All the prejudice he'd grown up with thinking they were an aggressive race of warriors who didn't care for the intricacies of politics were wrong. He knew he had a lot to think about when he returned home.

XLIII

Hroth made his way to the main square and stood by the fountain flanked by Pram and Jytte. Pram's braids were tied back in a high tail, a mace and scimitar held in each hand. The general bounced lightly on his feet, moving side to side in order not to be caught flat on his feet. Jytte underwent a complete transformation, the coffee and cocoa powder mixture having been scrubbed off of her body exposing her pale flesh. Her hair, tied in a high tail, was still darkened from when she dyed it.

The Flame was impressed that although the barbarian was slight, her arms were muscular and she held her battle axe casually in her hand. Like Pram, Jytte bounced restlessly on the balls of her feet, her eyes scanning around the square.

Reaching within, Hroth stoked the fire, preparing his magics for battle. He didn't know what to expect, but he knew that he would need to be ready to call on everything he had. Fyre's voice no longer spoke to him. The faint chatter that he'd grown accustomed to ignoring was replaced with a deafening silence that unsettled him.

"This is your last chance," Hroth said to the others. "I doubt Wyrd will hesitate to use either of you as a target."

"The Pshwani may be here," Pram replied. "There's no way you can take on Wyr-raji and a group of Pshwani."

"Besides," Jytte said, "I have some unfinished business with him. I may not be able to strike the death blow, but the Silver Wolf will not allow for me to leave one marked by Apophos alone. I must do what I can."

Hroth snorted and shrugged. He'd figured as much.

The morning sun slowly crept across the pale sky, working its way towards its zenith. Hroth began to worry that they'd miscalculated. People still walked around the main square, oblivious to the trio as they stood battle ready.

No, not oblivious. Ignoring us.

Hroth's eyes darted around, trying to find ways to draw Wyrd away from the crowd should things go bad. His options were limited, but he found a few side roads that led away from the main area.

"Perhaps we should go," Pram said. "Wyr-raji doesn't seem to be out today. I would've thought the Pshwani would have something to say though."

The general moved to sheath his scimitar. Hroth pushed off from the fountain he'd been leaning against and thought about heading over to the tavern for a bite before setting out to look for Wyrd when a movement from one of the less crowded streets caught his eye.

"The streets are emptying," Jytte said. "Look."

Hroth looked around and realized that the people who had been actively ignoring them all this time were suddenly nowhere to be found. The buildings nearby shut their doors; their lights were blown out to darken the insides in the middle of the day. He watched as the shopkeeps moved away from the windows, pulling their wares to safety. Glancing back to the side street, Hroth noticed a group of Pshwani making their way towards the main square. Viir led the group, his hand on the sheath of his scimitar as he walked. Wyrd traveled beside him, a smirk on his lips and his hands hanging loosely at his sides.

"Looks like someone's decided to join us after all," the Flame said.

Wyrd's eyes widened briefly before a look of anger took over. His hands clenched into fists. Raising both of them to chest level, they suddenly became engulfed in flame. Those around him darted away, giving the man some space as he lowered his still-burning hands once more. Balls of fire grew to the size of a melon in each hand. With a shout, he launched his attack.

Hroth jumped in front of the other two, his arms bursting into flame. Crossing them across his chest, but making sure to keep his face covered, he took the blasts. The heat seared his skin in a way no other Flame had. This was a power beyond Man. It was the power of gods.

Cries rang out as the Pshwani tried flanking them from the sides. Pram and Jytte sprang into action. The general swung his mace in an upward strike towards the nearest person, catching them unawares on the chin. The man crumpled to the ground instantly without even a grunt. At the same time, his scimitar hand shot up to block another man's attack. The blades clashed together, clanging as steel met steel.

To his right, Jytte could be heard letting loose a battle cry as she swung her battle axe at her nearest opponent. The man was not prepared for the small woman to swing so quickly or so fiercely, and caught the blade against his neck. Blood poured from his nose and mouth as she pulled the blade free with a grunt.

Pleased that he could count on the two of them to hold their own, Hroth focused his attentions on Wyrd. Wyrd faced the Flame, his hands still engulfed in flame and his orange eye sparkling. Taking a deep breath, Hroth reached deep within and tapped into his magical energies.

Fire shot from his shoulder and ran down the length of his right arm. His hand became engulfed once more. With a shake, he conjured his whip. The fire hung limply in his hand, ready to strike. Hroth snapped the whip, the tip exploding into a ball of fire on the road. Wyrd took a step back, but his flames did not shrink.

Hroth spun his arm over his head, the flame whip snapping around, before striking at Wyrd. Wyrd jumped back, his arms covering his face as the crack of the whip produced another explosive blast. Before he could recover, Hroth used his other hand to throw a ball of fire at him. Wyrd let out a cry as the flame caught him on the side of his face.

Refusing to stop his attack, Hroth spun his whip over his head. A second crack filled the air and Wyrd let out another shout as the end of the whip wrapped around his arm, the explosion catching him in the face. Hroth tried to pull Wyrd off balance with a tug. Taking a step back as he tugged, Hroth felt a moment of relief as Wyrd stumbled forward.

Pram swung his scimitar and his mace with deadly accuracy. Several Pshwani lay on the ground either dead or wounded. Pram tried to not make his strikes lethal, but he did not hold back. After the first two men fell without much of a fight, the other five approached the general with more caution. The remaining men attempted to circle around the general, entrapping him within their ranks, but Pram managed to dodge and maneuver his way out of their trap.

Viir inched towards Pram, his short sword brought up in a defensive posture. His four countrymen tried to keep themselves between the two, their swords pointed at Pram.

"Viir, call off your men," Pram beseeched. "Only death will come of this. Surely, we can resolve this without more bloodshed."

Several of the men's eyes darted in Wyrd's direction before returning to the general. A couple unconsciously lowered their swords a bit, exposing their neck to Pram. Viir shifted side to side, his sword still in a defensive position.

"Until Liir's death is avenged we will not back down." Viir's voice shook slightly as he spoke. He was not a fighter.

A man to Viir's right darted forward, his sword still in a defensive position. Pram took a step back as the man slashed at him. Using his mace, Pram slammed the weapon down on the blade as his body shot out of striking range of the sword. The weapons clanged together, the mace striking the sword with enough force to change its trajectory.

"We can make it right," Pram said as he brought his mace back up. He swung the mace at the man's head, his scimitar following up as it cut at an upward angle towards the man's heart.

The man threw his arms into the air, his feet scrambling to back up out of harm's way. His mouth hung wide in a silent scream as he barely missed being cut open.

Viir shot Wyrd another glance. "It's too late for that."

With a burst of effort, Pram watched as Viir launched himself at him.

Jytte danced nimbly around the Pshwani. Her battle axe sang in the air as she swung it in dizzying arcs to blocks strikes, while also throwing in a few herself. Three men lay dead around her, the remaining four keeping themselves out of arm's reach. One of them struggled to breathe from the broken nose she'd given him when she managed to land a punch to the face.

A feral smile spread across her face. She was finally free to enjoy herself without fear for the first time in a long while. Her barbarian bloodlust drove her to press her attackers, driving them backwards into the side of a nearby shop. None of them wanted to engage her.

"Come on," she teased. "Have you lost your spirit?"

One of the men sneered at her, his scimitar held up in a defensive position. "You're so smug thinking you've got the upper hand. The fight is just beginning."

A blast of heat slammed into Jytte, making her jump to the side. Her eyes darted to her left and saw Wyrd's arm wrapped with what appeared to be a whip made of flame tugging at the end and pulling Hroth off his feet. Jytte felt her stomach drop as another force of Pshwani soldiers approached them from the side street behind the battling flame-bearers.

"You didn't think we would come so unprepared, did you?" the sneering man asked. "Prepare to die."

XLIV

Hroth's arm shook as he struggled to pull his flame whip back. Wyrd held the tip in his fist, the end wrapped around his forearm, and was dragging the Flame forward step by step. Wyrd's orange eye gleamed as he twisted the whip around his arm, pulling him in closer. A feral grin played on his face as his bloodlust kicked in. Wyrd reached over and unsheathed his dagger with his free hand, flames still licking around his flesh. He wanted the ending to be personal.

The Flame grunted as he tried to pull his whip back, but Wyrd held on tight. Hroth tried to disengage, releasing the weapon as he shifted his energies, but Wyrd had created an extra layer of his own flame over Hroth's, linking their weapons together.

"This truly will be the battle of the assassins," Wyrd teased. "Let's see if you're as good as Pram thinks you are."

Hroth widened his stance in an effort to gain some leverage. He was rewarded as Wyrd gave a mighty tug, but was unable to send him lurching forward. Refocusing his energies, Hroth dissolved his whip. The two were only connected by Wyrd's flame rope. If the Qu'ari man wanted to see who was best, Hroth planned to give him what he wanted.

Darting forward, Hroth ran towards Wyrd. Wyrd's eyes widened in surprise and he took a step back. The fire binding the two together faltered, but Hroth didn't stop. When he was close enough, he shot out his leg and lunge kicked Wyrd in his thigh. The Flame leaned back so Wyrd couldn't cut him. The Qu'ari man was caught off guard as the blow landed on his leg.

The flame rope connecting the two dissolved as Wyrd staggered back and dropped to his knee. His muscle spasmed from the blow, making it difficult to support his weight. Spitting out a curse, Wyrd remained on his knee and launched a fireball at Hroth.

Hroth barely managed to dodge the attack and stumbled before falling. He quickly pushed himself upright, retaliating with a blast of flame. Wyrd brought his arms up to shield his face as the fire slammed into him. He grunted in pain as the heat seared him once more.

A loud cry rang out behind the kneeling Wyrd. Distracted, Hroth looked up and saw a second force of Pshwani warriors heading towards him and the others. The Pshwani broke into a run, their battle cries filling the air of the main square. A burst of fire slammed into him, knocking Hroth backwards and dissipating his attack.

Wyrd managed to make it to his feet, his hand held out in front of him with another blast of flame ready to shoot out any moment. Hroth glanced to each side and saw that both Pram and Jytte were keeping their current opponents at bay. The new force would overwhelm them.

<p style="text-align:center">~~~~~</p>

Pram and Viir's weapons swung through the air, whistling with the ferocity of their strikes. The Pshwani man's blows were wide and sloppy, but they carried weight behind them. Pram mainly worked at deflecting them. He didn't want to hurt the grieving Pshwan man, but he wasn't about to let Viir score a hit.

"Stop, Viir!" Pram called out, blocking a strike with the handle of his mace. "Nothing good can come from this. You *know* that."

Viir grunted with each swing, sweat beading on his brow and chest heaving with exertion, but said nothing. Instead, his eyes darted to the general's shoulder, giving Pram a moment to react before he swung his scimitar.

As the general blocked the blow once more, Viir's eyes widened in surprise before frustration took over.

"You elite think you can do whatever you want just because the Great Heart is one of your own," Viir spat. "We see everything as your Eyes."

"Then why hasn't Vaarden said anything?" Pram asked, bringing his mace up to block another strike.

As the weapons slammed into each other, Viir paused. Pram felt the change in pressure against his mace, but did not press his advantage. Instead, he matched the man's energy and waited.

"What do you mean?" Viir asked. His exhaustion finally hit him, and his voice came out in a soft gasp.

Pram did not allow any give. Instead, he lightly pushed back against Viir's scimitar, allowing the man to back away without feeling like he was being attacked. "Your leader, Vaarden, he hasn't said a word since we've returned. Why hasn't he spoken up about all that's gone on if he is as upset as you?" Viir opened his mouth to speak, but Pram cut him off. "What happened to Liir was horrible. But it was not our fault. Not Evenhand's fault. It all came because of Wyr-raji."

The general took a step back and lowered his arms. The men around Viir stood with theirs still in a defensive position, but Viir copied the general. Several of his counterparts looked around in confusion before lowering theirs a bit. They didn't completely lower their guard, however.

"We... I don't know," Viir said. He shot a glance at Wyrd. Wyrd struck Hroth with a blast of fire, causing the Flame to cry out in pain. The heat from the blow radiated outward, almost bringing Pram and the others to their knees.

Pram shielded his face with his arm. The metal of his weapons began to heat up, the leather grips becoming uncomfortable. He glanced over to Jytte and saw her lying on the ground, blood flowing from her head. The men surrounding her were crying out in pain as they backed away.

"He's the only one who's fighting for us," Viir tried to explain.

"He's using you to fight," Pram countered. "That's all he's ever wanted. To kill."

Despair passed over Viir's face. His weapon arm dropped completely, hanging limply at his side. The others looked at one another, confused. Pram took a step forward, sheathing his scimitar and holding out his hand.

"Brother," Pram said. "Let me help you."

Viir took a hesitant step forward. His hand twitched. Slowly, he raised his own to grab Pram's. His four comrades finally dropped their weapons, standing completely exposed. Their faces were nonplussed, but they made no move against Pram.

A thunderous roar behind them filled the main square. All heads turned to see a large Pshwani force running towards the group. Their weapons were raised high as they neared the fighting. Pram shot a look at Viir who seemed just as perplexed as him at the approaching warriors. The group that had been fighting Jytte called out to Viir, asking what they should do.

As the charge neared, Pram could make out several words being shouted amongst the general battle cry.

"For Vaarden!"

"Justice!"

"What happened?" one of Viir's men called out.

The charging force slowed down as they encountered the two dueling fire wielders. They stood with their weapons at the ready. Hroth shot a pillar of flame at Wyrd, causing the man to jump back the approaching warriors to break ranks. Hroth darted through the square, Wyrd following behind. A trail of blood ran down Hroth's mouth and over Wyrd's brown eye.

It was now just Pram and Jytte. The woman groaned. Pram looked over and saw one of her opponents lifting her up by her hair. Blood ran down the corner of her mouth and down her head. Her hand twitched as she gripped the handle of her weapon. Her other hand was twisted up behind her back, keeping her battle axe out of attacking range of the man gripping her.

"Vaarden is dead!" one of the new warriors shouted.

Viir and his remaining companions gasped. Pram felt his stomach drop as any progress he just made appeared to have vanished. Viir turned to face him. He looked defeated. Pram searched his eyes. The will to fight was gone. He did not believe whatever he'd been told anymore. Subtly, Viir shook his head, maintaining eye contact with Pram, before dropping his gaze.

Those who accompanied Viir broke out into cries of rage. Viir's hand dropped as he turned to face his brothers once more. The man holding Jytte up threw her to the ground, her arm barely making it up in time to shield her head from smashing against the stones. Pram ran over and grabbed her arm, dragging her away from them as she struggled to get back up.

Blasts of fire soared overhead, the heat waves radiating over the group. They flew fast and frequently, hitting nearby buildings and catching their roofs on fire. Black smoke billowed into the sky, darkening the main square.

Jytte clung to Pram's arm as he slowly guided her backwards. The Pshwani army began chanting and stamping their feet on the ground. Echoes rang in the air. And then, suddenly, they stopped. The silence was deafening, their shouts reverberating, even though they had gone still.

"Ready!" one of the newcomers called out.

With the exception of Viir, everyone shouted back in response. They stomped their foot twice.

"Pshwan!" the first man called out.

"Pshwan!" the rest called back.

Pram shoved Jytte behind him, shielding the wounded woman from the approaching Pshwani.

"It's been an honor," Pram said.

"We die as heroes," Jytte replied. "For the Silver Wolf."

"For the Silver Wolf."

Pram gripped his mace and scimitar, bracing himself for the onslaught. As the group advanced on the two, cries rang out. Men broke ranks as they scrambled to find safety as a hail of arrows rained down on them. Seizing his opportunity, Pram grabbed Jytte and pulled her to the safety of the Dancing Wolf's overhang.

In the distance Pram noticed another army approaching. Squinting his eyes, he saw the green livery of Zanir. The ground suddenly began to tremble. Pram watched as small pebbles started dancing on the ground as the earth shook. Men cried out in surprise as they fell to the ground, stumbling to find shelter. A stream of water flew towards the nearest burning building, extinguishing the fire.

"Archers ready!" A young man shouted, his sword pointing at the Pshwani forces. Pram recognized him as the young captain from the gorge: Brody.

A ball of fire flew towards the incoming forces. Pram watched as Wyrd stalked towards the forces of Pharn. Hroth lay on the ground, unconscious.

Dropping his sword arm, a redheaded archer led the others in raining down a hail of arrows once more. The ground began bucking as the Avalanche pulled on the earth. Pram dared to feel hope. The bones were starting to turn to his favor.

XLV

Tʜᴇ ɢʀᴏᴜɴᴅ sᴛʀᴀɪɴᴇᴅ and buckled as Alverick pulled at the bones of the earth. Another stream of water flew overhead as Cienna struggled to put out the fires. Screams sounded in the distance as people hung out of the windows of the burning shops. A baby cried as his mother held him out of the window, trying to keep the black smoke from smothering him.

Bows twanged as Caitlyn's second wave released arrows into the darkened skies. They flew true, striking a number of Pshwani warriors. Their cries rang out. Some dropped to the ground dead while others struggled to find shelter, arrows protruding from their bodies.

A Qu'ari elite, his double-handed weapons style marking him from his Xanan counterparts, stood guard in front of a pale skinned woman leaning on a battle axe.

Must be Swordbane's man. Seems to be outnumbered.

A second man approached them, his hands engulfed in fire. Alverick observed a single orange eye glinting in the light as the sun's rays began breaking through the black smoke. Alverick felt his body shiver involuntarily. They reminded him of Vahnyre's.

"Brody," Alverick said. "That Qu'ari over there and his female friend are on our side." He pointed to Pram as he took shelter under an awning.

"I almost want to say that pale man is as well," Brody said. He pointed to a Flame struggling to stand, blood running down his face. "Seems like they're a bit outnumbered."

"Those three," Alverick agreed. "Spread the word."

Thol and Ronan nodded their heads in agreement as well. Each sent a runner down the line to spread the news. Cienna crossed between the lines to put out some of the fires on their left, as she conjured water in her hands. With each blast of water, she looked more and more pale. Using this much was taking a toll on her body.

A ball of fire raced their way. Men shouted out as they scattered. Horses whinnied and pawed at the air, their riders gripping their necks to hang on. The ball exploded on the ground, scorching the earth and leaving a large indent. Soldiers cried out as the heat from the blast washed over them. Those who were closest saw their skin blister.

Emboldened by the presence of Wyrd, the Pshwani warriors began to regroup. Those on the sides raced towards Brody's forces, trying to flank them as they regained their bearings from the fire attack. Horses panicked, with one rider almost thrown from his mount, as the Pshwani charged with their weapons drawn.

Soldiers struggled to close ranks as the Pshwani's swords began cutting through their ranks. Metal struck metal, sometimes meeting flesh. Cries rang out from both sides as blade cut through flesh. Alverick raised his sword and charged into battle. He noticed the Qu'ari man and his female companion engage a couple of Pshwani nearby. The woman proved to be a formidable warrior despite the blood dripping from her head.

Alverick kept to the sides, making sure he had a building behind him. Arrows whizzed through the air, a few hitting their marks. Slowly, Alverick made his way over to the Qu'ari man until they were within a few arms lengths. The two fought ferociously. The Qu'ari swinging his scimitar and mace in dizzying arcs, much like Swordbane had during the battle at Pharn. The woman, on the other hand, seemed to prefer a more direct style of combat. She plowed through her opponents with astonishing results.

He was about to say something to the two of them when something strange caught his eye. Another person seemed to be fighting against the

Pshwani warriors alongside the Qu'ari general and pale woman. The third man wielded his scimitar in an unpolished fashion. His strikes were clumsy, but still managed to connect. Alverick was surprised at how the man succeeded in not getting hit despite leaving himself open several times.

"You've turned one of their own?" Alverick called out to the Qu'ari.

The man turned, startled that Alverick was able to get so close to them in such a short period of time. The second man, a Pshwani, held a blank stare as he fought his clansmen. There was no determination or even a will to live. He just fought.

"You couldn't have picked a better time to arrive, Avalanche," the Qu'ari replied.

The two maneuvered themselves until they were next to each other. The woman let out a mighty cry and charged the nearest person on their left, affording the Qu'ari a moment to talk.

"We almost reached an accord," he said, nodding to the Pshwani who fought with them. Alverick watched as any Pshwani who challenged the group was met with confusion at seeing one of their own standing against them. Many tried to move around the man, but he stepped in between his clansmen and the Qu'ari. "Wyr-raji has caused much chaos."

Alverick gave the man a blank stare.

"You're the one who was pulled into the abyss," the Qu'ari said suddenly. "You're full of surprises, Avalanche."

"Alverick," the Avalanche replied.

"Pram."

"Who is the leader of the Pshwani?" Alverick asked. Another volley of arrows rained down. This time, they were greeted with a pillar of flame that burned them before they could find their mark. Piles of flaming wood fell to the ground, quickly dying as the arrow was devoured by the fire.

Pram pointed to the man to their left. "It was a man named Vaarden, but we've just received word he's dead. Viir," another nod to the man at their left, "was leading the small group against us to avenge his brother's death."

"Who's driving the rest then?"

A pillar of flame shot through the air. It landed among a pocket of fighters. Both Pshwani and Zanirians screamed in agony as their bodies were burned, their charred corpses dropping to the ground in blackened heaps.

"Wyr-raji has done much damage," Pram said. "Jytte, Viir! We need to stop Wyr-raji. Help me clear a path!"

"That's madness," Jytte said, her heavy accent catching Alverick off guard. "You'll be killed."

"We're dead anyway," Pram replied. "We have to try and stop him. Hroth has failed."

"We'll never make it," Viir said. "There's only so much I can do."

Alverick watched the three struggle. His vision already clouded with red haze on his peripheries from his earlier exertions. He could feel his mind stretching. A Pshwani charged at him, swinging his blade. Alverick countered with his own. The metal clanged together. His opponent grunted as he tried to overpower Alverick.

With a swift kick, Alverick pushed the man in the stomach backwards. The man stumbled back a few steps. Seizing the opportunity, Alverick quickly reached down into the ground and set it shaking. Bits of rubble from the nearby buildings crumbled down, dropping to the earth and barely missing the fighters. Alverick's opponent danced around, trying to keep his footing. Next to him, cries rang out. Alverick looked over and watched as his allies' attackers jumped back, trying to keep their balance.

A ball of fire flew overhead. With a wave of heat radiating outward, screams rent the air as men were engulfed in a ball of god-fyre. Bodies flailed about, flame streaming from their limbs as they tried to extinguish it. They dropped to the ground one by one, unsuccessful.

Where's the princess? Alverick wondered. A ball of electricity flew in the direction of the fire. Men cried out as they began convulsing as the electric ball struck home. Alverick spied Caitlyn's red hair and a mop of curly blonde right beside her. A wave of relief washed over him. *Thank the gods. We can't have the Qu'ari finding her.*

"Lead the way!" Alverick called out to Pram.

The Qu'ari general looked over at Alverick. The Avalanche nodded his head, sheathing his sword and forming a ball of electricity in his hand. He also began pulling on the earth once more, sending fighters stumbling off balance.

"Jytte, Viir. To Wyr-raji."

"I'll check on the Flame," Jytte said.

"Let's go," Alverick said.

～～

With a groan, Hroth slowly came to in a pile of rubble. Clay and bits of stone covered his back. Something warm ran down his nose, tickling him as it moved. The Flame twitched his hands, causing pebbles and other bits of rock to roll off. With effort, he managed to push himself to his elbows. His arms shook under his weight. His head swam and darkness threatened to overwhelm him once more.

"Shit," he muttered.

Hroth tried to raise his head. In the distance, a blurry scene greeted him. A lone figure stood before a sea of fighting bodies. An orange glow encircled him, the light dancing around his hands. As he stood, the light grew in his hands. Suddenly, he launched the ball that he grew in his hands towards the mob in front of him.

Cries rang out as the flames expanded. A ball of blue met the fire. A swirling orb of water extinguished the blaze in a cloud of steam. Hroth blinked his eyes, trying to figure out what he just saw. Was there a Stream amongst the crowd?

Voices hovered over him. Hroth tried to turn towards them, but his arms gave way and he dropped to the earth once more. Before the blackness consumed him, he saw a pair of blue eyes staring down at him. Her mouth moved, but he couldn't hear what she was saying. Next to her, a Pshwani said something to her.

Hroth couldn't hear them, and soon, he couldn't see them.

XLVI

THE WIND BLEW GENTLY as Len and his retinue continued on their way to Xan. The sun shone overhead leaving them to walk in a pleasant warmth. The slight breeze rustled the grass and provided a breath of coolness. Len took the lead, pushing the pace. Despite their journey going quickly, a sense of unease gripped at him, leaving his stomach in knots.

The young general kept telling himself that it was because his wife was due any day, but a part of him didn't fully believe it. He'd been gone from Fa'Tinh for far too long. Too much time had passed and he'd left while Xan was in turmoil.

Pram and his Flame should be able to keep Wyrd and Viir's followers under control until I get back. Len told himself this several times ever since he'd left his home. Every time he said it, he felt less certain. *Mighty Freyna protects our people. She will not abandon me.*

Every time he thought about the blue-haired girl, he found a measure of peace. She'd come to him several times now, and he almost believed that the goddess favored him. She gave him strength. *I'll be damned if I lose everything to Wyrd and the Pshwani.*

A bump against his shoulder brought Len's attention back to the present. Beside him, Kayna held out a water skin. Len grabbed it and took a long drink. The cool water refreshed him. Wiping his mouth with the back of his hand, Len handed it back to her. The female pirate tied the skin back to her hip and began munching on a piece of dried meat. Len followed her cue and pulled out a snack for himself as well.

"How much further?" she asked.

"We're probably still a few days out."

Kayna's face darkened.

"What?" Len asked.

"The Scourge has been talking to his sister, the Tempest, and she seems to be hearing things."

"The woman is more trouble than she's worth," Len replied. "She talks to herself constantly. I almost think she's Snapped, but then she'll have moments where she's completely lucid and I always question myself. I can never tell if she's completely detached from the rest of reality or just touched. But she's strong. As much as I would say to ignore her, I think I need to have a word with her now."

The two walked along in silence. Len picked up the pace, concern causing his chest to tighten. Despite the speed, Kayna took in everything around her. Her lips were pressed in a tight line, but her eyes wandered about. Len glanced at her out of the corner of his eye and noticed that she was admiring the scenery. Butterflies flew about the tall grasses looking for a flower to rest on. The tall trees provided a welcome shade in the warm afternoon air.

A rustling in the grass caught his attention. He kept his gaze on the spot as he continued to move forward. After a short span of time, a rabbit jumped out of hiding. She sat on the road for a brief moment before returning to the tall grasses to hide. Kayna's mouth relaxed into a smile as she watched the rabbit hop away. Len noticed that her eyes darted to the next bit of nature, taking in everything.

No, he realized. She's on guard. She's worried. I'd wager it's that woman.

With an irritated sigh, Len shook his head. Wherever Dez was, there was always trouble nearby. Almost as though she were cursed. Her presence in the gorge led to Liir and his Shadow's death, as well as Wyrd's strange behavior. That woman had cost him a lot in such a short period of time.

"We need to talk," Dez said. Her voice startled Len. He hadn't even heard her approach.

"What do you want?" he asked.

"The winds are speaking to me. There's trouble in Xan and I'm afraid that if we continue at this pace, we won't make it in time." Dez's tone was strangely serious, nothing like the aloof exterior she had presented the few other times he'd seen her.

"What do you suggest? We don't exactly have horses to carry us."

Dez held up her arm. Len stared at the intricate collection of tattoos with mild curiosity. He didn't have much experience with magi; not many in Xan bore the tattoos of the gods. The bulk of his interactions came from the hired mercenaries he'd gotten from Ka'lev's Myrani. His unimpressed reaction must not have escaped her notice.

"I'm a Shadow," she said simply. "If you recall our time in Rydash, you'll know that means I can open dimensional doors for beings to travel through."

"I've had enough of your shadow magic," Len said, his eyes narrowing with distrust. "Every time I've had one of you open a gate it's resulted in more damage than it's worth."

"No." Dez's fingers wrapped around Len's arm tightly. The young general stopped in his tracks and stared blankly at the woman. He tried to hide his annoyance, but he was pretty sure it shown through.

Gods, these people will be the death of me.

"And what were to happen if I did not listen to you?" he asked.

Dez stared back into the young Qu'ari's eyes with a ferocity he hadn't seen. There was something different about this woman. Neither Kayna, nor Maya, nor even his wife could match the intensity of this Tempest's stare.

"Then I will go on without you and leave your people to die."

The matter-of-factness to her tone unsettled Len. He searched her face, trying to find any hint that she may just be rambling on like a mad woman. However, everything he saw appeared to be the truth. His stomach knotted. The sensation drove him crazy. He hated feeling like things were out of his control.

"You would live with death on your head?" he asked.

"I've lived with hundreds, maybe thousands of deaths," Dez replied. "What's one more village? Nations come and go, but Man has always managed to survive somehow. However, these would not be my deaths and it would not be me who had to live with them. Ask yourself, young one, can *you* live with yourself?"

Len balked at her answer.

"Think hard, young Len. You don't have much time."

Heavy footsteps announced someone's approach. Soft chatter among the pirates could be heard as they grumbled about their sudden stop. A few sat down, lounging about. Further towards the back, Len thought he could see a spirited game of dice beginning.

The footsteps stopped and Len forced himself to face the newcomer. Angh stood between Len and Kayna, the female pirate holding out a bit of flower blossom out for the young rabbit from earlier. The grey rabbit sniffed cautiously at the petals in her hand. Kayna was crouched over making little clicking sounds with her tongue as she tried to coax the rabbit to take them. Leaning against a tree off the road, Maya watched Kayna's attempt at making a friend with a bemused smirk on her face.

Angh towered over Len, his considerable size lending to his imposing aura. Len found himself unable to meet the man's gaze. Anger boiled in his chest as he fought the urge to submit to the mighty god. Len still struggled with the primal energies that emanated from the man. All he wanted to do was put distance between them, but his pride would not allow it.

"Follow me," the god said.

Len found his feet moving on their own as he shadowed Angh. The three walked away from the group. Len was surprised that no one seemed to notice that their leader was taking him and the Tempest to a secluded place. Dez's arms were crossed over her chest as she walked.

"Where are we going?" Len asked.

Angh leaned against a tree, the branches barely missing the top of his head, and folded his arms across his chest. "What holds you back?"

Len felt his eyebrow raise at the question. "What?"

"Clearly something is bothering you if you are turning down the opportunity to save your people. I noticed it when we first met. Your reluctance to join me when we went to confront Jylla. Is it because things are not under your control? Do you really need to be master of your own destiny that badly that you are willing to risk the lives of your people?"

Len watched the pirate lord with a careful eye. He felt himself seething at the man's words, yet he dared not show how he felt lest the god kill him. Len knew he was being pushed, but he couldn't figure out the end game.

"When I was younger, I went to a seer who read the bones for my future. I accomplished much, all at my own hand. He said my strength and cunning would be more than enough to get me whatever I desired. The bones never lie."

"The bones also do not take into consideration the motives of gods," Angh countered. "For centuries, we have been content watching Man as he went about his life. We had much to do to keep the balance. Things have changed and what worked in the old days is no longer. Will you bury yourself in the past or lead your people into the present?"

Len shifted his weight as he crossed his arms. He didn't want to admit it, but he had suspected as much. The seer had not spoken of the gods taking a role in his life. Len had seen firsthand how beneficial it was to have the mighty Freyna favor him in his ventures. It was something he hoped he'd continue to benefit from for the rest of his life.

"You call yourself a god," Len began. "Tell me, what awaits me back home?"

Angh's gaze dropped for the first time, a look of pain crossing his strong visage. Dez swallowed hard, as if she was fighting back tears.

"I cannot say," he said softly. "The balance is in jeopardy. When Eldest Brother Graak, oldest of us lesser gods, spoke to me on the ship, he said that his sister was punished for exposing the disparity. Sweet Freyna is now being tended to by another. Hopefully, she will be able to make it for what is to come."

"Freyna..." Len felt a pang in his chest. He had asked the goddess to keep an eye on his family and protect them from harm. If she was hurt, his family was exposed. "Tell me what you know."

Angh shook his head. "I can't."

Len felt himself sink into the ground. For the first time in a long time, he felt helpless, and it frightened him. All his life, he prided himself on being able to solve whatever problem came his way with a show of strength. Growing up, he'd climbed the ranks of the Qu'ari elite easily, earning him a following, and eventually catching the eye of Pram as he served the former Great Heart. Now, everything seemed to be spiraling out of control.

"I have heard things," Dez spoke up. Len snapped his head in her direction. "The wind, it speaks to me. It talks of the Ancients awakening, and an unspeakable darkness. I believe whatever is happening in Xan is only the beginning. I said earlier that you don't have much time. I need an answer. Do I open the door?"

Pushing himself up, Len unsheathed his scimitar and warhammer. Whatever was happening in Xan, he wanted to face it prepared. Spinning the warhammer idly in his hand, Len took a few deep breaths. He found himself easily returning to his training and becoming focused despite every-thing he'd gone through in the last few days.

"Open it." Turning to Angh, Len added, "Make sure your people are ready. Once the gate opens, we attack."

"They'll be ready," Angh assured him. "They've been through more than you give them credit for."

"But you've never encountered someone like Wyr-raji," Len replied. It felt weird to use his friend's true name. The man had gone by Wyrd since they were boys. "He's got the power of the gods and the temperament of a wild jackal. And his god powers came after being set on fire by Alazi. I'd hate you to lose one of your own because you underestimated him."

Angh's hand clenched the hilt of his sword. As Dez stood next to Len, she began summoning the dimensional gate. Her tattoos glowed silver on her arms and her hair began to whip about in an unseen wind. Angh stalked over to his crew and passed down orders. Kayna's crew crowded around Len and Dez, their weapons drawn and faces set.

The door opened and on the other side, Len could see Fa'Tinh's main square shimmering. Black smoke darkened the air, mixing with the screams of the dying and the cries of his people. Arrows flew through the air only to burst into flame and fall to the ground. Balls of fire and electricity slammed into each other, throwing anyone unfortunate enough to be nearby to the ground as the shock from the impact hit them. Walls of water sprang up as the fire targeted both warrior and soldier alike.

Kayna's mouth hung open, her hand covering it in horror. Tears rolled down Dez's cheeks as she observed the carnage. Somehow, she managed to keep focused enough to ensure the portal didn't close. A young woman scur-ried away from a burning building with her infant clutched to her chest as the babe wailed. Tears streaked the woman's smoke-stained face and she coughed as she ran. A distinct limp was noted, as though she'd fallen in her haste to escape. She almost didn't make it far enough before the building she'd been standing under crumbled.

Gripping his weapons, Len stepped into through the shimmering door.

~⁓~

Steam evaporated around her as Cienna barely managed to put up a water barrier in time. The princess gasped as blackness threatened to envelope her. She'd used up too much of her energy putting out the fires and keeping Wyrd's attacks from hitting people. Sweat covered her body, matting her hair to her red face.

The ground rumbled, throwing her off balance. With a cry, Cienna struggled to stay upright as she stutter stepped. A pair of strong arms grabbed her from behind, steadying her. She turned to see Brody holding her around the waist, his sword drawn and held in a defensive position in his other hand.

"Are you all right, Waterdrop?" he asked. His eyes scanned the area, keeping an eye out for one of Wyrd's attacks. It was less likely that he'd encounter a Pshwani. A number of them had broken away as soon as it was clear that there were magi fighting and fled the main square.

"Yes," she replied breathlessly. "Thank you."

"Stay close to me or Caitlyn," he said, turning his body and gripping his sword in both hands as an enemy approached cautiously. Blood spattered his clothing and stained his blade. He'd been busy today.

The princess stumbled as she tried to back away. The Pshwani charged and Brody brought up his blade. Steel met steel as the blades clashed together. Brody grunted as the other man's force pushed him back a step. His body trembled with exertion and his breathing came out in strained gasps. With a lurch, the ground shook once more, causing the Pshwani to pause his attack and giving Brody the opportunity to push his foe away. Brody followed up with a quick kick to the leg before cutting the man on the arm. The Pshwani cried out and backed away with a limp.

The shaking of the earth was getting more and more frequent. Cienna wondered if Alverick was still in control, or if he was on the verge of releasing something devastating. She hadn't seen him in action like this at the gorge, but she did remember how he made Caer Pharn shake. He was powerful, and it scared her.

~~

Wyrd grinned as he threw ball after ball of fire at the Zanirian army. He didn't care who he hit. A burning body was a burning body. All he cared about was taking his rightful place as the leader of Xan. He noticed some of the Pshwani attempting to flee from the main square down side streets and alleys. Every time that happened, an anger burned deep within, bubbling into rage. How dare they abandon him when he was about to bring them victory.

In the end, it made his decision easy. Xan did not suffer cowards, and with a thought, they were engulfed in a ball of fire.

Wyrd was amazed at how alive he felt despite expending much of his energy during the fight. He would've thought that he would be feeling fatigued, but his energies were still high. With a raised arm, he blocked another ball of electricity that flew his way. The electricity slammed against a wall of flame, the impact pushing him back a few steps.

He shielded his eyes as he tried to find where the Avalanche was. There were two of them, Wyrd knew. Two Sparks. One was the Avalanche. The other, he hadn't found yet. All he cared about was the Avalanche.

Wyrd had lost sight of Pram and Hroth early on. Once the Pshwani joined in the fight, both of them, along with his barbarian prey, disappeared in the sea of flailing bodies. Wyrd felt an initial spike of rage as he realized he lost track of them, but quickly let it go. It was no matter. He would find them soon enough.

The ground shook, causing him to lose his balance and stumble. Wyrd caught himself before he hit the ground. With a snarl, he scanned the fighters for his target. It took a moment, but he found him. The Avalanche stood off to the side with his sword drawn. He was alone despite the frenetic movements all around him.

Wyrd licked his lips as he locked his prey into his sights. He felt a hunger building up within him. He wanted that man dead. Fire exploded in both of his hands, growing with intensity until the burned brightly. Wyrd almost felt giddy as he pictured the Avalanche's flesh slowly melting from his body. He brought up both hands to chest level, ready to release his energy.

A shimmering light caught his attention. Several of the Pshwani called out as a circular hole appeared in the middle of the main square. The flames licking Wyrd's hands disappeared as he took a step forward, curious. The curiosity turned to surprise and before quickly morphing into rage as he watched Len walk through the shimmering portal. The Qu'ari general was accompanied by others, all with their weapons drawn. An olive-skinned woman with chocolate hair was with them, her tattoos glowing silver as she whipped up the wind around her.

"Hello, Wyr-raji," Len said with a smile. "I hope I didn't keep you waiting long."

XLVII

Baring his teeth, Wyrd let out a howl of rage as his hands burst into flame once more. Len brought his weapons up, assuming a defensive stance. The ground shook below them as the Avalanche tugged at the ground. Bits of rubble fell from the surrounding buildings and crashed into the earth around him. The stones barely missed him as Wyrd danced around, as much to keep his balance as it was to avoid the collapsing debris.

A gust of wind slammed into him, knocking the air out of his lungs and forcing him to take a step back. As the wind touched his body, he felt the fyre within shudder. The sensation left him feeling confused, but he chose to ignore it. Instead, he focused on Len and the Avalanche.

The ground beneath him shook. Wyrd widened his stance to keep on his feet. The newcomers cried out in surprise as they stumbled. More bits of stone fell from the buildings. The smoke was beginning to thin out as the shops were no longer burning. People stopped screaming, most of them having made an escape sometime during the fighting.

His new enemies fanned out, the bulk of the group engaging with the remaining Pshwani. Wyrd watched as the warriors struggled to meet the new threat, many of them falling quickly to the onslaught. Soon, it was only Len, the Avalanche, the Tempest, and a large man. He clenched his fists as he prepared to fight. The flames licked his flesh, begging for something it could consume. With a smile, Wyrd knew the fyre wouldn't have to wait long.

~

The winds around Dez built in intensity as she faced the Qu'ari man. She could sense there was something wrong about him. He had an inhumane energy that swirled around him. It felt familiar, but she couldn't place it. Her tattoos glowed silver, shining bright even in the light of day.

"Sister," Angh said.

"I know," Dez replied. "But it's the only way."

Angh touched Dez on the shoulder for a moment. She felt a surge of energy course through her. Aria smiled at her brother's tender touch; the sensation left Dez feeling both giddy and confused. Aria's emotions hadn't come through strongly in the past. Not like this, anyway.

The pirate lord raised his warhammer, motioning for Len to do the same. "This is it. As long as we can keep him busy, Aria and the Avalanche over there can do what needs to be done."

"I wanted to be the one who stopped him," Len said.

"It's not likely," Angh replied. "But you're free to try. Just don't get yourself killed."

Dez snorted. She knew the man's words weren't funny, but the nonchalant way he said it took her by surprise. Len shot her a withering look as he raised his weapons a little higher. Muttering an apology, Dez closed her eyes and began focusing on stoking her tempest. An image flashed in her mind. With a nod, she got to work.

~

Alverick watched as Swordbane and the large figure charged the Qu'ari man. Dez stood off to the side, her hair flying around her as she built her magical energies. The men didn't get more than a few feet away before the nearby rubble began circling Dez. Small bits of wood and stone smashed into the ruined buildings.

Beneath him, he felt the bones of the earth sliding about. They were ready for him to pull on them. He'd played with them a bit during the battle, giving them a little nudge here and there to help even the playing field, but the time was drawing close to when he would give them a tug.

Swordbane reached the Qu'ari first. The Qu'ari man launched a massive ball of fire at Swordbane, who barely dodged the attack. Alverick was sure that the heat from the fire had singed the general's hair. But he wasn't fazed. Swordbane's warhammer arced high as his scimitar sliced upwards from his knee to his throat. The Qu'ari man barely managed to evade the two strikes, stutter stepping backwards.

Alverick gave the ground a little push. He smiled as he watched the man stumble further, slamming into a building in an effort to keep himself upright. With a growl, he launched a pair of fireballs in Alverick's direction. Alverick dove out of the way, curling into a roll and emerging back on his feet. The shop behind where he had just been managed to not burst into flames, the stone walls not giving the god-fyre anything to hold on to. However, the intensity of the heat led to the windows exploding into tiny shards of glass.

By the time Alverick turned his attentions back to the fight, Swordbane and the tall man were raining blows down on the Qu'ari. The strikes fell fast and fierce, the man barely able to block and dodge the onslaught. Flames wrapped around the Qu'ari's arms, and a wall of fire separated the two, almost as though it were a shield.

The large man's hammer buckled the Qu'ari's knees as it slammed into the flame shield. The Qu'ari actually dropped one knee to the ground as the force of the blow pushed downward on him. Swordbane used that opportunity to dart around his fellow clansmen and take his back. His scimitar flashed in the sun as it sliced at his opponent's neck.

With a burst of light, flames erupted from the Qu'ari, shrouding him in a blanket of god-fyre. Both Swordbane and the large man were thrown away from the Qu'ari. Swordbane smashed into a nearby building, his weapons dropping from his hands as he lay unconscious on the ground. The large man landed in a sitting position against a shop near Dez. He appeared dazed as he struggled to stand up. Blood dripped from his head and he staggered as he tried to stay on his feet.

Dez didn't seem to notice anything going on. She stood motionless, her arms outstretched and a cloud of debris circling her. Her tattoos shone brighter. Alverick looked up and realized that the sky was darkening. Soldiers and warriors alike fled as the effects of her winds began to pick up. He could feel her maelstrom building, bits of stone at his feet dancing from her power. And still, she kept stoking her energy reserves.

The Qu'ari's hands were engulfed in flame once more. Stalking forward, he raised his arm to release his fire. Dez's eyes were still closed as she focused within. Alverick gave the earth a tug as he raced over to distract the Qu'ari.

Rocks bounced on the ground and curses filled the air as Alverick sprinted towards the Qu'ari man. His feet moved quickly, his momentum keeping him from falling over. His foe was beginning to regain his balance as Alverick launched himself into the man, shoulder first. The two fell to the ground, Alverick rolling over the Qu'ari and onto the ground.

His opponent spat out a string of curses in his tongue as he landed on his shoulder wrong. Alverick noted his adversary's discomfort as he gingerly put weight on his right side as he attempted to get up. One brown eye and one orange eye locked onto the Avalanche, glaring daggers at him. Alverick grabbed his sword and sheathed it. Red haze tugged at his periphery, steadily moving inward. With a deep breath, Alverick formed a ball of electricity between his hands. This was not going to be won with a sword.

～⌣～

Brody scrambled to his feet and pushed the dead Pshwani off him. The newcomers' arrival gave Brody and his men the upper hand, allowing for the Zanirian army to quell the Pshwani forces. Most of the Pshwani beat a hasty retreat, but some stayed, surrendering their weapons to Brody's soldiers.

Ronan limped his way over as blood ran down his arm and the side of his head.

The officer looked as bad as Brody felt. His leg ached from the wound he'd received outside of Pharn's gates a couple weeks back, having not given it the opportunity to fully heal. The muscle trembled, but still supported his weight. Wiping his face with the back of his arm, Brody noticed that there was some blood on him. He didn't give it too much thought, however. It could have been from him or someone else.

"Any word from Thol?" Ronan asked.

Brody shook his head. "I haven't seen him. No word that he's died though."

"Good enough," Ronan replied. "How's the losses? Should we regroup? Those new men, they almost look like pirates or something. I haven't seen any bandits dressed like that before."

"I think they're on our side." Brody tried to sound more confident than he actually felt. "They haven't made a move to attack us, at least. We can't be too sure though."

"Brody!"

The two officers spun around. Approaching slowly, Cienna struggled to make her way over to them. Caitlyn's barely conscious body hung limply at her side, the redhead's arm slung around the princess' shoulder. Caitlyn's eyes fluttered for a bit before continuing to stare blankly at the ground. Brody and Ronan hurried over to the princess and helped her with the red-head. While Ronan sat Caitlyn on the ground, Brody checked on Cienna.

The princess collapsed into his arms, her body trembling as she fought to remain awake. Sweat had matted her hair to her face, strands plastered to her cheeks. Her breathing was ragged and her body limp. Brody felt panic well in his chest as he held the princess. He had never seen her look so frail before.

"Brody!" Ronan called out over the ever-increasing winds. "She's in bad shape."

Cienna gave Brody's arm a faint squeeze to let him know she was okay as she gasped out something incoherent. Trusting that the princess would not topple over, Brody waited beside her for a few moments, his hands poised right next to her, to make sure she could hold herself up. Cienna lifted her head up just enough to meet his gaze and flashed him a weak smile. Her body swayed side to side as she sat.

Gently, Brody laid her down on the ground. She didn't protest, and closed her eyes as her head touched the earth. Brody checked her once more to make sure she was breathing, and as soon as he felt comfortable that she was not in any immediate danger, he made his way over to the redhead. His stomach knotted as he reached Ronan.

Caitlyn lay limply in Ronan's arms. Her limbs were splayed out like a rag doll's and her head rested gently against his shoulder. Her eyes stared blankly at her legs, the emerald green orbs having lost their sparkle. Caitlyn's mouth moved as though she were talking, but no sound came out. Brody's stomach clenched and he almost lost his breakfast. He'd seen this before when they rescued Alverick from Aramaine. Caitlyn's fingers twitched, as though she were trying to close her hand over something.

"She's bad," Ronan said. "Must've hit her head on something. We need to get her out of here."

Brody tried to swallow past the lump in his throat. He couldn't find it in him to say the words out loud. Brody hoped against hope that he was wrong. Caitlyn Snapped.

"Brody!" The urgency in Ronan's voice caught his attention. "We need to get her to safety. Now."

"Uh... yes. Yes. Ronan, take our wounded and dead back to the camp, along with the princess and Caitlyn. I'll keep an eye out for Thol. Once we get the chance, we'll head back and get you. If we're not back by nightfall, take shelter somewhere and retreat to Pharn before first light."

"Do you think things will turn?" Ronan's stared at Brody, his eyes full of concern. "I thought I saw that conjurer with the pirates."

"I don't know. I hope not."

Ronan scooped Caitlyn up and rose to his feet. Whistling to the nearest soldier, Ronan told the man to pick up the princess and head out. As word spread of Ronan's flank's retreat, soldiers began lugging bodies back with them. As the earth shook, many of them toppled over to the side, barely managing to keep their footing.

"See you tonight," Ronan called out as he fled the main square.

Brody watched as the main square began clearing out. Winds tore at his clothes. Looking up, he noticed that the sky was covered with black clouds. One particular cloud caught his eye. It was thin, almost like a finger, and was slowly extending to the ground. Brody's chest tightened and he felt his legs buckle as he looked at the strange cloud. There was something odd about it.

A powerful unseen force slammed into Brody, throwing him to the ground and knocking the wind from him. Turning his attention to the dueling magi, Brody saw Alverick and Wyrd locked in combat. Both were charging up their energies in their hands, larges balls of fire and electricity forming rapidly. Off to the side, he saw Dez lifting her head to the heavens. The large man who walked out of the dimensional door with her stood at her side, his hands resting on her shoulders. A crack of lightning flashed across the sky quickly followed by the rumble of thunder. The ground began rocking more violently than it had during the battle. Men fell to the ground. Cries ringing out as they hit the ground.

"Fall back!" Brody called out. His voice was ripped from his throat as the winds around him howled.

Soldiers from Pharn as well as the pirates and remaining Pshwani stumbled over each other as they attempted to flee the main square. Men tripped over the bodies of the fallen in their haste, the roiling of the ground making it difficult to keep their balance. Thol raced by Brody, a wounded pirate's arm slung over his shoulder, shouting orders to retreat to their rendezvous position with Ronan.

"Brody!" Thol shouted over the wind.

Brody looked at Thol, struggling to direct the fleeing men while juggling the wounded pirate at his side. Brody turned to look at the fight. Alverick and Wyrd exchanged magical attacks, the elements clashing together and sending powerful bursts of energy out as they collided. To the left, Swordbane was making his way to the fight, his warhammer poised in his hand to strike. The young general moved with a limp, blood running down his face. Brody found his body wouldn't move. Instead, he found himself taking a step closer to the action.

"Brody!" Thol shouted again. Panic was in the man's eyes as he silently implored Brody to follow him in retreat. When Brody didn't move, he called out again. "Come on!"

Thol slipped the injured pirate's arm off of his shoulder. The man was able to stand on his own as Thol ran over to Brody. Thol grabbed Brody by the arm and tried to pull him along with him.

"Please, Brody! We have to go!"

The desperation hung from every word as Thol pulled Brody's arm. His eyes stared into Brody's, begging Brody to follow him to safety. Brody found himself unable to move. He knew that he should, but something told him to stay.

Shaking his head, Brody gently pushed Thol's hand off of his arm. "I'm sorry. I can't."

Thol's eyes were pained. The captain did not want to abandon Brody, but his own fear pushed him to run.

Pulling the man in a tight embrace, Brody placed his mouth against Thol's ear. "Take care of everyone. I'll see you again."

With a rough shove, Brody pushed Thol away towards the injured pirate. Thol took a few hesitant steps away from Brody before speeding back over to the pirate and assisting him with fleeing the square.

Brody watched his friend retreat. He didn't spend too much time before pulling out his sword and moving towards the action.

XLVIII

Winds whipped around the main square sending debris flying into the air. The area was quickly emptying of living bodies, leaving the dead scattered on the ground. Dez's hair flapped around her face, her hair tie having snapped apart earlier in the fight. Her mind felt stretched to its limits as she continued to stoke the winds in her energy reserves. Just like in the past, she felt a comforting presence cradling her.

"It's too strong," Dez gasped. Her eyes snapped open as she stared into the sky. A long, black cloud tendril crept closer and closer to the earth.

Have faith. We can do this.

"I can't," Dez replied, her voice shuddering from the strain. "This is different. I'm at my limit."

Hold strong. I will get us to the end.

Tears ran down Dez's cheeks as she struggled to keep herself from falling apart. Her breathing came out in ragged gasps as she pushed herself further. A pair of strong hands gave her shoulders a squeeze. Glancing to her right, Dez saw Angh holding onto her as he raised his hand to the heavens towards the blackness.

"Have faith, Dzeara." Angh's gaze never left the sky as he focused on his efforts. "My sister and I are here with you. Keep going."

A lump formed in her throat as she tried to answer. Sensing her discomfort, Angh finally looked down at her. His eyes stared at her gently despite the chaos surrounding them. With a smile, he bent over and kissed her lightly on the top of her head. The simple action filled her with warmth.

Exhaling, Dez closed her eyes once more and focused on bringing her ultimate weapon down to the earth.

Sweat ran down Alverick's body, soaking him and plastering his clothes to his skin. His breathing was labored as he struggled to summon another ball of electricity while still manipulating the earth. The Qu'ari man barely seemed fatigued. His flames glowed strongly around his entire body. With a smirk, the man manifested two new balls of fire in his hands.

The Qu'ari man snapped one of his hands towards the ground. His ball of fire changed its shape into a sword. The blade covered his entire arm and almost touched the ground. Around the edge of the fire blade, bits of flame danced around.

Alverick considered pulling on the earth once more. There had to be a way to throw the Qu'ari man off and shake his confidence. He started poking around, searching for something closer to the Qu'ari man when something caught his attention. Without seeming too interested, Alverick glanced over his opponent's shoulder. Swordbane cautiously approached, his warhammer in his hand.

The two made eye contact and Swordbane nodded. Alverick took his ball of electricity between his hands and broke it into two smaller ones. He launched the two balls one after the other at the Qu'ari man. At first, his opponent smirked as he brought his arms up to shield himself. His eyes widened in fear as he realized the projectiles were growing in size the closer they came. He quickly dropped what he'd been creating and rushed to set up a wall of flame to absorb the attack.

As soon as the wall went up, Len broke into a run. The last few steps to his adversary were crossed quickly. His warhammer went up and down in quick succession as he struck the Qu'ari man on the temple. The man crumpled to the ground, blood running down the side of his head from the blow.

Wind continued to tear at them as Dez and the large man continued to summon whatever they had planned. Swordbane's arm dropped to the ground and he leaned on the warhammer. His body shuddered and threatened to collapse beneath him. Alverick suddenly felt exhausted as well. He released the energy in his hands and let go of his hold on the earth.

A voice shouted over the roaring winds. Alverick tried to turn his head, but his body wouldn't move. He just wanted to melt into the ground and sleep. It had been too long since he'd had a peaceful moment to himself and a nap sounded amazing at the moment. The voice called out again. Alverick managed to crane his head a bit. The red haze that had been hovering in his periphery at the beginning of the fight now tinged his vision almost completely.

A figure quickly approached him. In the red cloud, Alverick couldn't make out any features. They blurred together with the black shadows, obscuring everything. Another shout rang out before the figure was upon him. Brody.

"Al! Thank the gods you're all right," he called out between gasps. The howl of the wind carried his words away so that Alverick could barely hear them.

"Brody, what are you doing here?" Alverick blinked rapidly, trying to clear his vision and his head. "Everyone left."

Swordbane limped over, his scimitar now sheathed and his warhammer helping him walk. With each step, a grimace flashed across his face. Alverick moved to offer the Xanan a hand, but Swordbane swatted it away with a growl.

"I don't need your help."

The three stood together for a moment, looking at their downed opponent. Alverick found himself staring at the man. He couldn't explain why, but there was something about him that made the hair on the back of his neck stand up.

"We should go to Dez and figure out our next course of action," Alverick said.

Swordbane and Brody followed him wordlessly. It didn't matter if they tried to. The wind was howling so loudly that their words were carried away.

Another bolt of lightning flashed across the sky accompanied by the rumble of thunder. Fat drops of rain began falling. As they hit the ground, they quickly disappeared into the dry earth. Walking the short distance to the two under the eaves took forever. The trio fought to make progress against the gusts. As the rain started falling more heavily, they went from thick drops to small, thin ones that pelted their bodies.

"Stop!" Brody called out to Dez. "He's dead!"

Something felt off to Alverick. As he reached the shelter, he turned to look at the fallen form of the Qu'ari man. He heard Swordbane talking to the large man about the man, Wyr-raji. Through the sheets of rain, Alverick squinted his eyes. Wyr-raji's body was still on the ground. He couldn't be sure, but he almost thought that he could see a black smoke rising up from him. He also thought he saw steam.

The three spoke in the background, Dez still lost within herself as she brought her strange cloud to the ground. Alverick took a step forward, trying to see if he was imagining things. His stomach dropped as he saw the black wisps becoming thicker as they wafted off of Wyr-raji's body. Behind him, the talking stopped and the only source of sound was the elements. A sudden jolt pulled Alverick backwards, causing him to stagger.

"Back up," a deep voice warned. Alverick turned and saw the large man briefly before he was dragged behind the man.

"It's..."

Alverick didn't have time to finish his thought as he stumbled behind the tall man. In the rain, the steam and blackness that emanated from Wyr-raji's fallen body exploded into a wave of darkness. A shadowy figure stood up, followed shortly by the Qu'ari man. Flame engulfed his body, flaring out in all directions. Alverick gulped as he realized that if this happened a moment earlier, he would've been killed.

Another hand pulled Alverick back. Turning to thank Brody, he was surprised to see Swordbane. The Qu'ari general struggled pull Alverick back to safety as the large man stalked forward.

"Leave him," Swordbane said into his ear. "This is no longer a fight for us."

Alverick shot Swordbane a confused look. The general did not respond, but pointed to the large man as he approached Wyr-raji. Behind Swordbane, Brody stood with his mouth wide open.

"What do you mean?" Alverick asked.

"So, you come at last."

Alverick was surprised to hear the strange voice coming from Wyr-raji so clearly despite all of the noise around them. It was deep and gravelly, and familiar. Alverick tried to remember where he heard the voice before. A dark shadow stood behind the Qu'ari as he blazed in the rain. A pair of orange eyes stared out from the shadows.

"I thought you would have remained hidden, Ghan."

"By the gods," Alverick swore quietly.

Ghan swung his warhammer casually from hand to hand as he approached. "It's been a long time indeed, Vahnyre. I heard you tried to kill my brother."

"Czand was weak," Vahnyre's voice said with a laugh. "Just like your sister. I should just wipe out all of you."

A crack of lightning flashed in the sky, illuminating everyone in the darkness. The dark man behind Wyrd loomed over him, orange eyes blazing. Ghan stood facing his opponent completely relaxed, his warhammer moving in lazy arcs. The air around Alverick went still despite the electricity flowing through it. An eerie silence surrounded the group as the howling wind suddenly died down. Instead, as the thunder rumbled in the distance, a new monster emerged.

Having finally touched down on the earth, a swirling mass of clouds moved quickly on the ground. Bits of thatching and tile from the roofs lifted up and disappeared into the vortex as the nearby trees struggled to stay anchored to the ground. Leaves and branches ripped off only to be lost to the darkness.

The orange eyes behind Wyrd faltered as the two took a step back. Wyrd gazed up at the funnel, his mouth parted. Vahnyre clenched his fists and let out a cry of rage, sending an inferno erupting out of every pore of Wyrd's body. The aethren's scream melted into one from the Qu'ari man as his hair went up in flame until all that was left was his smooth flesh.

Ghan stopped swinging his warhammer and settled into a defensive stance. To his left, Dez walked up next to Alverick. Her entire body glowed silver. The tattoos on her arm were so bright that they almost appeared to be white. Her hair whipped around her and her eyes shone with a silver light, just like her body. Reaching out with one arm, she easily opened a dimensional door and pointed to the three to walk in. Without question, Alverick, Brody, and Swordbane crossed into the safety of the portal.

XLIX

THE PORTAL DOOR did not close after Swordbane walked through. Instead, the three watched as Dez calmly walked over to the two gods. The tip of her tornado followed behind her, the winds ripping shutters and roofing from buildings.

Ghan and Vahnyre leapt forward. The warhammer moved in dizzying arcs as Ghan launched a ferocious attack on Wyrd and Vahnyre. With Vahnyre acting outside of Wyrd's body, the pair were able to use their arms to block and deflect each strike. Shields of flame sprung up almost instantly. Sparks flew out every time the hammer struck. With their free hands, Vahnyre and Wyrd threw balls of fire at Ghan. Wyrd even recreated the flame whip Hroth had earlier that day, snapping it at the god and stopping his attacks.

With a crack, the tip of the whip snapped at the god. A sudden twist of his arm allowed Wyrd to wrap the whip around Ghan's leg. A feral smile broke out on the Qu'ari's lips as he ripped the whip back, causing the god to fall as his leg was pulled out from under him. Vahnyre didn't waste a second as he used both hands to send pillars of flame at the fallen god.

Both blasts struck Ghan with a blinding intensity. He barely managed to bring his arms up to protect his face. Ghan felt his skin blister as he was pummeled with the fire. Wyrd dissolved the whip and joined in on attacking Ghan. Unsheathing his dagger, Wyrd dove at the god and began slicing at his arms.

The blade cut through Ghan's flesh, red blood running down his arms. As Wyrd moved to stab him on his sides, Ghan attempted to protect himself, exposing his face to the fire. The god let out grunts of pain as he struggled to fight off his two attackers.

~~~

With a wave of her hand, Dez pushed the funnel in Wyrd's direction until it settled over him. The flames around his body whipped around in the wind. Using her free hand, Dez formed a ball of water and threw it in Ghan's direction, extinguishing the flames. With a rope of water, she wrapped it around the god and pulled him free from the two, knocking Wyrd to the ground.

As soon as Ghan was out of the tornado, Dez redoubled her efforts. The familiar presence of Aria hovered around Dez as she focused on tightening the winds around Wyrd and Vahnyre. The aethren howled, his voice getting lost in the gale, as he threw a ball of god-fyre at her. The flame entered the winds and transformed the funnel into a mass of flaming winds.

Dipping into her dwindling energy reserves, Dez released a pillar of water into the funnel, extinguishing the flames. She felt a twinge pull at her mind and she faltered. A grimace flashed across her face as she struggled to handle both styles of magic. In her mind, she could see the silver-haired goddess reaching out her hands, offering her help.

Ghan pushed himself to his feet, his knees buckling as his legs shook. As Wyrd moved to release another ball of fire, the god swung his warhammer in rapid circles before launching the weapon into the funnel. The projectile sped towards the Qu'ari man with deadly precision. Wyrd threw up his hands and dodged to the side. The warhammer smashed into the building behind him, leaving a large crack in the clay.

Flashing a feral grin, Wyrd created two new balls of fire. Dez struggled to maintain her energy as she engaged with Wyrd. Aria's added efforts aided in keeping her winds focused around the Qu'ari and aethren. His flames
~~~

licked around his body as his orange eye sparkled. Behind him, a dark figure loomed over him. Tendrils danced behind him as a pair of orange eyes pierced the blackness.

With a cry, Dez gave a tremendous push, tightening the winds around the two like a noose around a neck. A deafening crack rang in her ears and suddenly her head began to spin. Her body sagged as utter exhaustion gripped her. Dez's breathing came out in ragged gasps and her chest ached. As she stared into the tornado, she noticed Wyrd had fallen to his knees, grasping at his throat as his mouth hung open. The Qu'ari's eyes bulged as he struggled for breath. All fyre had been extinguished from his body.

～〜～

Panic gripped Wyrd like nothing he'd ever experienced. He gasped for air as he clutched his throat. However, in the vortex there was none to be found. Vahnyre's screams filled his head. Wyrd's body shook as a heavy force pushed down on him. He tried to rise up, but it was as though an invisible hand kept him down.

Wyrd looked to the side, trying to find a way to break free. His head swam as the lack of oxygen hit him. Blackness crept in to his peripheral vision, slowly moving inwards as each second passed. Wyrd struggled to form a ball of fire in his hand, as the winds kept him from creating anything. He shivered as the aethren's heat was leeched from his body. Wyrd's mouth hung open as he struggled for breath.

In front of him, a woman shrouded in silver walked towards him. Her long hair flowed behind her, undisturbed by the chaos surrounding her. A little further back, the Tempest dropped to her knees, her hands still held out in an effort to keep her winds blowing. A final thought entered his mind. Kill the Tempest.

His body shook as he bent over to try and pick up his dagger. The force pushed against him, making it near impossible. He managed to wrap his fingers around its hilt, the worn leather still warm in his hands, before a gust of wind knocked it out of his grasp and sent it clanging to the ground. Still doubled over and shaking from trying to straighten up, Wyrd's eyes darted to his right. His chest clenched as he saw Jytte and Pram supporting an injured Hroth.

Blackness closed in on Wyrd as the silver woman broke through the winds. He felt her gentle touch on his cheeks before he passed out.

Dez's vision blurred as she fought to hold on to her winds. The silver woman broke through the winds and gently held Wyrd's limp body. Vahnyre's screams filled the air as the silver glow engulfing the woman also traveled to cover the Qu'ari as well. Once Wyrd's body was completely bathed in silver, a mass of black shot out of him and into the sky.

A shudder coursed through her body and Dez collapsed onto the ground, releasing the winds and returning the square back to its calm. The rain stopped and the dark clouds quickly dispersed. Within minutes, the beautiful sunny day returned.

The silver woman hovered over Wyrd's unconscious body. Dez felt a pair of strong hands pick her up and carry her over to the silver woman. To her left, Dez noticed a few people watching her warily. Her head swam, the residual effects from the shock causing a headache to form in her temples. Dez felt weak. It was a sensation that she had never experienced before.

Footsteps pounding on the ground announced the arrival of Alverick and his group. The three caught up to them and the other newcomers. She heard Swordbane exchange a few words with the man holding the Flame. Dez couldn't hear what they said, but she realized that the man was the Qu'ari general's right-hand man. As surprised conversation broke out, Dez struggled to pay attention, but found she couldn't hear anything they said. Her eyes were drawn to the silver woman who now stood up.

Turning to face the group, there was a collective gasp as she revealed herself. Silver eyes. Silver hair. Dez felt a tear roll down her cheek as the gravity of what just happened sunk in. Aria had split from her, regaining a physical form. Dez was now on her own.

"I have removed Vahnyre's influence from him." Aria's melodic voice filled Dez with sadness. It was just like the voice she'd heard in her head all her life. Knowing it was gone forever left her feeling empty.

"What does this mean?" Len asked. "Vahnyre's free to inhabit someone else?"

"He will not inhabit anyone else. What was inside Wyr-raji was just a small portion of Vahnyre. What I've removed will go to rejoin his main body. Wyr-raji is now as he once was."

Blinking heavily, Dez struggled to remain conscious. As the sun shone down on the group, she found herself falling into the darkness. Dez tried to shake her head to keep awake, but she passed out mid-shake.

L

LEN SAT in the Dancing Wolf with his back to the wall. A plate of lamb and lentils lay on the table, the scent of the spices drifting up to his nostrils from the steam made his mouth water. A tankard of beer accompanied his meal. The tavern was packed as the soldiers of Pharn, the pirates, and the heads of each clan filled the tables. His family was seated by his side.

Viir and his followers represented the Pshwani. After Vaarden was found dead, Len learned that Viir worked to calm the Pshwan anger and helped convince them that Wyrd had been the cause of their suffering the whole time. Sitting next to him, Pram and his family, as well as Hroth and his guests, ate in silence. The children played together, but the adults were somber. Hroth and Pram were wrapped up after visits to the shaman. Len also paid the shaman a visit; he counted himself lucky that the worst of it was a sprained ankle.

A barbarian woman sat between Hroth's female companion and a young man. The young man spoke animatedly with her as he held her hand. To his right, Len's mother sat by Zaa'ni and his children. Len's newborn son, Heru, lay bundled in blankets fast asleep.

The Avalanche and his forces ate quietly, unsure of whether they could relax. To his credit, Alverick and Brody worked valiantly to engage their men in conversation. However, Alverick's enthusiasm was dampened by the redheaded woman sitting by his side. Her eyes lacked the sparkle that the rest of the group had. Len couldn't put his finger on it, but he knew she wasn't her usual self.

Dez sat by herself, as far from others as she could. She quietly watched Ghan and Aria as they spoke together. Kayna and the rest of her crew alternated between sneaking glances at the two gods and laughing uproariously as they downed their pints. Plates of food were continuously being replenished at their tables.

Len sat in silence, ignoring the need to address the issue. He was victorious. Wyrd had been defeated. However, it was a hollow victory. Wyrd was surrounded by a group of Qu'ari elite, stripped of all but a pair of trousers and shoes. His hands were tied behind his back with a rope that connected to his neck, pulling his arms up at an awkward angle.

The young general knew that he must address the room. But he couldn't. He failed. The shame ate at him. He couldn't bring himself to face his people.

A hand rested lightly on his back, snapping him from his thoughts. Pram motioned with his hand an apology for startling his leader. "Apologies, Evenhand. You seem troubled over your victory."

"Xan's glory is faltering," Len replied without looking at his general.

"Forgive me, Evenhand, but Xan's fortune appears to be growing."

Len shot Pram a nonplussed look, his eyebrow raising in silent question.

"Our people, though we hit a snag, have banded together after these unprecedented times. Viir did not order the Pshwani forces to attack. He was on the verge of surrender when they arrived. He then took over in the chaos after Vaarden's death and rallied the clan together. The rest of the clans have shown loyalty to you by not engaging in the conflict. And to top it off, our allies showed up and are still here to help us, despite our centuries-long differences. I see a strong future for our people. All we need now is to figure out how to deal with Wyr-raji."

With a sigh, Len ran his hands through his hair. "Our alliances appear to have grown, you're right. It just did not happen the way I thought it would. But Ghan was right. The bones do not take the will of the gods into consideration." Len lifted his head from his hands and gazed out across the room.

"We're in for some dark times, Pram. I fear Wyr-raji's actions are just the beginning."

Pram met Len's stare and the two shared a look. Len returned his attentions to the busy tavern. The owner smiled as he rushed to refill glasses and plates. The bar maids moved quickly to clear the dirty dishes and bring out fresh food. Laughter and conversation gradually filled the Dancing Wolf as the groups relaxed.

He watched as Alverick spoke to the redhead, her motions becoming more fluid and natural. The Avalanche's lines of worry slowly began to disappear from his face. But next to him, Brody's only deepened. He sat next to the princess, and the two of them were both stiff in their chairs as they stared down at their plates. After a while, the princess struck up a conversation with the redheaded archer, leaving Brody to himself.

The young captain rested his elbows on the table and buried his face in his hands. On the other side of the tavern, Dez mimicked the motion. Len's eyes traveled around the room until he found Wyr-raji, his childhood friend. The man sat quietly watching everything. Occasionally, he glanced towards the barbarian woman, shooting her partner a look of disgust.

Len stared at his friend for a while until Wyrd noticed him. Locking gaze, Wyrd flashed a feral grin at his friend. The once orange eye had faded to a muddy orange color. Breaking stares, Len focused on his food once more. The gods were making their move. The bones had been thrown. If he wanted to keep them in his favor, Len knew he needed to go on the attack. He had three gods on his side. Now was the time to hunt for Vahnyre.

Glossary

Anchor: A form of mental discipline that helps Sparks and Tempests prevent or delay Snapping. In order to Anchor properly, the mage must focus on a specific mental image or idea until their mind is clear once again.

Apophmet: One of the two Ancients. Is known as Apophos by those in the Northern realms.

Aramaine: An alternate realm inhabited by dragons, wyrms, and other evil creatures. Also known as the Abyss.

Avalanche: Practitioners of Earth magic. Their tattoos are thick and bulky, like the trunks of trees. Avalanches can trace the movement of others through the earth's vibrations. Strong Avalanches can cause earthquakes.

Draughting: The process of transferring the blood of one mage to another as a means to increase one's magical power and potentially acquire a new style.

Enlil: Ancient home of the gods. The land was believed to be deserted by all after the great collapse, but it was protected and preserved by the deep magic.

The Faceless: Thought to be old wives' tales, they are the demons of Enlil and part of Apophmet's army of darkness.

Flame: Practitioners of fire magic. Their tattoos twist into mesmerizing patterns and appear to dance on the mage's body like the flame of a candle.

Their personalities can be erratic, but they do not suffer from the mental instabilities like a Spark or Tempest would.

Flicker: A derogatory term for a Flame.

Ghost: Practitioners of night magic. Their tattoos are slim and a metallic black color. They can manipulate shadows. Night magi are used in Scrymme as assassins. They are found only in Scrymme.

Jyarl: A term for Ghosts in the land of Scrymme.

Halls of the Fallen: Thought to be the final resting ground for kings and great warriors. It is a neutral place where the gods meet to discuss the events regarding Corinth.

Konugrr: The title for the ruler of Grimmrheimr.

Liche: Practitioners of necro magic. Their tattoos are thick and sluggish-looking shadows. Liches can manipulate the dead either through animation of corpses or scrying through the dead. They are found only in Scrymme.

Naran: The title used in Scrymme for one's master.

Nannohav: A Scrymmen request for judgement by the king and Host of Scrymme.

Plague: Practitioners of biological magic. Their tattoos are a combination of fine lines and delicate swirls. They can use healing magics and bring about plagues.

Re'nukhtet: One of the original Ancients. Goes by Re'nukh by the Northern realms.

Shadow: Practitioners of shadow magic. Their tattoos are hazy. Strong Shadows can open dimensional gates and summon creatures to bring to their world.

Snap: The moment when a Tempest or Spark loses control of their mental faculties and succumbs to the erratic nature of their magic. Snapping usually occurs when a mage is fatigued or has recently draughted. In the case of Tempests, Snapping occurs when they lose their Anchor.

Spark: Practitioners of electrical magic. Their tattoos are sharp and jagged, like bolts of lightning. Those who use this style of magic are susceptible to mental destabilization but can control these side effects with great concentration and effort.

Stream: Practitioners of water magic. Their tattoos are graceful and flowing with rounded edges. Many practitioners of this style have calm demeanors and usually an interest in the healing arts.

Tainted: Those who tried to acquire blood magic, but failed. They are cursed with insanity.

Tempest: Practitioners of wind magic. Their tattoos are thin and branching with a hint of twisting or swirling. A practiced Tempest's mind is as fluid as the wind and constantly changing. This causes them to be highly mentally unstable.

Twinning: Taking two objects and linking them together with a mage's blood.

About the Author

K.N. Nguyen is a fantasy author and the founder of DragonScript, a group that offers an outlet for new writers. Growing up, she often found herself immersed in some imaginary world, conquering enemy nations, and saving the day. As time went on, her love for horrible puns and nerd culture pulled her out of these worlds and brought her back to reality.

It wasn't until she started working at her office job that she felt the itch to begin writing. Her first two books, *King's Blood* and *Oath Blood*, are part of *The Fallen* series, which draws on her love of ancient Mediterranean mythology and epic fantasy.

A native of Sacramento, California, K.N. Nguyen spends her time singing karaoke, playing taiko, enjoying rhythm dancing games, and traveling with her friends and family when she isn't writing.

Other Works by K.N. Nguyen

King's Blood
Oath Blood

Anthologies

New Beginnings: Science Fiction/Fantasy Anthology by DragonScript
New Adventures: Science Fiction/Fantasy Anthology by DragonScript
Coffins & Dragons by Dragon Soul Press
The Once and Future Kingdom by Irish Horse Productions
Towards the Sun by DragonScript
First Stain by Inked in Gray
Another World by SummerStorm Press

www.ingramcontent.com/pod-product-compliance
Lightning Source LLC
Chambersburg PA
CBHW070737190726
48292CB00002B/302